Praise for Lesley K

"'Times have changed.' We hear this a lot—but what if you lived the exact same story| much would really change? *Time Squared* has ...... answer. A love story that stays the same over different eras, this book by Lesley Krueger is a unique concept that ties in historical events, world wars, and women's roles in society . . . leading to a surprising ending."

—Rebecca Eckler, author of *Knocked Up*

"I'll dive right in and tell you that the novel, *Time Squared* by Lesley Krueger, which I've loved more than I've loved than any book I've read in ages, could be billed as Kate Atkinson's *Life After Life* meets Kazuo Ishiguro's *Never Let Me Go*, if we wanted to underline just how badly you really ought to read it. And oh, you really do."

—Kerry Clare, editor of *49th Shelf*

"Krueger's portrait of artists as young men and women is alive with wit and rebellion—an aesthetic vivisection of the young Victorian age."

—*The Globe and Mail* on *Mad Richard*

"Krueger's research is evident in every paragraph: from the use of authentic slang to richly sketched portraits of the lives of the era's rich and poor, the book confidently transports the reader to another time."

—*Quill & Quire* on *Mad Richard*

"The knitting together of Charlotte Brontë's and Richard Dadd's different trajectories worked like a dream. I was enthralled."

—Terry Gilliam on *Mad Richard*

"In this remarkable piece of historical fiction, Krueger (*Drink the Sky*) imaginatively delves into the life of Richard Dadd. . . . The two story lines . . . effectively juxtapose Dadd and Brontë, two very different people who travelled in similar circles during the same era and, more importantly, who were both entirely invested in what it means to be an artist. This question anchors the novel, adding depth and dimension to a terrific read."

—*Publishers Weekly* on *Mad Richard*, starred review

"There is much to ponder in this elegant novel about the potentially cata-strophic emotional toll of art, the irrational nature of love, the solitude of heartache, and what happens when one life touches another, however briefly."

—*Toronto Star* on *Mad Richard*

"By engaging us in two very different lives in a state of transformation, we become engaged in the process of what it means to become an individual, moral human being. It's a powerful story about human strength and frailty. It touches something deep inside."

—*Toronto Star* on *The Corner Garden*

"Lesley Krueger . . . has perfectly captured the laconic tone of an intelligent teen who can still offer moments of bracing lucidity and keen observation. . . . *The Corner Garden* is an ambitious book. It starts innocently as a contem-porary picaresque journey, then delves into a history lesson and the nature of evil."

—*The Globe and Mail* on *The Corner Garden*

"Part carefully-wrought thriller, part eco-excursion into the heart of dark-ness . . . a young woman struggles with questions of identity against the backdrop of modern Brazil. Her elegant prose is a pleasure to read, and when Krueger ratchets up the tension, we go with her, hearts in mouth. She has intriguing and serious things to say about human nature and the planet."

—*Quill & Quire* on *Drink the Sky*

"*Drink the Sky* captures both the precise local colour of Rio de Janeiro (where the author lived from 1988 to 1991) and the first-time visitor's wide-eyed wonder. Krueger renders the exotic beauty of Brazil's landscape and wildlife with rhapsodic authenticity. . . . The hidden story emerges piece by piece, as these things do, in a series of coincidences and unsuspected interrelations that weave the book's two parallel plots into a tense finale. As a cleverly plotted mystery, the book succeeds in hooking the reader."

—*Toronto Star* on *Drink the Sky*

FAR
CREEK
ROAD

FAR CREEK ROAD

a novel

LESLEY KRUEGER

Copyright © Lesley Krueger, 2023

Published by ECW Press
665 Gerrard Street East
Toronto, Ontario, Canada M4M 1Y2
416-694-3348 / info@ecwpress.com

All rights reserved. No part of this publication may be reproduced, stored in a retrieval system, or transmitted in any form by any process — electronic, mechanical, photocopying, recording, or otherwise — without the prior written permission of the copyright owners and ECW Press. The scanning, uploading, and distribution of this book via the internet or via any other means without the permission of the publisher is illegal and punishable by law. Please purchase only authorized electronic editions, and do not participate in or encourage electronic piracy of copyrighted materials. Your support of the author's rights is appreciated.

Editor for the Press: Susan Renouf
Copy-editor: Jen R. Albert
Cover design: Natalie Olsen
Cover image (house): "Lincoln homes: better homes by better methods" By Lincoln Homes (Booklet) [CC-BY-SA-3.0], via Internet Archive.

This is a work of fiction. Names, characters, places, and incidents either are the product of the author's imagination or are used fictitiously, and any resemblance to actual persons, living or dead, business establishments, events, or locales is entirely coincidental.

LIBRARY AND ARCHIVES CANADA CATALOGUING
IN PUBLICATION

Title: Far creek road : a novel / Lesley Krueger.

Names: Krueger, Lesley, author.

Identifiers: Canadiana (print) 20230467083 |
Canadiana (ebook) 20230467113

ISBN 978-1-77041-637-6 (softcover)
ISBN 978-1-77852-236-9 (ePub)
ISBN 978-1-77852-237-6 (PDF)
ISBN 978-1-77852-238-3 (Kindle)

Subjects: LCGFT: Novels.

Classification: LCC PS8571.R786 F37 2023 | DDC
C813/.54—dc23

This book is funded in part by the Government of Canada. *Ce livre est financé en partie par le gouvernement du Canada.* We acknowledge the support of the Canada Council for the Arts. *Nous remercions le Conseil des arts du Canada de son soutien.* We acknowledge the funding support of the Ontario Arts Council (OAC), an agency of the Government of Ontario. We also acknowledge the support of the Government of Ontario through the Ontario Book Publishing Tax Credit, and through Ontario Creates.

ONTARIO ARTS COUNCIL
CONSEIL DES ARTS DE L'ONTARIO
an Ontario government agency
un organisme du gouvernement de l'Ontario

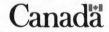
Canada Council   Conseil des arts
for the Arts   du Canada

Canada

PRINTED AND BOUND IN CANADA   PRINTING: MARQUIS   5   4   3   2   1

MIX
Paper from
responsible sources
FSC
www.fsc.org   FSC® C103567

Security is mostly a superstition.

It does not exist in nature,

nor do the children of men as a whole experience it.

Avoiding danger is no safer in the long run than outright exposure.

Life is either a daring adventure, or nothing.

—HELEN KELLER

PART ONE

1

I wish I had some of the furniture my father made for that house on Far Creek Road. He built a blond oak bedroom suite for the master bedroom with a headboard that was really a bookshelf one book high, my father being a reader. My mother would hide a chocolate egg there at Easter, and they kept a loud rattling alarm clock on my father's side of the bed, its numbers lighting up at night in a pale radioactive green. When my parents were able to afford a store-bought suite, my father and my Uncle Punk moved the oak set into the spare bedroom, and that was its first step out the door.

My father, Hall Parker, often withdrew to his workshop, which was built into the unfinished back end of the basement. The floor and the back wall were concrete, and pushed up against the rough wall was a workbench my father had built himself. The work surface was a wide slab of wood that Uncle Punk got for him at one of the mills, and its four iron legs were salvaged from a broken-down conveyer belt.

My father was a tall man who looked even taller in the basement. He had a slight stoop and wore black-rimmed Clark Kent glasses, and I thought both of these came from his job in the local railway headquarters over town. He said he was a bookkeeper but my mother called him an accountant, and she liked to say the Parkers were early settlers in the province who had once owned canneries and timber concessions. My father was older than most of the other fathers in our suburb, but he was popular, and always ready to fix anybody's car. People waved when they saw him, which made me proud, although it was also understood that Hall Parker—everybody called him by both names—Hall Parker had his moods.

My father usually went into his workshop on weekends, but sometimes he went there straight after work, not even coming into the kitchen, but going directly through the basement. Those were the times I had to leave his dinner on a stool outside his workshop. It didn't have a door, and when I put down his plate, he would keep his back to me and push things around on his workbench as if he didn't know I was there. I tiptoed, but that was politeness, too. It was because of the war, my mother said. But my father wasn't usually like that.

I was the youngest in the family and the only one at home. My brother and sister were born before the war, and at the time I'm talking about, my brother Bob had just hung out his shingle as a lawyer while my sister Debbie had been married for almost five years. I was born quite a long time after my father got back from overseas, where he had been a captain in the artillery. My parents named me Mary Alice, but everybody called me Tink. I was small for my age, which I got from my mother, although people said I got my personality from her brother, Uncle Punk, a lumberjack by trade, now settled in town as president of his union local. I never thought this was true, not feeling particularly united with anyone. I usually preferred to go off on my own, or maybe with my best friend, Norman Horton.

Norman and I were both interested in what went on in the world. That's the best way I can put it. He lived on a street at roughly a right angle to ours called Connington Crescent, where his family stood out, his mother still working as a teacher long after she'd married. Mrs. Horton taught grade five at our elementary school down the hill, while Norman's father taught history and geography at the biggest of the local high schools. After school, the Hortons left Norman with his older sister, Rosa, who let him run wild while she talked on the phone, lying on the kitchen

4

floor with her legs stretched up against the wall. Being a late child, I could do pretty much what I wanted, as long as I got home in time for dinner.

Usually, we disappeared into the forest at the back of my yard. Our street ran down the mountain parallel to Far Creek, and everyone's backyard ended in fences. Behind them, the forest marched in high stately fashion down to the creek, high trunks like giant's legs stepping politely around the huckleberry bushes and salal with berries we thought were poisonous, although it turns out they weren't. This was in the Vancouver suburb of Grouse Valley in the mountains of the North Shore, our houses set into a temperate rain forest at the far edge of the western world.

Some of the fences had gates in them, including the one my father built.

"She's going to go down there anyway," I heard him tell my mother, taking a cigarette break while he was building it.

"The whole point was to keep her out."

My father met my eye, and we acknowledged the futility. Since the creek was halfway to being a river, its dangers included spring run-off, when the thundering water was strong enough to carry children away. There were also older boys hanging around down there, at least according to my mother, Bunny. Everyone called her Bunny, including me. Bunny said the boys would start off by offering me a cigarette, and I had to get out of there as soon as the pack came out of somebody's back pocket. She was a little hazy on what happened next, and in fact I never saw any boys like that, but Norman and I sometimes played at being teenage murderers, usually when we'd laid out part of our allowances on a pack of candy cigarettes.

What we did see was a man in a raincoat who occasionally stood in the middle of a little bridge over the creek. This was farther down the mountain on the path that led to a small local shopping centre. He was a rectangular man in a grey fedora who opened his raincoat to show off his thing, making us scream and run away. Screaming at the Raincoat Man was like screaming on the rides at the Pacific National Exhibition. It was equal parts terrifying and fun, although we never talked about the terror part and pretended we enjoyed it, a clause in a silent neighbourhood agreement not to tell our parents what was going on. In a weird way, the man was ours.

My father built that new fence in the spring of 1962 when I was nine years old. I wouldn't remember the date except that it was only a few months before the Cuban Missile Crisis, when we thought the world was going to end, and there had been a real chance that it would.

This was when many of the most important things in my life happened. I would sometimes talk about it later with my father, although Bunny refused. That was done, she said. Gone. In the past. My leg had healed quickly, the scar down my shin barely noticeable to anyone except me. And if Norman had been bullied, well, he was the type to get bullied. Not that we needed to bring the Hortons into it.

Yet she couldn't deny what had happened, and it probably started the spring my father put up the fence. The Cold War was already underway, building toward the missile crisis, not that I knew what a cold war was. In fact, I only became aware that something was wrong one morning not long after the fence went up and the air raid siren went off.

I don't think this could have been the first time I'd heard the siren, but it's the first time I remember it, probably because my father hadn't yet left for work. I was eating my usual bowl of Corn Flakes, except that I'd poured on too much milk. The flakes were getting soggy, so I was wolfing, trying to get them down while they still crackled on the roof of my mouth. It was a sunny spring morning, warmth on my right shoulder nearest the window, and my lunch was ready at my elbow in its Dale Evans lunchbox.

Out of nowhere, a wail started, a rising mechanical howl that made me freeze with my spoon half raised. It happened so fast I wasn't frightened, at least not until I caught something out of the corner of my eye and turned to see my father diving to the floor, his glasses flying off.

"Jesus H. Christ!"

"It's all right. It's only a test," Bunny said, barely pausing as she put two slices of bread into the toaster. "They talked about it yesterday on CKNW."

The siren went on for what felt like a very long time. When it stopped, my father closed his eyes briefly then levered himself to his feet, his face red above his white shirt collar in a way that looked like blushing, although I didn't think fathers could blush. I was more worried about his red face than I was about the siren, and I was going to ask my father what was wrong when Bunny twitched her mouth in a way that meant I couldn't. After that, the toaster popped and I tried to go back to my Corn Flakes, but found I didn't want them anymore.

I could never get used to that siren. None of us could. It went off quite often that spring and summer, and I never saw my father duck and cover again, but if it went off while he was at home, he always looked as if he wanted to.

"Jesus H. Christ," he muttered. "Jesus H. Christ."

All this worried me, especially since my mother kept signalling me not to ask. For a long time, the only thing I learned was that they called it ducking and covering, the siren having gone off one time when I was at school.

"Under your desks!" the teacher called, clapping her hands. "Duck and cover!"

I crouched the wrong way under my desk. I learned later you were supposed to keep your body under your desk and your head on the chair, but I did the opposite. I was cramped and scared, yet also interested in the names cut into the underside of the wood with a ballpoint pen. Jack Baker. Peter Hardy. I'd never had occasion to notice them before and traced them with my finger. Jack Baker and Peter Hardy were older brothers of boys and girls in the school, and I wondered where they'd got pens. We still mostly used pencils in grade four. I also thought that when the siren stopped I'd finally learn why it was going off. Miss Atkinson would teach us.

When it finally ran down, Miss Atkinson let us crawl out from under our desks. I waited for her to say something, and she looked as if she might. Then she was distracted by a puddle spreading out from under Nancy Workman's desk. Nancy had wet her pants again and Miss Atkinson had to send Gord Brewster for the janitor, consoling Nancy by telling her, "It was only a test."

I loved Miss Atkinson, who wasn't anything like my awful grade three teacher, Mrs. Persson. It was true that Miss Atkinson hadn't answered my question about the siren, but I hadn't asked. As we walked uphill after school, Norman and I were both silent. He usually was, and I had to turn the whole thing over in my head. It finally came to me that Miss Atkinson had given me an excuse to ask my parents what was going on, or the siren had, and that was a good thought.

When I let myself in the front door, I heard noises in the basement. Heading downstairs, I found Bunny ironing in the rec room, spraying starch on the collar of one of my father's shirts.

I threw myself onto the chesterfield. "Why do there have to be stupid sirens?"

Bunny gave me a quick look and went back to her ironing. "Don't worry. It's only a test, just in case."

"In case of what?"

"Look in the cookie jar, and you might find chocolate chip."

I waited, but Bunny kept ironing, spraying one of the cuffs. I didn't understand why she didn't tell me, why nobody told me. Then she gave me a look that sent me upstairs, where the first cookie didn't taste that good, even dipped in milk, although the second one did.

That night, lying in bed, I heard my parents talking quietly in the kitchen, my father saying, "That damned siren." I slipped out of bed, creeping closer to my cracked-open bedroom door. But by the time I could pick up anything else, they were talking about my father's work and his boss Mr. German, who wasn't German at all but came from Seattle.

Uncle Punk called me Big Ears. After the second siren, I started using them all the time, sitting just out of sight on the basement stairs when my father got home and always leaving my bedroom door open a crack at night. I didn't always like what I heard. (Bunny: "Why we had children when Bob can't take five minutes to call." My father: "German's on a rampage.")

But there was nothing about the sirens until one day after school when I was downstairs and heard my father get home. The door closed softly, and his briefcase hit the floor over my head.

I crept halfway up the stairs. My parents were in the kitchen just around the corner, and while my mother made coffee, they started talking about when my father was overseas, the war, the Blitz and the wailing sirens in London. I picked up that an air raid siren had gone off at lunchtime over town, although we hadn't heard one here.

"That goddamn siren," Bunny said, since Bunny liked to swear, although not when we had company. Afterward, she said something about the Cold War, which struck me. I realized that everyone was talking about the Cold War, I just hadn't listened before, and I wondered what it meant.

At night we sometimes watched Walter Cronkite's *CBS Evening News*, eating our dinner on TV trays. I'd heard Walter Cronkite say Cold War, but I'd never paid much attention, being more interested in, for instance, what had got stuck on the bottom of my sock. Gum? *Gross*. Pick it off. ("Mary Alice! Wash your hands!")

After that, I started paying more attention to Walter Cronkite. He didn't say it for a while. But a couple of weeks later, he looked up from his papers to say heavily, "This Cold War."

Walter Cronkite's serious expression sent words tumbling around in my head. Overseas. Siren. Bombs. Buzz bombs. The Cold War. *This* Cold War. Sirens and . . . The nuclear bomb? Were the sirens warning us about the nuclear bomb? Was someone going to drop a nuclear bomb on us?

I was so terrified the words kept tumbling, churning themselves into a funnel like the tornado in *The Wizard of Oz*. I lost my breath, all the air sucked out of me. A tornado was going to pick me up and drop me on the other side of the rainbow, where an enormous tree was going to open its eyes and whip out its branches and trap me. Most kids hated the flying monkeys in *The Wizard of Oz*, but I hated those trees. I spent so much time down the creek that I could picture an evil tree tearing me to pieces exactly like the most famous Bomb. Hir-*ohhhh*-shima. They'd bombed Hiroshima, or we had, and the *ohhh* sounded just like the siren's wail.

Walter Cronkite kept talking under his little moustache, but I had to leave the room. I wasn't hungry. Remembered to thank Bunny for dinner. Went to my room, under the bed, where I picked at the cheesecloth on the bottom of the box spring, already shredded by our cat, Wilma. Usually, the pump in my aquarium put me to sleep but now it kept me awake after I realized that it could stop. My fish could die while I slept. I might wake up and they'd be dead.

I stayed frightened that whole long night—that whole tense week of breakfast, school, creek, home—while trying not to show it. You weren't supposed to talk about it so I couldn't, even with Norman, and lived inside that tornado of nuclear terror until one day as we walked home from school, I could barely breathe.

I knew I had to hold myself together until my father got home, and walked uphill as if I was walking on stilts. My legs weren't part of me and the road had gone untrustworthy, liable to drop away from under my feet. It was drizzling, so I had an excuse not to go to the creek, and I left Norman outside his house, barely able to say goodbye. I made it home, which I didn't thoroughly expect, going straight to my room where I pretended to read comic books until Bunny called me to dinner.

TV trays in front of the news. There was an autumn leaves pattern on those trays, and I felt as smothered as they were, half hidden under Bunny's woven orange placemats. She'd made meatloaf and mashed potatoes with peas, which was usually my favourite, but tonight I could only push the peas around on my plate. I waited for Walter Cronkite and his moustache to change to a commercial, and when he did, it was the Esso song, which usually got me singing along with your tires are humming and your motor purrs.

Instead, I asked my father casually, as if I didn't care, "What's a Cold War?"

It might have been the hardest thing I'd ever done, saying those words without being sure I'd be able to take a breath afterward.

My father was sitting across the room in his recliner with the footrest up, having settled back to read the *Vancouver Sun*. He read the newspaper cover to cover every night, and now he looked at me over top of it.

"Is that what's been bothering you?" he asked, his mild eyes made bigger by his reading glasses.

I managed to shrug, and my father looked at me for a long time. Then he made the paper crinkle as he put it aside and levered down the footrest.

"Well, Tink," he said. "it's a fight about whose system is going to control the world, capitalism or communism. The United States or the Soviet Union. I guess someone always wants to control things. But so far, it's a cold war because they're fighting it with words instead of weapons."

"Communists?" I asked faintly.

"Two systems of governance," my father said. "Ours far from perfect, but working better than theirs."

I didn't understand any of this but nodded seriously as if I did. And in fact, hearing my father speak about the Cold War in his usual voice melted some of the weight off my shoulders. Not all of it, but enough to calm me down. He said they weren't fighting the war with weapons, and my father would know. He knew the middle name of Jesus Christ, or at least his middle initial, which wasn't common knowledge. After he'd started saying it, I'd listened for his full name in church. But our minister, Mr. Culver, usually only referred to him as either "Jesus" or "Christ," or sometimes "Jesus Christ Our Saviour."

Now I saw that my father had it over even Mr. Culver. As he kept explaining things in his reasonable voice, I could see that he would protect me from the Bomb, from tornadoes and from trees with eyes, even from the Raincoat Man on the little bridge (if we ever told on him); protect me, protect our family, protect Norman and his family, despite the moods left over from the last war, the hot war, the Second World War where he'd got his medals.

Because my father usually wasn't usually like that, it was true.

2

There was a big world out there, but mainly I lived in a small one. The suburb, or our part of the suburb, was made up of a small T-shaped area consisting of our section of Far Creek Road with Connington Crescent running off it: Norman's street, one block long, a level semicircular sweep between a series of ranch-style houses.

Both streets had been ploughed through a dozen years before on land my father said was the traditional territory of the Squamish people. To me this meant hunting grounds, where people from the local band had stalked game and picked huckleberries the way I did. It meant forest, which was only cleared when people like my parents moved in. A family story had my mother carrying buckets of water downhill from a pipe at the top of the slope when it was cleared for our subdivision. There were stumps on every side, and deer leapt over them, and once when my mother came down the hill with her buckets, a cougar flitted across the road like a big golden cat. At the other side, it paused to look over its shoulder, and the way the cougar narrowed its eyes at her made the hairs on my mother's arms stand up. Then a car came grinding up the hill, changing gears, and the big cat bounded away.

Our subdivision was made up of people whose ancestors came from the Old Country, which usually meant Scotland or England or Ireland, Parkers and Coles and O'Neills, along with some Milewskis and

Krawchuks who had moved west from the prairies. There were even a few people with German names, although they were careful to mention family members who'd fought for the Allies during the war, even if they didn't have any.

A bigger difference was with the people on the reserves down the hill, where my father had friends who were members of the band living at the mouth of the Capilano River. Up the hill, the main difference was between Anglican and United Church Protestants, leaving aside a few Catholics, a family of Holy Rollers and the Shribmans, who were Jewish, Judy Shribman being in my grade at school.

We didn't worry about any of this, at least not in my family, although I was aware of a pecking order that put Anglicans on top. The Manners family next door was Anglican, and they were at the apex of local society. Like my father's great-grandfather, the earliest Mr. Manners had owned lumber concessions and canneries, the difference being that his family had managed to hang onto them. "The Manners Had Money": that's what everybody said. You could almost hear the capitals when adults were talking. Had Money. The War.

Belonging to one of these categories permitted certain types of behaviour. If you had money, you could drive your sports car as fast as Mrs. Manners, and the police let you off with a warning. But look out if you drove an old rust bucket over the limit. Men who'd been overseas could have moods like my father, but moods were frowned on in house-wives. All of this made the suburb a uniform place, and maybe kept it that way, but there was still low-level discord. My father explained it to me the time a boy in my class passed a mean comment about Donnie O'Reilly being a mackerel snapper.

"People will find differences, Tink. Even if they have to use a magnifying glass."

I wasn't sure what he meant. I knew that mackerel snapper meant Catholic, but wasn't sure why, or what Holy Rollers meant, or talking in tongues. How else did you talk? How could anyone talk *without* a tongue?

I wasn't sure about a lot of things, despite having a happy family, my brother Bob aside.

Middle class, Bunny called us. It was a prosperous time, although the prosperity didn't reach everywhere, including the reserves. I had also seen panhandlers over town and heard about unemployment. But there were jobs for white-collar men like my father, and working men like my Uncle Punk were in unions and they were well-paid. People talked about deserving this after the war. They'd earned their security. They were owed. This was a serious matter, what you'd earned and what you deserved. And while I wasn't sure what I deserved, I enjoyed what we had and never felt the lack of anything, especially after Norman arrived.

Norman Horton was two weeks and three days younger than me, both of us born in the rainy season leading up to Christmas. He and his family had relocated to our suburb the year before the sirens began. They'd bought the old Milewski place, moving in just before Norman and I were due to start grade four. Mrs. Horton started teaching grade five at the same time, while Mr. Horton had already been teaching at the high school for three or four years, having driven across the bridge from their old place over town.

I first saw Norman a couple of hours after the moving van pulled away. It was a sunny August afternoon, and he stood in the yard behind his new rockery watching us play Red Rover. Norman kept his hands clasped behind his back, sticking out his stomach in a way that made him seem hefty from a distance.

When I looked closer, I saw that Norman wasn't hefty; he was just solid. His brown hair stood up in a crewcut, and he looked as if he wore glasses, although that wasn't true either. It was more the case that Norman looked like a small father, standing there with his stomach stuck out watching us play.

We usually played Red Rover at school, but there was a crowd of people around that day, and someone had proposed it for the street.

We faced each other in two long lines, waiting for a captain to yell, "Red Rover, Red Rover, we call Somebody over." If they called your name, you had to take off, building up speed so you could break through the opposing line of linked hands. That day, I was too busy staring at Norman behind his rockery to hear the captain call my name. This was one of the Manners kids, who were always captains.

"We call Tink over," Harry Manners called more loudly. I came to myself and looked over at their line, deciding to break apart Jeannie Stevens and Cathy Cole, who were girly. Clenching my fists, I ran as hard as I could. But hitting their clasped hands was like hitting a wall, and I bounced back, landing on my rear so everybody laughed. Not meanly, since I was a pet. All the adults said that, not just Bunny.

I hated being a pet. I felt humiliated sitting on the road, hating the way I'd lost, taking a long deliberate time to push myself up and brush off my shorts. I didn't want to join the other side. I wanted to take a hostage back to my own. But I hadn't earned it, and when I finished brushing myself off, I made one of those decisions you never exactly make, swivelling and stalking across the road toward Norman's house, calling over at him, "How come you're just standing there snooping?"

Norman regarded me mildly. "I'm not snooping when I'm not hiding."

"So why're you just standing there?"

"Because I had polio, and I can't run."

Norman looked down at his pants—the rest of us were wearing shorts—and as I followed his eyes, I could see metal outlines on his left leg.

"I can walk fine now, but I still can't run."

I thought about this for a minute, before yelling to the others, "He had polio." Turning back, I asked, "So what do you like to do?"

Norman seemed to find this a reasonable question.

"I've got a bike, but it isn't unpacked yet."

"We've all got bikes," I said. "Didn't everyone have bikes where you used to live?"

He shrugged. Sure. Another shrug. Pretty much.

"I found my comic books, though," he said.

I went down the driveway and around the rockery to join him.

"I'm Tink," I said, putting out my hand for him to shake. He shook it gingerly, although there didn't seem to be anything wrong with his arm.

"Tink?"

"What's your name?"

"Norman."

"What do they call you?"

"Norman?"

At that moment, Norman and I became friends. Not that I actively needed friends. It was true that Jennifer Doherty had been my best friend and her family had moved to California in June when her father had been transferred by IBM. But even though I liked other people well enough, I mostly preferred being on my own. I liked to have projects, many of them down the creek. I was usually busy picking buckets of huckleberries for Bunny to make pies, building dams in summer, collecting leaves in the fall to iron between pieces of wax paper, a raggedy old dish towel on top to save the iron. You didn't need to talk when you did these things. You didn't want to have to keep telling people to be quiet, either.

Norman didn't care about talking. He cared for it even less than Jennifer Doherty, not that Norman was a follower. It was more that Norman was a thinker, and very polite. He didn't like to intrude, and he said he was used to being on his own, having spent a year inside an iron lung. Not that he could really remember it, he told me. After we went inside to look at his comic books, I got the story out of him, since sometimes I talked quite a lot.

We went through the basement door into what would become the Hortons' rec room. The house was on the south side of the street, meaning the front looked like one storey but the lot sloped down the mountain, and the back showed it was really two storeys, with the rec room looking out through big windows into the backyard. Mostly the windows were blocked with high brown boxes, but there was space open in the centre of the room. We decided to build a fortress there to keep from getting underfoot, the way Norman's father had told him. It didn't take long to pull five empty boxes into a circle, and after we went inside, I asked Norman why he'd got polio.

He hadn't got his shot? How come? Why didn't they have shots when he lived up north? Wait. You could get them now? So he'd lived in Prince George? How come his parents went to Prince George? What did he mean, he guessed they'd been sent? By who? Why wasn't he supposed to talk about it? Okay, but they must have had hospitals where he got sick. How small was small? Like a Dinky Toy? Ha, ha. What did *airlifted* mean? Wait a minute: I was born in Vancouver General Hospital. How old was he when he got here?

Four and a half. Norman couldn't remember much about it, but he could do a good job mimicking the *unh-uh, unh-uh, unh-uh* sound of the iron lung. Inside our fortress, the light was dimmed by the boxes at the windows. *Unh-uh, unh-uh, unh-uh, unh-uh.* Norman went on for so long that things started to feel weird, so I picked up a recent *Superman*.

"Who do you like better?" I interrupted. "Superman or Batman?"

Norman came to himself quickly. "Batman," he said.

"I like Superman. My father has glasses like Clark Kent."

"Everybody's father has glasses like Clark Kent. If they've got glasses."

I would have taken umbrage if someone else had said that. But you could tell right away that Norman just liked saying what was true.

"How come you like Batman?"

"He doesn't have superpowers," Norman answered. "So he has to be smart."

"I'd like to have X-ray vision," I said. "But I really like Lois Lane better than Superman, and she's pretty smart. So I guess I like Batman, too."

Norman smiled shyly and taught me to *unh-uh, unh-uh, unh-uh.* After I got it, we did it together while marching around the boxes, and I did it again as I walked home, then did it louder when I threw open the kitchen door.

"Lord lovely Jesus!" Bunny cried, dropping her wooden spoon. She was making pie crust, my father being fond of any kind of pie.

"That's from the new boy," I said, and explained about Norman.

"Too bad they don't have a girl," Bunny told me and dumped the pie dough out of her bowl onto some waxed paper to roll it out.

"What difference does that make?" I asked.

Bunny just kept rolling out her pie dough, being consistent in never answering anything important. My mother was one of the shortest of the local mothers, and she was usually on a diet, although most of the mothers went on diets at some point. As of today, she was almost back to her ideal weight, but only almost, which meant she wouldn't eat the pie she was making. In fact, I could tell she would ostentatiously not eat it for dessert tonight: a word I couldn't pronounce but understood very well, given Bunny's dramatic displays of *not eating* something she'd put on the table for my father, who could have eaten an elephant without gaining an ounce.

"*Unh-uh. Unh-uh,*" I said, breathing right up in her face.

Bunny used her hip to shove me away. If it had been cookie dough, I would have snuck in a finger and stolen a bite. But cherry pie for dessert was just fine.

Four weeks later, Norman put on another display of mimicry. Almost exactly four weeks, since we were on our way home from our first day in grade four, when he got Miss Atkinson down pat the first time we saw her.

I hadn't wanted to go to school that morning. I'd hated my grade three teacher Mrs. Persson so much that I'd pretended to get stomach aches all the previous year. I'd pretended so hard that sometimes I threw up, even though I had a strong stomach. My mother had promised me that I would never get Mrs. Persson again—my father had got rid of her—but I'm not sure I would have been able to make it out of the house if Norman hadn't unexpectedly knocked on the door. Maybe he knew how scared I felt, or maybe he just wanted to go with somebody himself.

In the schoolyard, when the bell rang to go inside, I followed the other girls through the Girls door and waited for Norman to come in from the Boys so we could go to our classroom together. I barely made it inside, slumping into a desk in the last row. After a moment's thought, Norman sat down next to me. There was an agonizing pause, then the front door of the classroom opened and Miss Atkinson strode in, clapping out a cheerful, "Well! People! Here we are!"

Miss Atkinson was slim and pretty, and she kept her hair in a ponytail with a barrette she changed every day, which became a matter for discussion. I loved Miss Atkinson from the first moment I saw her, when she smiled her perfect smile and carolled out, "Well! People!"

Not "Children!" But "People!" I watched mesmerized as she wrote her name on the blackboard. After "God Save the Queen" and the Lord's Prayer, she strode back and forth across the front of the classroom, her ponytail bouncing, burbling with laughter as she told us about her last Christmas vacation when she'd gone to Hawaii and eaten an octopus— that might have been the single most impressive thing I'd ever heard—and after lunch rewarded us for our excellent behaviour by taking us outside to the playground.

"Well! People! Who wants to burn off some energy!"

As we walked home after school, Norman got that, "Well! People!" down perfectly. I laughed, although it made me feel disloyal. I was also puzzled that Norman didn't seem to take school very seriously, even though his parents were teachers.

"You try it," he said.

I kicked the road with my new black patent-leather shoes, which were a bad call on Bunny's part. I didn't want to make fun of Miss Atkinson.

"Dare you," Norman said.

"Well. People," I said grudgingly.

"You've got to say it like her."

"Well! People!" I said more loudly, which was enjoyable.

"People!" he yelled.

"People! People! People!" I cried.

"Shorty people!"

"Booger-nose people!"

"Stinky-feet people!"

"Wet-Your-Pants People!" I cried, making fun of Nancy Workman.
I knew that was mean, but Norman bent over laughing his silent laugh,
which was sort of like gasping.

"You don't have asthma, too, do you?."

Norman shrugged, which meant yes.

We didn't go down the creek that day. I was under orders to go straight
home and tell Bunny how school had gone, and for once I wanted to.
After dropping Norman off, I burst into the kitchen yelling, "Well!"

I stopped right there. My sister Debbie was sitting at the kitchen table
with Bunny.

"Hey there, little Tinker," she said, signalling me over for a kiss. "So
it went okay? I needed to come see."

Debbie was beautiful, wearing eyeliner over her big blue eyes and
putting her fair hair into a bouffant. One time I'd seen a man walk into
a telephone pole, he was staring at Debbie so hard. And she wasn't
just beautiful. My sister was also such a nice person that she'd driven
over from West Vancouver for no other reason than to ask about
grade four.

"Our new teacher is called Miss Atkinson," I said. "And she's really,
really nice."

"*Is* she?"

"Miss Atkinson took us outside to burn off our energy. We did
jumping jacks and then we had a race—a dash—and she took off her scarf
and waved it like a flag."

"That's smart. Burning off energy," Debbie said, and regarded me mock-seriously. "Now you need to build it back up."

My sister got up to make me a treat, heating milk on the stove and stirring in half a teaspoonful of instant coffee.

"Since you're so grown up," she said, bringing it over. "Grade four!" Debbie put the cup down in front of me and leaned her arms flat on the table, cupping her chin in her clasped hands so she could watch me at eye level, being comical. When I sipped the coffee and grimaced at the bitterness, she didn't say anything but sat up and took the cup, stirring in a heaping spoonful of sugar, then another, using her own spoon before handing it back.

Another cautious sip, and it proved to be almost as good as hot chocolate. I nodded slowly, thinking I might be able to get used to coffee. Debbie nodded just as slowly back, then sat up in her chair and knuckled a tear out of the corner of her eye, laughing in such a strangled way that Bunny clucked her tongue. I didn't know why, although I'd heard the words disappointed and disappointment attached to Debbie. I knew this somehow involved children and was afraid I'd disappointed her by not liking coffee without sugar.

"It's really good coffee," I told her sincerely, so she laughed again, and dried her eyes.

Debbie was married to Ed, who was blond too, and looked like the movie star Tab Hunter. Ed's father was a Dutch immigrant who owned a nationwide appliance chain. Ed worked as an executive for his father and was being groomed to inherit. That was why Debbie lived in West Vancouver, where an architect had designed their house. My sister's name was Debbie Brouwer now. She'd met Ed at the country club five years ago when she was twenty and playing tennis with a friend who was a member. My father had decided we couldn't afford to join a country club but it turned out not to matter. Deb had Married Up anyhow.

Married Up. Another Disappointment. I heard all those verbal capitals because I knew the words meant more than I could understand, they had nuances, and I was bookmarking them to understand later.

"You want to go outside and kick a ball around?" Debbie asked.

I was already on my feet when my mother said, "Are you sure?" To Debbie, not to me.

"Yeah. Too bad," Debbie said. "Regular as clockwork."

We had a big backyard, although it was shady. Bunny did her gardening in the front yard, where she'd planted azaleas, rhododendrons, and hydrangeas in the rockery. Closer to the house, she'd dug in a rectangular bed of roses like the rose garden in Stanley Park. My favourite was a Peace rose that was both pink and yellow. Bunny always said she didn't love gardening but liked having a garden. The backyard was my father's job, and he seeded the grass frequently enough that it was a uniform green, with none of the brown spots other people ignored.

I picked up a soccer ball in the basement and we kicked it around the yard, making *Ha!* noises as we booted it back and forth. Miss Atkinson looked quite a bit like Debbie, although I hadn't noticed that yet. Norman would be the one to point it out after meeting my sister, and I would overhear Mr. Horton say something about the trend for little bottle-blond Barbies. This puzzled me, since my sister didn't need to dye her hair, and she was tall. When I asked my father about this, he told me that Mr. Horton was sardonic, and for once explained what that meant.

But this was pure innocence, two sisters booting a soccer ball back and forth, no matter what our ages. When Debbie got off a particularly hard shot, it made such a big wow in the chain-link fence she said, "Daddy better budget for a new fence," and I burped coffee.

3

G rade four was shaping up to be a golden year. The hated Mrs.
Persson was thoroughly behind me, and I had a new friend. But
then, Grouse Valley was the sort of place where things usually turned out
properly, like a fairy tale. It felt reassuring to know that, and I hoped for
Norman's sake his parents would quickly figure it out.

Norman's parents were my one worry that fall, since they were so different. No sooner had the Hortons moved into their new house than they
took off on a ten-day camping trip, which made for more excitement in
one month than most people cared for. That meant they missed the Pacific
National Exhibition at the end of August, which the rest of us looked forward to all year. And of course, there was the fact that Norman's mother
still had a job when most mothers couldn't wait to quit work when they
got married.

Mr. Horton turned out to be like other fathers in driving off to work
every day. But Mrs. Horton proved to be eccentric, striding past everyone's windows early in the morning, heading downhill to the school
with a canvas rucksack on her back. Not long before dinner, she'd stride
home again and disappear inside, and on weekends no one saw her, since
Norman said she did her marking and class prep.

This put Mrs. Horton outside neighbourhood life. Few people had
two cars, so most of the mothers spent quite a bit of time in each other's

houses, meeting for coffee, maybe exercising together to Jack LaLanne on television, no one going very far afield without their husbands and not really needing to.

The milkman came every Monday and Thursday in his square yellow Dairyland truck, rattling cases of milk bottles. The egg man from the Fraser Valley pulled up Tuesday in his station wagon, and on Wednesday, the fruit and vegetable truck lumbered up the hill, the man and lady from China selling produce out the back that smelled of good earth. My father let the egg man and the fruit and vegetable people park in our driveway, meaning that Bunny got to chat when the neighbours came by.

But since Mrs. Horton worked, she was never there for the egg man or the fruit and vegetable people, much less for a chat. She didn't even go to the supermarket. Instead, Mr. Horton did the shopping on Friday after school, when it was open late. Bunny shopped on Thursday, but for three weeks running, one of her friends saw Mr. Horton at the local SuperValu, pushing his cart up and down the aisle as if it was natural for a man to shop for groceries after work.

When Bunny told my father, he had to pause to think things through.

"That boy's going to be teased," he said finally.

"Children are mean," Bunny agreed, which interested me. "His mother ought to pave the way. She ought to know that. Otherwise, I don't see how she can claim to be a teacher."

"Because she teaches grade five?" I asked.

This proved to be a mistake, my parents having forgotten that I was lying on the floor behind my father's recliner.

"Who's supposed to be in bed?" Bunny asked, and I had to scramble.

Yet what she'd said stayed with me: paving the way. My mother made it sound as if Norman was a car, and you paved a road ahead of him, allowing him to drive his Normanness forward. Paving the way meant making the suburb fit Norman instead of making Norman fit in. Yet it seemed to me that Norman would be better off if he did things the way other kids did, at least as far as his polio let him. I never did myself, but

Norman was new and he didn't have as much leeway. Lying there, I decided on a fall project: to help Norman belong.

As a first step, I brought up Norman's allowance on the way to school the next morning. I'd already learned that Norman got a dollar once a month instead of a quarter every Friday like the rest of us. Everyone had quiet time on Saturday mornings when we didn't bother our parents, getting our own cereal and watching cartoons. Afterward, they paid our allowance and the younger kids went down to the shopping village while the older ones went to the Park Royal mall.

"Don't your parents make you have quiet time on Saturday?" I asked, as we walked down Moore Road.

"I get lots of quiet time," Norman said. "They've always got their marking."

"But you watch cartoons?"

A shrug. Of course.

"And you like to come to the village on Saturday."

This was a statement rather than a question, since we'd already established that he did.

"So why don't you get your allowance beforehand like everybody else?"

"I get a dollar, and I divide it into a quarter a week, so I get a quarter a week same as you do. It teaches me willpower."

"But you didn't have any left last week, and it's only halfway through September."

"That sometimes happens," Norman said, and I could see how it could, although I felt on the edge of something else.

Then it broke through.

"But some months have five weeks!" The injustice struck me hard. "So we get a quarter each week and you only get a dollar! That's not fair!"

Norman sucked on this, getting my point and slowly going sad. We walked on like that for a while, with me kicking my shoes on the road.

Bunny polished them every night but the patent leather was already cracking, so that she was starting to see them as a bad call, too.

"I can't," Norman said finally.

"You can't what?"

"Ask my mum and dad."

"All right," I said, calculating that I couldn't talk to Mrs. Horton at school, but I could wait at Norman's until she got home. I might have been the only one in the neighbourhood to speak with Mrs. Horton, since I often went to Norman's house and we'd formed an acquaintance.

"Here you are again, Tink," she'd say, hanging up her knapsack on a hook beside the front door.

The idea of turning this into an actual conversation made Norman nervous. But I refused to budge, insisting on going home with him, building a fort out of sofa cushions in the Hortons' rec room and staying inside it stubbornly until the front door opened and closed.

When I ran upstairs, trying to explain properly, Mrs. Horton took off her knapsack and put it on its hook. She listened as I spoke, but kept walking into the kitchen to get dinner underway. Mrs. Horton was a calm person. She was the usual size for mothers, but she wore her light brown hair braided and coiled around her head like a grandmother. There was also something powdery about her hair and complexion, and when she'd come in, she'd kicked off her shoes and put sandals on top of her socks, not slippers. I knew her name was Marian, having heard Mr. Horton call her Maid Marian. It looked as if they were having fried chicken for dinner.

"That's a good point, Tink," she said, once I'd argued my case. "But you know, Norman can very easily do long division, dividing up his dollar to find out how many cents he has to spend each day. Can't you, Norman?" she asked. "In months with thirty days, he can divide his dollar by thirty to get one daily figure—can't you?—and in months with thirty-one, he can divide by thirty-one. And February is a bonus month, isn't it? With only twenty-eight days. Then you multiply each daily number by seven to get his allowance each week. I wonder if it makes much of a difference. What about you, Tink?"

The arithmetic boggled my mind. Nancy Workman was a genius at arithmetic even though she wet her pants. But I wasn't, and most people weren't. Mrs. Horton was being a teacher, which wasn't fair when school was out.

"We're only grade four," I said, my voice wavering a little. "*Not* grade five."

Mrs. Horton considered this for a while, and to my surprise, she nodded. I thought she was going to say she'd ask Mr. Horton, but instead she told Norman, "It looks like you've got yourself a raise."

Norman's shoulders drooped in relief, although I felt disregarded.

"*I* got it," I said. "I'm the president of Norman's union local. Which is made up of him."

Mrs. Horton didn't seem to know how to take this.

"My Uncle Punk is president of his union local."

"Which union?"

"The woodworkers?"

"The one who's on the radio all the time?" When I nodded, she asked, "Isn't his name Donald Barnham?"

"He's my mother's brother," I said. They'd started calling him Punk because he went to work as a lumberjack when he was just a punk kid, and I wasn't surprised that Mrs. Horton had heard of him. My uncle was famous, although the newspapers didn't like him, much less Jack Webster on his radio talk show.

"Everybody's heard of Uncle Punk," I said, savouring my second victory.

It proved to be more than that. When we went down to the village the next Saturday, Norman had an extra quarter, which his mother had thrown in so he could treat me to fries and a milkshake at the Riverine Restaurant. Union dues, she said. We were too young to presume to a booth at the Riverine, which was a diner. Instead, we sat at the counter on the red leatherette stools and decided to save a quarter by sharing an order. The Riverine gave you so many fries they fell off the plate, and the shakes came in an icy metal container that filled a soda glass one and a half times, and they were big glasses. We were both in the mood for vanilla, so it worked.

Afterward, Norman used his saved quarter to buy two extra comics in the drugstore, where they were displayed on a revolving metal rack that squeaked when you turned it. We could share those, too. The comics were twelve cents apiece, leaving Norman enough to buy himself a penny candy in the fruit and vegetable store across the street, which stocked gum and chocolate bars on shelves below the counter and kept penny candy in jars on top.

Having bought just one *Superman*, I had enough money left to buy a package of red licorice. Norman took a long time to decide on a gummy bear. Afterward, we picked up our bikes from outside the drugstore, taking a tour past the hardware store, where they sold marbles, then past the library, where Norman already had a card. Further on were the doctors' and dentists' offices, where we stopped at the stop sign.

"My mum says I'm going to keep seeing my old doctor in the Marine Building over town," Norman said. "But he's okay."

"*Unh-uh. Unh-uh. Unh-uh,*" I replied, and we both said it as we turned right and rode past the Anglican Church, which wasn't the one we went to, and said it even louder as we circled back through the village. People turned to look at us, including the jeweller who stared out the window with an eyeglass in one eye that made it look enormous. It looked exactly the way the dentist's eyes looked through his glasses before he bent down to hurt your mouth, the thought of which made me pedal faster, like Dorothy trying to escape the tornado that carried her to Oz.

Two weeks later, the Hortons came to dinner, which ended up making my plan for Norman feel crucial. Bunny had invited the Hortons as soon as they'd arrived. But first, they had to settle, then they went camping, then school started, and it was almost the end of September before they found a date. I heard Bunny tell my father she felt insulted. At least she would have, if they hadn't turned down invitations from everyone else.

There was a knock on the door the next Saturday evening and there they were: Mr. and Mrs. Horton, Norman and his sister Rosa. They were late, but Mrs. Horton made up for it by holding out flowers, having picked a bouquet of sweet peas from Mrs. Milewski's garden. It was their garden now, but I still thought of it as belonging to Mrs. Milewski, who had planted the sweet peas before selling her house. Getting them was a bit of a coup. Mrs. Milewski had never given them to anyone, although I'd been known to sneak into her backyard and pick some, at least until she caught me.

"How lovely!" my mother cried, using her company voice. "Mary Alice, go get the small cut-glass vase."

"So you have a real name," Mr. Horton said, fixing me with his teacher's eyes. I'd seen him around Norman's house, and he'd looked at me just as piercingly once or twice but had never spoken to me before.

"What's yours?" I asked.

"Mary Alice!" my mother cried.

"Jack," he said. "But you can call me Mr. Horton."

That was strange, since of course I had to call him Mr. Horton. I still thought it was a valid question, and looked at him again as I went for the vase. Seeing Mr. Horton beside my father made me realize that he was tall, although not as tall as my father. He was also darker than my father with black curly hair, and I thought he looked more like a principal than a teacher.

"I'll take a beer," he said, before anyone had asked.

"Please and thank you," Rosa said lazily, as I came back into the kitchen with the vase. Rosa was like Norman in being a slow-moving person. She moved like syrup, and after seeing her for the first time, my mother had said Rosa was a little *too*, without going on. Maybe she meant a little too grown up, since Rosa was already busty at not-quite-fifteen.

Mrs. Horton was busty, too, although she was otherwise slender, and she wanted a beer as well. Afterward, she stood watching my mother jam the flowers into the vase, not taking over the way some mothers did, Bunny being the first to admit she wasn't artistic. I wondered if Mrs. Horton was the observant type, as Miss Atkinson called Norman. He must take after someone, and he wasn't like his father, who had already left the kitchen with his beer.

Feeling curious, I followed Mr. Horton into the living room, where I found him frowning out the picture windows as if he were planning to grade the view.

"Flitting around, Tinkerbell?" he asked. Like all teachers, he had eyes in the back of his head.

"It's Tink."

"And you don't know where it comes from?" he asked, turning to face me.

"My sister," I said. "And the movie. And the book, *Peter Pan*."

I knew I had to stare him down, the way I would a kid like him. I remembered my father's word *sardonic*. Mr. Horton scared me, and I refused to let him know it, holding my ground until he turned amused, his grey eyes sparking.

"Tink it is," he said.

"Are you teasing her, Jack?" Mrs. Horton asked, coming in with her beer. My mother had a highball, my father his ginger ale. Norman and Rosa each had Cokes, and I hoped I hadn't missed the boat on the Coke front.

"Mr. Horton likes teasing people, Tink," his wife said. "He doesn't mean anything by it."

"Yes, he does."

"Mary Alice!"

"Yes, he does," Rosa echoed. "Ignore him."

Mr. Horton smiled broadly. So Rosa was his pride and joy, just like I was my father's and Debbie was my mother's. Not that they were ever as obvious about it as Mr. Horton.

"I got a new *Batman,*" I told Norman. "We can go read it in the rec room." Raising my voice slightly: "After I get my Coke."

Hearing no objection, I turned politely to Rosa. "You can come if you want."

"You've got a cat!" she cried, spotting Wilma by the fireplace.

"No," her father said.

"Rosa wants a cat, but Jack can't stand them," Mrs. Horton said.

"It's okay. I'll get one now we're out of that cruddy apartment."

This was new information, and I lingered while Rosa crouched down beside Wilma, who was a tortoiseshell. My father called her long-suffering. I had no idea why.

"She has kittens twice a year, so you can have one the next litter," I said, conscious of scoring a point on Mr. Horton, then taking off to get my Coke.

Norman was naturally polite. A born gentleman, my father called him. But as we sat down at the dinner table, it turned out that his parents and sister didn't have any company manners, which involved asking people how they were and being concerned about the answer. People always said they were fine, couldn't be better, but then you had to ask were they *sure.* The Hortons didn't ask anything, although it's true that Mrs. Horton showed herself to be as bookish as my father. While my mother served the starter, Mrs. Horton mentioned how much she'd enjoyed a novel she'd just finished reading.

"*The Carpetbaggers,*" my mother agreed, putting out fruit salad in sundae-type dishes, which was the latest fashion. Mrs. Horton looked so uncomfortable that you could tell she hadn't read it.

"*Catch-22,*" she said.

My mother didn't seem to have heard of that one, although my father nodded.

"That's how it felt," he said. "Overseas."

I knew the name of one of the battles where my father had fought during the Second World War. Ortona. He'd got a medal there, the biggest of his medals. One time, after he'd stayed in his workshop for almost a week, my mother had taken them out of a crumpled old brown paper old envelope to show me. Ortona had been fought exactly fifteen years before.

"Although I can't say I've ever heard things spoken about in quite that way," my father said. "And wonder if they ought to be."

"How do you think they ought to be spoken about?" Mr. Horton asked.

"As little as possible," my father said, and there was an awkward pause.

"My latest was *Franny and Zooey*," Rosa said. "Which I *l-o-v-e-d*."

My mother sat down uncomfortably. Once you'd established that everyone was fine, the polite subjects for conversation at dinner were the weather, TV, and the outrageous prices charged by shopkeepers. Books weren't discussed any more than politics and religion, although at least the Hortons hadn't got into those.

It was also true that children didn't have opinions, even teenagers like Rosa, who were expected to either wolf down double helpings (boys) or push their food around on their plates (girls) then excuse themselves from the table to widespread mutual relief. My mother didn't like Rosa smoothing things over, especially since you could see that Bunny hadn't heard of *Franny and Zooey* either, although it turned out my father had read that one as well.

"*The Carpetbaggers*," my mother repeated, her feathers ruffling. "Was a real page turner."

It wasn't that my mother didn't read. She drove me to the library on days she had the car and sometimes took out a book for herself. But Bunny only really had time for one big book a year, and this year it had been *The Carpetbaggers*, which was a Hollywood novel that all of her friends adored.

"What about you, Tink?" Mr. Horton asked, emphasizing my name. "Did you read *The Carpetbaggers*?"

My mother had swatted my hand when I'd reached for it. But you couldn't say so in front of company; even I knew that.

"I like *Anne of Green Gables*," I said.

"You like Anne," Mrs. Horton said, smiling agreeably. "So do I."

"And *A Wrinkle in Time*. I got it out of the library last week, and I've already read it twice. And my Aunt Magda gave me *Little Women*, and that was absorbing." Aunt Magda was married to my father's younger brother, Uncle Ray, and she was absorbed by many things.

"So you like Jo Marsh, too." Mrs. Horton was still smiling.

"She's okay. Except that all the girls in that book keep running after boys. After *Laurie*. You'd think they'd have more brains."

"*Ha!*" Mr. Horton laughed, which was startling. He pushed his fruit salad aside and leaned on the table to fix his eyes on mine, ready to quiz me, I could tell.

I tried to avoid him, concentrating on my salad, having lucked into four pieces of pineapple. It occurred to me that getting teachers for parents must be tiring. Maybe that was part of the reason Norman moved so slowly. Polio wasn't all of it.

"In the nineteenth century . . ." Mr. Horton began.

"History lesson," Rosa said.

"Historically, *Tink*," he went on, almost ignoring his daughter, but not quite, "young ladies of the middle and upper classes weren't allowed to hold jobs. Their economic positions were determined by whomever they were able to marry. So getting themselves a rich husband was fundamental to their comfort. Marriage was their job. In writing a novel about young women, Louisa May Alcott was writing a how-to guide for getting the job you wanted, which in Jo's case, wasn't what people expected. Giving advice. An agony aunt. The nineteenth-century Ann Landers."

My mother looked bewildered, my father amused, although his eyes were sharp, too. He took Mr. Horton's measure in full, which was one of his sayings.

Farther down the table, I thought about what Mr. Horton had said.

"I get that," I replied.

Mr. Horton looked me over. "I actually think you do." Turning to his son, he asked over-politely, "What about you, Norman?"

Norman was eating his way through his fruit salad. He liked all kinds of fruit but especially cantaloupe, so he'd lucked out, too.

"I haven't read it," he said.

"No. Because you only read comic books."

"I plan to start reading science fiction."

"Oh. You *plan*."

Mr. Horton sounded like my brother Bob needling our father.

"My brother is sardonic, too," I said, making Mr. Horton swivel toward me.

"Mary Alice has a vocabulary," Bunny said, sounding pleased with me, which wasn't usual when we had company.

"Mrs. Horton knows Uncle Punk," I said, trying to smooth things over.

"No. I'm sorry. Who?" Mrs. Horton asked. Then she corrected herself. "You told me Donald Barnham is your uncle. Yes, I've heard him on the radio."

"Airing his many opinions," Mr. Horton said. He didn't seem to like Uncle Punk's opinions, which struck me as a rude thing to say. I looked at Norman, who was taking his time with his fruit salad. Beside him, Rosa had an expression on her face I didn't understand, almost as if she felt superior to her parents.

It was the strangest evening I'd ever spent, although Norman and I enjoyed our meal. After the fruit salad, Bunny served a fine roast pork and scalloped potatoes with cheese.

"Daddy?" I asked afterward. I hardly ever called him that, but I was sitting on his lap keeping Bunny company while she did the dishes. I couldn't think how to ask him what I wanted to know. I didn't even know what I wanted to know.

"The Hortons are intellectuals, Tink," my father said. "They're readers. Thinkers. Fish out of water, at least around here. They're not bad people. They're just different."

I didn't think they were bad. I didn't think Mrs. Horton was bad, anyhow. She paid union dues. But it took Uncle Punk to ask my real question two weeks later, which I recognized as soon as he asked it.

"What are they doing here?"

This was on a Sunday, when he and Auntie Nita had come over to watch the B.C. Lions football game, my brother Bob in tow.

What are they doing here? That was Uncle Punk's overall question, at least about our neighbours. One time, we'd all been standing in the driveway out front, saying goodbye to him and Auntie. They took up a lot of room. Auntie was big, and Uncle Punk's shoulders were as wide as a refrigerator, although his bulk was softened by a comic's rubbery face.

Just as they were about to leave, Mrs. Manners ran out their front door in her tennis clothes, waving at us cheerfully as she ran down the steps. She got in her little red sports car, honked the horn and backed out of their driveway. It must have been summer. The top of her convertible was down, and Mrs. Manners looked like a movie star turning into the road and roaring around the blind corner.

"How come they live here?" Uncle Punk asked, watching the empty road.

My mother bristled, because why wouldn't you want to live here?

"Most people live where they can afford to live," my father answered peaceably.

"Not in the British Properties, or Shaughnessy, or Point Grey," Uncle Punk persisted. "Even when they can't afford it, people like that live there."

Rich people lived there; even I knew that. Uncle Ray and Aunt Magda lived in the British Properties. I was perturbed that my parents didn't seem to know the answer, although I could tell that my father had thought of the question and felt a little perturbed as well.

Now he answered Uncle Punk, "The Hortons were working up north when their lad got sick. I don't think they intended to move down here, but the boy was admitted to Vancouver General. Marian Horton quit work to look after him for three, maybe four years. It sounds as if she schooled him at home. Her husband found a job at the high school, and when the boy was well enough, Marian took a job down the hill."

Uncle Punk grunted. He was inclined to dislike the Hortons after Bunny's story about dinner. Stuck-up, he'd decided. Full of themselves. Even though Bunny had told the dinner as a funny story. "I'll take a beer." When nobody had asked!

"You can shine a good light on it," Uncle Punk said. "But I've got my questions."

"You've always got questions," I said. That was my way of defending Norman, and I was ready to argue the point. But Uncle Punk just broke into a smile.

"You got that right, pet," he said.

I wasn't a pet, but Bunny signalled me to let it go. We were in the rec room watching the game, although it was halftime and we had the sound off. Uncle Punk and Auntie Nita were on the chesterfield while Bunny sat on the arm. She had to get up and down, refilling bowls of potato chips and dip, especially the sour cream and chives dip, which was popular, mainly with me. My father was in his old recliner, which had migrated downstairs, while my brother Bob slouched in an armchair. Only Debbie and Ed were missing. They had tickets to the game.

My father was the one who wanted to keep the TV in the rec room rather than the living room. That meant we didn't use the living room as much as most people, although my mother was happy since it saved the furniture. It was October by that time, so the rec room fire was lit and crackling. My father had built the fireplace surround with big round stones he'd hauled up from the creek and lined the room with knotty pine. He'd also built bookshelves into the wall facing the picture window. They were overflowing with books, newer books laid on top of long rows of older books. My father had more books than anybody, even the Hortons, which I knew from snooping.

Outside the rec room was a small covered patio where the coals in the portable barbecue were burning down nicely. As the game headed into the fourth quarter, my father would be in and out cooking hot dogs and hamburgers. Some people wouldn't miss one flat second of the fourth quarter. But my father found it tense and preferred to be moving, especially if it was a close game and it looked as if the Lions might bunk it.

"They won't be here for long," Uncle Punk said. He'd left a pause long enough that it took me a second to remember that he was talking about the Hortons.

"Dog with a bone," Bunny said.

"Get jobs in some fancy-schmancy private school."

"Norman is Tink's friend," my father warned.

"He fills a gap," Bunny said. "With the Doherty girl off to California."

"He doesn't *fill a gap*," I said, indignant on Norman's behalf.

"Private schools don't pay as well." That was my brother Bob, levering himself up in his armchair. Bob was a Parker, tall and rangy with a lawyer's sharp eyes. He got lost in his thoughts and didn't always listen, although he listened to Uncle Punk more than he did to our father, whom he resembled so closely. "Part of your pay is supposed to come from the prestige of working there."

"From what they said," our father told him, "they're planning on staying where they are."

"I didn't get the impression you'd become confidential," Bob replied.

"No, and I don't think we will."

"So you don't have any particular insight into their intentions."

My brother sounded as if he had our father in the witness box. That's how my father sometimes put it, although pointing this out didn't make Bob any happier.

"I've met them once, counsellor," he replied. Bob looked ready to snap at him when Bunny shook her head.

It was well known in our family that my brother had a grievance against our father for having signed up, enlisting in the army as soon as Canada declared war on Nazi Germany. There wasn't conscription, Bob would say. No one had made him sign up. A married man with two children. No one *expected* him to sign up. But there he was, first in line.

Bob was usually quiet, but sometimes he arrived even quieter, as gloomy as an overcast sky. This was a sign that at some point he'd go after my father, which Bunny would always tell me later wasn't my father's fault. It had probably started earlier in the day when a professor was too hard on Bob. After university, it might be a judge, a client, a girl. Bob couldn't seem to take life easily. Bunny wished he would, although if she tried to forestall things by telling him so, Bob was guaranteed to go off. It frightened me, hearing my brother's voice go thin and needling as wire.

A married man, he would say. Two children. No conscription. They weren't going to grab him off the street. But he'd been gone for six years, starting when Bob was five years old.

"*Six years!*"

The worst times were when Bob goaded my father into answering back in that same whipping voice. Our father, I mean to say. He'd get out of his chair and stand what Bunny called ramrod straight, which frightened me even more.

"And would you be happier if Hitler had won?"

I didn't understand why Bob cherished such a grievance, especially since he'd got Uncle Punk while our father was away. Uncle Punk and Auntie Nita had a family of seven and Bob was the same age as their middle son, Darren. He'd been over there all the time during the war and had been close to our uncle ever since. Debbie had gone there too, Bunny having worked as an executive secretary during the war, although Debbie always got left out of Bob's story. He had to leave her out. Debbie had lost her father for six years, too, and she was a happy-tempered person.

"I suppose Norman is a family name," Auntie Nita said, out of nowhere. I figured she wanted to change the subject before Bob went off, Auntie being a peacemaker, as warm as a bath.

"He's going to be a doctor," I began.

"Good for him!" she said. Auntie would have said that about anything up to, "Norman's going to be a teenage murderer." In which case, she probably would have answered, "Well, he probably has his reasons."

"I guess having had polio means he wants to cure it," Bunny said.

"They *have* cured it," Bob said, still ready to take offense. "Or at least they've got a vaccine."

"So if he's cured—which he isn't, by the way, not with that leg brace. If he's cured, he must look up to the doctors for doing it."

Bunny didn't take Bob lying down, although he accepted more from her than he did from our father.

"He was named after a famous doctor. That's why," I said, still trying to answer Auntie's question. "A famous Canadian doctor. I guess he was one of the missionaries Mr. Culver talks about in church. He helped the poor people in China. Norman wants to be like him."

For some reason, this made my family go silent.

"Bingo," Uncle Punk said quietly.

"Looks like it," Bob agreed.

"Let's not jump to any conclusions," my father said.

"Oh, come on," Bob told him. "They're hardly going to name their kid after Norman Bethune if they're not communists."

"Communists?" Bunny asked faintly.

"Dr. Norman Bethune, the famous communist," Bob said. "Put it together and what do you get?"

"I repeat: What are they doing here?" Uncle Punk asked. "Who sent 'em?"

"Auntie just asked me a question," I said.

"And you done good by answering, sweetheart," Uncle Punk replied.

Did. I thought you were supposed to say, You did good by answering. Did well. But I wasn't sure, and I didn't think I'd done any good at all. Not with my father turning into a ramrod in front of the window.

"I'm not going to have this," he said. "We know very little about these people. We're going to drop this right now."

Bob got up to face him, but it was Uncle Punk who spoke.

"Chairman Mao's favourite doctor, Norman Bethune," he said, still on the chesterfield. His voice got low and carrying when he wanted to make a point. You leaned forward to listen, even though you didn't have to. "Norman Bethune, toeing the commie line during the Spanish Civil War."

"You should be the last to cast aspersions," my father said. "Given the way they slander unions."

"Some of 'em deserve it. Little too pink for comfort. My comfort, anyways," Uncle Punk said. "But in our union, we ain't commies, and we don't like 'em one bit."

"Aren't," I said, sure about that one, anyway. Then I realized that my uncle had used bad grammar for a reason, although I had no idea why. I hated the way my family could bristle into parts. The men could, anyway. It didn't seem to take much in my family for the men to bristle. Right now they were like a forest of angry trees. There were only three of them, but they felt like a forest.

"What's a communist?" I asked. But maybe I didn't say it very loudly, and no one was paying attention to me anyway.

"If we suppose it's true," my father told Uncle Punk, "when you're young and idealistic, you can make mistakes . . ."

"I imagine that's intended for me," Bob said.

". . . but a great many people left the Communist Party after the Soviets invaded Hungary in '56. It's on the public record. Not that we have any indication that any of this applies to Jack Horton."

"You mean that he left the Party," Bob said. "No, we have no indication of that."

My father held my brother's eye.

"People move here to get away from things," he said. "How many men around here fought in the war? From what he said, Jack Horton signed up as soon as he turned eighteen. People come here to lead a quiet life. We're going to let them."

"So," Bob said. "At least we know why you're defending him."

My father went even more ramrod. "They have children."

"They *teach* children," Uncle Punk said, in his low and deadly voice. It snaked around the room like mist.

"They have children," Auntie Nita repeated.

My brother and my uncle turned in surprise. Auntie stood up nimbly. She may have been a big woman, but as Bunny said, she was a good dancer and light on her feet. As soon as she'd secured their attention, Auntie Nita sat down again on the arm of the chesterfield, as if it was high enough for what she had to say.

"Senator Joseph McCarthy," she went on in a humorous voice, addressing Uncle Punk. "Here you go again, off on a witch hunt. Why in hell's bells do you want to stir the pot?"

"Well, that's true," Bunny said nervously. "We don't need any trouble around here."

"No one's going to say anything," Auntie said. "They probably came here to get away from it all, the way Hall says. Not that membership in any party is illegal. We have a democracy in this country, I would remind you."

Bob looked as if he was going to answer but he didn't. Uncle Punk sucked his cheeks. I looked at my father, who was very still and straight. He didn't get like this very often, but when he did, it didn't go away easily, and sometimes it required time in his workshop.

I thought unhappily of the barbecue, and my hot dog, and of Norman.

"Will Norman be all right?" I asked.

"With a sister named Rosa," Bob said. "No doubt in honour of Rosa Luxemburg, the famous Marxist."

That seemed to be a last gasp. Looking at the TV, my brother said in a fake voice, "Oh good. Joe Kapp just completed an eighteen-yard pass."

The third quarter had started and we hadn't even noticed.

My father swivelled on his heel and went outside to tend the barbecue. Bunny turned the sound back on and everyone stood down. I didn't really understand any of this, and no one had answered my question about whether Norman would be all right. I had an idea I would need to double down on helping him fit in. It also occurred to me that ramrod must be a military term, although I had no idea what it meant.

4

Down the creek the next day, Norman and I played Knights of the Round Table, which we'd read about in *Classic Comics*. This involved sneaking up on each other and sword fighting. Hiding behind a tree, waiting for Norman to sneak up, I tried to figure out how to ask if his parents were communists, even though I still had no idea what that meant. I wasn't sure if I even wanted to know, afraid I'd blurt out the answer at the wrong time. I was known for my blurting.

Hiding meant I wasn't moving around much, but the afternoon was warm for October, all soft air and fallen leaves. The creek was lively, the wrens chipping happily. We didn't have long to play outside after school anymore, with evening smudging in early. It would smudge in soon, the colours fading, the forest turning great and dark. The wild animals would take over as soon as we were gone, bears lumbering across the creek.

We still had time to play, but Norman was being slow about sneaking up, and I was getting restless. Nor could I decide whether to ask about communism or not, and that was an irritation. There was also the fact I'd found an excellent sword that I was keen to use, an old piece of wood as long and wide as a blade, although not particularly pointed. Flat across the top, actually. I held it against my leg as I waited for Norman to give himself away.

Yet Norman was moving slowly, and walking as softly as the Lone Ranger stalking bad guys across the cactus mountains. We were playing knights, but it occurred to me that the Lone Ranger was a knight. That was an interesting thought, and I wondered whether it excused Norman's lateness.

Crack of dead twig. Norman was behind me. I swivelled and yelled "Ha!" and he yelled "Ha!" and we each put one hand on our hips like Zorro and started fighting our swords. Norman had a long skinny fallen branch that whipped around nicely. Ha! Ha! His sword made a *zizzing* sound as we jumped around. Or I jumped. Norman held his ground, swishing his stick. When he caught my sword head-on, I felt a quiver up my arm.

"Careful you don't put an eye out."

An adult voice. Mrs. Manners, we saw when we turned. Not that I'd needed to turn to recognize her voice. Mrs. Manners spoke with laughter underneath everything she said, as if she was constantly joking.

We drooped down our swords as she made her way over, picking a path delicately around the wettest ground. Adults didn't come here, although there was a track down the mountain beside the creek that led across the Raincoat Man's bridge to the little shopping mall. Teenagers used it, but adults on our side of the creek took their cars.

Yet Mrs. Manners always did what no one else did, including not dyeing her hair. She was getting close to us, but she would have been easy to spot halfway up the hill. Mrs. Manners had thick silver hair and wore it in a bob like Jackie Kennedy. The mothers said she'd had black hair when she was younger, which you could tell from her black eyebrows and her grey-green eyes. But they said she'd gone white during the war, and I pictured her waking up one morning and looking in the mirror to find that her hair had turned to snow. After recovering from her surprise, she'd said to herself, I won't dye it. I'll just wear it in a bob like Jackie Kennedy.

But President Kennedy hadn't been president during the war, which meant that Mrs. Kennedy hadn't been around then, either, so maybe Mrs. Manners had been the one to get the bob idea first. She did what other mothers didn't do. Ahead of the times, Bunny said. It wasn't a compliment.

"Hello, Mrs. Manners."

I spoke in my best company voice as she reached us, her fists balled up under her arms as if she was cold.

"Here you are, Tink," she said. "Indescribably filthy as usual."

I had nothing to say to this since it was true, and in any case, she didn't seem to hold it against me.

She turned to Norman. "You're the new boy, aren't you?"

Norman nodded, which is all he usually did.

"He's Norman," I said. Speaking to strangers was hard on him. "This is Mrs. Manners," I told him, and Norman surprised me by putting out a hand, which Mrs. Manners shook. Not all mothers would have done that. I was a little in awe of Mrs. Manners, and not just because of her hair.

"I hear you're the same age as my Harry," she said. "You should probably be friends."

"But Harry's on the track team," I said. "And Norman can't run."

"And he's your friend, isn't he Tink?" she asked, in her laughing voice.

I didn't answer, thinking it must be obvious.

"We should probably have your parents over for dinner," Mrs. Manners told Norman. "I'm a little negligent on the dinner front, aren't I?"

My thoughts fell into a welter about dinner being a bad idea because of communism, which I'd forgotten about while sword fighting. I wished I could forget about it entirely.

"But I suppose your parents are bohemians, aren't they?" Mrs. Manners said. "So I've been told. And they probably don't want to come over, anyway. A little busy for everyone's invitations, aren't they?"

Still in a welter, I told her, "No, Mrs. Manners. It's my Aunt Magda who's a bohemian. That's what you heard. Aunt Magda comes from a place that used to be called Bohemia. It's got a longer name now."

"That's not what I meant, Tink," Mrs. Manners said, her fists back up under her arms. She was wearing a cardigan over her blouse so she couldn't have been cold. "Although you're right. I find your Aunt Magda entirely alarming."

Turning back to Norman, she said, "I suppose your parents are, too. I gather your father's the tall one who teaches history at Cal and Andy's school."

Norman nodded. The oldest Manners boy, Cal, was quarterback on the football team and the big man at school, even though he was only in grade eleven. Her daughter Andy, on the other hand, was always in the principal's office, having a tendency to let the air out of teachers' tires. Mrs. Manners said they should probably send Andy to the nuns; I'd heard the mothers talking about it. Some of them thought it was a good idea, others that Mrs. Manners was only joking, the Manners family being Anglican.

The two younger boys, Jamie and Harry, went to our school. The Manners family had enviable nicknames, especially Andy. Mr. and Mrs. Manners were Jim and Pat. You'd think they were a household of six boys, especially since their house was a disaster area. A cleaning lady had to come over once a week to fix things up, arriving from the bus stop with a grim expression on her face. Her grimness was a private joke in our neighbourhood. Or at least, a joke shared by the mothers who didn't have cleaning ladies, meaning most of them.

Mrs. Manners looked at Norman with her head to one side, making a blush rise up his neck.

"You *can* speak?" she asked.

"Yes, Mrs. Manners," I answered.

"But I'm a complete terror," she said, still looking at Norman. "I freeze your blood."

"No, ma'am. You don't," he replied, not even muttering, but speaking very clearly.

"You're just alarming," I said, so Mrs. Manners snapped her head toward me. I reassured her, "Like my Aunt Magda."

"I'm not as sophisticated as your Aunt Magda, Tink," she said. And that seemed to be the end of it, with Mrs. Manners saying, "On with you then," and walking down the path.

As soon as she was out of hearing, Norman sang the *Twilight Zone* song. *Dee-dee-dee-dah. Dee-dee-doo-dah.* He was right. The whole episode was so strange I couldn't encompass it.

"She looked like she was crying or something," Norman said. "Her eyes were all red. But it's probably just allergies." ·

Norman noticed things that no one else did, meaning me.

"How come they live here?" I asked. "How come their kids don't go to private schools over town? Like with nuns."

"My dad says you'd think Andy Manners was smart, but she's just like her father. Cal Manners is the one with brains. It's not fair, when he got his mother's looks, too." Norman stopped, looking caught out. "I'm not supposed to say anything about school."

I shrugged, letting him know I wasn't going to pass it on. I also wondered again if this was the time to ask why the Hortons lived here, and if I could tell my father his parents had given up on communism.

Norman saw I was going to say something, which put me on the spot.

"Did you ever go to school before this year?" I asked. "I never got that."

"I went last year over town," Norman said. "They beat me up pretty bad. It was kind of a rough school. So we moved."

I felt relieved. "So *that's* why you came here."

Norman shrugged. But it was the sort of shrug that didn't mean, Of course. There was a shimmer in there which made it more along the lines of, Sort of. I wasn't sure I liked that, and sat down on a log to think.

Norman sat down beside me, seeing that I might say something else. I felt annoyed at being put so continuously on the spot. It was probably better not to know about communism, but I was running out of other questions.

"Mrs. Manners really comes from the planet Krypton," I said. "Her superpower is being super-weird."

"My dad says she dyes her eyebrows black instead of her hair."

I was completely thrown. "They can do that?"

Norman nodded slowly, his bottom lip sticking out.

"Holy jumping Jehoshaphat," I said, using one of Uncle Punk's expressions.

"Holy shirttails," Norman said, which sounded like one of his mum's.

"Holy *shit*." Bunny.

After that, we sat on the log swearing happily until there was a commotion up the hill. Bunny, calling me to dinner, making me realize I was famished. We'd been down the creek for long enough that colours had faded out around us. The air was chilly and the seat of my pants was wet from the log. I would hear about that from Bunny, but I'd heard it so often that I didn't really listen anymore. Nor did I ever get colds, despite her threats. Or hardly ever.

Leading Norman up the hill, I realized I was every bit as filthy as Mrs. Manners had said. I also had an idea that October was too late for allergies, but thought I may have been wrong.

It happened again that night. I never talked about it and didn't know why it happened or if it happened to anyone else. But sometimes at night as I lay in bed I would float out of my body.

Usually, I went as far as the hot-air register. When I was my normal self, I liked to hunker down there on winter mornings under a blanket to eat my mandarin orange, the hot air blowing under the blanket like summer. That was a happy time.

But when I floated out of my body, I usually stopped beside the register like a forgotten toy. From my place just off the floor, I could see myself lying in the bed and feel the dark room around me looking large and empty: empty even though I was in it, both in bed and in the air.

At first, the feeling was exciting, although a little lonely. But when it didn't stop, I always grew frightened that this time I wouldn't be able to make it back into my body. I would slip anchor like a lost little dory and drift away forever.

The fear was bad enough, but the worst part came when the floating started. I would find myself rising, heading toward the ceiling, knowing I could slip through it and be gone. Panicked now, I would urge myself through the air like a swimmer without arms, willing myself toward my body. Then I was just outside it and falling and . . .

I don't know. I was back, sitting up in bed, and the world was enormous.

It was worse the night after Mrs. Manners, the worst I'd had so far. I was awake when it began the way it always did, my lights out, the night light on. My parents wondered why I was so afraid of the dark. My mother said my sister never was, although my father told her in a warning voice that people were different.

This time I didn't go to the register. Instead, I found myself slowly floating up from the bed in a way I'd never done before, rising toward the ceiling and slipping through it. I was in the attic amid its collection of trunks and boxes and heading for the rough wood beams above. Then I floated through the beams, too, and up through the roof and shingles until I drifted into the dark night sky.

I drifted gently, rising more slowly now that I was outside the house. The suburb was laid out below me, the peaked roofs of the houses widely spaced along the curving streets. Smoke came out of the occasional chimney, flowing at an angle, so there must have been a wind. Yet I was conscious of neither wind nor cold and felt surprisingly unafraid. Instead, I had a sense of the strangeness of the world as I gazed down at the suburban streets, seeing the way they curved up the mountain like animal trails.

After that, I started drifting along like the smoke, floating slowly over the houses. Streetlights made round pools of light on the main road below and cars sped through them. Softer light shone out many of the windows, golden light and the flickering blue of television screens. It wasn't late. I had an early bedtime. Drifting on the wind, or becoming something like it, I passed westward over Mosquito Creek. On the other side, I saw another subdivision. More curving streets, one with a deep black line drawn down the side of it. A ditch, I supposed, where they hadn't yet put in the pipes. House lights shone behind it.

Remembering this, I picture the husbands and wives behind those lighted windows. The children are in bed and their parents are slouched down on the chesterfield watching TV, the husband with his feet on the coffee table, the wife curled up, her stockinged feet underneath her. The husband gets up to pour himself another scotch. Sure you don't want one?

The people I see in house after house aren't the older parents I registered as a child. These days they look young, most of them in their thirties. Many smoke, even though they know what it's doing to their lungs. Often they drink too much, especially at parties, and husbands sometimes drive home drunk even when they have children in the car. A few of them are having affairs, and divorce is becoming more common. As a child, I never knew the real reason behind some of the sudden disappearances from the classroom, a girl or boy I'd known all my life permanently gone.

My parents weren't gossips. My father refused to hear it, growing so distressed when people turned malicious that he sometimes got up and left the room. Bunny stayed and listened, so she knew where all the bodies were buried. But she disliked repeating things, and it took me years to get her to tell me which children had left the neighbourhood because of a divorce. Years to learn that the father of my best friend Jennifer Doherty had taken a transfer to California hoping to rescue his marriage. His wife had caught him having an affair with Mrs. Milewski, whose house the Hortons would buy.

I'd thought of Mrs. Milewski as an old woman chasing me out of her garden the times I'd picked her sweet peas. But when I asked Bunny to take me through the old family photograph albums, the one picture she found of Carrie Milewski shows her as little more than a girl. A healthy girl with thick ankles in a flowered housedress squinting up at a bright summer sky.

Carrie Milewski trained her sweet peas on twine like a farm wife. An awkward, freckled, hopeful young woman, childless when everyone else had children. Jennifer's father must have been moved by her, although in saying that, I'm probably underplaying her part in the affair. Her agency. My friend Jennifer hadn't wanted to move to California, although I imagine she was happy once she settled in. Not that I have any idea, really. We lost touch.

Yet I've never lost that aerial picture of the suburb. It's still inside me, those streets curving like animal paths, although when I see them again with an adult eye, the forms rustling along them at night don't belong to deer and bears. I've never forgotten what my father said about men moving to the suburbs to lead quiet lives. But not all of our neighbours fought in the war. Many of them had been too young and some had been exempted from service. It's true they all had brothers or cousins or even fathers who'd fought overseas, and that had left a mark. But I would guess that a decent percentage of them preferred excitement to quiet. Some even had a taste for violence, or at least a tendency toward violence, and that would play a part in what happened during the missile crisis.

Mr. Milewski was one of them. I don't know his first name. Bunny claimed not to know it, although she found his picture in an album, too. It made me remember the time he had leaned against his yellow Pontiac as my father worked under the hood. I think it was summer. I can still see the sun glinting off the passenger-side door handle. When he fixed people's cars, my father often took me along to hand him his wrenches, at least until I got bored or he sent me away.

I don't know why he didn't send me away that afternoon, at least when Mr. Milewski started talking about the war. Maybe they forgot me in the sudden switch. Mr. Milewski went from talking about getting a pure-bred cocker spaniel to claiming the Japs hated dogs. Without any transition, he was talking about his three years as a Japanese prisoner of war after the fall of Hong Kong. He was just a kid when Hong Kong fell. Corporal Milewski, nineteen years old. *Nineteen years old.*

The Japs, he kept saying. Even as a child, I could recognize racial prejudice, which wasn't permitted in our house. But I didn't know enough not to
dislike the aggressive self-pity in Mr. Milewski's voice, or how to get beyond
disliking it. I only saw my father straighten up gravely to listen, even though
Mr. Milewski wasn't speaking to him, not exactly. He was telling his front
lawn that he had no idea how he'd got through three years and eight goddamn months as a prisoner-of-war. No idea in the goddamn world.

Then he noticed me, looking startled as he met my eyes. I remember
a feral look in his, still able to picture that mangy, restless coyote of a man
looking down at me wildly. I also have an idea that he knew exactly what
he'd done to survive, things he'd had to do and thought he shouldn't
have done—things he believed a better man wouldn't have done—and he
couldn't get past it.

Bunny also told me that the Milewskis hadn't sold the house to the
Hortons to move back to Kelowna. They'd put it up for sale when Mr.
Milewski had found out about his wife's affair. Or at least, after Mr. Milewski
beat up his wife so badly the neighbours had called the police.

She must have been screaming very loudly for a very long time. It
took a lot back then for people to call the police in a case of domestic
violence. You'd think I'd remember the police car pulling up at their door
when it would have been an event. Maybe the Mounties didn't use their
siren. Maybe their neighbours kept it quiet for years.

In any case, after her beating, Carrie Milewski moved back in with her
parents in Kelowna and the house was sold. Of Mr. Unnamed Milewski,
all Bunny would say was that he had gone to the bad, end of story. Even
though it was really the beginning of the story of how I met Norman, and
of everything that would follow.

Our other local prisoner-of-war lived next door. I think of him as another
piece of the puzzle that slowly assembled itself that year. Mr. Manners, Jim
Manners, Flight Lieutenant Manners, had been a flight instructor during

the early years of the war. He finally shipped over to England in 1944 and was shot down while flying his second mission, spending the rest of the war in a Nazi POW camp. I heard my parents talking about it one night. I can't remember when, but Mr. Manners had said something Bunny thought was condescending and she complained about it to my father.

He was shot down on his second mission, my father replied, as if that explained everything.

"Second or twenty-second," Bunny answered impatiently.

"You might feel a little foolish if it's your second," my father said. "Especially when you'd spent most of the war as an instructor. Picking away at it. Lots of time to pick away at yourself in a POW camp."

I was listening from inside my cracked-open bedroom door, not understanding everything they said. This must have been after Norman arrived and I'd started eavesdropping in earnest. But I've lost the sequence of events, and it might have been earlier. Logic puts it earlier, Mr. Manners explaining himself to my father not long after the Manners family had moved in next door. But I'd been only three at the time, and since our families were never confidential, it might only have happened after the missile crisis, when an explanation of Mr. Manners's behaviour would be called for.

"He was a pilot," I remember Bunny saying, although she didn't sound certain. She believed Pat Manners was expecting their first when he was shot down. The first boy. Cal.

"He says they took out his gunner," my father replied. "They always aim for the turret. Aimed for it."

There was a good amount of damage, Mr. Manners had said, and they found themselves with an electrical fire. They were going down. When Jim Manners jumped, he'd seen three parachutes open below him, the pilot being the last one out. But only Mr. Manners and his navigator made it. They were lucky enough, my father said, landing in a pasture. Mr. Manners had kept checking later on in the camps, asking any of the new men if they'd seen the rest of his crew. No one had. There was never any sign of them. Not to this day, my father said.

My parents thought about this for a while.

"The headlights coming toward them were German," my father said.

"In the movies, it's always the resistance," Bunny answered. "In a skirt."

Their conversation was as much thinking as talk. Bunny finally murmured something about how long, meaning how long was he a prisoner. The answer was eleven months, which called for another pause.

The guards marched them east at the end of the war, my father said. Mr. Manners said that his navigator didn't make it through.

"The man was starving to death. They all were. Fell and he wouldn't get up. 'Bugger off,' he says, and Jim keeps going. At least he knows he had to."

"No, he doesn't," Bunny told him. "Like all the rest of you."

They didn't say anything else for a long while.

"Time for bed," Bunny said finally, and I had to scramble into mine. Afterward, I lay there picturing Mr. Manners floating to earth in a parachute. He had broad shoulders, a bullish man filling up his tailored suits. Most of the times I saw him, he was coming home from work, so that night I pictured him wearing pinstripes and holding his briefcase as he parachuted into occupied France. I think it was France. My parents might have said that, too. Maybe I heard it somewhere else.

Lost, I would say of him now. Say it not without rancour and not without pity, given what would happen, beyond his wife's tears.

Floating over the suburb that night, above its peaked roofs and curving streets, I was ready to keep going. Even the sense of lightness had gone. Everything had left me, and I was only a diminishing thought in the air. I felt peaceful. Easeful death; that might have been it. Or maybe sleep was overtaking me.

Then I reached the edge of the Capilano River and found myself unable to cross it. I slowed, looking ahead at the dark water shimmering with moonlight. I became a child again as I hovered over beauty. Then something pushed me away. Enormous propulsion as I was thrown back toward our street, our house, tumbling down through roof beams and ceiling until I found myself in bed and sat up screaming.

Bare footsteps ran toward me. I wanted my father but Bunny got there first, and that was all right, being bundled into her arms.

"Nightmare," she said. "You had a nightmare. It's all right. You're all right."

I panted, trying to say what had really happened. But it was Bunny and I couldn't.

"It's all right," she crooned. "Nothing's wrong. You're at home. You're in bed. You're all safe."

My father, who was standing in the doorway, flipped on the overhead light. That was a relief. I blinked, seeing both my parents waiting for me to speak sensibly to show I was back. Not that they knew I'd gone anywhere.

"Mrs. Manners," I said, doing my best. "Mrs. Manners down the creek. She was down the creek today. Holding her arms like "—I wriggled out of Bunny's embrace and balled my hands into my armpits—"and she was *crying*."

My parents exchanged a glance over my head.

"I'm sure she wasn't," Bunny said.

"She *was*. Her eyes were red, and Norman said it was allergies. But nobody has allergies in October. Even Norman."

Bunny didn't say anything for a while, then took my hand.

"What are you going to be for Halloween?"

My mind went blank. Halloween? My father shifted unhappily in the doorway.

"You've got to make up your mind pretty soon if I'm going to sew you a costume."

I had no idea. "The Lone Ranger?"

"You can't be the Lone Ranger, Mary Alice. Girls aren't the Lone Ranger."

"I want to be the Lone Ranger," I said, immediately stuck on the idea. "I *want* to."

"What about . . ."

"She can be the Lone Ranger if she wants," my father said angrily. It was as if Bob was here and he'd gone from zero to sixty. My parents never argued, but I could see that this was close and it was my fault. I needed to get a handle, which was one of Uncle Punk's expressions.

"Why did Mrs. Manners call Norman's parents bohemians?" I asked.

A second glance between my parents. So that had worked.

My father came over and sat down on the other side of the bed. I plumped over and cuddled him the way I always did. This time, though, I figured that Bunny might feel bad and took her hand. They both seemed to like this.

"Remember how I told you they're bookish," my father said. "They like to read and talk. They're intellectuals. Bohemian is another word for that. Roughly."

"Also arty," Bunny said. "It means kind of arty, too."

I hadn't noticed that the Hortons were arty. "But they're not like Aunt Magda."

"Not even faintly," my father said.

"Not one solitary inch," Bunny agreed.

Now they were almost laughing, and things were starting to be all right. The nightmare was past, although it hadn't been a nightmare. The flying had flown. Instead, we were a happy family, a girl cuddled between her parents, the aquarium bubbling pleasantly on my dresser.

"Norman wants to be Zorro," I said. "I need to make sure he has a good costume. So he can fit in."

"You fit in fine," Bunny said.

"*Norman*," I told her.

"Oh, *Norman*," Bunny said. "Well sometimes pigs grow wings."

That was one of Bunny's expressions, but I'd stopped even trying to figure out what it meant. Anyway, it was warm. They were warm, and as they went comfortably silent, I found myself drifting off to sleep.

5

E very year before Halloween, my Aunt Magda gave us a suitcase of old clothes. It was a smart well-packed suitcase, and my aunt always said it would give me a good selection for costumes. She wanted to take the suitcase home, so we had to go through it in the living room, the suitcase lying open on the coffee table. Bunny would pull out last year's poodle skirt or an old cocktail gown, exclaiming over everything in her company voice as Aunt Magda watched, leaning against the mantlepiece, her black eyes like caves behind her cigarette smoke.

"Oh, so *chic!*" Bunny cried. "I'm sure she can use it for *something.*"

What neither of them said was that the clothes were mainly for my mother. Bunny would spend the next few weeks tailoring them to fit, making sure she had something grand for New Year's Eve. I was puzzled by the whole process. Bunny never thanked Aunt Magda and wouldn't wear one of the alterations in front of her. In fact, my mother always seemed annoyed by the process, turning as grim as the Manners family's cleaning lady as the Halloween phone call approached.

"That will be Magda," she'd start to say when the telephone rang.

"Parker residence," she'd answer, as she never did.

I would know it was my aunt when her voice went even higher. "Oh, how *are* you? What a *surprise!* It's been *ages.*"

A pause. "Yes, yes, of course she would. How very kind of you."
With a grimace. "Aren't you lovely? Yes, of course we'll be here."

Muttering about charity after she hung up. Ray wouldn't have got
anywhere without . . .

"Actually, she wants to be the Lone Ranger," she said this year. "Hall
has an old white shirt gone at the elbows . . . Well, the actor wears blue in
some of the colour pictures but it looks white on TV . . .

"Oh, *aren't* you kind? I was *wondering* about trousers. But white gets
stained so easily . . . Of course one has to be careful. We *do* get bored with
our old things, don't we?"

Hanging up, she told me, "Lady Foofaraw will be over on Tuesday. I
hope you still want to be the goddamn Ranger."

I liked Aunt Magda. She stalked through life like a panther, thin and
faintly savage, her black hair pulled back in a bun. I'd seen a ballet dancer
like her once at the Queen Elizabeth Theatre. The dancer was playing a
stepmother, or maybe a witch, and she was thrilling in the same way Aunt
Magda was thrilling. I think the dancer was Russian, so they both had
foreign accents, too.

In fact, I never disliked anyone unless they were mean to me, which
came down to my grade three teacher, Mrs. Persson. And Aunt Magda
wasn't anything like a witch. She was just sophisticated, as Mrs. Manners
had put it. Generous, my father said. She would spray me with perfume
as she sat at her dressing table, making me smell like the shadows in her
garden. Nor did I believe that Bunny disliked her, given the way her voice
quivered if anyone said anything against my aunt. This included the word
intimidating, which I learned the week before Aunt Magda brought over
her suitcase.

Bunny's friends were over for coffee. I was home sick, hunkered
just inside my bedroom door hoping for a chance at one of the squares
she'd baked. Nanaimo bars were the best, brownies a close second and
date squares a distant third, given the way they stuck to the roof of
your mouth.

I had a slight fever, suffering mildly from a cold I'd caught down the creek when Norman and I had stayed too long. Bunny had told me she'd predicted this and wasn't happy about keeping me back from school. She'd already invited her friends and wasn't going to cancel. I would have to stay in bed and be quiet, not even watching TV in the rec room. There was nothing suitable for children on weekday mornings, anyway.

Yes, there was. Being cut off TV was a punishment, which was unfair when you were sick. But in this case, I accepted it, Norman and I having got interested in swearing after we'd sat on the log. Our minister, Mr. Culver, didn't approve of swearing. When I got sick, it occurred to me that Our Lord probably didn't care for it much either, which made me wonder about Bunny's chances of escaping my cold.

"I saw your sister-in-law last week in Eaton's."

It started with Mrs. Oliver. She was a redhead like her daughter Lucy, who was in my class. Mrs. Oliver had been a news reporter before she was elected to the PTA—I thought it was the PTA—having written a column called Comings and Goings in the local paper.

"I'm sorry, Buns. But whenever I run into her, she always manages to convey the impression that I'm doing something wrong."

"Intimidating," someone said, amid the rattle of coffee spoons. I wasn't sure who was speaking and hadn't heard the term before. But if it meant someone who thought you were wrong, that was both interesting and useful.

"She *surveils*," Mrs. Oliver said. "And finds the world inadequate."

"She always makes me conscious of what I'm wearing." That was Mrs. Armstrong. "Which probably has spit-up all over it."

"Those legs! Good Heavens. Glen sure notices." Mrs. Winters. She was married to our dentist Dr. Winters, who was far too old to look at Aunt Magda's legs.

"Not that she absolutely *has* to wear French stockings," the unknown person said.

"*Sun*glasses," Mrs. O'Neill added; I had no idea why.

"All of which is terribly superficial of me," Mrs. Oliver said, as if she'd been the only one speaking. "But I always think the sign of true quality is the ability to put other people at their ease. No matter how glamorous you are, or how damn cultivated, you don't lord it over the peasants."

"I don't think she's lording it over anyone," my mother said, her voice doing its quiver.

"Well, I don't suppose her people were in the position to be lords," Mrs. Oliver said. "Financiers, I would imagine. I'd say rich as Jews, except . . ."

They all tittered, making Bunny say with even more of a quiver, "You know Hall doesn't like that, Irene."

"Oh, *Hall* doesn't," Mrs. Oliver replied.

"After all she's been through," Mrs. Armstrong said peaceably. She was a nice, curly-headed lady. I'd never seen a significant amount of spit-up on her clothes, even though she had four children younger than me.

Rattle of plates. From the sounds of it, Bunny was passing squares. "Who hasn't had enough sugar?"

"Me," I called, making everybody laugh.

"Well come on in, pet," Mrs. Oliver said. "Your mother's a pet and you are, too."

Nanaimo bars still on the plate. So that had worked, even though Bunny didn't look pleased to see me.

Aunt Magda had packed an old pair of white pedal pushers on top of the other clothes in her suitcase. That might have been a mistake. Bunny took them out and closed the suitcase, saying in a voice as bright as tinfoil, "Thanks so much, Magda. She already knows she wants to be the Ranger."

Aunt Magda drew on her cigarette. She never looked surprised, only as if she had to consider what was being said. I was the one who felt surprised. Bunny didn't have a new dress for New Year's Eve and wasn't likely to get one, my father's boss Mr. German being on another rampage. Among other things, this meant cutting paid overtime. Yet Bunny always said you needed a new dress for New Year's Eve to bring in your luck.

"Of course, Tinker might change her mind," Aunt Magda said, the words blown out with the smoke. I was going to say that I wouldn't when she caught my eye.

"People do," I agreed, which was truthful.

"Then I wouldn't have time to sew it, would I?" Bunny asked. "And I've already cut down your father's shirt." Smiling even more brightly, she asked Aunt Magda, "Coffee?"

Shrugging. "Sure."

The word didn't sound like slang when my aunt said it.

"Sure," I echoed. When Bunny swivelled, I reminded her, "Debbie made me some." Adding, "Two sugars."

The sugars sounded very satisfactory, like one of the old movies my parents watched on TV. Yet when my mother left the room, she stalked out in a way that puzzled me.

"What happened?" my aunt asked. She wasn't like Mrs. Manners, forgetting to treat me as a child. Aunt Magda treated everybody the same. Leaving aside the idiots, of course, who were legion. You didn't want to be an idiot around Aunt Magda.

"Her friends said things the other day." But since the things concerned Aunt Magda, I didn't think I should repeat them, even though she kept staring at me.

"I see," she said finally and drew on her cigarette. "That bitch Irene Oliver."

I was astonished. It wasn't even a question.

"Your mother needs new friends." Aunt Magda stubbed out her cigarette, even though she'd only smoked half of it. "But of course she's known them forever. It's interesting how fond one gets of people after knowing them forever. Even without liking them."

"Mrs. Armstrong is nice," I said. "She said, 'After All Magda's Been Through.'"

Aunt Magda's eyelids flickered. The *Been Through* phrase was always capitalized when people spoke about my aunt, although in this case I knew what it meant. She had a number tattooed on the inside of her arm. I saw it every time we went to swim in her backyard pool. One memory I have from being very small was the way I was fascinated by the number and reached out to touch it.

"Mary Alice!" My mother's jarring voice.

"It's all right. She can."

Tracing it with my fingertip.

When I was older, she told me, "The Nazis did that." She neither hid the tattoo nor flaunted it. "You must never hate anyone in your life. Except Nazis."

"My father says I can't hate anybody."

"Then just this once ignore him."

Aunt Magda had been held for most of the war in the camp at Theresienstadt. My father had told me the names and said it was respectful to remember them. Toward the end of the war, my aunt was transported to Auschwitz and liberated from there. Afterward, she was a Displaced Person, there being a lot of capitalizations in Aunt Magda's past. She came from Prague but didn't want to go back there, not with all her family gone, and Aunt Magda had seen them go. Instead she came to Canada, where she married Uncle Ray.

My uncle's eyesight had kept him out of the war. Bunny always said this gave him a leg up, although they never said which leg, so I didn't know how my uncle got started. He must have done it on his own, since the Parker money was gone. Not long gone, but gone. He became a commercial real estate developer, owning the first of his shopping malls. When Bunny said he couldn't have made it without my father, she meant that my father had quit school to support the family after his own father died, his and Uncle Ray's, and that he'd sent my uncle to university when he didn't go himself. My father often spoke about his lack of a university education, but I never thought he was lacking in anything. Uncle Ray wasn't either, although in a different way, while Aunt Magda said the Nazis had emptied her out.

"Coffee cake!" My mother came back into the living room with a tray that included two cups of coffee and a glass of milk. I decided not to say anything about the milk, afraid of jeopardizing my piece of cake. Bunny's cakes were famously light, and her coffee cake was topped with a crumble of cinnamon and sugar that was an excellent way to ruin your teeth.

"Now, Muriel," Aunt Magda said as Bunny served. "Mary Alice and I have been talking. And even though she will be the Lone Ranger, she can use the other clothes for dress-up, and you'll oblige me by taking them. You're afraid she's becoming too much of a tomboy. Well, here. Let her play with some old rags. And if she doesn't, do me the favour of throwing them out. I don't have enough closets."

My aunt's entire speech shocked me, starting with the way she called my mother Muriel, which no one did but my father, and extending through the fact—which I knew instantly was true—that Bunny was afraid I was a tomboy. I wasn't a tomboy. I was Tink, and being called anything else made my fists clench.

"I suppose you'll want your Louis Vuitton suitcase back," Bunny said. "Don't think I don't know what it is."

"Oh, I don't care. Let her have the suitcase, too. Why not?"

I brightened. There were many things you could do with a suitcase. But Bunny was shaking her head, ready to say something else.

Aunt Magda gripped her by the wrist.

"Don't let them get to you," she said, holding on tight.

They'd forgotten me. I watched my mother's posture droop. The way she puddled down to gaze up at Aunt Magda. She looked like a pet, it was true.

"I'm just an ordinary person," she said.

"You can choose to be."

Aunt Magda let go of her wrist and gave my mother a handkerchief, a big square white men's handkerchief like the ones my father used.

She and Uncle Ray had one son, Simon, who was three years older than me and exceptionally polite. He went to private school and wore a blue blazer with a gold crest on the pocket. I decided that I would be as mature as Simon when they noticed me again, remembering not to wolf my coffee cake.

"Oh, thanks for the clothes," Bunny said, sounding tired. "Really. I can use them, the way Hall's boss has been acting lately."

"And the suitcase," I said, forgetting my resolution.

"It's Aunt Magda's suitcase, Mary Alice," my mother said, blowing her nose.

"Your daughter has good taste. Who cares for silly girls?"

But here's the mysterious thing. When my aunt left, the suitcase went with her. She must have forgotten what she'd said, or maybe she was used to taking it with her so she just did.

Yet I had my Lone Ranger pedal pushers and Bunny had her New Year's Eve dress, or at least a taffeta skirt and pretty silk top. They'd make sure she was lucky next year even though she was an ordinary person, which was fine. You wanted your mother to be ordinary, although I didn't tell her so, and decided on reflection that this was a good call.

After school on Halloween, I checked out my costume in the full-length mirror on the sliding doors of my parents' bedroom closet, twisting and turning to see it from every angle and feeling very proud. The shirt looked as white as the Lone Ranger's, especially since my mother was making me wear two undershirts against the cold. I also thought my black rubber rain boots did very well as cowboy boots, despite the red line around the top.

Most important, I had a black mask and a white fedora we'd found in Woolworth's Five and Dime. I could push the fedora back off my forehead like a gunslinger even though I didn't have a gun, Bunny having drawn the line while we were at Woolworth's. When we got home, my father said that I could use my imagination, and it was true that pointed fingers could be guns. I stood with my legs wide apart looking in the mirror. Yanking my fingers out of my pockets, I fired them off until I was satisfied, then I fired them few more times for good measure.

It was still early when I ran along Connington Crescent to Norman's house, holding my pillowcase balled up in my fist. It was drizzling but not really raining, the sky still light and none of the other kids out yet. Running up the Hortons' walk, I rejected trick-or-treating, thinking it would be rude. Norman opened the door when I knocked, and as we crowded into the kitchen, I saw he made an impressive Zorro, dressed in black from head to toe.

"You found a hat at Woolworth's!"

"It's an old one of my dad's," Norman said. "Mum wound an old tie around inside it so it wouldn't slip down. And I've got a big head."

Auntie Nita would have said, "Filled with brains." Norman's mother was there but she didn't say it. She was too busy drying her hands on a dish towel.

"You got your cape," I said, walking around him. It was a wonderful cape, swishing and shiny, made with lining from the fabric store. I envied Norman that cape and had to stifle a small whispered feeling that I should have been Zorro instead.

"And Rosa's old sweater that doesn't fit her anymore," Norman said, looking down at his chest. "And they're my good pants, so I have to be careful. But they're just my ordinary shoes."

I held up one of my feet to show off my black rubber boots. Mrs. Horton made a sound as if she had a fly caught up her nose. I turned to see what was the matter, then did a double-take as Rosa came in, dressed for the high school dance. Rosa was being Marilyn Monroe in a blond wig and the famous white dress that blew up to reveal Marilyn's legs. The costume made it very clear why Rosa's old black sweater didn't fit her anymore. She held out her arms and turned a circle to show it off.

"No," Mr. Horton said.

I hadn't heard him come in, but he was standing behind me in the kitchen doorway.

"Oh, come . . ."

"No," her father said.

They had a staring match that ended when Rosa turned back toward her bedroom. She held her arms horizontal and shook her hands in protest as she retreated.

"How's she going to hold them in when Marilyn Monroe never can?"

"Tink," Mrs. Horton began. She seemed to be trying not to laugh.

Mr. Horton was still concentrating on Rosa. "Remember I'm working the dance," he called. He didn't seem to think anything was funny and was still angry when he left the room. Mrs. Horton looked after him for a while, then told Norman to get his bag.

"Pillowcase," I said. When she looked confused: "He needs a pillowcase to carry all his loot."

"No one needs that much candy," Mrs. Horton said.

"Our parents steal half when we're at school. Don't think we don't notice." I liked Bunny's turn of phrase, although the look on Mrs. Horton's face made me feel apologetic. "I don't mean that you do."

"Yes, she does," Norman said. "He doesn't, but she does. Before I get up."

Mrs. Horton blushed up her neck to her powdery cheeks the way Norman did, although she remained close to laughing.

"Tink, you've been sent to try us," she said.

No, I hadn't. But she went and got an old pillowcase, so I had no real complaint.

The drill, as I explained to Norman, was to get to the O'Neill house at the far end of Connington Crescent before everyone else did. Mrs. O'Neill may not have liked Aunt Magda's sunglasses, but she handed out homemade candy apples that were even bigger than the ones at the PNE. The problem was, she didn't make enough for everybody, so you had to get there fast.

There was no point telling Norman to hurry. We were making slow progress down the block, but I could see he was trying, rocking forward as fast as he could between his braced leg and his usual one. We skipped the houses between his place and the O'Neills, even though most of them had lit pumpkins beside the front door. Mrs. O'Reilly had carved a cat face with excellent whiskers, but I told Norman we'd do Connington later.

I had my route: Mrs. O'Neill at the end of the block, then down Moore Road as if we were going to school. But instead of carrying on downhill, we'd turn left at Derriton Crescent, going along Derriton on one side and doubling back on the other. Afterward, we'd go down Moore again to Egerton Crescent, going back and forth across the street, remaining aware that our principal lived in one of the houses. After that we'd go uphill again on Far Creek Road and do Connington down and back until Norman was home, not bothering with Bennington Crescent farther up the mountain, much less Alderton at the top. Our pillowcases would rip if we got too greedy, which had been known to happen.

"They're alphabetical," Norman said, trying to hurry. "The streets. Alderton, Bennington, Connington. I never noticed that before."

I stopped. Alphabetical, and they all end in *ton*. I hadn't noticed that either, and I'd lived here all my life. I looked at Norman, and he nodded proudly at having figured it out. It reminded me of one of Mr. Culver's sermons, how the Bible said all things should be done decently and in order. I got an eerie sense of the hidden order of the world, how things were structured in a way you never noticed, life ticking around you like a clock. My father had opened his watch for me once, all the wheels and gears. There, in the middle of the road, I felt locked inside a giant clock, its gears whirling around me, its hands clicking down the minutes of my life. My mind stuttered to a stop as I realized I was trapped in a world far stranger than I'd known.

An astronaut and a cowboy ran past me down the rainy street. Devils and ghosts grinned from either side of the road while a cat-whiskered pumpkin burned fiendishly. It was all so strange, I felt in danger of floating out of my body right in the middle of Halloween.

"What's the matter?" Norman asked. He looked at me more closely and must have seen how I was quivering.

"Nothing's the matter," he added kindly.

But I couldn't get free of it, all the gears grinding around me.

"Everyone's coming outside," Norman said. "We'd better get going."

He pointed and I followed his arm, registering the fact that the astronaut and the cowboy were only Harry and Jamie Manners in their store-bought costumes. Children were melting out of the houses on either side, the little ones with their fathers, staggering down their front walks like kittens and puppies learning to walk. Two big girls swished out of one house as a princess and a witch—Jeannie Stevens and Cathy Cole—with Judy Shribman emerging behind them as a butterfly flapping her tissue-paper wings. The girls started off by skipping the Connington houses. Jamie and Harry Manners were skipping them too, and I realized that everyone was heading straight for the candy apples.

"Come on!" I cried, spurting forward as if Norman was the hold-up. When we landed on the O'Neills' front steps, I wasn't entirely sure how we'd got there.

"Trick or treat!"

"Well don't you look grand!"

Mrs. O'Neill bent down and gave each of us a candy apple wrapped in waxed paper and tied around the stick with curly red ribbon. A sigh of pleasure escaped me. I fell back to normal, the weirdness and tension sliding off my shoulders now that everything was the way it always had been and always would be.

Leaving the O'Neills', we followed the plan, joining waves of kids heading down Moore and along Derriton, trick-or-treating every place they'd put out a pumpkin. We got candy bars and Rockets, black licorice and packets of Twizzlers. There were also little brown folded-over bags, which we opened as soon as we reached the street. Some were penny candy, some filled with cheap Halloween kisses in their orange and black wrappers. I thought the kisses tasted like ear wax, but Norman liked them all right, and I was surprised at how happy he looked when the lady on Egerton Crescent gave us her popcorn balls. He pulled his out of his pillowcase afterward and marvelled over it.

Popcorn balls! Why hadn't I told him there were popcorn balls?

Because they tasted like puffed-up paper. Because everyone thought they tasted like puffed-up paper, and you had to be careful not to get hit later on when the bigger boys started pegging them like snowballs. Because the lady made so many popcorn balls you didn't need to worry that she'd run out before you got there. In fact, she'd give you seconds, maybe because she had popcorn brains and didn't recognize you— didn't recognize snowball-throwing boys getting seconds—although it was entirely possible she pretended she didn't recognize them because she'd made so many popcorn balls she needed to get rid of them any way she could.

Or maybe the lady made so many popcorn balls because she thought we liked them. It came to me suddenly that the lady was being nice. It was another example of gears turning in a way you'd never noticed, although figuring it out this time didn't stop me dead in the street, probably because I was so jittery from eating candy that I couldn't have stopped dead if it killed me.

"We can go back if you think I'm lying."

"You and me have different tastes," Norman said. "You don't like gummy bears."

This was true. But we couldn't go back right away or the lady would be hard-pressed to pretend she didn't recognize us. There was also the fact our principal, Mr. Eisenstadt, was looking out the doorway of his house across the street, craning his neck up and down Egerton, looking as if he was checking the number of kids against the amount of candy he had left.

By this time, the little ones had all gone home. But kids our age were out in droves, and we'd been joined by bigger kids in last-minute costumes: thirteen-, even fourteen-year-olds wearing scavenged masks who were too old for trick-or-treating but couldn't stop themselves from wanting free candy.

I usually snuck past the principal's house. But with Norman slowing down, he and I were walking between two waves of kids. As he craned his neck, Mr. Eisenstadt spotted us. Without even exchanging a glance, Norman and I knew we had to go over, dogging our way toward the principal's pumpkin. There was a Mrs. Eisenstadt, but I only ever saw her in the medical complex, where Bunny always said she looked pale.

My father called Mr. Eisenstadt a fireplug, he was so short and broad. He wasn't popular, even though his name sounded like President Eisenhower, who was a war hero and admirable. Mr. Eisenstadt yelled over the P.A. system every day after "God Save the Queen" and the Lord's Prayer and was known to enjoy strapping. There was also the fact my father had gone up against him over my grade three teacher, Mrs. Persson, and Mr. Eisenstadt hadn't liked that.

Now he ignored me and grunted at Norman, "Marian Horton's boy."

"Yes, sir," Norman said very clearly and held open his pillowcase. "Trick or treat, sir."

Mr. Eisenstadt grunted again and threw in a chocolate bar, hesitating for a half second before throwing one in mine.

"Now there's a little girl who isn't as smart as she thinks she is," he said, as if speaking to himself.

I wouldn't have dreamed of answering. With principals there was an unusually wide gap between what you thought and what you said; even I knew that. But since blurting was always a possibility, I was glad when he shut the door quickly, as if he wanted to keep out the rain.

I headed back down the principal's walk, my pillowcase hitting against my legs, heavier than usual with candy. I turned to say this to Norman, but found him behind me, his limp having visibly gotten worse.

As soon as he reached the road, Norman said, "'She isn't as smart as she thinks she is.'"

We were still a little close to Mr. Eisenstadt's front door for one of his imitations.

"I'm smarter," I said, trying to joke him into moving along.

"You can't talk to a pupil like that," Norman said, sounding like an irritated adult. Leading him off, I pointed out that principals were like the weather, and my father said it didn't do any good to complain about the weather. You might not like it, but complaining wasn't going to change anything.

"People are supposed to change," he said. "You're supposed to *grow up*."

That struck me as funny. "A principal growing up."

"You *have to*."

I'd never heard Norman sound so irritated.

I'd never seen him drag his leg so badly, either.

"We're almost at my street," I said. Norman rolled his eyes exactly like Rosa. He knew where we were. But I still thought it polite to add, "We can go home if you want."

"You don't care because you've got all the things you like," Norman said, his voice quavering. "But maybe the other houses have things I like."

It would just be ordinary candy, but all right. I stole glances at Norman as we trudged uphill, watching the way he dragged along. Luckily, we had several childless neighbours in a row who ignored Halloween. A few other people had blown out their pumpkins after running out of candy. Reaching the house of the Manners family was a relief. We were almost home.

There was also the fact that Mr. and Mrs. Manners gave out excellent treats, different every year. And Mrs. Manners dressed up, which none of the other adults did. I'd forgotten to mention this to Norman, which made it a surprise.

"Trick or treat!" I yelled.

Norman gaped. Mrs. Manners was being Bernadette from *The Song of Bernadette*, which made Bunny cry every time we saw it on TV. There

73

was a short striped kerchief tied around her neck and a filmy white scarf over her hair. I wondered if she was one of the nuns who were going to take her daughter Andy, which didn't make sense.

Far too much candy. It was obvious even to me.

"Well, my goodness," Mrs. Manners said. "Tink and her friend Norman." Calling: "Jim, come look."

Mr. Manners appeared behind her, a glass of ice cubes in one hand. He was wearing his business suit without the jacket, his tie loosened and his sleeves rolled up. He could be playing Humphrey Bogart in any number of movies, although he only played tennis, at least as far as I knew.

"Black and white," he said, taking in our costumes. "What have we got here? Let me guess. Martin Luther King and the Ku Klux Klan."

"The Lone Ranger and Zorro," I said.

"A Freedom Rider," he said, jabbing his glass toward Norman. "And a Night Rider." He stumbled a little as he jabbed, as if he'd fallen off the sides of his shoes.

Mrs. Manners gave a burbling teenage giggle. Despite her white hair, she looked girly as she stood behind his shoulder, one arm around his neck. Norman stared as if they were an alien species.

"You get to give them the candy," Mrs. Manners told her husband.

"*Dr.* Martin Luther King," he said, not seeming to hear her. "Forgive me, Doctor. As you and your boys, by which I mean *boys*, ride your freedom down to Alabam."

Mrs. Manners stepped out from behind her husband and picked up the bowl of candy. She was still burbling as she dropped handfuls of chocolate kisses into our pillowcases. Great heaping fistfuls as Mr. Manners started singing.

Nobody knows the trouble I've seen.
Nobody knows my sorrow.
Nobody knows . . .

He had a very handsome voice. As he sang, Mrs. Manners urged him back with one hand until he was behind her. Then she gave us a wide smile and shut the door in our faces, leaving me and Norman stunned. We walked back down the steps and the few feet uphill toward my house. When we stopped in my driveway, I was the one to sing the *Twilight Zone* theme song.

Norman didn't echo it back, remaining as quiet as he'd been at the front door.

"At least she gave us lots," I said.

Norman shook his head, looking as tired as anyone I'd ever seen.

"No one needs this much candy."

As tired as an old person. As an old person wanting their bed who couldn't get out of their chair. I gestured up our steps, inviting Norman to come in. We could look at our candy, then Bunny would give us some sparklers to take outside before the fireworks began.

"I want to go home," Norman said.

I could see that. The problem was, too many big kids were out now with their popcorn balls, and it was best to go around in pairs.

I offered to take my pillowcase inside and walk him home.

"Then how are you going to get back in a pair? If I don't go back with you and you don't go back with me. And if I don't go back and you don't go back. And if I don't . . ."

He stumbled to a close while I failed to find an answer. Waving one hand, Norman limped off silently toward Connington Crescent, his pillowcase dragging on the damp asphalt behind him. I stood watching until he turned the corner. Then I ran up our front steps, dropping my loot as I ran past Bunny, who was stationed just behind the door. Ran into the living room and jumped up onto the chesterfield where I picked out Norman trudging along his dark and shadowy street—smudged with costumes, barbaric with pumpkins—wanting to make sure he was all right. He'd done a good job so far at Halloween, and I needed to make sure he didn't bunk it right at the end.

My father was sitting in his chair reading his newspaper. Seeing what I was doing, he rustled down his paper and came over, picking me up around the waist so I could track Norman all the way home. No one threw popcorn balls. His pillowcase didn't rip open. Norman dragged his leg up his walk, the Hortons' pumpkin out, their door opening on a brief flare of light as he disappeared inside.

Halloween wasn't usually like this. I had no idea what had just happened, the world's gears turning and churning. I fit in there snugly, it was true. But I felt caught up in things I didn't recognize, and when Bunny gave me some sparklers to take outside, their fizzing and cracking spoke a language I didn't understand.

6

y cat Wilma had kittens two days after Halloween, which was a relief from human perplexities. "Come see," Bunny called when I got home from school, and I hung over the cardboard box near the furnace that my mother had lined with clean rags. Wilma was giving us three kittens this time, all of them treats, but one especially: a tortoiseshell in ginger, white and black, with a little black nose and tiny white feet.

The second was a black-and-white kitten and the last was a striped ginger tabby. All three of them nuzzled into Wilma, who lay curved like a crescent moon with her babies nursing at her underside. Their eyes were still closed and their ears pressed flat against their heads as their tiny paws worked at her. She'd licked them dry, but their coats remained spiky and tousled. Now she looked half asleep, and when I scratched her ears gently, she let out a faint half-hearted purr that hiccupped quickly to a stop.

"Good girl," I told her. "You're the best girl."

Turning to my mother: "Rosa will want the tortoiseshell."

"Well, someone will," Bunny said. Wilma could keep having kittens as long as I could find homes for them, which usually meant putting a notice with a Polaroid picture on the bulletin board at school. Free Kittens! There were always more phone calls than there were kittens, especially for the ones ready to go just before Christmas.

Sometimes Wilma had four in a litter and sometimes three; eighteen kittens so far, since I'd got her when I was five years old. Kittens were my favourite thing in the world, even better than comic books and far better than candy. Only two days after Halloween and I was already sick of candy, although Bunny wasn't. Settling down cross-legged by the furnace, I watched Wilma's new kittens. They weren't really doing anything, just nursing and sleeping. But with Wilma's apparent permission, I picked up each in turn, all of them feather-weights in my palm. The tortoiseshell would be female since they always were. But it was too early to tell with the other two, their rears remaining as swollen and private as their eyes.

Bunny leaned over my shoulder frequently. She liked kittens almost as much as I did, although my father claimed not to care for pets and called Wilma "the cat" or, when addressing her directly, "Cat." However, Wilma was sometimes seen on his lap while he read the paper, and I knew he'd come downstairs when he got home.

"Norman!" I remembered, scrambling up. "Rosa will want to see them, too."

"You might want to wait until their eyes open," Bunny said. "If you want to be a real salesman."

This struck me as shrewd.

"But how can I bring Norman over without letting on to Rosa?"

"By bringing him tomorrow straight after school?"

Bunny raised her eyebrows as if we were hatching a conspiracy. I nodded significantly, and she brought me milk and my after-school cookie, still warm and melting with pieces of Hershey bar from Halloween. I ate my warm cookie, drank my glass of frosty cold milk and watched the newborn kittens. I had an idea that life didn't get any better than this.

Nor am I sure, now, that it ever has.

Norman proved to have no interest in the kittens. The next day, when I promised a surprise, he looked in their box and said, "I thought you meant the new *Superman*."

"But they're real," I said.

"They look like rats."

"They look like kittens."

"Rats." He sounded proud of himself; I didn't know why.

There had already been a coolness between Norman and me starting the day after Halloween. His mother had kept him home from school, and for some reason, Mrs. Horton seemed to think this was my fault, shaking her head at me sadly during recess. When Norman showed up after lunch, he used the term *Over-Exertion*. But that just sounded like a capitalized way to say he'd been tired, and since Norman had been the one who had wanted to keep going, I didn't see how it was my fault.

This made me a little tired of Norman, too. It was funny how words could start kicking around in your head. Now that Norman wasn't interested in the kittens, we kept walking home after school but said goodbye at his house, which seemed to be fine with both of us. After a few more days, we didn't even bother walking home together. I was especially anxious to see the kittens once their eyes were open and they could walk, or at least blunder into each other like bumper cars, so I leapt out of my desk at the three o'clock bell, punching my arms into my jacket and running home.

There was also the fact that November was skipping season. It always rained so much all month that going down the creek was impossible. So was playing marbles beside the ditch at the edge of the schoolyard, where it got too muddy even for me. But the rear of the school was built with a covered playground, and when the rains came, girls started skipping there, making me remember that I was a girl, too.

As soon as the skipping started, or at least after the kittens' eyes opened, I found my old rope in the rec room and got to it, both at recess and lunch. That weekend, Debbie brought over a long two-person rope made of white cord with wooden handles at each end, calling it a pre-birthday present, and saying it would provide some variety.

Popularity, more likely. Owning a rope like that made girls come over, since two people had to turn it while others jumped in and out, so you gathered a crowd. I didn't mind being popular for a while, but I saw how you could get tired of that pretty quickly too and go back to being on your own.

I remember that fall as a clamour of skipping rhymes, chanted alone or in groups.

> *Cinderella, dressed in yella,*
> *Went upstairs to meet her fella.*
> *What they did I cannot tell ya.*
> *How many bones did the butcher break?*

I know that isn't the classic version, but it's what we always chanted, jumping pepper to count out the number of broken bones until someone's feet got tangled in the rope. I wonder now if we got our bowdlerized version from someone's too-resonant, How many bones did her father break? The chant might be a memory of child-beating, one of the shadows in our suburb that no one ever mentioned, a bruise we weren't supposed to see. Maybe it was similar to the way "Ring Around the Rosie" supposedly remembers marks raised on the skin by bubonic plague.

> *Hush-a, hush-a, we all fall down.*

We had other chants for Chinese skipping, done with rubber bands tied together into a loop ten feet long and held over two girls' ankles. *Lou, lou, skip to my lou.* My favourite, though, wasn't skipping, but putting a tennis ball into the toe of one of Bunny's old stockings. Holding onto the top of the stocking, I would bounce the ball side-arm against the outside wall of the garage, flicking my wrist to keep up a strong and regular rhythm, which is harder than it sounds.

A, my name is Alice, my husband's name is Al,
We come from Alaska and we sell apples.

B, my name is Barbara, my husband's name is Bob,
We come from Burnaby and we sell beatniks.

That was the only chant tied to the bouncing ball. Extemporized, obviously.

C, my name is Cathy, my husband's name is Carl,
We come from Canada and we sell candy.

C was an easy one, especially after Halloween. Other letters were harder, although I could usually make it to *Q* without too many problems, when trying to remember a man's name starting with *Q* often proved impossible, and that was usually the end of it.

Yet one day, when the kittens were two and a half weeks old, I kept getting tripped up right from the start. Over and over, I had to backtrack after bunking the rhythm, the ball skittering on the wall. You needed to start over if you broke rhythm or couldn't think who sold what, and for some reason, I kept bunking *A*. So it was *A, A, A,* then *C, C,* after which I had to repeat *D* several times before finally getting on a roll.

G, my name is Georgia, my husband's name is George,
We come from Germany and we sell guppies.

"Tink, you're driving me mad," Mrs. Manners called, throwing open her basement door.

I was startled into losing my rhythm. "I'm sorry, Mrs. Manners."

"You'd better come in and play Scrabble with Harry. Go wash up. Everyone's out and he's bored."

"I don't like Scrabble, Mrs. Manners. Thank you. I always think of words I *almost* have and they get stuck in my head because I enjoy them."

I was breathless from saying it but she didn't seem to care.

"Snakes and Ladders. Monopoly. Anything but that damn ball."

"Harry can come see my kittens," I called, but Mrs. Manners had already shut the door.

"Have a good snoop," Bunny said, when I told her where I was going. We'd lived next door to the Manners family for five years but none of us had ever set foot in their house.

"I don't want to," I said. "Harry Manners is always so *clean*."

"He's what?"

It was a laugh, not a question, and Bunny ran a comb through my hair as I stood rigid in protest. November was for kittens and skipping and not for boys, especially not Harry Manners. Yet a few minutes later, I was heading next door for the second time in three weeks, my fingers crossed as I muttered get-me-out-of-here-before-Mr.-Manners-gets-home.

The house was like nothing I'd ever seen. Aunt Magda and Uncle Ray had a modernist house, meaning they didn't have much furniture. They also had large abstract paintings on the walls, which were white. Everyone agreed that Aunt Magda had Good Taste. Debbie had gone shopping with her after she got married so Debbie's house was similar, although her armchairs and chesterfields were more comfortable and the art was chosen by Ed, paintings by famous artists who were only famous in Vancouver, at least so far. There weren't people in any of Ed's paintings, so Aunt Magda approved. People didn't seem to be in Good Taste.

The main floor of the Manners family's house had a ceiling as high as my aunt's and similarly clad in cedar. But the living room, kitchen and dining room were all one huge room with small flights of stairs dividing them. And while it wasn't crowded, the room had far more furniture and not all of it was new. The dining suite looked modern, and so did the chesterfield and armchairs, but the carpets were patterned and surprisingly worn. There was also a large cabinet of heavily carved pale wood that looked as if someone had taken a metal chain to it. A pew seemed to have walked out of a church, picking up coats and umbrellas along the way, and there were a couple of dark paintings of dead-looking people. I knew the word antique. Nice Mrs. Armstrong with her four children younger than me had mentioned it once to my mother. "We're making do with my grandparents' furniture and calling it antique."

The Manners place was messy, it was true. There were newspapers thrown everywhere and coats and math tests dropped where they fell. But there was something perfect standing in front of the picture window: a small tree with glossy leaves that was covered in miniature oranges. They were the most precious things. I walked over and touched them, finding that they were soft and slightly squashed at the top and bottom like mandarin oranges.

"Can you eat them?" I asked Mrs. Manners.

"I couldn't really have them around if they were poisonous, could I?" she asked. "I know someone who freezes them into ice cubes, but I find that a little Frou-Frou."

Frou-Frou. Capitalized.

"They're ornamental, Tink. Rather like me."

I cast a glance back at the oranges as Mrs. Manners led me over to the Monopoly board, which Harry Manners had set up on one of the rugs, pushing a coffee table aside. He had one ankle wrapped in a bandage, which explained things. Harry didn't look particularly happy to see me, but he seemed to realize I wasn't particularly happy to see him either, so we were all right.

"I'm always the banker," Harry said. I didn't care, although I wasn't happy when Mrs. Manners sat down on the rug to play with us. Not that I could say anything, and I could see that Harry couldn't either. It made me wonder what he'd done to make his mother punish him with me. There was nothing in his eyes to tell. They were bright blue, and you couldn't see through them any more than you could see through the noonday sky.

It began with Mrs. Manners grabbing the thimble as her token and Harry taking the cowboy on his horse. After some consideration, I chose the Scottie dog. When we started rolling the dice, it turned out that Harry liked buying up expensive properties like Boardwalk, and that he was lucky about landing on them, as you would expect. I always tried to buy up railroads and yellow properties, especially Marvin Gardens. I liked yellow. Meanwhile, Mrs. Manners didn't really seem to be paying attention. When she rolled a seven, she would shove it forward eight places, or maybe only six. Then she would buy wherever she landed on, even if it was Baltic Avenue.

"Mrs. Manners, I think you really landed on Go To Jail," I said once, and she widened her blue eyes at me and whipped out a Get Out of Jail Free card.

"Mrs. Manners, I think you really landed on Park Place. You need to pay Harry his rent."

Harry seemed to know that, but I supposed he couldn't correct his mother in front of a guest, even if it was only me.

"Mrs. Manners, I think . . ."

"My goodness, you *do* keep track, don't you Tink? Are you going to be a policeman when you grow up?"

I was surprised at her irritation and could only shrug, not being sure what I wanted to be.

"You must want to be something."

"Grown up?"

Norman told jokes like that, but Mrs. Manners didn't seem to get it.

"I'm going to be a lawyer," Harry said.

His mother swivelled. "Where did that come from?"

"From Cal." His oldest brother, the quarterback.

"Cal wants to be a lawyer?"

"Yes, Mother, Cal wants to be a lawyer."

Harry sounded as bored as a teenager, and we exchanged a secret look, with me thanking him for getting me off the hook. I didn't say that my brother was a lawyer. I wanted to get this over with and go home, although Mrs. Manners turned away from Harry to look at me pointedly.

"That was a nice Halloween costume, Tink," she said.

I shrugged, not liking this at all.

"Mr. Manners made a joke about it. He likes making jokes. I wonder if you know that. Your father probably knows it was all a big joke. I bet you told him. Didn't you."

I remembered when the Hortons came to dinner, and Mrs. Horton said that Mr. Horton liked to tease people even though he wasn't teasing.

"Are you listening to me, Tink?"

"Yes, Mrs. Manners. Mr. Manners likes making jokes." I couldn't keep myself from adding, "Ha, ha."

The words had such big elbows they took up the whole room. I couldn't remember ever saying anything as bad before, not to an adult. I couldn't remember people as strange as the Manners family either. My remark made Mrs. Manners look disorganized, as if she couldn't remember where she'd left her purse.

Harry hated me. You could see behind his eyes after all.

"It's your turn," I told him, holding onto those eyes. You couldn't do anything about anyone's mother, but you couldn't let another kid get the whip hand over you. I had to stare him down, even though he had the advantage of being in his own house.

After a long moment, Harry looked away, telling his mother, "I'm bored of Monopoly."

"Bored *with* Monopoly," Mrs. Manners corrected automatically.

Harry swept his hand over the Monopoly board, knocking the tokens and houses flying. I was shocked, and Mrs. Manners looked even more disorganized. Without pausing, Harry got up clumsily to leave, favouring his bandaged ankle. This was going to make being in school with him tomorrow a bit dangerous. Being in school with him forever.

"I'm sorry," I called, even though it wasn't my fault.

The funny thing was, Harry turned and nodded at me before limping out of the room. So it wasn't me he hated, although I had no idea what it was.

Debbie was with Bunny when I got home, and they questioned me as thoroughly as any *Daily Planet* reporter about the inside of the Manners house. As Mrs. Oliver with her Comings and Goings column in the newspaper. Apparently, the worn carpets were antiques too, called Persian like the cats. The pictures of dead people made them agree that the Manners family must have Had Money even back in England. All of this was interesting, and maybe it lulled me into staying in the kitchen. That and Debbie getting up to make coffee.

Staying was a mistake. As Debbie gave me my coffee, two sugars, she asked casually what Harry and I had been doing.

"Playing Monopoly which was boring," I said all at once, hoping that would end it, and blowing on my coffee for emphasis.

"Who won?"

Debbie liked winning at tennis, so of course she would ask.

"Nobody," I said. "Harry got bored of playing, too. *With* playing."

"And his mother let him quit?" Debbie asked, sitting back down. "'Cause you shouldn't be a quitter, right, little nickens?"

"He kind of pushed over the board so we couldn't play anymore."

"What a brat," Debbie said. "Guess he was losing, hey?"

I didn't know if he was losing. We didn't get far enough. I didn't care either, I told her, although I still wanted to know what the Manners family was doing here. Why didn't they live in West Van like she did or in Shaughnessy over town? That way, all the Manners kids could go to private schools like my cousin Simon, and Harry could get a gold crest on his pocket, which he'd probably like as much as Boardwalk.

Bunny still wanted to know why they shouldn't live here. But Debbie hesitated, my sister being unable to skirt the truth, the same as our father.

"Your friend's dad, Mr. Manners, Jim Manners, doesn't get along particularly well with his own father. The old man. Who runs the family business. Tyrannically."

"Why not?"

Debbie hesitated again. "You can never know what goes on inside families, nickens. Not from outside. I think Jim Manners would like to get along. But he got himself a bit . . . cut off."

"Is that right?" Bunny asked.

"Of course his friends are going to get him a job. But as far as an inheritance goes, or the lack of one . . . Ed hears things. Old Cal Manners being a subject of conversation."

"Tyrannicalus Rex," I said, which made Debbie smile.

"Guess you aren't going to ask Harry Manners to your birthday party," she said.

"We've got a list," Bunny answered, although I wasn't aware of one. "She was invited to a *lot* of parties this year. More than a dozen. I was going to ask you . . ."

"And Norman," I interrupted. "His birthday is in December, so I didn't get invited yet."

My mother pursed her lips. "Girls go to girls' parties, Mary Alice. Boys go to boys' parties. You know that."

I stared at her and felt tears gathering in my eyes and spilling down my cheeks. I never cried, but I felt sad about Norman, and how we hadn't seen each other lately. How he was nicer than Harry Manners, at least when he hadn't over-exerted himself. Although Harry Manners had been over-exerted by his mother, so it wasn't a fair comparison. Harry Manners was all right. At least he would be if he wasn't dangerous at school in the morning. It was Mrs. Manners who was *Twilight Zone* and Mr. Manners who was worse, since he hadn't been joking on Halloween, despite what Mrs. Manners said. I was scared, I didn't know of what. Astronauts and cowboys and principals let loose in the night-time streets and being caught inside gears that turned and churned even though you couldn't see them and didn't understand anything.

"Why not? Why can't Norman come to my party? Why can't he?"

"Oh, hey there, little sweetheart," Debbie said, crouching down and putting her arm around me. "Hey there. Hey. Here's the deal, okay? I'll take you and Norman to the movies. How's that? We'll have a birthday matinee the Saturday after your party. Deal? Is that a deal?"

I had to nod, not wanting to disappoint her. Also, there would be popcorn. Not popcorn balls, but real popcorn with butter and salt. Bunny seemed to think that settled things, although it didn't. But at least I'd got two birthdays out of it, and that was all right.

My father came home so late that night I was already in bed. He and Bunny spoke quietly for a long time, and I heard the word Monopoly. Afterward, he spied through the half-open door as if he thought I was sleeping.

"I hope you got paid overtime," I said.

My father came and sat down on the bed, kicking off his shoes and swinging his legs up alongside me, which wasn't usual. Stretching his arms above his head, he said, "For some of it."

"German's really on a rampage," I said. When he looked surprised, I corrected myself: "Mr. German."

My father thought about this but didn't say anything. He was Ruminating, as Bunny put it. Your father likes to Ruminate. I wasn't sure, but I thought it meant percolating, the way a pot percolated coffee.

Thoughts had been percolating in me, too.

"Mrs. Manners cheated at Monopoly," I said. "She kept trying to move her token past bad places to land, and when I counted them out, she got mad at me."

My father went a little ramrod. "She got mad at you how?"

"She asked if I wanted to be a policeman when I grew up."

He paused. "And that's all?"

"Harry said he wanted to be a lawyer and she got interested in that." I thought about it. "Harry's okay. He probably won't fight me at school. Even though his mother over-exerted him."

My father swung his legs off the bed so he was sitting beside me as usual. This time, he let out a sigh that was part laughter and part something else. Tiredness, maybe.

"She wanted me to tell you about Halloween," I said. "To say that Mr. Manners was joking when he said I was being the Ku Klux Klan. You know I was being the Lone Ranger. And Norman was being Zorro in his dad's hat. But Mr. Manners said Norman was being Dr. Martin Luther King riding his boys down to Alabam, and Mr. Manners *did* mean boys, and then he sang 'Nobody Knows the Troubles I've Seen.'"

My father went more angry than tired and waited a minute to speak.

"Mary Alice . . ."

"Tink."

"Mary Alice," he repeated, and rubbed his eyes again. "I'm not sure what to say."

"You can Ruminate," I said, and he smiled.

"Harry Manners is in your class at school, isn't he?" To which I agreed. "But he's not your friend." To which I also agreed. "So there's no reason to go over there anymore, is there?"

"But what if she makes me, like she did today?"

"Here's a good word for you. *No.* You say, 'No, thank you.' Do that whenever something feels wrong, in your heart. Will you do that for me?"

"In my heart or my stomach?"

"There," he said, and tickled my ribs. Tickled and tickled so I howled with laughter, laughing and screeching until Bunny stuck her head in the door.

"She's supposed to be going to sleep."

"You're supposed to go to sleep," my father told me, and tousled my hair.

The next morning, when it was still a bit early to leave for school, I showed up at Norman's house. Mrs. Horton opened the door wearing her knapsack. She looked at me a moment then turned and called, "Norman!"

When Norman appeared, he nodded at me thoughtfully and went to get his coat. This was the difference with the Hortons. They treated me like a person, meaning politely, even though I was a person who'd been sent to try them. Mr. and Mrs. Manners treated me like something else, I wasn't sure what. Maybe something to play with, like a Monopoly token. Mr. Manners did that, and Mrs. Manners was prone.

"No," I said, testing the word. "No thank you, Mrs. Manners."

When Norman reappeared, I told him, "My sister is going to take us to a movie." As we left the house, I remembered that I'd never asked, "What did you think of the popcorn ball?"

"Paper," he said.

"Glued-together paper."

"Puffed-up, glued-together paper," he said, and we walked downhill to school.

7

I had my two birthday parties that year, and Norman had his. Looking back, I remember a great weight of parties. After Norman's came the Christmas explosion, and then the New Year's celebrations for 1962.

New Year's Eve had never played a big part in my life, aside from Bunny's new clothes and a teenage babysitter my parents hired so they could go to the neighbourhood party. But this year, one party leading to another and another all through late November and December seemed to gradually stretch something too thin. Maybe self-discipline. Peoples' ability to be their best selves rather than their worst ones.

The calendar is so arbitrary. Wherever I've lived, the New Year really starts when children go back to school in September. Yet I think I'm not alone in using dates to pitch myself. "If I can make it through Sunday dinner." "I can keep it together until January." Then a deadline arrives and resolutions grow attenuated. Stretched out, self-discipline failing. Which is how I account for what happened that year, tensions snowballing toward the missile crisis in a winter when it didn't even snow.

My ninth double-birthday went fine. The big party with the girls took place partly in the pool at Debbie's club, which got loud with shrieks and splashes. Playing water tag made me feel like I was eating too much candy when I hadn't even eaten too much cake yet. I also wasn't sure what to do with the Barbie doll that redheaded Lucy Oliver gave me afterward in the party room. Bunny said it was an extravagant gift, telling my father later that it was really an apology from Mrs. Oliver of Comings and Goings, not to me but to her. I think that confused my father as well as me, since Bunny's only explanation was that Irene Oliver had been flip the last time she'd been over for coffee, end of story.

The next weekend was my real birthday party, since it was what I wanted to do rather than what Bunny thought I should do. Debbie took me and Norman to a movie theatre to see *One Hundred and One Dalmatians*. I had loved it when it first came out and was excited to see it again, especially now that we had a black-and-white kitten in the house. What made things even better was that Norman hadn't seen the *Dalmatians*, and that Debbie bought a popcorn tub for each of us at the concession stand instead of making us share.

She also bought one for herself, since Debbie parked around the corner and came into the movie theatre with us, putting her feet up on the back of the seat in front. This was forbidden, but the usher didn't ask her to take them down because she was beautiful. At least, that was why Auntie Nita said my sister got away with everything, and good for her. The usher leaned against the side wall for most of the movie, watching Debbie instead of the *Dalmatians*, only waking up when some boys started throwing popcorn. The usher was a teenager and spindly, and he waved his arms at the boys like a sea anemone I'd seen over town at the aquarium.

Afterward, Debbie took us home in her two-door coupe, which was coloured an enviable traffic-light green.

"You should probably call your sister after we eat my cake," I told Norman. "She can come and see the kittens. And she can have a piece of cake, too, if she wants."

Norman didn't seem to want Rosa to come to my party. Then he looked startled, and his slow blush rose up his neck.

"I forgot your birthday present," he said. "So I have to go home anyway."

"You didn't need to get me a present," I replied, which Bunny had drilled me in saying before my girls' birthday party. When someone walked in the door of the club and handed me a present, I had to say, "You didn't need to do that." That felt uncomfortable at first, but it turned out to be one of those things that everyone knew meant the opposite, so you weren't lying. "It doesn't hurt." "You go first. I don't care."

Rosa said she'd come over soon. Meanwhile, my present turned out to be an illustrated book, *The Lion, the Witch and the Wardrobe*, the lion part of which looked promising. As I flipped through the illustrations, Norman disappeared into my new comic book, *The Fantastic Four*. We ate the chocolate cupcakes Bunny had made instead of a cake, and after Debbie left, the doorbell rang with the day's surprise. The book hadn't been a surprise, since it had been wrapped like a book. But when I opened the door, I found not only Rosa but Andy Manners, the girl who let the air out of teachers' tires. They stood on opposite sides of the front step, the space between them vibrating with friendship.

Andy Manners was much thinner than Rosa and taller, so she had to look quite far down to acknowledge my existence. She had her father's male jaw and black eyes, to which she added dungarees and big lace-up boots that looked as if someone even younger than me had tied them, not a big girl like her. Andy and Rosa were fifteen.

"So. Kittens," Rosa said, sounding like Marlon Brando.

When I agreed there were kittens, the two of them crowded inside. Andy ate a cupcake silently as Rosa talked far too sweetly to my mother in the kitchen—"Thank you so *very* much for the invitation"—making Bunny's jaw clench as she suggested I take them downstairs. Rosa ordered Norman to come with us, using a jerk of the head that I decided to practise later in the mirror. Afterward, Andy clattered her boots down the stairs, which was also enviable, in its way.

The kittens were four weeks old and lived in the rec room, where my father had made a step-over board in the open doorway to keep them contained. I'd cut the side off the cardboard box so they could still go and nurse whenever Wilma chose to lie there. But she was weaning them, and they were lapping up dishes of condensed milk mixed with hot water and a plate of kitten food that Bunny chopped up. The three of them bumbled quickly toward us as we stepped over the board, their little legs clumsy, their round eyes staring, looking surprised to be alive.

"Such *sweeties!*" Rosa cried, sounding as exaggerated as she had with Bunny. Only after she and Andy plumped down on the rug did they turn human, letting the kittens climb up on their laps and murmuring to them and each other. I sat down on the chesterfield beside Norman, who was back into the *Fantastic Four*, only looking up occasionally over the top of the pages like my father looking over his newspaper. I'd learned that when people came over to think about kittens you let them, trying not to push one over the other since all of them needed homes.

"Black and white," Andy said finally. It was a *Twilight Zone* echo of her father, although she couldn't have known, having been at the high school dance on Halloween.

"That's the one I like, too," Rosa said, picking it up.

"The dichotomy between good and evil. Light and darkness," Andy said, enjoying her vocabulary. It was interesting to find we had something in common. "The dualistic fight in the universe. *For* the universe." Not that I understood a word she was saying.

"Eyes as wide as saucers, Tinkerbell," she said.

"Tink," Norman told her, without putting down his comic book. He hadn't been thrown by seeing Andy Manners with his sister, but he didn't like it, either.

Andy leaned back on her arms and crossed her boots on the rug in front of her.

"Surprised to find I've got a few brains, Tink?"

Now Andy was being Marlon Brando. I was about to tell her what Norman's father had said when I remembered I wasn't supposed to repeat what his parents mentioned about school.

"I heard you got your father's brains as well as his looks."

I felt proud of myself for putting it that way, which was complimentary. But Andy was so angry that her eyes turned into sparklers and she spoke angrily, standing up.

"I've got my mother's looks and my grandfather's brains."

Rosa stepped in peaceably. "We'll call him Tommy for dichotomy."

"It's a girl," I told her, watching Andy nervously. But she only threw herself down in an armchair, balling her hands up into her armpits like her mother down the creek. I supposed she looked a bit like Mrs. Manners, although Andy's eyes weren't her mother's bright grey-green but two black holes even when she wasn't furious.

No thank you, Mrs. Manners, I practised. No thank you, Andy.

Not that she'd asked me for anything.

"When are they ready to go home?" Rosa asked. "Meaning," she said, raising her eyebrows at Andy, "how much time have I got to work on my father?"

"They need to be eight weeks," I said. "Which is Christmas."

"We're going skiing as soon as school gets out," Rosa said, making Norman fumble down his comic. "But they need to be home for New Year's, seeing as how we're thrown back in the dungeon on January second. So you have to keep her until then."

"No one told me about skiing," Norman said.

"You're getting your brace off next week," Rosa said. "I told them to tell you. They won't put you on skis yet, but they figure you can probably go snowshoeing with Mum. Anyway," she said, turning back to me, "like I say, you have to hold onto her over Christmas. Presuming I can wheedle my father, which I can. Unless I just bring her home," she added, turning back to Andy. "What do you think? Fait accompli."

I didn't know where to go with my divided attention. Norman was looking upset, as if his brace was a pet they were going to take away from him. Meanwhile, Rosa was speaking French as well as our teacher Mademoiselle Tremblay, who came in twice a week now that we were in grade four. It sounded as if the Hortons had been to Quebec, although Norman had never said. I wondered if it was connected to communism, in which case I didn't want to know. Plus I had to tell Rosa that Bunny wouldn't hold the kitten without her parents' permission, and Andy looked like a firecracker waiting to be lit, and I didn't know what to do about any of it, especially when Andy levered herself up in her chair ready to speak.

"They should have said something," she told Norman, sounding entirely reasonable.

"They were afraid he'd get all worked up," Rosa said. "Nightmares. Wetting the . . ." Catching herself. "And you're gonna help me work on Dad, right?"

"It's going to cost money to get her spayed," Norman said, still sounding upset.

"Babysitting. I'm going to haul it in on New Year's Eve." Telling me, "Inform your parents."

"I thought you'd like the tortoiseshell," I replied, feeling lost. "But Judy Shribman liked hearing about the tortoiseshell at my party. My other party. Which maybe leaves the tabby," I told Andy. "If you want."

"I want a wolfhound," Andy said.

"I only wet the bed when I was a baby," Norman said, back behind his comic book.

"Everyone wets the bed when they're a baby," Andy said. "I still do."

"You *don't*," I said, and her eyes bored into me before she shrugged.

I was left puzzled, especially when I remembered for a second time what Norman's father had told him. You'd think Andy Manners was smart, but she was just like her father. Cal Manners was the one with brains.

What I was seeing of Andy didn't add up to what Mr. Horton had said, and I sat there wondering in which way I was wrong.

After my birthday party was over, Bunny and I went into the kitchen so she could cook dinner. Finding a home for one of the kittens had made me bounce. That and two cupcakes. I told Bunny that Rosa wanted the black-and-white, which would be named Tommy even though it was a girl. She was going to ask permission, and then Bunny could call her parents.

"Norman said his mother was at home, didn't he?" Bunny asked.

"Mr. Horton is the one who doesn't like cats. He's the one who has to agree."

Bunny raised her eyebrows at me and picked up the phone. My mother usually wasn't in any hurry, so I was surprised by her speed. Mrs. Horton answered, and after some company politeness, Bunny brought up the question of permission, afterward repeating half sentences from Mrs. Horton for my benefit. So you spoke *before* she came . . . Responsibility, yes. Learning to be responsible . . . Fallen in love, has she? Just as well it's a cat.

Seeing that they were taking the kitten, I did a sugar dance around the kitchen.

"One more thing," my mother said urgently, when I thought she was about to hang up. "I understand we might get Rosa to babysit on New Year's Eve." This was a surprise, since I hadn't mentioned a word about babysitting. Bunny must have been eavesdropping, and it felt uncomfortable to find that my mother took after me.

She also sounded brave when she mentioned the idea, so there must have been some question about my parents' plans. This wasn't unusual, since my father preferred to stay at home on New Year's Eve. He preferred to stay at home most of the time, and with his boss on such a rampage lately, this included work. Step, pause. Step, pause. His morning walk out the door.

"That's a lot of money," Bunny said, and sounded braver. "Tell her it's fine."

After Bunny hung up, I wondered whether Mrs. Horton had sounded brave as well, taking the decision about the kitten without consulting Mr. Horton, the way she'd done when she'd given Norman the raise in his allowance.

"Why can't you hear both sides of a phone call the way you can on TV?" I asked.

"It's probably just as well," Bunny said.

That was her usual answer, the one that percolated out when she wasn't listening. Then she helped herself to a cupcake, making a bratty face at me as if I'd said she couldn't have one, and taking an exaggerated bite.

Norman's birthday party was two weeks later, and at first it looked as if it was going to be a copycat of mine, except without a party for boys beforehand. Mr. Horton drove the two of us to the same movie theatre as Debbie, while I carried a present hidden in a grocery bag to disguise the fact it was a book wrapped like a book. But instead of joining us for the movie, Mr. Horton dropped us off and drove away, not even waiting to see us safely inside. Norman paid at the ticket booth and we went through the big glass door like Hansel and Gretel trekking alone into the woods. I enjoyed being an unsupervised party orphan, although it also felt strange.

The movie was called *The Absent-Minded Professor*. Neither of us had seen it before and as we walked into the theatre, it proved to be popular, the red velvet seats already packed with kids. We were late enough that we had to sit almost too close to the screen, but only almost, and it was fine to share a tub of popcorn. You didn't need that much popcorn anyway; Norman was right. And the movie was a comedy, which gave everyone a chance to laugh and hoot and howl when it was funny and throw popcorn when it wasn't. This happened frequently, keeping the usher busy waving his tentacles in the stream of projected light.

The real difference in our parties came afterward. Once the movie was over, instead of leaving with Debbie, we walked outside looking for Norman's father. A crowd of parents waited on the sidewalk and a long lineup of cars idled at the curb. But his father wasn't chatting with the other parents, and when we walked down the lineup, he wasn't there, either.

Embarrassed at being abandoned, we went silently back to the theatre. I remembered my project of making Norman fit in when it became clear that his father was working against it. We waited as the first kids flooded away, and while the next group trickled off with acceptably late parents, then while a final party of girls broadcast relief when a harried-looking mother drove up in a station wagon honking her horn.

This left us alone on the chilly sidewalk, the lady in the ticket booth glaring at us through her tinted window. She seemed to think that being forgotten was our fault, which was unfair.

"He's late sometimes," Norman said.

"Maybe your mother can come get us."

"My mum can't drive," Norman said, which was new information. "He's late all the time," he added, as if he didn't want to lie.

It was cold. Not raining or windy but cold. I had my coat on over my dress but only wore a thin white leotard and my party shoes. At least Norman had pants. He'd also got his brace off, which was a good thing, since he'd told me the metal turned icy in the cold. I wondered if that was why his father was late. He knew that Norman didn't get cold without his brace so he didn't need to hurry, either forgetting about me or punishing me for being sent to try them.

Being punished sounded right. You didn't forget about your own son.

"They gave me a dime to call for emergencies," I said.

"You can't. They'd get angry at my dad."

"I've got choir practice after the cake," I told him, and worked it out. "Except there won't be any time for cake."

"There isn't any cake," Norman said. "The popcorn was the cake. My mum says sugar is White Death."

I felt exasperated, which was one of Bunny's favourite words.

"Did she say that before or after she ate all your Halloween candy?"

"After," Norman said. "And she didn't eat all that much. Rosa got most of it."

"Here's your present, then," I said, and shoved it at him.

That immediately felt mean, even though Norman perked up as he took the present. His father must have been late all the time if he was used to this degree of *Twilight Zone*. Norman didn't seem to understand that you couldn't open a birthday present in the middle of a sidewalk, or at least that you shouldn't have to. He tore the wrapping off eagerly, the wind catching shreds of tissue paper and wisping them away.

"What on Earth are we going to get Norman?" my mother had asked.

As I eavesdropped, I'd heard my father remind her that when the Hortons came to dinner, Norman had said he wanted to start reading science fiction. Maybe we could get him a book they'd written up in the newspaper.

"Give Jack Horton a reason to praise the boy's reading," he'd said, which puzzled me. Norman read all the time. He had the best collection of comics in the neighbourhood.

The book my father chose had planets on the top of the cover and a red spaceship on the bottom that had crashed into a desert. *A Fall of Moondust*, it was called, by Arthur C. Clarke. Seeing it, Norman got so excited that I thought he was going to sit down on the sidewalk and read it right there.

"He's famous," he told me. "Arthur C. Clarke. *Arthur C. Clarke!*"

"What does the *C* stand for?" I asked.

Before Norman could answer, his mother pulled up in a taxi cab.

"Here we are," she called through the window. Calling louder, "Car problems!" to the lady in the ticket booth, who looked disgusted and left through a door in the back of the booth.

Norman held up his present, ready to speak.

"You can show me later," Mrs. Horton said. "Come on. Let's get out of here."

"My father can fix your car," I said, although Mrs. Horton didn't seem to hear me.

"Back home?" the cabbie asked.

"Yes," Mrs. Horton said.

"She needs to go to choir practice," Norman said.

"Where?" his mum asked, sounding as ragged as I felt. When I told her the name of our church, the cabbie nodded, and Mrs. Horton promised she'd phone my mother from home.

"So what have you got?" she asked Norman, before taking his book and answering her own question. "Arthur C. Clarke!"

I was going to ask about the *C* again, but Mrs. Horton and Norman huddled over the book like two girls sharing a secret, even though neither of them said a word. They were shutting me out. I knew what that looked like, and went as cool as Marlon Brando to prove I didn't care.

I probably didn't want to know what they were protecting, anyway. It might have concerned communism when I already needed to keep too much about Norman's party a secret from my parents. If I told them what had happened, Bunny would box me in with rules about seeing Norman, whose dad had forgotten us and whose mum had pretended not to hear what I'd said about my father fixing their car, even though we both knew perfectly well that she had.

The cab dropped me off alone outside the church just as Mr. Horton had dropped us off alone outside the theatre. It was a strange day, yet not a bad one. Being around the Hortons was like visiting a different city, bigger than any I'd visited so far.

After hopping up the church steps, I walked through a second set of tall double doors of the day. The church's carved oak doors led into the lobby, which I had been told to call a vestibule since the church wasn't a theatre, even though I still privately thought it was. The thick carpet was patterned green and white and there was a big bouquet of flowers on a round table at its centre, flowers being the responsibility of the Church Ladies, of whom my mother wasn't one.

I'd never come into the church alone before, and took the opportunity to drag my feet on the carpet as I headed through a side door toward the auditorium. Our church had a children's choir good enough to enter competitions. Walking down the deserted hallway, I had somewhat mixed feelings about my life as an unsupervised party orphan. My footsteps echoed with a lonely sound, but I also liked opening the door and walking into the auditorium on my own like the older choristers.

Mrs. Culver looked over her half glasses as I took off my coat, nodding at my arrival. She was our minister's wife and the choir leader, and she'd learned about my singing when I was seven years old. I was a little girl with a big voice, and the Culvers' daughter had been teaching Sunday School when I'd opened my mouth for a hymn. Afterward, Mr. Culver took advantage of being a minister and invited himself and his wife over for coffee, with Mrs. Culver wanting to know if my parents realized what they had.

"Not knowing her own daughter. Who did Mrs. Culver think she was?"

Bunny only said this after the Culvers had left, although her attitude toward the choir was probably part of the reason she wasn't a Church Lady. My mother disliked people making a spectacle of themselves and at first she wouldn't allow her daughter to join them. I hadn't started my serious eavesdropping at that point so I never knew how they wore her down, but in the end it was agreed that I would sing in the choir on charitable occasions, although I wouldn't become a year-round member until I was older, and only if I expressed a real interest.

I think the charitable aspect probably convinced my father. This meant joining the choir before Christmas when it sang in hospitals and nursing homes. The old people drooling in the homes terrified me almost as much as the ghost-faced patients in hospitals, and sometimes I had nightmares. This meant my membership in the choir was always up in the air, not like November skipping or kittens and certainly not like Norman. It was never inevitable.

"You don't have to sing in hospitals if you don't want to," my father would tell me, sitting on the side of my bed when I woke up screaming.

But I insisted, Mrs. Culver having let it be known you got good marks in heaven for being charitable. I'd finally figured out that meant you did what you ought to even when you didn't want to, and my father told me I wasn't wrong. More secretly, I loved playing to an audience, even if it drooled. Bunny's position made this impossible to admit, but my mother's position was also indefensible, not least because I'd got my voice from her.

My mother had a lush, sooty, untrained voice that she'd unleash when we were alone, singing along to her records of *Oklahoma!*, *Brigadoon*, and *Seven Brides for Seven Brothers*. She and I loved those old musicals and watched them every time they came on TV, hoofing it around the rec room as we belted out the songs.

Bunny could do all the dance steps even when we weren't watching the actors on TV, just playing her records in the living room. I followed half a beat behind her the first time through, hesitant, a little out of focus, although I picked up the moves quickly. She taught me how to harmonize as well, getting me to belt out the melody while she embroidered her voice around it.

"Now you," she'd say, and we'd switch.

I wanted the neighbours to see us, hoofing it in perfect smiling-faced rhythm across the beige wall-to-wall, our faces always turned toward the invisible camera. Bunny was usually preoccupied with cooking and cleaning and laundry, but sometimes I could get her to put on one of her records, and then we would fly.

Years later, I would wonder if the combination of Bunny's voice and her reluctance to let me perform meant that she'd tried for a career as a singer and failed, and it had gutted her. I didn't see when she could have done it, since she and my father married when she was nineteen and she'd got pregnant with Bob right away. Then it occurred to me she might have gone after it when my father was overseas, because why not?

I asked my father, which was always my first line of inquiry.

"No," he said, looking puzzled.

That was the end of it for a while. But it bothered me, and eventually I found what I thought was a good time to ask Bunny.

"Where did you get that from?" she asked.

Which isn't a denial.

I may be wrong about the singing, but I'm certain my mother had suffered some sort of trauma that made her want life to be smoothed down and quiet and predictable, a wish that grew frantic during the missile crisis. But no one gets through life without trauma, and I'm not sure anyone else can ever know the true nature of someone else's hurt, or if we're even sure what happened to ourselves.

"Mary Alice," Mrs. Culver said, after I'd put down my coat. "Come over to the piano. I've got a job for you."

A solo. I vibrated. Mrs. Culver sang songs she wanted soloists to learn, accompanying herself on the piano. This time it was "O Holy Night." She sang it for me as I concentrated, quickly picking up the beat and starting to pat my thigh. Mrs. Culver had a sweet thin soprano that could break on the high notes, and it broke in the second verse, when "His power and glo-oh-oh-ry" overwhelmed her. I couldn't help wincing and hoped she didn't notice, being happy to get a more challenging solo than "Away in a Manger" or "Jesus Loves Me," which she said people liked to hear little children sing.

"Again, please," I asked when she'd finished.

"You'll have the first verse on your own, and the choir will come in on the chorus." Raising her voice: "Are you listening, Choir?"

They weren't. After I had my verse, she formed us into rows so everyone could learn the new song. But the choir was restive, shuffling, school holidays having grown fingers and started beckoning from the exit. Long after I'd got the "Night" down, others were still fumbling, especially the altos, and Mrs. Culver finally rapped her baton sharply on her music stand.

"Mary Alice, you'll also take the beginning of the third verse," Mrs. Culver said, glaring at the altos, particularly her former favourite Tammy Wharton, who had a new-found interest in boys. Maybe a fraction of Mrs. Culver's decision came from the fact Bunny had just walked in to join other parents in a line of chairs around the outside of the auditorium. In any case, there was punishment involved, although not of me.

"Can you please show the others how it goes, Mary Alice?" Mrs. Culver asked, and the accompanist played a bridge so I could sing the lines I knew my father would like.

Truly He taught us to love one another;
His law is love and His gospel is peace.
Chains shall He break for the slave is our brother;
And in His name all oppression shall cease.

"Choir!" Mrs. Culver called, and the rest came in smartly, not all of them liking me.

Sweet hymns of joy in grateful chorus raise we,
Let all within us praise His holy name.

"Practise, practise, practise," Mrs. Culver said after we finished the song, although I never had to and never did.

By the time Norman left to go snowshoeing, I was so busy with choir and our annual Christmas customs that I barely noticed he was gone. *The Wizard of Oz* came on TV as it did every year, and I was reliably frightened by the trees. Bob's childhood train set went up in the rec room, supposedly for me, although Bob and Ed hogged it the way they always did before getting bored and letting me play. We went out to family parties and hosted Christmas dinner, and two days later Judy Shribman came over for the tortoiseshell kitten. A pair of random parents had taken the little tabby pre-Christmas, so aside from the black-and-white kitten we were holding for Rosa, we were done with kittens once again.

Yet in the middle of this, there was also the choir performance on Christmas Eve, one that cast a shadow over everything. We gathered that afternoon in the lobby of the newly opened Grouse Valley Hospital. Many had carpooled there, while our parents had dropped some of us off for our final Christmas performance. My father took me into the lobby, but he had to pick up something at work and arranged with a neighbour to bring me home: Mrs. Winters, the dentist's wife, whose youngest daughter, Ingrid, was a soprano. The concert was well enough advertised that patients in their blue hospital gowns were already crowding into the lobby, many of them guided or wheeled out of the elevators by family members looking relieved they could do something besides stare at one another.

Mrs. Culver was busy arranging us into ranks when I got there, and I slid into my place in the front row on the right side, where I stood both in choir and in school photos. Other choristers were still arriving, and in the confusion, a man who looked like a doctor recognized Mrs. Culver, walking over to greet her so they chatted and nodded. Then Mrs. Culver looked back to see that we were ready and turned to smile at the audience. After giving her standard introduction, she raised her baton and dropped it on "Hark! The Herald Angels Sing."

It being a normal concert, "O Holy Night" was the final hymn, with my solo. "Merry Christmas," she said afterward, which led to the applause that I loved and the audience filtering away. Our last concert seemed to be over when Mrs. Culver rapped her baton on a metal chair arm.

"Choir," she called, and we had to stop, even though we were already at home in our heads. "We've been invited to sing one or two songs in the Rehabilitation Wing."

Some of the parents looked askance—members of the choir certainly did—so she added evenly, "Where people need cheering up."

The Rehabilitation Wing turned out to be the old General Hospital next door, a damp brick building that Grouse Valley Hospital was meant to replace. The doctor-looking man Mrs. Culver had talked to earlier met us outside. Somewhat mysteriously, he took us up some back stairs to a door he had to unlock, letting us into a green corridor with empty hospital rooms off it. We ended up in a small lounge with green Naugahyde chesterfields. Ladies in dressing gowns were standing and sitting around the room, not all of them awake.

"In ranks," Mrs. Culver told us quietly.

"I'm rank!" a lady called, raising her arm. "Wanna smell?"

"We'll start with 'Hark! The Herald Angels Sing,'" Mrs. Culver said quickly and dropped her baton. From my place in the front row, I saw a tiny old lady start to sing along, which wasn't unusual, although she seemed to be singing a different hymn. A few sleepers woke up and others drifted off. I also saw someone darting around the back of the group, looking over shoulders and bobbing back down. It was strange, but I thought I recognized the lady, although I couldn't place her. Only when Mrs. Culver announced "O Holy Night" and I stepped forward for my solo did I see who it was.

"Hello, Mrs. Eisenstadt," I called, waving energetically since she needed to be cheered up. It was the principal's wife, whom we usually met at the medical offices. Horror bloomed on her face before she hunched her shoulder to angle away, looking like a sailboat turning into the wind. "O Holy Night," I sang, as she pushed through a pair of metal doors and disappeared.

Mrs. Winters brought me home later than expected, so my father was already back from the office. She and my parents held a whispered conference at the door while I rummaged in the fridge. I heard several unknown terms and frequent mention of the word mistake.

"Thanks, Audrey," my father said. "We'll take care of it at this end."

I was looking over the rim of my glass of chocolate milk as he closed the door.

"What's a psych ward?" I asked, speaking into the glass. It gave a nice echo.

"Never mind," Bunny said. "You're going to forget all about that." Before I could say anything, she answered, "Because I told you to."

"The psychiatric ward," my father told me, "is for people who have mental problems instead of physical ones. There's nothing wrong with that. They can't help it any more than someone can help having asthma. But some people don't understand that, and we're not going to gossip about who you saw today." Hopelessly he added, "We don't gossip anyway."

"Well, we don't," Bunny said.

"We listen," I said, thinking of the way Bunny had eavesdropped on Rosa Horton about babysitting on New Year's Eve. She knew it too, and we held each other's eye, neither looking away, both of us as stubborn as rain.

8

Bunny proved to have good reason for sounding brave with Mrs. Horton on the phone. Mr. and Mrs. Manners had stepped forward to host the annual neighbourhood New Year's Eve party, and my father refused to go. The alternative was to join Uncle Ray and Aunt Magda at Trader Vic's nightclub over town. After Aunt Magda phoned, Bunny said she preferred Trader Vic's anyway. But Uncle Ray had reserved a table for a group larger than my father was comfortable joining, and he said the place was too noisy.

"Maybe we could spend a little more time thinking about it," Bunny said, although it sounded as if my father had already said no, and I heard him turn the page in his newspaper.

That seemed to be the end of it, at least until a few nights after Christmas. As soon as I'd gone to bed, I heard Bunny sit back down at the kitchen table and tell my father they had to make up their minds about Trader Vic's. My father was surprised, saying he thought they'd already decided. Why couldn't they just enjoy a peaceful night at home?

Because Bunny spent most of her time chained to this house and deserved a night out. Because she *liked* going out. Because she had a new outfit, and she *liked* dancing, and she was far from the only person in this world who actually *enjoyed* having a good time.

Bunny never went off like this, and I didn't want to hear it. My father didn't either. He scraped back his chair and padded his slippers toward the stairs down to his workshop.

"Besides," Bunny said, coming after him, closer to my door, "I've already hired a babysitter, and we'll be on the hook for that anyway. It's too late for the girl to get another job."

When she named Rosa's price, my father stopped at the top of the stairs, and I calculated that it would go a good way toward paying for the black-and-white kitten to be spayed.

Not that I wanted to hear how much they were paying. I didn't want to hear any of it. My parents never argued, and I felt sick when they did. When they kept at it near my bedroom door, I had to put my hands over my ears to block it out. I didn't want to know that Bunny was chained to the house, or that my father's job took everything out of him. It scared me to learn that he'd like to enjoy his home in peace, since it was all he could do to hang onto it, and what alternatives did Bunny propose for *that?*

My mother had no answer. After a long pause, my father went down to his workshop. And that, finally, seemed to be that.

When the telephone rang the next evening, we were sitting silently in the kitchen long after our usual dinnertime. I was under orders to finish my tasty chipped beef biscuit from Bunny's new cookbook, owing to the fact I looked pale.

The caller proved to be my Uncle Ray, phoning out of the blue.

"Your brother," Bunny said and held out the receiver.

My father shook his head.

"He can't come to the phone right now, Ray," Bunny said, and listened for a while. "So you're saying that one of the couples has had to cancel . . . Oh, good. Mike and Jo Duprée are going to come instead. We haven't seen them in ages." She held my father's eye. "I'd love to see them, and of course Hall would, too." To my father, she added, "Wouldn't you?"

He was getting up when he noticed me hunched over my tasty biscuit, looking up at him from under my eyebrows, although I quickly looked down. There was a long pause as he watched me, one hand on the back of his chair.

"I would," he said, and sat back down, so I felt a weight drop off my shoulders that I hadn't even known was there.

Mr. Duprée was my father's oldest friend. They'd grown up next door to each other and signed up together when the war was declared. The difference was that Mr. Duprée wasn't married back then, having gone to university instead. He and Mrs. Duprée only met after he was shipped home two years into the war. She was a nurse at Shaughnessy Veteran's Hospital and he was a Burn Case. Not that you'd know it, since Mr. Duprée wore pants and long-sleeved shirts even in summer. The Duprées had two sons, the younger being the same age as my cousin Simon.

My uncle had known Mr. Duprée all his life, too. But having boys the same age had drawn them closer, especially since the Duprées lived only ten minutes from my aunt and uncle in West Vancouver, not in the British Properties, but down the mountain near Ambleside Beach. My aunt and Jo Duprée both possessed what my mother called a cynical turn, while the men were used to running things. Mr. Duprée was the principal of our local high school. I don't think either the Hortons or the Manners family knew this, but my father's oldest friend was Mr. Horton's boss, and it was his office where Andy Manners was sent after letting the air out of tires.

"What are you going to wear?" Bunny asked my father, after hanging up.

"Clothes," he replied, and disappeared behind his newspaper.

New Year's Eve ended up feeling frayed that year. Stretched thin. Yet things started out well, at least for me. Rosa showed up at our door with Norman, saying that if it was all right with my parents, she thought we could entertain each other until bedtime. Then she'd call her mother, who would come and take Norman home, along with the kitten. Her parents never went out on New Year's Eve, so they'd be home whenever we got sleepy.

"That's very thoughtful of you, Rosa," my father said, while Norman rolled his eyes at me behind my parents' backs.

What happened, of course, was that Rosa ordered us down to the rec room while she got on the phone in the kitchen. From the sounds of it, she was talking to Andy Manners, who was helping out at her parents' party next door. At least, Andy was supposed to be helping. Rosa had the black-and-white kitten with her upstairs, and I imagined they were happy. The black-and-white was a friendly kitten, although the tabby had been friendlier. Judy Shribman's tortoiseshell was the stand-offish one, but it was also the prettiest, so that was her bargain.

I didn't care that Rosa had taken the kitten upstairs and wouldn't miss her when Mrs. Horton took her home. After two months, I was as bored with kittens as I usually was, and both Norman and I had our books. My new book from Aunt Magda was called *Tell Me a Riddle*, which was about old people. It didn't have any riddles in it that I could see, so it was hard going. When Norman finished *A Fall of Moondust* again, we turned on the TV, where they were playing a movie about a woman in a wheelchair looking out her window. We didn't understand what was going on, but you could tell from the music that it was tense. We screamed, then held a screaming contest, so Rosa shouted downstairs, "Shut *up*."

By then, the clock showed 8:30, which was my bedtime. Soon it was nine o'clock, which was an enjoyable length of time after I was supposed to be in bed. But as the hands crept toward 9:15, I wanted to sleep, even though Norman showed no signs of slowing down. Not that he ever moved quickly.

It seemed best to hint. "What time do you go to bed, anyhow?"

"Whenever I want," Norman answered, barely looking up from his comic book.

"So when's your mother coming to get you?"

"She isn't," Norman said. "Our parents think everyone around here is a hopeless coddler. I can walk half a block on my own."

"Okay," I said, and stood up.

It took him a moment, but Norman got the point and stood too, tottering a little on his un-braced leg. When we reached the kitchen, Rosa looked over.

"Ready?" she asked, and put down the receiver without hanging up.

Norman only shrugged, not at all happy with me.

"It isn't that cold," Rosa said, "but you'd better wear your toque. And take the kitten, all right? Everything's ready in my room. All you have to do is put her in there and shut the door."

That woke me up. I always felt that the kittens were my responsibility until they were safely in their new home, at which point I could forget about them completely.

"You mean Norman's going to take her?"

"It's all right. He can manage," Rosa said, although after Norman got his coat on, he held the kitten awkwardly, looking as if he was going to drop it.

I wouldn't have been a hopeless coddler about Norman going home on his own, but I was worried about the kitten. As I walked him to the front door, I could see how easily it could squirm free and run away to be eaten by a cougar. Which would be cannibalism, in a way.

"Call me when you get in," I said, telling Rosa, "You need to hang up."

Norman liked that, either asking him to call or telling Rosa how to behave. I went to the window to watch him home, although without my father to lift me, I couldn't see him go inside.

The phone rang almost immediately, and I ran back to the kitchen to answer.

"Hello?"

"It's Norman. I got here."

"You've got the kitten."

"Yes."

"Okay. Bye."

Norman hung up. I didn't get many phone calls, so that was satisfying. Afterward, I celebrated New Year's Eve by not washing my face and going to bed.

A crash. Bolting upright, I realized the crash had come from inside and there was a man's voice in the rec room. Not awake yet, hugging myself, feeling confused and frightened, I wondered if someone had broken in and was going to hurt me and Rosa. Then I heard Rosa laugh, after which Andy Manners said something that made her laugh even louder, and I realized the man was on TV. When music started, I recognized Guy Lombardo and his Royal Canadians playing their New Year's Eve show on CBS.

Andy and Rosa were having a party in the rec room. I didn't even have to be awake to know that my parents wouldn't like it. But if I went downstairs to say so—or maybe to join them—I knew that Andy and Rosa would send me straight back to bed. They were having fun, sounding silly, being big girls. I thought I could hear a couple of boys as well, although they were being shushed silent. From what I could make out, they seemed to be dancing and weren't very good at it, bumping into things and scraping chairs across the floor.

That's where the crash must have come from, an overturned table. It made them go sardonic about Guy Lombardo, as if their bad dancing was his fault. I thought that was unfair, especially since my father had wanted to stay at home and watch the Royal Canadians on TV. Instead, he was at Trader Vic's, which was too noisy. Andy and Rosa's party was too noisy for me, especially since I wasn't invited, the laughter and giggles and scraping furniture making such a clamour in my head that I couldn't get back to sleep.

Except that I must have, since I was woken again by the sound of my father's voice in the rec room. The house was otherwise silent. No TV. No sound of boys. I wondered where Bunny was, then heard her speak sharply, with Andy answering in a slovenly fashion. Creeping to the top of the stairs, I heard my father say, "The reason I'm concerned about the amount you've had to drink is that there's something called alcohol poisoning. I'm looking at a great many empty bottles."

"She had to clear, clear, clean her parents' party. Put out new ones. So she saved the drags," Rosa said.

"Anyway, she spewed a lot of it," Andy added.

"Yes, I can see that."

Andy sounded insulted. "She hit the bucket."

"I've brought your coats," my mother said. "Mr. Parker will take you home."

"No!" Andy shouted. Controlling herself. "I can make it. Next door."

But my father insisted on taking them home to their parents, his voice gone ramrod. I ran to the living room window and saw the three of them walking into the driveway, having left the rec room through the basement door to the garage. My father's posture looked ramrod, too. Rosa was trailing behind him like a scolded puppy. But my father was making Andy march ahead of them toward her house next door, her legs moving obediently even though he didn't so much as lay a finger on her back.

"Mary Alice! Why aren't you in bed?"

Bunny had come upstairs. I ignored her, watching my father march Andy Manners up her front steps.

"Mary Alice . . ."

Mr. Manners opened the door, looking the way he'd looked at Halloween with a glass of ice cubes in his hand. He didn't fall off his shoes this time. Instead, he took in the sight of his daughter and his hand shot out. He grabbed Andy by the upper arm, jerked her past him and threw her into the house. She must have fallen on the floor but I couldn't see. All I could see was the angry face of Mr. Manners under the porch light, and how deeply he scorned my father. I heard him say, "let this happen." Then he slammed the door in my father's face.

I couldn't have said why, but that's when I knew Andy Manners still wet the bed. She hadn't been lying. Andy was many things, but she wasn't a liar.

"Happy now?" my mother asked. "Back to bed."

I shook free. "No! Rosa!"

Sighing, Bunny held me up so I could watch my father walk Rosa up her front steps. My father knocked and Mrs. Horton answered, her back straightening in surprise. She didn't seem to have expected Rosa back so soon. Our mantle clock had just chimed midnight.

"So there you go," Bunny said behind my ear. Her breath smelled like a highball. "Now, if we're lucky, they'll turn down the babysitting fee. Which your father will insist on offering."

I didn't understand why.

"Because in the best of all possible worlds, the money would be decently offered and decently refused. And that's where your father lives, in the best of all possible worlds."

"What if they take it?"

A pantomime at the Hortons' door. A hand held out, a head shaken, a hand pulled back. So the fee had been decently refused, and Bunny carried me to bed.

"Daddy?"

He was walking past my cracked-open door and only put his head in.

"Go to sleep, now."

"Why did you come home before it was midnight?"

A long pause, then my father sighed just like Bunny and came to sit on my bed. He was wearing his pyjamas. It took a while before he spoke, and he sounded very tired.

"New Year's Eve can be a night when adults behave badly, too. Some people at our table got a little . . . difficult. People we don't know, and that your uncle doesn't really know. Business types. Your mother and I found it uncomfortable, the way they were behaving."

"But they didn't say anything about Bunny wearing Aunt Magda's old clothes."

My father ruminated on that one. "You were worried people might do that."

I shrugged.

"Well, they didn't. But these . . . types were unkind to people working in the nightclub."

"If the people were idiots, Aunt Magda would have told them."

My father smiled. "They weren't idiots. There was one young lady who hadn't the benefit of as much education as I'm sure she deserved. So her way of speaking was a little incorrect."

"Like *ain't* and what Uncle Punk puts on when he's being silly. Except that she wasn't."

"Putting it on. No, she wasn't. She told your mother she'd been hired for the New Year's rush, and this was all new to her. We thought she was doing a far better job than anyone had any right to expect. Your mother and I did."

"So the *types* were the idiots."

"They had her in tears," my father said quietly.

A thought occurred.

"So if the types hadn't been idiots, you wouldn't have come home before midnight, and Andy would have had everything cleaned up before you did."

My father's conversation was full of pauses tonight.

"*Andy* would have," he said.

"Mr. Manners doesn't like Dr. Martin Luther King."

Another pause. "No, I don't think he does."

"Why not?"

"Well, that's a hard one," my father said, and paused again. "I think it's because Dr. King says all men ought to live together as brothers. He said that back in '57 down in Washington, how God is interested in freeing the whole human race, so we can live in a society that respects the dignity and worth of the human personality, whether of a black man or a brown man or a yellow man. Or a white man, I like to think, every man being equal, none above the other. But there are people who are used to being on top, and they'd prefer to keep it that way."

"You don't want to stay on top."

"I'm not on top, Mary Alice. I'm not on the bottom, either. I'm not exactly sure where I am. But feeling equal for once would do me fine."

"Okay," I said, and turned over to go to sleep.

"Okay? I'm dismissed?"

He bent down to kiss my forehead, and in the morning when I woke up, it was a whole new year.

PART TWO

PART
TWO

9

M r. Eisenstadt had never liked me, so after school got back, it was hard to tell whether he liked me any less for having seen his wife in hospital. My father had asked me to tell him if Mr. Eisenstadt said anything to me, the thought of which was frightening. Usually, a principal didn't talk to pupils unless they were Andy Manners.

But when we'd been back a little more than a week, I saw Mr. Eisenstadt across the playground at recess watching me climb the jungle gym. It was a sunny day and not too cold, and he was far enough away that he looked like a lonely man in a wartime movie watching an airplane take off. You saw him from a distance, his hands in his overcoat pockets and his face hidden by his hat. It was impossible to know what he was thinking.

I told my father about that, and afterward, I didn't see Mr. Eisenstadt much anymore. What had gone on before school got back in came to feel distant and ready to be forgotten. My father had also asked whether Mr. Eisenstadt knew I was friends with Norman, but because Halloween had been such a long time ago, I hadn't remembered that we'd trick-or-treated his house. That only came back to me in late January when I was watching the Lone Ranger on TV. But I didn't mention it then either, not just because more time had passed, but because I didn't see why it was important that I was friends with Mrs. Horton's son. Norman didn't know about Mrs. Eisenstadt being in the psychiatric ward. I'd done what they'd told me and never said.

Besides, the rainy winter had turned to Vancouver's early spring, and the snowbells came up, as pretty as kittens, and the crocuses and daffodils burst out in the rockery, and the cherry trees foamed pink all over the city. I wanted it to be a different year, and it was.

More than that, I wanted it to be a real new year, the old one thrown away like last year's calendar. The problem was, the past refused to stay in the past. Wheels kept turning, life not running in a straight line forward and not circular either, but stubborn and repetitive and urgent. I felt increasingly caught up in something that was building around me, echoing more loudly instead of more softly, even though I had no idea what it was.

For one thing, as soon as it got dry enough to go back down the creek, the Raincoat Man returned to the bridge, as if he'd been waiting for the weather to improve so he could air out his thing. I saw him again on a Saturday in late February when Norman came down with a bad cold. Having spent my allowance and read my comics, I'd gone to the creek alone and was busy hitting the tree trunks with a cedar branch when I saw the Raincoat Man on the bridge.

"Who's that?"

Andy Manners spoke behind me. I turned to see her and Rosa for the first time since New Year's Eve.

"How come you're down here?" I asked.

"Eyes as wide as saucers, Tinkerbell," she answered. "The guy on the bridge?"

I was surprised she hadn't heard, and told them how he was a known factor who opened his raincoat.

"Disgusting," Andy said, and suddenly yelled, "You're disgusting! *Pervert!*"

The Raincoat Man turned, looking startled, and I caught a glimpse of his face. Andy grabbed my cedar branch and heaved it toward him. It fell far short of the bridge, but it made the man take off. Andy ran after him, yelling "Pervert!" as she picked up a piece of deadfall and shagged it toward him. When she reached the creek, she started throwing rocks. She was enjoying herself so much and so grimly that I started doing it, too. I would have felt guilty about hurting someone if the Raincoat Man wasn't already halfway up the far slope, our rocks falling far behind him as he disappeared over the top.

Once he was gone, Andy and I walked onto the bridge, where I pointed out a branch swirling downstream and Andy spit on it. You'd think we were friends. Rosa soon joined us, having hung back from the attack, acting a little girly. It occurred to me it wasn't an accident that she'd been Marilyn Monroe at Halloween.

"We should tell our parents," Rosa said, leaning on the railing.

"Nobody does," I said. "They'd make rules about coming down the creek even if they catch him."

"She's right," Andy said, not even having to think about it. She and Rosa held a silent conference until both of them nodded, agreeing not to tell their parents. That meant I wouldn't have to tell mine either, which was a relief. Rosa's parents were busy and Andy's disorganized, but mine would have actually done something, and that would have hemmed us in.

The Raincoat Man was one sign that things weren't different, but the bigger one was that Andy and Rosa were still friends. Before getting a cold, Norman had told me that his parents sat Rosa down on New Year's Day despite her headache, taking the opportunity to suggest she find other people to spend her time with.

"They told her loser kids always grab onto the new kids at school," Norman said. "Rosa said Andy isn't a loser, she's better than all the rest of them. So our mum said maybe Andy is an outlier, but Rosa can still do better."

"Andy doesn't lie," I said. "I figured out she wets the bed the way she told us."

Norman thought about this. "Because she's got bad things that worry her?"

I wouldn't have thought of that, but I had to agree that she probably did, like being thrown onto the floor by her father. Not that I could mention seeing that happen any more than I could say the words communism or Mrs. Eisenstadt. When Norman was finally over the worst of his cold, well enough that I could visit, I didn't even tell him that his sister and Andy were still friends. I wasn't sure why I was keeping so much to myself. I started to feel weighed down by things I couldn't say, although I soon learned that both the Hortons and Mr. Manners had changed their minds about their daughters being friends, and that lightened the load.

This was new information, something I saw on the other side of the creek. By then, I could visit Norman for an hour after school, his post-cold asthma keeping him home after any desirable absence from class. His mother came home at lunch when she could, but otherwise he had a teenager from the Home for Unwed Mothers to look after him, which he didn't enjoy.

Norman being sick meant I'd been spending too much time alone, which I wouldn't have thought possible. Comics, creek, library, *boredom*, followed by Bunny telling me to go outside and whine at the trees. At least my fantail guppies were breeding and I could watch the new little babies hiding in the weeds. Their parents would eat them otherwise. Which would definitely be cannibalism.

Then one day I decided to look for the Raincoat Man. I was kicking a ball around the backyard after school when it occurred to me that I could find him and warn him off being a pervert. I'd glimpsed his face when Andy had startled him, and we'd watched him run up the path from the bridge to the other side of the creek. It led to the little mall and another subdivision, and I figured if I snooped around over there, I might be able to find him. I had no idea where to look and felt scared at the thought of actually flushing him out. But it was something to do, and before I lost my nerve, I let myself out through the chain-link gate and skipped down the hill to the bridge, the creek still in spring flood beneath it. I paused to spit at a passing leaf, and that felt satisfactory. Afterward, I set off up the slope.

Years before, someone had cut a road from the mall to the little bridge. An access road, they called it, although by now there were too many potholes for it to really be a road, and most of the gravel had long since washed away. The Raincoat Man had run up it, and now I followed, emerging between two high wooden fences, each belonging to one of the houses backing onto the creek. The front of the houses looked across the street at the strip mall. Or at least, at the back of the mall, where trucks unloaded boxes and the shopkeepers came out for a smoke.

Now that I'd reached the Raincoat Man's territory, I peered out from behind the fence like the Lone Ranger stalking a bad guy, not through the cactus mountains but into Dodge City itself. I thought I looked professional but didn't know what to do next, uncertain how close I could get to the houses. If I crept up to a front window, I might see a telltale raincoat thrown on a chesterfield. I might even see the man himself. But I also might disturb a housewife doing her dusting, and that could get complicated.

I was feeling a little lost when I glimpsed a car up ahead that made me do a double-take. Mr. Horton was sitting in his parked car along the house side of the curving street. He was facing toward me so I was sure it was him. It was as if he was waiting in the lineup outside the movie theatre, where he ought to have been after Norman's birthday party. Except that this was a gap-toothed lineup, with enough space between him and the other parked cars that I could pick him out easily.

Mrs. Manners sat beside him, her white hair unmistakable. Now that I had something definite to stalk, I crept slowly closer, slipping out from a front yard hedge to dart behind a tree, then risking a run to a telephone pole not far from the car. In the passenger seat, Mrs. Manners was crying into a handkerchief. Mr. Horton was leaning toward her from the driver's side looking sympathetic. Watching them, I thought I knew what was going on. Mrs. Manners was upset that Mr. and Mrs. Horton had forbidden Rosa to be friends with Andy, and she was asking him to change his mind.

It seemed to be working. Mr. Horton looked so sorry for Mrs. Manners that he reached out and put his arms around her. Mrs. Manners collapsed against him, her shoulders looking relieved. Bunny would have called that a bit much, and I agreed. Something felt wrong about what they were doing, although I didn't know what. I was glad that Rosa and Andy could be friends again, in public as well as down the creek. But I also felt itchy to get out of there. Melting back from the telephone pole, I retreated from tree to hedge until I was safely behind the fence at the top of the path. Then I ran downhill as fast as I could, fleeting over the bridge, zigzagging up through the forest and making it safely home.

A couple of weeks later, the neighbourhood was busy with more new information. Mrs. Manners had dyed her hair. Auburn, she called it. Mrs. Manners told several neighbours that black hair dye was so stark it killed the complexion, even for people like her who had been born with black hair. But she was ready for a change, and here she was.

"Red," Bunny said, as we looked out the window, watching Mrs. Manners patter down her front steps on the way to her convertible. She'd got her hair cut too, short enough to show her ears, although she'd kept it curly on top, and it had been backcombed and hair-sprayed into making her look even more like a movie star.

"She doesn't match her car, though," I said, which Bunny found so funny she repeated it to my father when he got home.

"Doesn't match her car!" She laughed even though I hadn't been making a joke.

Bunny was preparing dinner and my father was keeping her company while I did my homework at the kitchen table, or eavesdropped while pretending to do my homework, since it had been easy and I'd finished.

"She looked pretty happy, though," I said.

"Very pleased with herself," my mother agreed.

"Mrs. Manners fixed it so that Rosa and Andy could be friends again," I said, wanting to drop more of the weight off my shoulders.

"They had a tiff, did they?" Bunny asked. "Why am I not surprised."

"Norman said on New Year's Day, their parents told Rosa she could get a better friend." Bunny seemed to agree with the Hortons' opinion. "They said when someone is new in a school, the losers always grab hold of them."

Her expression changed. I thought it was nice of my mother to get angry for Andy. "That boy . . ."

My father's hand shot up to stop her, and I looked from one to the other.

"Rosa said Andy is better than all of them," I said. "And she isn't a liar. Andy told me and Norman she wets the bed, and that wasn't a lie."

It felt good to let it out.

"Rosa made a mistake and said Norman wets the bed, which he said he used to when he was a little kid. And Andy said everyone wets the bed when they're little kids, and that she still does. So anyhow, Norman said Andy must have bad things happen that upset her, I guess because he does, and I remembered Mr. Manners throwing her on the floor. But I didn't say anything. I promised."

My mother and father failed to say anything either, my mother continuing to make dinner and my father looking down at his clasped hands.

Finally, Bunny said, "When she came for the tortoiseshell, I thought that nice Judy Shribman wanted to be friends."

"Judy is best friends with Jeannie Stevens and Cathy Cole."

"They were at your birthday party, weren't they?" Bunny asked. "And the Cole and Stevens girls may be friends, but Judy looked like a third wheel."

"They aren't *may be*. They *are*. They're all girly, and they're all best friends." I could see where this was headed. "And Norman is *my* best friend."

"You've got lots of friends, Mary Alice," my mother said. "Look at all the parties you're invited to."

That my mother's daughter was invited to. I wasn't stupid.

It was also true that people liked me and I liked them. I was the local pet, even though I hated being one.

"But it's *important*," I said. "Andy and Rosa being friends again. And Mrs. Manners fixed it. I saw her with Mr. Horton in his car near the little mall over the creek. And she was crying like before. I *said* it wasn't allergies. And this time it was because she was sad Mr. Horton didn't want Rosa to be friends with Andy and she wanted to fix it. Anyone could see that. So he gave her a big hug and she hugged him back"—I mimed it, although my parents were both looking down now—"and she looked happy. I *said* she looked happy. And now Andy and Rosa can be friends again."

My father and mother looked at each other, and my mother shook her head slowly for a very long time. Afterward, my father cleared his throat, which wasn't usual for him.

"Mary Alice," he began.

"Tink."

"Tink," he agreed, which wasn't usual either. "Sometimes we stumble onto people's private business, and it's best not to mention . . ."

It broke out of me. "I'm tired of not mentioning," I cried. "I can't say anything about communism or Mrs. Eisenstadt. Now I'm not supposed to say anything about Mr. Horton and Mrs. Manners, either?"

It was only a partial catalogue of what I wasn't allowed to say, the rest of which I couldn't even mention to my parents. Mr. Horton not picking us up at Norman's birthday party. The Raincoat Man.

Bunny didn't look impressed.

"Sometimes in this world, you've got to bite your tongue," she said. "And it's past time you started learning."

For once, my father didn't say anything. In the pause, all I could think of was to read out my homework before Bunny asked me. Anyone could see she was going to.

"Dear Miss Atkinson. Aunt Magda and Uncle Ray went to Hawaii like you did. They didn't eat octopus, which would have been a most inpressive thing. They ate too much pineapple and Uncle Ray got a sore stomach. They swam in the ocean and saw surfer boys like in *Gidget*. We have to go next year. It's inperative. Yours truly, Tink. (Mary Alice Parker)"

"It's imperative, is it?" Bunny glanced at my father. "Then I guess we'd better go."

He smiled, but only slightly. "That's a very good composition," he said. "Did Miss Atkinson ask you to write her a letter?"

"She said if we couldn't figure out how to write a composition, we should think about just saying it to her. And if you're talking to someone on a piece of paper," I told him with scorn, "it's called a *let-ter*."

My father paused. "That was a good thing for her to suggest. But let's think about a word called analogy . . ."

"I'm sick of thinking!" I yelled.

Running into my bedroom, I still couldn't see why it was so funny that Mrs. Manners's hair didn't match her car. It was just a fact. And facts weren't funny at all.

Back then, I'd never stopped to think who my father would have called a friend. With Bunny it was easy. She had friends all over the neighbourhood, even if some of them were friends she'd become fond of without liking them, as Aunt Magda had said. Bunny might have also had friends who didn't like her, although I can't think of anyone in particular. In any case, the dynamic worked if you were as intent on maintaining a social circle as Bunny was, and most of her friends were. They were team players, they liked to say. Joiners.

But my father's friends were different. For one thing, most of them had fought in the war. They didn't see each other very often, but when they did, they took up where they'd left off. Or maybe they met up in a place they'd never really left. There was Mr. Duprée, the high school principal, and Mr. Hague, who had bought land in the Okanagan Valley when he got home and grew peaches. He plays little part in this, and Mr. Warren plays no part at all, having been laid off from his accounting job at the railway company the previous fall, moving on to sell cars at Jimmy Pattison's new dealership over town.

Yet there's someone who would be important: my father's friend Mr. Lake. Mr. Lake had been a commando, plucked out of their regiment and sent to Scotland for training. My father told me when I was older that Mr. Lake had become an elite sapper, an explosives expert who slipped ahead into enemy territory to blow up targets and booby-trap bridges. Mr. Lake was a long-legged man with wild eyebrows and a runner's angular face. My father said that he'd had close calls, and Mr. Lake showed me once how he'd lost the tip of his right index finger. But the Nazis had never caught him, even though my father said he was a vexation to them and they'd tried.

I don't think my father and Mr. Lake had known each other very well overseas. Both had started out as enlisted men, but my father was chosen for officer training at around the same time that Mr. Lake had been sent to Scotland, and they only became friends back home. They might have met up again at the Legion, where my father went sometimes for cards and a couple of beers. But I have half a memory of someone saying they'd run into each other at the bus stop not long after my parents moved to the North Shore, and that might have been what happened.

My father got paid every second Thursday, which made it Bunny's day with the car. She'd drop my father off in the morning at the bus stop in the turnaround at the corner of Capilano Road and Marine Drive, where they eventually built an A-frame tourist booth. On Thursday afternoon, Bunny would pick me up at school and we'd drive over the Lions Gate Bridge to my father's office, where it was my job to go upstairs and get his cheque. Afterward, we'd drive back over the bridge and cash the cheque, then go to the library and do our big biweekly shop at the SuperValu before it closed at six o'clock. I wasn't supposed to say anything, but we had to do the shopping on Thursday because the prices went up on Friday and Saturday, and Bunny said she preferred to spend what we could actually afford. Once she'd put away the groceries, we'd pick up my father at the bus stop on Marine Drive, and then we'd have dinner.

In any case, the stop was close to the reserve and Mr. Lake was a member of the Squamish band. He drove a pickup truck, but his wife used it too, and because of sharing among band members, so did a lot of other people. That could leave Mr. Lake with the bus, so he and my father might well have run into each other at the stop. Mr. Lake was a carpenter in the construction trade, building things rather than blowing them up, which might have been the point, although it might just have been a job.

What happened with Mr. Lake started one Saturday in March when my father and I drove down to the reservation to help him fix his truck. Bunny never came with us when we went there, and I'm afraid racism might have been involved. There was also the fact that Mr. Lake's wife was a tough woman with crossed arms and a formidable frown. She may have scared my mother, or left her feeling small and tangential. I also think Mrs. Lake might not have liked white people very much, and with every reason. Whatever the combination of factors, my mother and Mrs. Lake didn't mesh, although in Bunny's favour, she never tried to stop my father from visiting the reserve or from taking me with him, which happened two or three times a year.

Mr. Lake didn't really need my father's help fixing his truck. It was something they liked doing together, and that March afternoon, they had bent down happily under the hood on a sunny, breezy afternoon. The reserve was down on Burrard Inlet, and the breeze was pungent with salt and seaweed and diesel fumes. I stayed by the men ready to hand over tools, having learned not to rush out looking for children to play with but to let them find me, and allow things to develop from there.

The first time my father had taken me to the reserve, I'd made a mistake, running up to a group of kids and saying, "Isn't it a beautiful day!"

The kids looked down, scuffing their shoes on the road. They were my age and a bit older, a few younger, and they'd been playing tag. There was a long silence. I can still hear what happened, with Mr. Lake's oldest son Daniel speaking up from the back of the group.

"We don't say that."

Since Bunny had told me it was always a good thing to say, I was a little belligerent.

"Why not?"

Daniel was older than the oldest kids, and I assume now he'd been told or was simply expected to look after me. He took a while to answer, looking down and then looking away.

"When you say that, we think you're saying we're too stupid to notice."

I had to think about that.

"I only think someone's stupid when they do something stupid."

Daniel nodded thoughtfully, and with a quiet signal he told the others to play with me. They weren't happy about that, but we were kids and eventually everyone just played and it was fine, and it continued to be fine every time I visited.

That morning, I didn't find handing out wrenches particularly interesting, since my father and Mr. Lake didn't talk much. I soon felt bored and wondered whether the kids had gone over to the Capilano River or down to the railroad tracks that ran between the houses and the beach. I could hang around one place or the other until they noticed me, which happened more quickly these days, especially now that I'd met a girl named Sheila with whom I would have been friends if we'd gone to the same school. Tracks or river? I was trying to figure it out when a car drove past.

"That's Norman's car!"

The men looked up to watch the car drive down the road.

As if Mr. Lake had asked a question, my father said, "I don't imagine he's mentioned him. Norman is Jack Horton's son."

Mr. Horton parked and walked up to a house, not seeming to notice us. I'd hoped he brought Norman with him but he was alone, carrying a fat black binder. Norman's post-cold asthma had retreated and he'd returned to school, although he still had to go straight home afterward. I walked with him and often went inside to read comics, so things were roughly back to normal. Even the girl from the Home for Unwed Mothers had left to have her baby. When I'd asked what happened to the baby, Bunny said it would be dealt with, end of story. This was the only part of Norman's illness that still troubled me, and I'd had a nightmare about the girl being mother to a school of fantail guppies swimming in the air around her head. It was otherworldly and siren-like and awful.

"Jack showed up last fall," Mr. Lake said, as the door of the house opened and Mr. Horton went inside. "He offered to tutor a few of the older boys for their exams, see if they could get the marks for university. Scholarships."

"And he chose which ones he'd help?" my father asked.

"He said he'd see what he could do if another boy asked."

They worked for a while longer, the problem being the truck's suspension, which was greasy. My father wiped his hands on a rag and handed it to me. Part of my job was to take their dirty rags and hand them clean ones. Or at this point, the cleanest ones. The work hadn't got any more interesting, but I wanted to stay now they were talking.

"Missionary," Mr. Lake said out of the blue. "Converting the heathens."

They both thought that was funny, although I wasn't sure how they could be talking about Mr. Horton when he was a teacher, not a missionary, or whether the subject had got switched at the same time as the rag.

"The wife takes a position against anything that removes children from our culture," Mr. Lake said. "Forcing them into the white man's world. You're never going to fit. Then you don't fit in here, either."

"Jan takes the position or you do?"

"I have what you call a nuanced understanding of the subject."

Nuanced Understanding, I thought, bookmarking it.

"Jan calls it defeatist, but I reserve the right to disagree."

My father took this in. "Your boy Daniel was one of the ones he chose? Unless he was too young. He'd be what? Grade ten?"

"Daniel asked. Told his mother we're going to have to educate our leadership, and he's probably right. 'Oh, you're the leadership,' she says. I admire the kid for standing up on his hind legs. He manages his mother better than I do."

"Wait till he gets married and then we'll see."

They chuckled for reasons I didn't understand. That was the problem with eavesdropping. You couldn't ask about things you overheard or they'd turn off like a faucet.

"So what was the decision?" my father asked, and corrected himself. "Well, he's here."

"Up to each boy to decide. And I guess they've got to keep deciding each step of the way. One kid has already told Jack he's had enough. Not that his reasons were any good."

"Ambition," my father said. "Wears you down."

"Whose ambition is that?"

I waited for my father to respond, but that seemed to be it. Yet there was so much I hadn't understood that I wanted to step in. Conversations between my father and Mr. Lake were different than the ones Bunny had with her friends, who liked to give their opinions. The two men exchanged information instead, and the fact I wasn't allowed to mention any of the information I'd picked up half killed me.

"Mr. and Mrs. Horton named Norman after a missionary," I said.

I thought that was safe enough. I also knew it was blurting, especially when my father gave me a considered look before turning back to Mr. Lake.

"Norman Bethune," he surprised me by saying. "The communist doctor. The boy's nine years old, and a lot has happened in nine years. People are changing their colours, leaving the Party. But if it comes back to bite him . . . You'll know better than me whether it might have some consequences here."

Mr. Lake looked at me thoughtfully and I blushed, which didn't happen that often. He gave me a wink and told my father, "Still trying to save the world. At least he stays the course."

"I'm not sure about staying the course," my father said. "But that's gossip."

Mr. Lake looked as puzzled as I felt. But that was all they said, even when Mr. Horton left the other house and walked over to the Lakes'.

"Hall Parker. You're here," he said, stopping briefly in the driveway. "Dan," to Mr. Lake. And a precisely said, "Tink," before going inside.

"Daddy?" I said afterward, in the car.

"Don't start."

"But why doesn't Mr. Horton like you anymore?"

My father was watching traffic in the side view mirror.

"Well, *Tink*," he said, imitating Mr. Horton. "I'm not sure he ever did."

"But . . ."

"Your dessert is in jeopardy," he said, which shut me up for the rest of the drive home.

I was worried Norman wouldn't be my friend anymore, not if Mr. Horton didn't like my father. That made it a relief when Norman was finally allowed to go outside after school and we went back to doing whatever we wanted. Nothing had changed, so I decided it must be true that Mr. Horton had *never* liked my father. I wondered about his reasons, but I didn't have the least idea why anyone would dislike him. In fact, I had no idea why one adult might dislike another. It had never occurred to me before that they could. Adults were a different species, elephants bumbling through the jungle, protective and demanding and unpredictable, while we were a flock of noisy, busy, unsafe sparrows pecking around their feet.

Yet Norman and I were still friends, and that was the important thing, and so were the plans we started to make about my aquarium. Norman had never shown much interest in the fish. He didn't disdain them the way he did kittens, but he usually only glanced their way as we went downstairs to the rec room. Then he got better, and I dragged him into my room to see the baby guppies. Something shifted when I lifted the hood to reveal the tiny silver eyelashes curled up in the floating weeds, flicking and shying as we loomed over them.

"You're kidding," Norman said. Eyes wide, he leaned in close to watch the babies try to hide, counting seventeen, eighteen, nineteen, before crouching down in front of the tank to take in the whole show. A mixture of awe and tenderness bloomed on his face, and I knew from the movies that this was what it looked like when you fell in love.

The aquarium was on the white-painted dresser my father had made, a glowing tableau of fantails, neon tetras, zebrafish, and red swordtails swimming amid the broad-leafed plants. Norman took a particular interest in my whiskered black-and-silver catfish as it worked its way along the bottom, vacuuming the gravel. Debbie and Ed had given me the twenty-gallon tank with the overhead light, filter and heater for Christmas the year before. Afterward, Ed had helped me set it up and took me to the pet store for the fish and plants. He had an aquarium himself in his study, a big one with coral and saltwater fish like a reef in the *National Geographic*, Ed being drawn to beauty. Well, he'd married my sister.

The fantail guppies were my favourite. They were even brighter than the neon tetras and trailed their long silky tails as they swam, looking as if they were followed by rainbows. Some of them were green and yellow with black spots that turned into black-bordered windowpanes on their tails. Others had silver and blue bodies with scarlet, pink and orange brushstrokes down their length onto their tails, which were spattered with black.

"You're kidding," Norman repeated. After that, he visited my fish every day.

One Thursday, when I needed to buy some frozen brine shrimp, Norman even came with me and Bunny on our biweekly errands, which this time would end at the pet store. First we had to drive over town, but Norman was a patient person and didn't mind joining me in picking up my father's cheque. While Bunny idled the car outside, we rode the elevator up to the ninth floor where I nodded at the receptionist, who often changed but was always pretty. Taking Norman down the main hall, I knocked on my father's door.

"Norman's here, too," I called.

"Is he?" my father asked, opening the door on a small square room. It had a high ceiling, but my father always looked a little stooped there, crowded in between the filing cabinets.

"A couple of freighters in port," he said, and stood aside to let us in.

The best thing about my father's office was the big window, which had a view of the harbour and the North Shore mountains. I liked freighters all right, but I particularly enjoyed tugboats, the way they scolded their log booms into port.

"Any tugs?" I asked, just as my father's boss, Mr. German, put his head in the door.

"Parker," he began, before seeing me and Norman, and opening the door wide.

"Well, if it's Thursday, it must be Mary Alice," he said, speaking in the joshing voice of someone who didn't have children. Mr. German had a red face and a big paunch hanging over his belt. He wore his watch on his right wrist, which I thought was a mistake until my father said he was left-handed.

"Hello, Mr. German," I said.

"And today, let me see"—noticing Norman—"today you brought your boyfriend."

"No, Mr. German. Norman is a boy and he's my friend, but he isn't my boyfriend."

"So you're like your pops when his head gets into the clouds," Mr. German said, looking at my father. "And one and one don't make two. Which can be a problem when you're doing the books."

Norman glanced my way and saw how little I liked Mr. German. Afterward, he looked patiently at his shoes, but I could hardly wait to get out of there, wishing I could whirl into a tornado like Superman, ripping my way down through the floor and pulling Norman down after me.

The problem being, I knew what I was going to say.

"Who needs a boyfriend, Mr. German?" I asked, my tone of voice skating dangerously close to impertinence. A parent would have known that, but luckily Mr. German thought it was cute.

"That's what they always say, isn't it, Parker? The ladies, giving us the brush-off."

"Well, at nine years old, I would hope so, Art."

"You would hope so, would you?" Mr. German asked, which didn't seem to mean anything specific but was also an insult. He looked down at some papers in his hand.

"Now, see here, Parker," he said, walking toward him. "I'm not going to stand for any more of this."

My father signalled with his pinkie finger to grab an envelope that had magically appeared on his desk.

"Goodbye, Mr. German," I said loudly, sweeping up the envelope and hurrying Norman out the door. We were lucky. The elevator was just arriving, letting out a teenage messenger with pimples the same colour as his uniform. Being alone inside, we made faces in the mirror on the back wall as the floors dinged down, and felt a rush of air on our backs as we reached the lobby. Turning, fleeing, we made it safely outside, Norman singing the *Twilight Zone* song on the sidewalk while I echoed it back. Since Mr. German had been so awful, we sang it again as we tumbled into the back seat of the car.

"What's all that about?" Bunny asked, putting the car into gear.

"Mr. Pukey German came in."

Bunny's hand froze on the gear shift and she spoke sharply. "I hope you were polite."

"I know how to behave," I said, aware of being truthful. Knowing wasn't a guarantee that I had.

"Was she polite, Norman?" Bunny asked, not in the least bit fooled.

"Yes, Mrs. Parker," Norman said. "But Mr. German is insolent."

Bunny raised her eyebrows in the rearview mirror.

"My dad says there's far too many insolent pupils at school."

"What's insolent, though?" I asked.

"It means someone thinks they're better than you are when they're not."

"You figured that out, did you?" Bunny asked, although she looked worried as we drove back down Hastings Street toward the bridge.

Norman's patience was rewarded by a pet store that had aquariums three decks high along the back wall. Puppy dogs were woofing as we walked in, and indignant birds screeched from their cages. It was a large, noisy, crowded store. In a sudden break in the clamour you could even hear crickets. I always liked to visit the puppies, but Norman headed straight for the aquariums, taking a slow stroll in front of them with his hands clasped behind his back.

After I'd asked the teenage fish and bird manager for my brine shrimp, I joined Norman in checking out the tanks. Inside were several dozen small tableaux of shipwrecks and windmills with every type of fish swimming among them. There were bright, big enviable fish for saltwater aquariums like Ed's, and goldfish, which I found too staring, and different species of small tropical fish for aquariums like mine. Black mollies were particularly enticing. They reminded me of Aunt Magda, although I didn't think this was something I could tell her. They were two inches long.

"Your fantails are better than theirs are," Norman said, going back to the tank where they kept the guppies. "Is this where you got them?"

"They bred prettier."

I didn't know what that meant but Ed had said it.

"The store ought to buy your fantails and sell them."

"I've given some away to people with aquariums," I temporized. You had to be at least a teenager like the bird and fish manager to handle a business operation.

"Sell them your fantails," Norman insisted. "Then you can save up and buy another tank, so you can put the babies where their parents won't eat them. Then you can sell those ones. And then," he added shyly, "if I can get an aquarium, I can have some, too."

We exchanged a sad glance, both of us far too aware that having your birthday around Christmas meant you didn't get presents spread throughout the year. At least Halloween and Easter were five months apart in terms of chocolate.

"You've got some fish to sell us, have you, Tinkerbell?"

Turning, I saw a man I half recognized, which meant he was someone's father.

"Tink," Norman said, and stuck out his hand. "Yes, sir, she does. I'm Norman."

"Well hello, Norman," the man said, shaking his hand. The mothers I knew, the fathers I only recognized. A glimmer made me think he was probably redheaded Lucy Oliver's father, married to Mrs. Oliver of Comings and Goings. Mr. Oliver had been in something called public relations, but that might have come and gone. He might be like my father's friend Mr. Warren, who was selling cars for Jimmy Pattison, except that the unknown father was selling fish. I was still trying to work him out when the fish and bird manager came back from the freezer with my brine shrimp. When he saw the man we were talking to, the fish and bird manager straightened up in a way that said the talkative man was his boss.

"Kevin," the boss said. "This little girl has some fish she's going to bring in next week."

"They'll be ready in a couple of weeks," I said and thought of the car. "Two weeks exactly."

"Take a look, Kevin, and see if you can give her a quarter apiece. Something like that. Do the trick for you, Tink?"

I nodded, my eyes as round as quarters.

"Then you can save up and buy Norman his tank," he told me, and Norman's eyes grew even wider than mine.

This is how the aquarium idea got started: the pet store boss suggesting it. Back in the car, Norman and I did the arithmetic. Nineteen times twenty-five cents was almost five dollars. We'd neglected to check how much a ten-gallon aquarium set cost, but there were also our allowances. Plus we could set up a lemonade stand now it was warmer.

"Lemonade and cookies," I said, angling my voice toward the front seat.

"If you want," Bunny replied, agreeing so easily that I grew conscious of how many times Jennifer Doherty and I had made plans for a lemonade stand and never got around to having one. Drawing up plans was satisfying. Doing things was hard work, and it didn't always get done.

Yet Norman turned out to be a dog with a bone. Over the next few days, lying on the rug in our rec room, he drew up plans for a lemonade stand that kept making him say, "My contribution."

"My contribution can be the poster board for the signs. They get it at school."

"My contribution can be the paint for the poster boards."

"My contribution can be a tablecloth, once I ask."

Norman made a very thorough list on a piece of lined paper torn from a workbook, chewing his bottom lip as he added more plans, not even in pencil but in ballpoint. I'd never seen Norman so excited about any-thing. He turned into an alien version of himself, maybe sent in from the *Twilight Zone* or escaped from a comic book, one of the mad professors who pushed up their hair, leaving a cowlick in front, telling me that my contribution would be lemonade, cookies, drinking glasses, our driveway, the card table and chairs.

It was a happy time, and it lasted until I arrived at his house on Monday morning to go to school. When the door opened, Norman came out looking cloudy. He only grunted hello, and his lunchbox weighed down his arm. I didn't think he had another cold or they would have kept him home. But he didn't say anything as we walked down Connington, or even Moore.

Finally, I asked, "Won't they let you use the tablecloth?"

Norman shrugged. "I can't have an aquarium."

I had to think about that. "Does it give you asthma?"

"Summer vacation. Who's going to look after it?"

Alarmed, I asked, "Who's going to look after the kitten?"

"Andy Manners is going to have a key and feed it. But it's too much to ask her to take on an aquarium without paying her, and she isn't allowed to get a summer job. My mum says it's too Plebeian."

I didn't know what Plebeian was but was glad of the confirmation that Andy and Rosa were allowed to be friends in public, even if I didn't like how they got there. I saw a flash of Mrs. Manners with her head on Mr. Horton's shoulder and had to look the other way, even though the picture was only in my mind.

"You could always bring the aquarium over to my place."

"That's only part of the reason. My dad doesn't believe in pets."

"Rosa got her cat."

"I'm not Rosa," Norman said.

Something hurt in my chest. I didn't like that at all, and started walking more briskly.

"So what happens," I said. "The aquarium lives at my house all the time, but it's your aquarium. You get to pick the fish and buy the fish, and you're the one who has to clean it." Which was not my favourite task. "But it will be *your* aquarium."

Norman looked at me shyly. "We can do that?"

"I don't see why not."

That was one of Bunny's favourite expressions, and it impressed Norman.

"If we did," he began, and paused. "If it happened, we couldn't tell them. You couldn't call it my aquarium when you came over. They wouldn't like it."

I didn't like him asking me to lie. To be fair, it wasn't exactly a lie, it was just keeping things quiet, and I was already keeping a lot of things quiet. But I wasn't keeping the other things quiet so I could fool someone, and we would be trying to fool Norman's parents, and that's what I didn't like. Norman saw it in my pursed lips.

"Only if you want to," he said.

His face made me remember how Rosa could get what she wanted and Norman couldn't.

"They don't care if we have a lemonade stand?"

Norman could see I was teetering.

"They said it would be good for me. They said we won't make any money. But having a lemonade stand teaches you something."

He tried to remember what and failed, which made him look miserable again. But I'd already decided to go ahead.

"It teaches you arithmetic," I said.

"I'm already good at arithmetic."

"Then it teaches me," I said, with school just ahead.

Over dinner, I told my parents that Norman and I had chosen this coming Saturday for our lemonade stand. We were sitting at the kitchen table eating spaghetti with meat sauce from a new recipe Bunny had found in the newspaper. I thought it was extremely tasty, although my enthusiasm had raised concerns about laundry.

"Lemonade and cookies," I said, remembering to add, "If that's all right."

"It's too early for a lemonade stand," Bunny said. "You better wait till summer."

"Norman says this way we wouldn't have any competition."

My father smiled. "He really wants that aquarium," he said, amazing me with the way he was able to put things together.

"The tank is for here," I said. "But that's okay. Norman's going to clean it."

My parents went silent, looking at me over their spaghetti. I couldn't lie. Keeping quiet in front of Norman's parents was as far as I could go. At least, trying to keep quiet.

"His dad won't let him have one," I said. "He doesn't believe in pets, even though Rosa got a kitten. But Norman can't have an aquarium. He isn't Rosa. It's like that."

"Is it?" Bunny asked, her voice gone flat.

I felt hurt again for Norman but wanted to sound capable of running a lemonade stand.

"I said we could save up for another one here. It could be his. He could choose the fish and come over every day. And clean it. That way it wouldn't bother his dad."

"This was your idea?" my father asked.

I was a little worried about that, but shrugged yes.

"Then I'm proud of you," my father said.

I hadn't expected that. Meeting his eyes gave me a warm feeling, like getting a present in the middle of the year.

"But it can't work like that, Mary Alice," he said. "Norman needs to speak with his parents."

"Or you do," Bunny said.

"All right," I agreed, then realized she wasn't talking to me.

"She'd do a better job than I would," my father said, pushing up his glasses to rub his eyes. We both knew that meant yes.

"Talk to his mother," I advised.

"Mary Alice . . ."

"Good idea," Bunny said. "Ginger snaps or chocolate chip?"

"Both?" I tried.

The aquarium could go in Norman's house and come to our place when they were on vacation. That night in my bedroom, I overheard, "The poor woman was embarrassed half to death," and, "She honestly didn't know the boy was so set on it," and Bunny's, "I don't suppose Jack Horton thanked you for it," which was followed by, "I was surprised. He shook my hand."

The lemonade stand was a success, our greatest profit coming at the end when Mrs. Manners pulled into her driveway. Jumping out of her sports car, she looked over at our sign. "Lemonade 5¢. Cookies 10¢. Chocolate Chip. Ginger Snap. Delicious."

Walking over, Mrs. Manners let out her easy laugh to find our trays nearly bare.

"Apparently I'm late to the party," she said. "But I had to get my roots done, didn't I?"

Norman looked confused. Clearly, his mother's roots didn't play a large role in his life.

"I can't see them, Mrs. Manners," I assured her. "Your new hairstyle is very fashionable. It makes you look like a movie star."

"*Do* I, Tink?" she asked. She was exaggerating her pleasure but you could tell she felt it. "Which one?"

I meant movie stars in general and had to struggle.

"Katharine Hepburn," Norman said.

"Katharine Hepburn!"

"Except younger," I said.

Percolating with laughter, Mrs. Manners dug into her purse, pulling out a five-dollar bill and putting it firmly on the muffin tin where we kept our cash.

"You worked hard for that," she said, and turned to leave.

"Would you like a ginger snap, Mrs. Manners?" I asked, holding out the tray.

"Don't be silly," she said, and ran up her stairs, slamming the door hard enough that my father came out of the garage, where he'd been busy all day.

"What in heaven's name was that?"

"Sales," Norman and I said at the same time, and linked pinkie fingers to make a wish.

10

The next Friday, someone knocked on the door just as we were sitting down to dinner. This was shortly before the first air raid siren, the first one I would remember. I answered the door reluctantly, famished after the school track meet and afraid a door-to-door salesman would hold things up.

Mr. Horton stood on the doorstep shifting nervously from foot to foot. He looked as if he wanted something, which puzzled me.

Mr. Horton's arrival was another part of the avalanche of puzzles that were starting to bother me. Him and Mrs. Manners, Mrs. Eisenstadt, communism: all these things that only happened once but never went away either. They were like the seals we saw sometimes while we were eating a picnic on the rocks at Lighthouse Park. One would raise his dog face from the waves, looking around until he saw us, all bright eyes and whiskers. He'd stare at us a moment then dive back under, gone but still swimming around in the seaweed, liable to surface again unpredictably.

"Is Norman all right?" I asked.

"Now why would I run over here if he wasn't?" Mr. Horton asked, and rapped his knuckles on my head. "Use those brains, Tink."

"Jack," my father said, arriving behind me. He put one hand on the door above my head and blocked the entrance with his body, which was his friendly way of keeping people out.

"Hall Parker," Mr. Horton replied, and reached out to shake. "Thought I might rescue you. Couple of beers at the bar. If you don't have any other plans for the evening."

This put my father on the spot. He never had plans for Friday night, not after a long week at work. But with Mr. Horton putting it that way, his only possible response was to agree that he had nothing on, and that was a trap.

"I need him to play Rummoli with me," I said, and got interested in the idea. "Rummoli and hot chocolate."

"Maybe you can sacrifice Rummoli for one evening," Mr. Horton said. "Seven thirty? I'll pick you up."

He was gone before my father could reply, and all we could do was go back to the kitchen and sit down for dinner.

"What was that all about?" Bunny asked.

My father rubbed the back of his neck. "I have no idea in the world."

I put my head down and cleaned my plate, except for turnips, meanwhile seeing that I needed to stay awake and eavesdrop when my father got home. After he left to get dressed, I cleared the table without being asked, trying out the Rummoli idea on Bunny and throwing in hot chocolate to make it more popular. Either would have answered my purpose, but both together were guaranteed to keep me awake: overexcitement followed by sugar.

The fact that neither worked should have gone into my arsenal. I could have asked later: Remember when I had hot chocolate the night Mr. Horton asked you to go for a beer? But I couldn't keep my eyes open even for Rummoli.

What made it worse was to wake up the next morning and realize it was Saturday, my parents' morning for sleeping in. I got up to a sunny day and helped myself to cereal, no one to question what had happened last night even when I rattled the bowl. Afterward, Norman knocked on the door the way his father had. But seeing him standing on the doorstep with his cowlick and shorts, I found I couldn't ask him what was going on. I wasn't sure what was worse: that Norman would tell me something I didn't want to know or that he wouldn't have any idea that his father had dropped over, making him feel forgotten once again.

We spent the day down the creek, not even making a trip to the village, with Norman saving his allowance for the aquarium. Despite Mrs. Manners, our take from the lemonade stand had fallen short of what he needed for a ten-gallon tank, and I'd ended up having only eleven fantail guppies to sell, cannibalism having been an issue. The pet store boss had been jolly about rounding it up, maybe because he really *was* Lucy Oliver's father. He'd given me three dollars for the eleven, but Norman still had to save for eight more weeks, barring additional births.

That meant I only saw my father when we sat down to dinner on Saturday night, a full day after Mr. Horton had knocked on the door. I'd had all day to think about what I was going to say, knowing that I had to be polite and that this would be hard. But the problem was, I couldn't remember the question I'd thought up earlier, not with Bunny serving fish fingers. I liked fish fingers. They were distracting.

"Is something the matter?" my father asked.

I gave up. "So what did Mr. Horton want last night, anyhow?"

My father took some time to ruminate while unfolding his serviette. "You're quite concerned about Norman, aren't you?"

I didn't get the connection, but he was looking at me as if I needed to say something.

"He doesn't fit in. I'm trying to make him fit in."

"Does he care?" my father asked.

I'd never thought about that and didn't know the answer.

"What he wanted was to talk about himself," Bunny said, sitting down. "The way most men do. Put that in your pocket for when you start dating. One question: So what about you? Then they're yours, presuming you want them."

My father smiled. "Mr. Horton is from Winnipeg," he said. "If that's what you wanted to know. From a pretty rough-and-tumble part of Winnipeg called the North End. He joined up in January of '43. The Winnipeg Grenadiers. They shipped over to England a few months later, but he doesn't seem to have seen much action. Nothing he spoke about, anyway. The Grenadiers fought in Hong Kong back in '41, and that didn't go very well. I imagine the brass decided that Winnipeg had lost enough boys and kept them out of the fighting in Europe."

"Boring enough for you?" Bunny asked.

Above my head. I knew where Winnipeg was, in the middle of the prairies. We drew grain fields around it on poster-board maps of Canada, poster board being a big part of education in grade four. But I didn't know anything more than that.

"Is Mrs. Horton from Winnipeg?"

"He didn't say," my father replied. "He mentioned that her family is Ukrainian, and there are Ukrainians living all over the prairies. He just said they met at a club when he got back."

I pictured the nightclub, Trader Vic's, where the girl had said *ain't* on New Year's Eve, although Bunny muttered something about communist clubs that I didn't quite hear.

"Do they speak French in Winnipeg?" I asked. Seeing how this threw my father, I told him, "Rosa says French words just like Mademoiselle Tremblay."

"Does she?" my father asked. "Well, Mr. Horton went to McGill University in Montreal. If you were in the army, the government paid for you to go to university. Lots of men did that."

"If they didn't have a family," Bunny said.

"He had a family," my father said. "Rosa was born before they went east, from what he said. She's, what? One of the fifteen-year-olds born after demobilization."

"Well good for them," Bunny said. "Managing both university and a family."

I didn't understand the sudden tension between them, which caused my father to take off his glasses and rub his eyes. Nor did I recognize his peace offering in the rare bit of gossip.

"I think Marian Horton might be a few years older than Jack," he said. "She was already teaching when they met. I gather she found a job in Montreal and supported the family while he went to McGill. I imagine they found someone to take care of Rosa, and the person, the girl, probably spoke French."

"When her mother should have been taking care of her," Bunny said.

"It's one of the decisions people make."

"Most people make the right one."

I wanted them to stop. "Norman got polio in Prince George."

"Well," my father answered, looking as if he wanted it over with, too. "I gather they moved around for a while. Sudbury, Prince George. Following jobs, I would imagine. Then they came here." He smiled at me. "Happy now?"

I wasn't, still not getting it. "But why did he want to go out for two beers?"

My father smiled again. "Your mother's right. People like to talk about themselves. Explain themselves. Be seen in a good light. Maybe after all that business about Norman's aquarium."

I gave this some thought. "But he didn't explain about Dr. Norman Bethune."

"You're supposed to forget about that," Bunny said.

"You said *communist*," I pointed out.

"No, he didn't explain," my father replied. "And your mother's right. There's a lot in people's lives that's over and done with before we ever meet them."

"And a lot that isn't," Bunny said. "But that's their business, and doesn't need to be any of ours."

That's when I got a sense of seals swimming underwater, something not yet done with, and wondered if Mr. Horton wanted to be friends with my father. That's what someone my age would have wanted, behaving like that. And if they felt that way, they didn't let up, wanting to play. A loser kid would do that anyhow, the way Mrs. Horton said. I wondered if

Mr. Horton had been a loser at my age. I wouldn't have said so. I would have put him down as one of the Marlon Brando types who made girly girls whisper in a corner, making all of this a puzzle.

"Are you going to go out for another beer?"

"Oh Lord, I hope not. That was far too much work."

My father bit it off quickly, as if he'd caught himself blurting.

"But you're friends now, right?"

My father ruminated on that. "What does having a friend mean to you?"

I didn't know exactly and shrugged. "Helping them get an aquarium?"

"Then your father and Jack Horton are intimate friends," Bunny said. "Considering the amount of money we laid out on that lemonade stand."

"Muriel . . ."

"Lemonade and four batches of cookies. I'm just saying. Now eat your dinner, Mary Alice. I've had just about enough of the Hortons."

I grumbled, "Everyone always telling me to eat so much dinner I'm going to have to go on a diet."

But I really did like fish fingers, especially with tartar sauce. It also occurred to me that Mr. Horton and my father were the type of friends who didn't like one another, the way Aunt Magda had said. That was satisfying, to find a category, although there remained the question of future beer nights. Also the fact that tartar sauce was different than the tartar on your teeth in toothpaste ads. But there was lemon meringue pie for dessert, and that was just fine.

We got Norman his aquarium a couple of weeks later, ten days after the first air raid siren went off. My terrible week was over by then, my father having explained about the Cold War, making me feel a little better. Not entirely better. Jangled, and more than normally puzzled by all the unexpected events that kept raising their heads. Or maybe I just noticed them more, and questioned them more, made nervous by the sirens and the Bomb and the way my eyes could melt any minute, life becoming a calm before the storm.

Still, Norman got his aquarium. Technically, he'd needed to save more of his allowance, and that was just for the tank. But Rosa had topped him up after a good weekend babysitting. My parents' failure to gossip about New Year's Eve had allowed Rosa to launch a lucrative business. It was a piece of luck to be among the first of so many children born after the war. Rosa gave Norman enough money not only for the ten-gallon package but for aquatic plants and as many fish as he wanted, at least once the aquarium was up and running.

"I thought that saving your allowance was good for you," I said. "Isn't that what your dad said?"

We were out for Thursday errands, with Bunny just pulling into a space in the pet store parking lot.

Norman shrugged. "Rosa decided, so he couldn't say anything."

"You can't feel sorry for yourself all the time about your sister," Bunny said, looking in the rearview mirror after she pulled to a stop.

I was surprised, but Norman was listening.

"In this life, you need to toughen up."

"I already did," Norman said.

"Fair enough," Bunny replied, and yanked on the emergency brake. "Go get your aquarium. They can help you carry it. I need a smoke."

I wondered if she needed a smoke because she'd gone into my father's office with us. Mr. German had been there, and he'd called her Maureen. "Well, look. Here's Maureen shepherding the lambs." I'd wanted to say, "Muriel," but knew I couldn't and it nearly killed me. Bunny didn't seem very happy either, but she'd only said, "Hello there, Art. Nice day, isn't it."

Inside the store, we looked for the boss, with Norman having an idea that he might give us a discount. But all we saw was the fish and bird manager, gangly and officious, a word I'd heard my Aunt Magda use about his particular type of idiot.

"Where's Mr. Oliver?" I asked.

The fish and bird manager didn't know who I was talking about.

"The boss? Mr. Oliver? Lucy Oliver's father?"

"Mr. Duffy," he said, and the penny dropped. Mr. Duffy was the man who'd got divorced and moved back home to take care of his mother in the house at the top of Far Creek Road. I'd only ever seen him from a distance riding his bicycle in shorts and knee socks and the type of sandals Mrs. Horton wore. But my mother's friends liked to talk about him over coffee, opinions ranging from his wife being a tramp to not being able to blame her. The one who said that was Mrs. Oliver of Comings and Goings, whose real husband must still have been in public relations, whatever that was.

Mr. Duffy's mother was elderly and verging on senile. My mother's friends agreed he took excellent care of her, making sure she got to the beauty parlour once a week for her wash and style, where Belinda the hairdresser said the old lady was sharp enough about money. Mr. Duffy had two children, two boys, but his wife had got custody and taken them to Portland, Oregon. No one knew why.

"Mr. Duffy," I agreed. "Is he here?"

As if summoned, Mr. Duffy huffed out of the stock room and beamed when he saw us, veering over.

"Well, here's Norman and Tinkerbell. Come to buy our aquarium, are we?"

"Tink, sir," Norman said, shaking his hand. "And it's my tank. We decided. The ten-gallon set."

"Kevin here'll fix you up," Mr. Duffy said. "And get you your fish. Employee discount. Tink being one of our suppliers."

Kevin and I started explaining at the same time that Norman couldn't get his fish, not until the aquarium was up and running, which meant four days (me) and five days (Kevin). Underneath it, Norman said, "Thank you," so there was a confusion that took Mr. Duffy a moment to work out.

"Well, pick out your fish and we'll hold them for you," he said. "Take your time."

"But we can't come back for two weeks," I said. "And if they die, Norman will know the difference."

Mr. Duffy looked at Norman, who nodded solemnly.

"And my mother's in the car with the groceries. So we need to hurry."

Mr. Duffy found this amusing. "She can wait while you pick out your fish. I think we can keep them alive until I drop them off at your place next week. The old Milewski place on Connington, isn't that right?"

I pictured Mr. Duffy riding his bicycle with some plastic bags of fish held in one of his hands. I supposed he missed his children in Portland, Oregon, and felt sorry for him, which was strange because he was an adult.

As soon as Mr. Duffy left, Kevin turned officious. Norman had already decided on the type of fish, and while he picked out the individuals, Kevin hovered fussily by the tanks, noting the look of an especially active catfish, three neon tetras, two red swordtails (male and female) and two small but nicely-striped black-and-silver angelfish. I pressed for black mollies but Norman didn't want them, although he offered to get me a pair. Even after buying his plants, he'd have more than enough left over, given the employee discount.

"He means a discount on the fish," Kevin said. "She isn't an aquarium supplier."

I was inclined to argue the point, but Norman said it was all right, and Kevin started netting out Norman's plants and the mollies, then carried the tank set to the cash desk.

As we fell in behind him, Norman said quietly, "My dad says pick your battles."

I didn't see why.

"I've got more than enough money," he said. "Rosa gave me ten dollars."

"I bet I could have got a discount on the plants, though," I said. "I'm still president of your union local."

Norman considered this. "Then the mollies are my union dues."

He ducked his head and bit his lip. Norman made jokes like that, drier than cactus mountains. They weren't funny but you enjoyed them anyway. At least, I did.

After dropping off the mollies, I helped Norman set up his aquarium, and Mr. Duffy brought the fish over the following Monday, knocking on the door after school. Mrs. Horton had come home early and called us out of Norman's bedroom, where we were reading comic books bought with the dregs of Rosa's ten dollars. The pet store was closed on Mondays so we were surprised, but it turned out Mr. Duffy still had to go in. The animals needed to eat, which was something you didn't think about.

"Where do you want them?" Mr. Duffy asked, holding out three plastic bags of fish.

"Do you want to see?" Norman asked, and the three of us took the bags back into his bedroom, where we floated them on top of the tank so the water temperature would equalize the way Ed had taught me.

"Well there you go," Mr. Duffy said, putting a hand on Norman's back, as if he was one of his divorced children.

Back in the kitchen, Mrs. Horton offered Mr. Duffy a cup of coffee. Of course she would, the two of them preferring the same sandals, even though Mr. Duffy was wearing brogues.

"Thanks, but I'd better get home to Mother," he replied, before leaning in to say something weren't supposed to hear. "Your son is a smart little fellow. Knows his business."

"What business?" I asked, after Mr. Duffy had left.

"It's an expression, Tink," Mrs. Horton said. "It's just another way of saying that Norman is smart. He's astute."

"So why did he have to say it twice? Especially since Norman is smart."

"Because he's a creep," Rosa said, looking up from her homework. She was doing a page of complicated-looking math that made me not look forward to high school.

"He's nice," Norman said.

"He's divorced," I told them. "His wife took their boys to Portland, Oregon. That's why he takes care of his mother."

"The poor man," Mrs. Horton said.

"Creep," Rosa said.

"How long before the water temperature is ready?" Norman asked. He wasn't usually in a hurry, but it was already May, and he wanted to get as much out of the fish as possible before his summer vacation.

I told him it wouldn't be long, so we went back into his bedroom to watch the bags until it was time to let out the fish. They were the angelfish and catfish Norman had picked out, which he knew from the markings, and certainly he'd got a male and female swordtail, the male being smaller and having a sword. But it was hard to tell about the neon tetras, which flicked around as quickly as the northern lights.

Aurora borealis, my father said. I'd seen them the previous year at his friend Mr. Hague's peach farm, where we went on vacation every year. My father had got me up past midnight, carrying me outside when no one else was awake, and we'd watched the sky ripple with green fire.

By the time Norman's fish settled in, life was sliding toward summer, which usually meant freedom. But by this time the sirens were going off more often, and the Raincoat Man appeared down the creek again, and Andy Manners threw more rocks at him, and Wilma didn't have kittens for the first spring since we'd got her. Bunny said it was because she'd infected her paw and we'd kept her inside, which didn't make much sense to me. All this might have seemed normal if not for the Bomb. But the threat of the Bomb made the world feel noisy and frightening, as if a Monopoly game had started talking.

There was also the fact that Miss Atkinson asked us to draw a picture. I think it was a Thursday when we had to guess what special thing she was going to do when school let out. She refused to give any hints, and after some thought, I drew a picture of her back in Hawaii eating another octopus, which stood up on all eight legs on its plate with a friendly smile. I was proud of that octopus, which you couldn't mistake for anything else.

Also pleased that after we handed in our drawings, she said, "Now, people. I'm going to hold them up one by one so everyone can see."

Wedding dress. Wedding dress. Wedding dress. It soon became clear that everyone else had drawn Miss Atkinson wearing a wedding dress, even Norman.

"Well aren't you all smart?" she asked, leaving an invisible asterisk hanging in the air, which was me. "I'm getting married this summer, and you're my last class!"

I threw up my hand. "Last class forever, Miss Atkinson?"

She nodded as slowly and emphatically as Norman had at the pet store. That hurt my heart, which stayed hurt even as we slogged uphill after school.

"We'll get my mum for grade five," Norman said. He spoke as if this was the best thing in the world, although I couldn't agree. There was the way his mother had kept after Norman about long division while we'd negotiated his allowance. How she'd said I was sent to try them when I wasn't. Those sandals she wore, which said she was bohemian without coming from Bohemia. That still confused me. And there was also my recent confusion about whether his identical sandals made Mr. Duffy a bohemian, too.

"I still would have seen Miss Atkinson in the hallway."

"They always forget their last year's class."

"They don't forget me," I said, which seemed to raise private feelings in Norman as well.

"What?" I asked.

"My mum can help you with your arithmetic more than Miss Atkinson."

But I knew with great certainty that whatever she tried wouldn't work, and when the air raid siren went off the next day during class, it jangled me badly.

"All right, people! Duck and cover!" Miss Atkinson cried, clapping her hands.

After scrambling under my desk, I found myself in a mood to carve my name on the bottom alongside Jack Baker's and Peter Hardy's. Grade four had progressed to ballpoint pens, and since I was holding one when the siren wailed, I managed to scratch T-I-N-K in lightly, then got the *T* in deeper before the siren ended just as abruptly as it always did. Perhaps the word for what I felt wasn't *jangled* but *rebellious*, and not just because Miss Atkinson was leaving. It had also occurred to me that the Bomb wasn't fair.

"Just another exercise!" Miss Atkinson said brightly as we crawled back out, this time without a wetting incident. I'd heard one day when eavesdropping on my mother and her friends that Nancy Workman was seeing a doctor about her weak bladder. "Are they doing an operation?" one of the mothers had asked. "Not that kind of doctor," Mrs. Oliver had replied.

It was also true that as we sat back down, Nancy distinctly said, "Stupid," under her breath. That was an event in itself, a half event, a stub of an event, and it puzzled me until Cal Manners's party on the weekend, which was an event of a bigger sort.

"Duck and cover," a boy said in the same cynical tone as Nancy. "Give me a break."

I was spying on Cal's backyard party through the picture window in our living room. It was warm enough that I'd opened the door to the small sundeck over the garage so I could hear what was going on. Cal Manners was holding a barbecue in his backyard to celebrate passing grade eleven. I didn't see why he had to celebrate when he was guaranteed to pass, at least if he was as smart as Mr. Horton had said. Yet there was another asterisk hanging in the air: Mr. Horton had also said Andy Manners only inherited her father's brains, even though she seemed clever to me.

"As if ducking under your desk is going to stop a nuclear bomb," another boy agreed.

"Melting the flesh off your bones," someone else put in. "Like ice turning to water."

"Going all poetic on us, are you, Shribman?"

That was Cal himself, and it was a warning. Michael Shribman was the older brother of Judy Shribman, the one who'd taken the tortoiseshell kitten. I wasn't sure what Michael was doing at Cal's party, since he wasn't on the football team. Then I remembered that he'd won citywide medals in track and field, and wondered if it was true that the Bomb would melt me like the Wicked Witch of the West, making me drain through a hole in the floor.

"Let's leave the boys to their party," my father said, appearing behind me. Feeling his arm on my shoulder made me realize how nervous Cal and his friends were making me.

The boys, the Bomb, duck and cover. The fact Miss Atkinson would go away in two weeks and I'd never see her again. The fact that all these things occurred unpredictably. Seals raising their heads. Clocks *tick-tick-tocking* all out of rhythm.

"But is it true?" I asked my father. "Is it stupid to hide under your desk?"

Without speaking, he urged me away from the window and sat me down in the kitchen, where he did something he never did, pouring each of us a glass of milk.

"I don't suppose they explained it," my father said, giving me milk and taking his own to his usual chair at the head of the table. "But I don't think it's a wrong thing to do. Not exactly."

I took a sip of milk, looking at him over the top of the glass.

"In 1917," my father began.

History lesson, Rosa Horton had said. Everything echoed in my head lately, nothing forgotten or staying in its place.

In 1917, my father explained, there was something called the Halifax Explosion. My grandfather, my father's father, had survived it when he was in uniform for the previous war. The Great War, they'd called it. The War to End All Wars. Two ships collided in the Halifax harbour, one of them loaded with explosives. Both of them went up, and so did a big part of Halifax. Two thousand people were killed and even more were injured. Many of the injuries came from people standing by their windows, looking out at what everyone could see was about to happen, the two ships steaming heedlessly toward one another.

"That's what they're trying to prevent now," my father said. "Secondary injuries."

"But if they dropped the Bomb right on top of us?"

"Yes," my father said, answering the part of the question I hadn't asked. "But I don't think we're that big a target. The brass are thinking, I suppose, that it might be dropped a ways from us, far enough away that the city would survive. And so we'd want to," he paused for a pained moment. "Protect our eyesight."

"So we don't go blind like Helen Keller," I said, having got her autobiography last year from Scholastic Books.

"Like Helen Keller. In a sense."

"So they'd bomb Seattle?"

"It's unlikely, Mary Alice. All of this is very unlikely. And while it's a port, Seattle isn't all that close. We're a port, but I don't think they'd . . ." He paused again. "It would be a mistake, if anything landed here, or near here."

"And the Russians aren't going to make a mistake."

My father thought for a long time.

"Come on, now," he said, as if waking up. "Drink your milk."

Which I did, although I was still preoccupied by the fact that never in my life had I succeeded in looking away from anything.

One more important thing happened after that. Two, although I didn't recognize the initial one at first: the fact that Mrs. Horton had appeared in the newspaper. I saw it one day when I brought the afternoon paper inside. On the front page was a photograph of a meeting about nuclear weapons. The way one person stood made me look closer.

Mrs. Horton. It was her, standing outside with a small group of people. The lines under the photograph said they had gathered by the

War Memorial, although it was night and you couldn't see the memorial. A demonstration, the newspaper called it. Most people held signs made with wooden sticks topped by poster board. On them were written Ban the Bomb and Nuclear Tests Cause Cancer and Stop! and Women Strike for Peace. Mrs. Horton had one saying No Nuclear Arms for Canada. I supposed she'd got the poster board from school, maybe for several of the signs, although probably not for all of them. One lady near the front wore a checked coat and a striped scarf, which Bunny would have said was a fashion mistake.

"Here's Norman's mum," I said, taking the newspaper into the kitchen.

"Where?" Bunny asked. She was making shortbread.

I pointed to Mrs. Horton, who was looking away from the camera as if being photographed made her shy.

"Good eyes," Bunny, making me think of the way the Bomb would melt them. The Bomb had become the only capitalization in my life. Everything else had shrunk in significance.

Bunny wiped her hands on a dish towel and took the paper, looking at the photo before pausing for a long time and folding it neatly.

"You didn't see that," she said.

I didn't know what to answer, because I had.

"And don't so much as mention the word *newspaper* to Norman. We don't want to know even a tiny bit more about this."

An echo came to me from the previous night, when I'd overheard Bunny meeting my father at the door, sounding as excited as I'd ever heard her.

"News," she'd said, although I didn't understand their half whispers until now. I can't say why it came to me wholesale, the second big event.

"Is Debbie going to have a baby?"

Bunny's eyes lit up, although she pursed her lips, trying to hold it in.

"Where did that come from?" she asked.

I grouched, "I guess I can't say anything about that, either."

"Not yet," Bunny told me, pushing my hair back from my face and looking down at me with the most extraordinary expression in her eyes.

Love. It was love. I felt loved. My eyes would melt if I looked out the window, as I did all the time. But I was loved, and I leaned into my mother's floury embrace.

11

S chool let out two days later and Norman left soon afterward on vacation. His mother had learned to drive that spring, raising comments. One Saturday afternoon, as I lay on the grass out front, I'd seen the Hortons' car turning onto Connington, jerking as if it was having seizures. Mrs. Horton was at the wheel. She stalled it in the middle of Connington, stalled while she was turning into their driveway, then stalled a third time in the driveway itself. Afterward, she kept turning the key, making the engine growl in protest.

Fathers stopped mowing their lawns to watch. Mothers came to look out their windows. When the engine flooded and the car ground dead, Mrs. Horton threw open the driver's side door and stalked into the house. Mr. Horton got out afterward and pushed his hair back sheepishly, as if it was his fault.

"Women drivers!" Mr. Wall called from across the street. The fathers all chuckled, the only hesitation involving Mr. Wall himself. He was a policeman who had given Mr. O'Neill a speeding ticket even though they were neighbours, and Mr. O'Neill had been going only eight miles an hour over the limit. Maybe ten.

Nevertheless, Mrs. Horton had got her licence, and the first Monday after school let out, she was going to drive Norman and Rosa to northern Ontario, where they would go to summer camp on a lake. It was a sleepover camp, which we didn't have on the coast. We didn't need them, Vancouver being a citywide recreation centre, with beaches and parks and mountains. It was true some people went to Europe, including Aunt Magda and Uncle Ray. But in our suburb, Europe was considered unnecessary and on the edge of showing off.

Rosa had gone to camp even when Norman had been sick with polio, and now she was going to be a counsellor-in-training while Norman would be a camper for the first time. He told me this as we walked home on the last day of school, saying that his mum would stay back east all summer, although he didn't say why. His dad would stay home to teach summer school.

"You mean I won't get to babysit your aquarium?"

We were coming home late after playing marbles at the weedy edge of the schoolyard. Norman had won a couple of steelies but it didn't make him look happy. I could see he wasn't looking forward to camp, where he would be the new boy for a second time in a year.

"My dad won't have time to take care of the fish," he said. "I mean, to feed them, okay. He's going to feed the cat. But not to clean the tank."

"So we can bring it over in my wagon," I said, just as happy to have a temporary tank as I was to have temporary kittens.

"On Sunday," Norman said, as firmly as if there was some question. "I can pack on Saturday. I can do my laundry myself on Saturday morning."

In the end, Norman delayed the handover until Sunday afternoon, when we bagged the fish and plants, drained the aquarium and loaded up the wagon to bring everything over to my house. Afterward, we floated his bagged fish in my tank to equalize the temperature. They were going to visit my fish until Thursday, hopefully without incident, when the new water in his tank would be filtered.

"See? You can tell my catfish from yours," Norman said. "He's just a little guy."

He still had almost everything from the pet store: the prized catfish, two angelfish, the two swordtails and four of the neon tetras. There had been an unexplained tetra fatality, after which cannibalism had briefly occurred, or at least nibbling, before Norman was able to net the body.

"I know how to take care of them," I said.

"I just don't want any more surprises," Norman said. "They never told me about camp. It was just like my brace, when they're supposed to be teachers and tell you things."

I had no answer, and we walked uphill for a while.

"Why are they making your dad teach summer school?"

Norman hesitated. "I was expensive when I got that cold. Hiring the girl from Unwed Mothers. He has to work, which means it's pretty much my fault he misses our vacation. Except I'm not supposed to say that, and we weren't having a family vacation anyhow."

Seeing the misery around Norman's jaw was like opening a curtain on the Hortons' private life. I glimpsed pursed lips and sulking, as if shadows raged through that well-known house: the shadows of Norman's parents arguing and of Norman thinking it was his fault. I wondered whose fault it really was, and had a very distant understanding that fault wasn't the real issue. Fault was a curtain, and there was more drama behind it than I could begin to imagine.

"I never thought you had to pay the girl," I said. "I thought you were giving her a home."

It was another question, but Norman only shrugged. It was one of those times when I didn't know if he'd shrugged because he thought the answer was obvious, or because he didn't know, or because he preferred not to say. I didn't think this one had anything to do with communism, although Norman was so firmly vague about his mother's plans back east, I thought that might be connected. It was either communism or the Bomb.

"What happened to the girl's baby?"

"Adopted into a good home," he said promptly.

"She didn't want to be a mom?"

"I don't know. She never said anything. Mainly she just cried."

Norman seemed to hear himself and turned toward me with widened eyes. "There was a tragedy going on right underneath my roof and I didn't even know it."

I shook my head in sympathy, and decided to give it one more try.

"What's your mum going to do back east?"

"Stuff," Norman replied.

They drove off the next morning. We left three weeks later, although not before I'd seen Mrs. Manners slip out of her house and into the Hortons' back door four separate times, always holding a book in her hand as if she was returning it. She went after Mr. Horton got back from teaching and before Mr. Manners got home. This left her a good deal of time, since Mr. Manners had started coming home later and later. Eavesdropping on my parents, I heard that he could stay out half the night, and the words, "driving drunk."

In Norman's absence, I was left to entertain myself not just with the creek and fish, but with spying on Mrs. Manners, all my questions about adult complications having settled on her shoulders. The first time I saw her was coincidental, just a glance out the window as she slipped out their garage door. But she was being so cagey that I ran to the front window to see her walk down Connington Crescent, then turn abruptly into the Hortons' driveway, crossing her arms and hugging herself as she usually did despite the book, and going down the side of the house toward the back door.

After that, I had to spy on Mrs. Manners, who became as itchy a subject as the air raid siren. The two were mysteriously connected, since the siren had gone off only a few minutes after the first time I'd seen her go to the Hortons'. Once she'd slipped through their back door, I'd come out on the front lawn to look for a four-leafed clover, and possibly to see what time she went home. There was no sound aside from buzzing bees and little kids being called inside, the occasional slammed door. Then the awful metallic horn revved up and howled, making me leap to my feet, panting more than breathing, and running to duck and cover under the hydrangeas.

After that, late afternoons often found me waiting by the window, checking to see if Mrs. Manners left again, and worried about sirens. It bothered me to see her only half open the door, slip through it sideways and be careful about closing it. She walked away hurriedly, and I ran to the front window to watch her head up Connington, holding her book. I didn't know why I had to keep watching, but I did, and I hid what I was doing from Bunny.

Each time it happened, I tried to tell myself that Mrs. Manners had pretended to borrow a book so she could check up on Rosa's kitten, making sure that Mr. Horton was feeding it. The kitten was now a cat, a black-and-white tuxedo cat, and spayed. Each time I heard the voice in my head, it sounded more sprightly and absurd. There goes Mrs. Manners again, checking up on Rosa's cat!

I knew you had to distrust a voice like that, which was covering up something soiled, like unexplained blood. I wanted to find another explanation for her visits than the cat, but I couldn't. I also knew that Bunny would tell me the same thing in the same sprightly voice. She's just checking up on the cat. You can't trust a man to feed it, can you?

The only person I could ask was Andy Manners, and she was never around. Andy left at ten o'clock in the morning four days a week to play tennis at the country club. Her mother drove her and random brothers, with Andy wearing a short white skirt and white blouse the way Mrs. Manners did. Another couple of days a week, Andy left in dungarees and running shoes so she could take sailing lessons. In Rosa's absence, Andy had turned athletic, although it didn't seem to make her happy. She left the house with her arms crossed exactly like her mother's and got moodily into the back seat of the convertible, hunching down as if she didn't want to be seen.

We were getting ready to leave on vacation when I finally found Andy down the creek. She was sitting near the edge looking even more moody than she did in the car, leaning over her bent knees as she flicked pebbles underhand into the water.

"What do you want, Tink?" she asked, not bothering to turn around.

"It's just," I said, and dared myself to say it. "I don't understand your family."

Andy looked at me keenly over her shoulder without answering. Afterward, she turned around again and ignored me, even though I hovered. Only when I was about to leave did she speak, mostly to herself.

"My grandfather," she said.

I stopped, but knew enough not to walk back to her.

"Aren't you smart as he is?"

"He's pretty smart," Andy said. "Hating my father like that."

She turned toward me again.

"How would you feel if your father thought you weren't up to it, Tink? Not suitable for command. What do you figure?"

I didn't know what to say.

"So it's all good old Granddad's fault," she said, and heaved a stone at the creek.

I hovered some more, but this time Andy had left me, her attention following the stone into the creek and staying there, trapped underwater.

I remember well that our vacation was two weeks long that year. My father had reached a new level of seniority at work and got elevated from one week's annual vacation. When he told Bunny, he said it was a miracle he'd lasted this long. I had no idea why he wouldn't have, and none of my eavesdropping explained it.

Yet somehow our summer vacation that year was suffused with the idea of prevailing. I slowly untensed, forgetting the sirens, and the vacation grew flawless. Those two warm weeks stretched on endlessly, and the rising sun shone so affably that opening my eyes each morning was like opening the door on a field of wildflowers. Running outside, lying on thick grass or the sandy shore of a lake, I felt no boundary between the clemency of the world and myself, but a flowing into and out of. My fears leached into never-ending nature, never-ending life. During the approach of that long-ago crisis, I sensed that the great wide world would last far beyond us, and that was a gift.

We spent the first week of that vacation in the luxury of our own motel cabin on the shores of Okanagan Lake, a large blue lake surrounded by the shrugged shoulders of low golden mountains. My father wanted to retire to the Okanagan, and he was always at his happiest there, saying it was the only place he slept well outside his own bed. I think he became the person he wanted to be, his war memories wiped clean, unworried and undisappointed.

When we left the motel, we camped for a few days on a forested site in a provincial campground, having borrowed a tent from the Duprées. From there, we went for our final weekend to the Hagues' orchard, where the peaches were ripe and the harvest underway. Handmade wooden ladders leaned against the trees, shifted around by local farm-hands, many of them kind slow-moving old men. The peaches were huge and warm, and I was allowed to pick one anytime I wanted.

Those peaches were the highlight of my visit to the orchard. I think my father's was the peace he discovered in the cool clear mornings, when I'd find him sitting outside on the porch no matter how early I got up. He didn't have a book or a newspaper but sat there smiling mildly. Bunny's favourite was the Saturday night dance at the local community hall, where my parents went with the Hagues. A live band was playing, and my father promised Bunny beforehand that he would dance, which is all she wanted in the world.

They left me with the Hagues' daughters, who were fourteen and fifteen. The older girl wanted to be a hairdresser, and after discussing the shape of my face with her sister, she said she was going to give me an Audrey Hepburn pixie cut. She sat me on a couple of dictionaries on a kitchen chair and flipped a towel around my shoulders professionally, even though I was looking at the refrigerator instead of a mirror. My hair wasn't very long but she cut it shorter, and in the morning when I came downstairs, Bunny said "Oh, oh, oh," like the chug of a train. When I got to a mirror, I was just as pleased. I thought I looked more like *Leave It to Beaver* than Audrey Hepburn, but that didn't matter. What mattered was that I was becoming more firmly Tink.

Then we went home, and the brilliant late August days rolled on peaceably. I'd forgotten about sirens, and Bunny's garden was perfect even before she weeded and trimmed. I spent most of the day in the yard or down the creek, having little call on my time with Norman still at camp. His father had never left to go back east, even though summer school had finished. I saw him randomly around the neighbourhood, and was even more surprised to see Mrs. Manners visit him one day without even needing to spy. I'd forgotten her too, but there she was, walking openly down the street in the late afternoon as if she hadn't a care in the world before turning matter-of-factly down the Hortons' walk. And that was the end of my summer vacation, or at least the best part of it, although I couldn't have said why.

By that time, we'd reached the dog days of summer. Bunny accused me of mooning around, which was true, and told me I needed to get back to school, which wasn't. This tended to happen toward the end of every August, but for once Bunny did something about it. To my surprise, she invited Judy Shribman over to play. Bunny didn't give me any warning, and I was deep in a comic book when Judy and her mother arrived. Mrs. Shribman sat down for a cup of coffee with Bunny in the living room, and since it was raining, they told us to go downstairs and play.

"You didn't invite me, did you?" Judy asked, as we walked into the rec room.

I couldn't lie, and couldn't think of a non-lie, either. Stuff, Norman had said, when I'd asked what his mother would do back east, but it wasn't the right answer for Judy. She and I exchanged a sideways glance, both of us knowing that our mothers had decided we ought to be friends, no doubt for insulting reasons, and that it wouldn't work.

"I brought my Barbie," she said eventually. Because I was the hostess, and Bunny had drilled these things into me, I went to get mine out of the toy box, where it was jumbled in among skipping ropes and boxes of Lego, building blocks and my soccer ball. The way I pulled it out of the mess surprised Judy, whose dark-haired Barbie was in a plastic lunchbox case with several different outfits. Mine was the blond Barbie that Lucy Oliver had given me for my birthday, and her dress had got pushed off one shoulder.

"I don't have a dollhouse," I said, trying to fix the dress.

"That's okay," Judy said. "My Barbie just wants to invite your Barbie for a gossip."

I was surprised at her confidence. Judy was never in charge when she was with her best friends, Jeannie Stevens and Cathy Cole. I supposed we had been thrown together since the Stevens and Cole families had gone on vacation together the previous Saturday, driving south in their identical wood-panelled station wagons, headed for a Heritage Hotel on the Oregon side of the Columbia River. I hadn't registered until this moment that the Shribmans hadn't gone with them.

"So you don't have any furniture either," Judy said.

She went silent to think, then headed over to my toy chest. Taking out some blocks, she set up her Barbie and mine on make-do chairs. I watched her silently. Judy's dark hair was tied back with a red ribbon, and she had big blue eyes and liked pretty things: crinolines and tortoiseshell kittens and invisible cups and saucers.

Pouring some invisible coffee, she asked, "What does your Barbie think about Mrs. O'Neill?"

I wasn't used to talking like that, but remembered that I was the hostess.

"I guess she likes Mrs. O'Neill's candy apples at Halloween."

"But what does she think about the weight gain?" Judy asked. "When it turns out that Mrs. O'Neill isn't expecting."

Too many candy apples? But Judy didn't seem to need an answer, and carried on to say, "My Barbie thinks she needs to go on a diet *right now*."

In the absence of Jeannie Stevens and Cathy Cole, all the neighbourhood gossip seemed to have backed up inside Judy, pushing against a Columbia River dam that burst into my rec room. I didn't need to say anything. Judy just made her Barbie drink from her invisible cup and talk. What did my Barbie think about the Howards on Egerton Crescent having a Mongolian for their Late Child? And say they were keeping him instead of putting him in an institution where he belonged. And didn't my Barbie think Andy Manners was going to disgrace her family any day with that *mouth*. Did I hear what she'd called her tennis coach at the country club? Well, Judy's Barbie couldn't possibly repeat it.

Of course, Andy's mother had disgraced the family too, with her red hair like a Scarlet Letter. Sneaking over to visit Jack Horton while his poor wife was back east, she *said* visiting friends. Except Mrs. Manners didn't even bother to sneak around anymore now that everyone knew about the affair except her poor husband. Although he probably *did* know because of the way he lifted a glass. Not that Judy's Barbie thought that Mr. Manners was a very nice man. She knew you were supposed to feel sympathetic, but he'd called out "Jew banker" when Judy's father had honked his horn after Mr. Manners didn't notice that the light had turned green. And Mrs. Enderby on Bennington was such an awful cook that when the Eisenstadts went over for dinner, Mrs. Eisenstadt took a bite and said, "Pre-masticated cauliflower."

Judy left a pause, finally wanting an answer.

My head in a flurry, I told her, "My Barbie doesn't know what pre-masticated means."

"Well, she's only little. It means overcooked. Your Barbie doesn't know it because her grandmother is such a good cook. She makes excellent ginger snap cookies. What does your Barbie think about her aunt expecting?"

I was entirely confused, wondering if she meant my sister, which led to a pause.

"Well, she's showing now, so you can say. Do they want a boy or a girl?"

"Girl?"

"A girl then two boys," Judy agreed. "People want that." Even though her family was two boys and a girl. "But of course she had all that trouble getting knocked up. So probably they want a boy first, really, in case it's a Lonely Only."

"What's a Scarlet Letter?" I asked.

Judy didn't seem to know the answer.

"My Barbie doesn't know what an affair means, either."

"More coffee?" Judy asked, pouring it invisibly.

When the Shribmans finally left, I threw myself in a kitchen chair, telling my mother, "That was far too much work."

"She seems like such a nice girl," Bunny said.

"She's mean," I said. "Talking about Mrs. O'Neill getting fat and the Howards putting away their little baby and Mrs. Enderby's pre-masticated cauliflower." Mimicking her: "What does *your* Barbie think?"

Bunny's mouth did a twitch, and then another, but she couldn't contain it.

"Joyce Enderby is a *dreadful* cook!" she carolled. "Don't tell your father I said that. And Ellen Shribman is discreet. Your friend Judy didn't get that from her." Thinking it through. "Isn't Judy close to Cathy Cole? She probably gets it from Josie Cole. Josie couldn't stifle if her life depended on it."

"Judy Shribman is *not* my friend."

"Not yet," Bunny said absentmindedly, before breaking out again.

Norman arrived home four days later, when the Pacific National Exhibition was underway. Both these things were lucky. The dog days of summer had been going on for too long, and not only because of Judy Shribman. Walter Cronkite had started to look worried on the *CBS Evening News*, reading reports I didn't understand about Soviet Russia. People around the world were marching against the Bomb, and against testing the Bomb atmospherically. Seeing pictures of the mushroom clouds and the signs at the marches brought back my jitters, since I knew that nothing was more likely when you took a test than to make a mistake.

There was also my disappointment about the PNE. For the past few years, I'd gone twice, once with Debbie and once with my parents. This year, even though Debbie came over quite frequently, she never mentioned the PNE. I knew it was impolite to beg for an invitation, although I made a point of meeting her at the door with puppy-dog eyes. But Debbie only swiped her hand over my pixie cut and called me pet. After they made coffee, she and Bunny settled down on the living room chesterfield to whisper, with Bunny telling me to play outside.

"Pet," Debbie said, not snickers or nickens or Tinker. When she said it again at a family barbecue in the backyard, my brother's eyes flicked between us, although he usually paid no attention to sisters, either her or me. As Bunny and Debbie drifted in and out of the kitchen, carrying chicken to be barbecued, I spent my time kicking the grass, until I accidentally stood with my arms crossed beside my brother's wooden lawn chair.

Bob was slouched down, hands in his pants pockets, his long legs crossed out in front of him.

"She was just practising on you," he said. "Don't take it personally."

I flopped down on the wide arm of his chair, scratching a mosquito bite, not knowing what he meant. Bob glanced up at me.

"Practising how to be a mom. Handling a *nickens*."

I knew he was right and felt stung. "So I guess you're doing it now, too."

"Nah, I don't want kids."

"It's probably just as well."

Bob gave me a warning look. Or at least, a look we'd learned to be warned by. Bunny would have said, *I was only agreeing with you. Pacify him*, she'd tell my father. To me, she'd say, *Your brother wants it both ways.*

"I've got eyes in my head," I told him. I'd forgotten until this moment that the Bomb was likely to melt them, although it came back to me now.

"You've really got a mood on, haven't you?"

"I guess I take after you."

"Maybe in more ways than one."

I didn't like that, which amused him, and he cupped an invisible crystal ball between his hands. "I can see into the future," he said in a wavering voice. "You're going to do whatever you want to in this life."

I thought that was the point of being an adult, that you could give yourself permission.

"Not like Dad," he said, dropping his hands. "Boxing himself in with scruples."

We both looked at our father, who was putting the chicken on the barbecue.

"I don't know what scruples are."

"That makes two of us," Bob said. "Which is useful for a lawyer."

He levered himself up in his chair and smiled crookedly to himself, not taking his eyes off our father.

"They're a definition of being civilized, really."

Norman was a welcome relief after my puzzle of a brother, running over as soon as he got home, bursting through the front door, scarcely knocking, desperate to see his fish. Another of his neon tetras had been lost and nibbled a few days before. After some consideration, I'd decided to replace it with one of mine, not wanting to spoil his return. I chose the one with the nearest markings, but they were all pretty much identical, and I didn't think even Norman would be able to tell the difference between them.

The bigger news was that there had been a birth of swordtail babies in his tank, tiny see-through minnows hiding up in the weeds. His female swordtail had started to get chubby and then actively fat. I'd learned a few things from the Debbie situation, and even before the swordtail babies had been born, I'd worked out that Norman's female was expecting, not just eating too many candy apples like Mrs. O'Neill.

"Oh, wow," Norman said when I showed him, leaning over the tank. Norman looked different after his summer outdoors, taller and hardier, with a deep tan and bleached-out hair. He looked so much older that I realized I felt older too, although I couldn't have said why.

It might have been the air raid sirens. But the sirens also made me feel younger, especially at night, so I spent my time moving back and forth between the person I would be and the person I'd been without ever stopping in the present. Watching Norman watch the fish, I also realized that while he looked older, he sounded the same as he always had. I thought maybe Norman would always be the same person, just taller.

"How was camp?" I asked.

"See, I can sell them and save up for a bigger tank."

"Judy Shribman said your mum was visiting friends."

"Sixteen babies. That's four whole dollars! And I didn't even have to do a thing."

I only got more out of him a few days later when my parents took us to the PNE. Since there were two of us and we were almost ten years old, my parents gave me five dollars and Norman's parents had given him a two-dollar bill, meaning we had seven to split, and my father said we should go enjoy ourselves. We only had to check in every two hours at the bumper cars, where they would be waiting. Norman wore a watch, which made this possible.

It was early afternoon. We wandered among families eating candy apples and candy floss and buttery bags of popcorn; among teenagers clutching big plush toys, and little kids who butted into us like miniature horses as they galloped toward the baby rides. Left alone, we could crane our necks up at the Tilt-A-Whirl and shiver at the long-falling screams coming off the giant roller coaster, which we said we would go on and knew we wouldn't. Instead, we wandered inside the buildings past corrals of farm animals and automobiles, and paused when we were back outside to watch the logging show, where lumberjacks like Uncle Punk fought a logrolling competition in a square manmade pond.

I liked the midway best, even better than the rides, and led Norman toward a covered aisle of booths with bored jokey carnies shouting at us from both sides. "Hey-ya, hey-ya, hey-ya, little gentleman and lady." But Norman wouldn't let me try my luck, saying the games were rigged. Instead, he insisted we walk along watching people throw rings at bowling pins and missing, throw basketballs at hoops and missing, throw darts at balloons and missing (dull points, Norman said) until I had to admit he was right.

"Did you like summer camp?" I asked, speaking loudly above the excitement.

"It was okay," he called back.

"What did you like best?"

"Swimming." Norman stopped in the middle of the midway, making people eddy around us. "You could float in the lake and it held you right up, and your leg didn't get tired."

I wondered if his leg would get too tired for the PNE the way it had for Halloween, although he'd been carrying a brace around then.

"What *didn't* you like?"

"Crafts." Norman looked disgusted and started walking again. "And campfire songs. 'Kumbaya.'"

I got that, catching up to him. "Mrs. Culver's daughter made us sing 'Kumbaya' at Sunday School. It's pretty boring. Like 'Jesus Loves Me.' Did they make you sing 'Jesus Loves Me'?"

From the look on Norman's face, I could see that Jesus hadn't been on the menu. It made me wonder if he'd gone to a communist camp. They wouldn't care if Jesus loved them since Jesus wasn't a communist. At least, I didn't think so. He hadn't been born in Russia.

"Bingo!" Norman cried.

I was confused until he pointed to the Bingo tent ahead.

"Isn't Bingo rigged, too?"

"It gives you a chance," Norman said, heading over quickly. "All you need is a chance. My grandma took me to Bingo in Prince Albert when we were driving to camp."

Prince Albert?

"Saskatchewan," he said, as we reached the tent.

"Is that where your mother comes from?"

"Not really," Norman replied, and led the way inside.

Bunny had taken me to Bingo in other years at the PNE. I liked the shadows inside the tent, and the smell of the sawdust covering the floor, and the lady who sat on a platform at the front pulling balls out of a tumbler. It was often the same lady. She called the numbers into a microphone without taking the cigarette out of her mouth, which was an enviable skill.

"Under the B, five," the lady called. Norman and I bought our cards and corn kernels and took them to a table near the front, where we sat down to wait for the next game.

"Is your mum getting ready to be our teacher this year?" I asked.

Norman surprised me by drooping.

"She can't. Mr. Eisenstadt told her yesterday she isn't allowed to have her son in her own class." A painful pause. "My mum says that's the correct decision."

"And me?" I asked, panicking.

"He says my mum can't have you, either. Not when you come over to our place. Mr. Eisenstadt knows you do. We both get the new teacher."

That was a lot to process before a Bingo game.

"What's her name?" I asked. "The new one."

"Miss Something," Norman said.

Hope flared. "Maybe Miss Atkinson didn't get married."

"Probably she did. My mum gave her a bud vase," he said, at a call of, "Under the O, sixty."

"Anyhow, this lady's old. She worked for Mr. Eisenstadt a long time ago, and now he's bringing her back. My mum says it's hard to find qualified teachers. There are so many new schools, everybody needs them."

I didn't want an old teacher, and drooped a little myself before remembering that my grade one teacher had been old and she was nice. Miss Barnes. A sweet little old maid, my mother had called her, not being fully aware of the frequent descent of the Barnesian ruler on male knuckles. But Miss Barnes still taught grade one, so they couldn't be bringing her back.

"Bingo!" someone called.

Norman and I turned to look at the excited old lady waving her hand.

"Maybe it's her," I said.

"There's no reason it couldn't be," Norman replied, and we watched the lady's win being verified until the microphone crackled up front.

"All right. Eleven o'clock special," the Bingo Lady called. "What have we got?" She waggled her cigarette between her teeth at the prize booth, where the man held up something red. "A three-piece luggage set. A fine red luggage set. Who's got the travel bug?"

From the sound of it, everybody did.

"If you're ready," she called, and people went silent, "Under the I, sixteen." And without ceremony, "Under the B, four."

The extraordinary thing was, Norman had the I, he had the B, and he had the O that came after it. He didn't get the next call, or far from all of them, but he got a surprising number, and quickly covered his squares with corn kernels. No one yelled Bingo, and in the increasingly intent silence, Norman's card was filling up.

Mine wasn't. At least, I didn't get very many calls by the time I stopped paying attention, when Norman was looking down at a card with only three squares left uncovered.

"Under the *B*, number eight."

Two squares.

"Under the *O*, sixty-one."

Someone startled us by shouting, "Bin . . ." And then, "Excuse me, please."

"Under the *G*," the Bingo Lady called, giving the man the stink eye. "Number fifty-two."

Norman didn't have fifty-two, but he had five, under the *B*, which meant he had only one square left.

"Under the *N*, forty-four."

And there it was. Norman's last empty square. He was so stunned, I had to be the one to yell, "Bingo!"

Norman had won the eleven o'clock special after only one game, and he'd won it under the letter *N*, which probably meant something magical. We'd paid for three games, but as the man verified Norman's card, we decided to get out while the going was good. Padding across the sawdust to the prize booth, we picked up three suitcases of diminishing size, the three bears in red leatherette. Norman took the big one and I took the medium and small ones, and we left the tent to batter our way through the midway crowd.

"Miss Oliphant," Norman remembered. We were taking the suitcases back toward the Modern Living building, where I thought we'd find my parents. "My mum calls it a regrettable name for a teacher."

"Miss Elephant," I agreed.

Norman stopped in the middle of the crowd, which pushed every which way around us. "I was supposed to tell you her name but I wasn't supposed to joke about it."

"She's got a trunk and you've got suitcases," I said, since no one had forbidden me from joking. Norman hunched his shoulders in amusement, and we continued on our way.

"What have you got there?" my father asked, tall enough to see us battering our way through into Modern Living crowd, suitcases in hand.

We explained, talking one on top of the other until my mother said, "You know they're nesting suitcases? You can put one inside the other."

Norman and I exchanged an astonished look. Eyes as wide as saucers, Andy Manners would have said. And it was true: life didn't get any better than this.

12

I felt no particular trepidation as I walked to school. Norman dragged his feet at my side, in his case not because of either trepidation or polio, but his continuing disappointment that he wasn't in his mum's class. It was September 4, the Tuesday after Labour Day.

The morning was warm and breezy, and I liked my grade five shoes, two-tone Oxfords in brown and cream leather. I also had a new lunchbox featuring Mr. Ed, the talking horse on TV. Since Mr. Ed was brown and cream, the lunchbox matched my Oxfords in the way Bunny liked her purse to match her shoes. Even my school uniform was new, a navy blue tunic and white blouse. I felt ready to take on the school year, even with sirens.

The new teacher was writing her name on the board as we walked into the classroom, her back to us, the chalk squeaking. At first glance, nothing worried me about Miss Oliphant, aside from the possibility of calling her Miss Elephant. I had more important worries, and chose a desk at the end of a middle row as far away from the window as possible, protecting myself from blindness in case of a nuclear explosion.

Miss Oliphant wore a tweed skirt and twin-set sweaters of the type worn by every lady teacher in the city. It made me wonder if there was a store where only teachers could buy clothes. Maybe they even sold teachers. I felt happy at the thought when the teacher turned around, lowering her piece of chalk.

It was Mrs. Persson. She'd changed her name, but it was Mrs. Persson, my hated grade three teacher. A volcano erupted inside me. I couldn't see through the whirlwind of sparks, or feel anything besides the lava flow in my chest, going dizzy from nothing more than a glimpse of Mrs. Persson's broad, strong face. She'd lost so much weight that I hadn't recognized her from the back. Permed her hair, got new glasses, what Bunny called harlequin glasses. But it was Mrs. Persson, reserves of scorn and sarcasm packed into her pigeon breast, ready to burst out unpredictably.

"Good morning, children," she said, looking around the room without seeming to notice me. "I'm Miss Oliphant, and you will confine your jokes about my name to the playground. I know a few of you"—still not looking my way—"although far from all of you, from the time I taught here before. So after the announcement, we'll start with attendance, and I can put faces to your names."

The loudspeaker crackled as if she had ordered it to, and we sang "God Save the Queen." When the Lord's Prayer began, I prayed fervently. Norman was the one to look at me, not Mrs. Persson, Miss Oliphant—the teacher—as I asked the Lord to deliver me from evil.

Attendance. In my hot confusion, I heard "Here" all around, including from Norman, and managed one myself. Judy Shribman was in the class but not Jeannie Stevens and Cathy Cole, and I felt a flash of sympathy for Judy, seeing that her trio would break apart.

There were a few people I didn't know, but the only new girl who drew my attention was Mary Anderson. The fact her name was Mary had been a relief when the teacher called it at the start of attendance. In our initial grade three attendance, when she'd got to my name, Mrs. Persson had called, "Mary Parker."

I hadn't known she meant me until half the class had turned to stare.

"Mary Alice, ma'am," I had said belatedly.

"Well, that's unnecessary, isn't it?" Mrs. Persson had replied. "Mary will do."

She'd been ready to call the next name when I put up my hand. Without waiting for her to nod, I said, "If you don't want to call me Mary Alice, ma'am, you can call me Tink."

I was aware of walking the boundary between information and insolence. It was such a narrow path that I felt brave walking it. But she was in the wrong, and I knew it.

"That's not a good first step, is it, Mary?" Mrs. Persson had asked. She didn't take her eyes off me as she called, "John Roark."

The strangest part of my grade three year was that Mrs. Persson insisted on calling me Mary all the way through. I heard my father tell my mother one night in great exasperation that Angela Persson had no sense of how much was enough. From what he heard, she aspired to be a principal, but she kept undercutting herself with her lack of political acumen, or at least by her failure to understand the uses of either compromise or insincerity.

"Dog with a bone," Bunny had replied, which is the part I understood.

During our first awful grade five recess, I stood with Norman at the edge of the schoolyard. Getting Mrs. Persson back was such a blow that I felt miserable and small and unlucky. It had never occurred to me before that you could behave well and things could still go wrong. And with a teacher like Miss Elephant, I knew things would keep going wrong, and that I would pass an unlucky year.

"She's got a real Mary this time," Norman said, trying to console me. "Maybe she'll hate Mary Anderson instead."

"Teachers aren't supposed to hate pupils."

"Okay," Norman agreed.

He couldn't seem to think of anything else to say, and we kicked dirt for a while on the path that ran around the schoolyard. We would soon be playing marbles there. I enjoyed marbles, and I was trying to let the thought of them cheer me up when I realized that Mrs. Horton was watching us from the playground.

Seeing that I'd noticed her, she walked over.

"Is there a problem, Tink?"

Under her crown of braids, Mrs. Horton looked more curious than sympathetic, but it was enough to choke me up.

"She had Miss Oliphant before, in grade three," Norman said. "She was mean, and Tink didn't like her."

"I thought you told Tink she was getting her grade three teacher," Mrs. Horton said.

"I told her we were getting Miss Oliphant," Norman said, bristling to an extent that made me look up. "How was I supposed to know she had her in grade three? You never said."

"I would have thought I did," Mrs. Horton answered mildly, before turning to me. "In any case, Tink, you knew you were getting Miss Oliphant. Which *is* rather a memorable name."

"She used to call herself Mrs. Persson."

Mrs. Horton didn't seem to know that, and thought for a while.

"I imagine she called herself Mrs. Persson because it was her name," she said finally. "This should have been handled better, Tink, and I'm sorry. I shouldn't have been used as a conduit to get a message to your parents."

Her vocabulary made me even more miserable.

"I don't know what a conduit is."

"A sewer pipe," Norman said. I was shocked by the degree of dislike in his voice. It wasn't his mum's fault she couldn't be his teacher.

"That's enough, Norman," Mrs. Horton said.

"People not hanging onto their husbands," Norman sang, as if he was a commercial. Looking straight at her, he chanted, "Mrs. Persson then Miss Oliphant. Divorce on the table."

Mrs. Horton looked down. When she looked up, she held my eyes steadily, as if I was the only one in the world.

"We'd better get you to the office, Tink. I'll tell them you're sick, and they can call your mother. Norman," she added, and glanced at him briefly. "You can do whatever the hell you want."

Mrs. Horton swivelled and walked so quickly toward the school I had to run to keep up.

When my father got home from work that night, he was perturbed about something that I didn't understand. I picked up "Cuba" and "White House announcement" as my parents talked briefly in the kitchen, but for once I had no interest in eavesdropping. I was lying on my bed reading comics, and it wasn't long before my father's slippered footsteps approached my room. He knocked and came in, sitting down on the side of my bed. After a brief silence, he put his hand on my forehead to see if I had a fever.

"I've never liked surprises myself," he said, taking his hand away.

"I need to go into Mrs. Horton's class," I said.

My father looked at me steadily. "I called Mr. Eisenstadt from work. You can go into Mrs. Horton's class if you want. *But*," he cautioned, as I elbowed up excitedly, "Norman can't."

I slumped back down.

"You have a choice, Mary Alice," he said. "You can stay with Norman, or you can transfer into Mrs. Horton's class. It's your decision, and I think you can see it comes with consequences either way."

I felt so hot I might really have had a fever, and choked on my words. "That's not fair."

"This hasn't been handled very well. But I would say you've been given a fair choice." When I was about to protest, my father held up his hand. "That doesn't make it an easy one. Fair and easy aren't the same thing."

It all spilled out in a jumble. How I didn't know why Mr. Eisenstadt had to go and bring her back. How I didn't know why he hadn't found another teacher at the teacher store. How everyone knew that Mrs. Persson was mean. Miss Elephant Oliphant with her big fat trunk. When the fact she'd got a divorce meant she couldn't even hang onto her husband . . .

"Mary Alice! Where on Earth did you get that?"

I looked away, but had to mumble, "Norman."

My father seemed pained and didn't answer.

"His father and Mrs. Manners are having an affair," I said, my personal dam of gossip bursting. "Judy Shribman says so. She says everybody knows. She says Mrs. Manners dyed her hair like a Scarlet Letter, which means divorce is on the table. And Norman figured out that Mrs. Persson got divorced, and he hates it because his mum can't hang onto her husband, either."

My father pushed his glasses up on his forehead to rub his eyes. "Oh my good Lord."

"What's a Scarlet Letter?"

"How much of this is from Norman and how much did Judy Shribman tell you?" Bunny asked, coming into the room. Breaking the rules of eavesdropping, by the way. I didn't like it and didn't want to answer, not least because Bunny was the one to ask and not my father.

"I said I won't be friends with Judy Shribman. Even though she's in my class again, and Cathy Cole and Jeannie Stevens got Mrs. Horton." Thinking of Judy sitting there all alone made me feel guilty. "Okay, so she likes kittens. But she likes Barbie better."

Bunny had no answer. After a while, my father said, "*The Scarlet Letter* is a novel by Nathaniel Hawthorne about Puritans in the old days. It's been a long time since I read it, but the main character is a woman who has to wear a scarlet-coloured letter on her dress, an *A* that stands for adultery. It means everyone knows who she is and they can shun her."

"'Thou shalt not commit adultery,'" I said. We'd learned that much in Sunday School. "What's adultery?"

"It's the same as having an affair," my father said. "Which you seem to have heard of."

"Judy Shribman never told me what affair means, either."

My father cleared his throat and stood up.

"I think you're going to have to handle this one," he told Bunny.

"Too early," Bunny said, and my father stopped in place, looking trapped.

"But it's happening." I sat up further and clasped my feet, which kept me balanced. "I saw how Mrs. Manners goes over to Norman's place. I mean, how she did when Norman was at camp. Several times."

"So what do you think that means, Big Eyes?" Bunny asked.

"That she isn't supposed to?"

"Okay. So there's no mystery, is there?"

In living colour. But I didn't even know what to ask, and stayed upset until my father sat down on the bed again, sighing.

"You're right in saying your teacher got divorced."

"Norman said."

"Norman said. If we're establishing a chain of provenance."

"What's . . . ?"

"Divorce," he said, interrupting me, "is an upsetting thing. It happens when there's disappointment in a marriage, and the disappointment may have been going on for a long time. When you first met Mrs. Persson, it turns out that she was suffering badly from disappointment. She shouldn't have brought that into the classroom, and you know Mr. Eisenstadt and I discussed her behaviour at the time, even if I didn't realize what caused it. But he tells me that she's come through her divorce. And even though Mr. Eisenstadt and I have had our differences, he's right in saying that people deserve a second chance. He's giving her one, and you might find you have a different teacher if you give her a chance as well."

"She isn't any different," I said. "She just got new glasses and a perm."

"A perm, did she?" Bunny asked. "The last one in the universe."

"Except Mrs. Horton."

"Fair enough."

"Different in other ways," my father continued, looking helpless. "She's strict, I know. But she prepares her students well. It turns out that your class has some ground to make up, and she's the best option."

I didn't know what he meant.

"I know you liked Miss Atkinson," he said. "I did, too. But there's some question about how much of the curriculum she got around to teaching. So there's a fair bit of ground to make up, and Miss Oliphant turns out to be the best available option. You need to stay on top of the curriculum, Mary Alice, to get into university."

I hadn't known I was going to university. I thought he was the one who'd wanted to.

"Garbage at their age," Bunny said. "The girl gave them the basics. Who cares if they know the capital of Nigeria?"

"Muriel . . ."

"What's Nigeria?" I asked.

"These endless questions, Mary Alice . . ."

"What do you think it is?" Bunny interrupted.

I tried to put two and two together. "If it has a capital, it has to be a country."

"So if you need to know the name of the capital, what do you do?"

"Look up Nigeria in the encyclopedia?"

"I rest my case."

My father looked amused. Confounded, but amused.

"Mrs. Horton is a good teacher as well," he said. "Mr. Eisenstadt says she's excellent. So it's on the table, Mary Alice. Whether you want to transfer into her class."

Norman had said "on the table." I'd repeated it. Now my father was saying it, as if he'd picked it up from Norman through me. I found that interesting. I also wondered who was disappointed in the Hortons' marriage, whether it was Mr. Horton or Mrs. Horton, and how Mrs. Manners came into it. Not that I was clear what it meant for divorce to be on the table.

Then I remembered transferring into Mrs. Horton's class was a possibility, a decision not yet taken. So maybe the Hortons' divorce was only a possibility, too. It frightened Norman terribly, I could see.

"I can't leave Norman on his own."

I hadn't known I was going to say that.

"Feed him to the elephants," I added, trying to joke it away.

"I've always liked elephants," my father said.

"Don't," Bunny told him, and turned to me. "If that's what you want, you've got a case. I'd be just as happy if Norman wasn't your friend. But since he is," she said, talking over my objections, "you'd better stick by him. If old prune face gets too bad, you can change teachers later on. That stays on the table as far as I'm concerned. Now can we drop this, please?"

My father and I both kept silent. I was questioning my decision. Maybe he was, too.

"Now isn't forever," Bunny said. "Especially when dinner's getting burned."

Meatloaf. We ate at the kitchen table, and I didn't notice that we weren't watching Walter Cronkite. I didn't care where we ate or what we ate. I usually liked meatloaf, especially with ketchup, but this time I could barely choke it down.

As I failed to sleep that evening, I heard my parents talking in the kitchen. They spoke quietly at first, so I knew they were talking about me. But gradually their voices grew louder. They probably thought I was asleep, although it was possible they'd forgotten about me, which was worrying.

By this time, my parents were talking about the White House announcement. From what I could pick up, President Kennedy's spokesman had read it this evening, Washington time, and it was so important the whole world was talking about it. The spokesman said that as far as the president knew, there were no Soviet troops in Cuba. There weren't any ground-to-ground missiles, either. My father said this meant the president thought the Soviets might have put both of them in there. Why else would he have brought it up?

"Logically," I heard him say.

"I thought we were talking about politics."

"We know the Americans have some pretty impressive spy planes. So, logically, the CIA was flying U-2s over Cuba and got a pretty good look. I imagine he's giving Nikita Khrushchev a warning to stop whatever it is that he's up to."

"You don't mean nuclear missiles?" Bunny asked, which hit me like a truck.

There was a long pause.

"One thing I learned overseas," my father said finally. "'Battle plan' is an oxymoron. You can set battles in motion. But no matter how well the brass hats plan, anything can happen after that."

I pulled my pillow over my head, terrified of the Bomb. If it went off, I'd be unable to look away, since I could never look away from anything, and the window glass would shatter, and I would go blind like Helen Keller. I whimpered under my pillow, and maybe the air whimpered for me, or for itself.

"What was that?" Bunny asked.

"It's only wind in the chimney," my father replied.

Taking off the pillow, it occurred to me that I would have to behave very well to fend off disaster. I couldn't have explained it, but I always felt responsible for what was going on in the world. Step on a crack, break your father's back. I knew that was superstition, but how could you be sure it wouldn't come true? I hadn't behaved badly, and it wasn't enough. I'd still got Miss Oliphant. So I'd have to do my part against the Bomb by being perfect, and spit in my palm as a promise that I'd try.

The next morning, I walked over early to Norman's house, wanting to speak very politely to Mrs. Horton before seeing her at school. I would thank her for offering to take me in her class, even though I wasn't sure she'd been the one to make the offer, or if she even cared.

I hadn't expected Mr. Horton to open the door.

"Tinkerbell," he said.

"Tink," Norman called from inside, sounding as irritated with his dad as he'd sounded with his mum. He arrived beside Mr. Horton, struggling to put on a knapsack.

"I hear there's some drama at school, *Tink*," Mr. Horton said, ignoring Norman and leaving me even more confused. *Drama* was the word I'd given to the Hortons, or at least to what was going on behind closed curtains.

"Don't tease her, Jack." Mrs. Horton came to the door, saying what she'd said at our dinner party almost a year before, but this time impatiently. She sounded as if I'd caught them in the middle of another argument. Putting her hands on Norman's shoulders, she moved him aside, so she stood next to Mr. Horton in the doorway. She looked as if she wanted to ask me something but couldn't find the words.

"I wanted to say, Mrs. Horton," I told her, "I know you're an excellent teacher, like Mr. Eisenstadt says. But I think I'll stay with Norman in Miss Oliphant's class, if that's all right."

"Planning on herding elephants, are you, Tink?"

"Jack!"

"Good speech," he said. "Prepared it beforehand, did you?"

I shrugged, caught out. Mr. Horton had teacherly eyes not only in the back of his head, but all around it.

"So Eisenstadt said you could transfer," he said.

"To my father." Adding a little desperately, "I came to get Norman."

"So what was your problem with the formerly sibilant Mrs. Persson?" he asked, refusing to stand down.

"Jack, that's really uncalled-for."

"Tink can give us the scoop on the elephant. If Norman's going to be in her class."

I didn't know what to say, but Norman saved me by answering from behind them.

"She called her Mary all grade three."

Neither of his parents turned, but they went alert as dogs to listen.

"Not even Mary Alice," he went on, "which she said was unnecessary. And when Tink forgot and turned in a test saying Mary Alice, she took off marks. So Tink got mad and turned in a test saying Tink, and teacher gave her zero."

His parents' faces took an identical look of distaste, shifting invisibly in the doorway so their bodies fit more naturally together.

"Then Nancy Workman forgot to put her name on it at all," Norman said. "A composition they'd worked hard on. And Mrs. Oliphant held up the paper saying so many mean things that Nancy Workman wet her pants right in the middle of the floor."

Seeing his mum wince, I assured her, "It's all right, Mrs. Horton. Nancy Workman doesn't wet her pants anymore. She went to see a doctor. She doesn't even wet them during air raid sirens. I guess she's in your class now. She's really, really good at arithmetic."

Norman's parents went quiet for a moment, then his dad said, "It's good of you to say so, Tink."

His voice sounded less like a slangy Marlon Brando and more as if Mr. Horton might be good himself, at least underneath. I wondered if he was going to shake hands with me the way he'd shaken hands with my father. Instead, he stepped aside, bumping into Mrs. Horton.

"Jack! My foot!"

"Always in the way."

They glared at each other with such renewed irritation that divorce climbed back onto the table like a little gnome. Without saying goodbye, Norman pushed between them and came outside. As we walked down Connington, I couldn't sing the *Twilight Zone* song, not about his parents. I couldn't think of anything that would help, either.

Norman shifted something on his shoulder, which distracted me.

"Isn't that your mum's knapsack?"

"It's mine now," he said. "For all the homework we're going to get. Since Miss Atkinson was such a lousy teacher."

Now he sounded as if he disliked me, too. I controlled myself, intent on being perfect, and tried to concentrate on whether Norman had inherited the knapsack. I wasn't sure if you could inherit something when the previous owner hadn't died. Nor did I think you could get hand-me-downs from your parents the way you could from an older brother or sister. Being unable to find the right word upset me. I was going to have to find the right words in class, picking them like sweet peas in Mrs. Milewski's garden.

Mrs. Horton still grew sweet peas. She'd found she liked gardening so much that a friend had come in from over town once a week to weed while Mrs. Horton was back east. Mr. Horton had mowed the lawn, at least when he remembered, or when a neighbour passed a remark about the wheat fields of Saskatchewan. But the lady had weeded, never introducing herself but wearing sandals like Mrs. Horton, in her case without socks.

"Can't your parents afford to get you a new knapsack?" I asked.

"Mortgage," Norman replied.

I understood, having heard my parents talking about mortgages, which involved the bank owning everything in the house except the front doorknob.

"It makes things even worse," Norman said.

"What?" I asked, busy picturing our round brass doorknob.

"Bourgeois capitalism," Norman said. It was one of his jokes, drier than tumbleweed, although I was so far from understanding what he said that he might have been speaking French.

School was a blur those first two or three weeks as I struggled to be perfect, which chiefly meant keeping quiet. Miss Oliphant continued to ignore me and I put up my hand only occasionally, even though I knew a decent number of the answers. To keep her from suspecting us of joint stupidity, Norman often put up his hand. A verb, Miss Oliphant. The Nile, Miss Oliphant. It makes seventy-eight, he would say, and I would nod judiciously.

Yet nothing memorable happened in the classroom those first few weeks. The only thing that really happened was my family eating dinner every night in front of the *CBS Evening News*. The White House announcement had left us fixated on Cuba, and we ate downstairs on TV trays that were always set with ironed placemats. I'd heard Bunny tell Debbie she found it soothing to do the ironing. Mr. Wall, the policeman, seemed to find it soothing to dig a hole in his backyard.

Bomb shelter, I heard my father say. Hope he doesn't plan to blast when he hits bedrock.

My father laughed strangely after making his joke, his laughter gone too high. He'd also started talking more when he got home from work, although my father was usually a quiet person. This made me go alert as a grasshopper around my parents, noticing their tones of voice, their sudden busyness, and my mother's new bursts of speed.

On our first biweekly shop after the announcement, Bunny flew down the aisles, only pausing to throw food into the cart, far more of it than usual. I refrained from questions, only selecting a big bag of potato chips that she frowned at when I showed her but let me put in the cart. At the check-out counter, when the girl gave her the total, I saw the same bravery on Bunny's face as she'd shown when agreeing to pay Rosa Horton's babysitting fee on New Year's Eve. Afterward, she quickly wheeled the cart into the parking lot and crammed so many brown paper grocery bags into the trunk that she had to take a couple out so she could shut it, handing them to me to put in the back seat.

At home, we carried the groceries into the basement, not upstairs to the kitchen. Following my mother like a baby duck, I helped carry sacks of flour, powdered milk and sugar into my father's workshop. Several shelves had been cleared above the bench, which explained my father's workshop time the previous night. The heavy sacks went onto a small

cleared table nearby. Afterward, I used the stepladder to stack up bags of
dried peas above the workbench, and cans of pork and beans that Bunny
handed me, which I thought was an excellent choice, and cans of green
beans, corn and mandarin orange slices, which Bunny said contained
Vitamin C.

When we were finished, I jumped off the ladder and stepped back to
look at an impressive display, bright cans in store-like ranks lined up on
shelves against the concrete wall.

"The salt!" Bunny cried, and ran back to the car, where she found that
her restaurant-sized box of salt had tumbled out of the bag into the dark
back end of the trunk.

Climbing back on the ladder, putting the salt beside a bottle of yeast,
I had no real sense of what we'd done, but I knew I wouldn't like the
answer if I asked. Why did we stop at the drugstore on the way home, and
what were iodine tablets, anyway? Why were there jugs of water under
the bench? Why was the camping stove there, too, instead of under the
stairs where it belonged? They hadn't yet explained that the workshop
had been blasted into the side of the mountain. What I was seeing were
the thick concrete retaining walls holding up the house, making it a bomb
shelter as useful as any Mr. Wall could dig. Or as useless, once the bombs
started to fall.

The shopping trip came not after President Kennedy's first announcement, but after Chairman Khrushchev gave his answering statement a
week later. I only heard it over dinner that night from Walter Cronkite,
although Bunny already knew, having picked it up from the radio earlier
that day. Part of the strangeness we were suffering came from the time
difference, the West Coast lagging three hours behind Washington D.C.
and half a day behind Moscow.

The American provocations, Mr. Khrushchev said that night, could plunge us into World War Three. Or as Walter Cronkite put it, "Into the disaster of a universal nuclear war with the use of thermonuclear weapons."

I realized that must have been what sent Bunny flying to the supermarket. The words began to echo in my head. The disaster of a universal nuclear war. Disaster. War. Nuclear . . .

"He's lying," I burst out.

"Quiet! I want to hear this!"

My father never talked to me like that, and I shrank into silence.

"Our nuclear weapons are so powerful in their explosive force," Mr. Khrushchev said, or an American voice said over his photograph, "and the Soviet Union has such powerful rockets to carry these nuclear warheads, that there is no need to search for sites for them beyond the boundaries of the Soviet Union."

He seemed to mean Cuba. I desperately wanted to ask if that's what he was saying, but I remained still until Walter Cronkite finally told us, "And that's the way it is." He always signed off that way, although I took very little reassurance anymore in the world being the way it was.

My father turned off the TV, then looked around the rec room as if he'd lost something. When his eye landed on me, he went still as a deep well.

"Are they talking about this at school, Mary Alice?" he asked.

No one said much, at least not much that I had heard. But I didn't think it would get us anywhere to mention eavesdropping, much less the way I was keeping a close eye on both him and Bunny. Instead, I answered with some dignity. "Do I have to make a chain of provenance?"

A ghost of amusement in my father's eyes. But only a ghost, and I realized that World War Three was on the table after all.

"Have they been talking about this at school, Mary Alice?" he insisted.

"I don't talk anymore. Not in class, anyhow. I'm being perfect."

The word seemed to vibrate in the air. Bells vibrated, making a beautiful sound. I was very fond of bells. But my father didn't find my answer beautiful.

"Mary Alice," he began, and didn't go on.

"Bath time," Bunny said, and sent me upstairs.

Two days later, President Kennedy told the world he wouldn't invade Cuba. Afterward, when reporting on his statement, Walter Cronkite said the president had also advised that he would do whatever he had to do if Cuba became a significant military base for the Soviet Union. As I understood it, this meant he wouldn't invade Cuba unless he did.

"It's a chess game," my father told me, as Bunny cleared the dishes.

He paused before going on.

"I know you're worried about this, Mary Alice. But the leaders are speaking to each other through their announcements. We have to hope their officials are talking behind the scenes as well. I imagine they are. But the fact that the leaders are speaking at all is a very good thing."

"About World War Three," I said.

My father looked pained, and his pause was longer this time.

"Your friends at school are probably repeating what their parents tell them," he said. "But they might have been hearing it wrong, or repeating it wrong. I'd like you to bear in mind what I said about chess. It's a game of strategy."

"You mean you tell big fat lies."

At least this made my father smile.

"There's an element of misdirecting your opponent," he said. "I can teach you to play, if you want."

I didn't see the point of learning to play chess if we were going to go blind during World War Three. It also sounded as if chess involved battle plans, when from what my father had said, battle plans were moronic. Once you started to fight, anything could happen.

I was about to say this when Bunny startled me by coming downstairs so heavily she sounded like two people. When she'd gone upstairs with the first load of dishes, her footsteps were a quick normal patter. So this was puzzling, and things got stranger when Mr. Manners followed her into the rec room. He was wearing his business suit and held a sheaf of papers. I hadn't heard him knock, although of course he would have knocked on the front door upstairs. As far as I knew, this was the first time Mr. Manners had ever set foot in our house.

"Hall Parker," he said.

"I was just in the middle of clearing," Bunny told him, embarrassed by the dirty dishes, "Mary Alice . . ."

"Communists in the schools," Mr. Manners said, and the window glass seemed to shatter.

13

B ourgeois capitalism wasn't the phrase that got Mr. Horton in trouble, even though Norman must have heard it from him, or maybe from his mother. What happened stemmed from a lesson Mr. Horton taught Cal Manners and his grade twelve history class about Old Imperialism and New Imperialism. Capitalizations were very much involved. So were Cal's suspicions, raised when he didn't find these terms in his history textbook. Looking back, I think Cal must have been as angry as his sister, since he reported his suspicions to his father as soon as Mr. Manners got home.

Old Imperialism meant the ancient Greek and Roman civilizations, Mr. Horton told the class, writing a series of dates on the chalkboard in review. New Imperialism meant the United States after the recent war. The U.S. wasn't creating an empire by occupation, he said, but through economic expansionism. The Marshall Plan in Europe, for example. Cal told his father that Mr. Horton seemed to think there was something wrong with the U.S. having a sphere of influence. Or Sphere of Influence, as I heard it at the time. And because Mr. Horton was against the United States, he had to be in favour of the Soviet Union. You were on one side or the other. And what did that make Jack Horton?

I caught all this in snatches as Mr. Manners talked to my father in the rec room. Bunny had signalled me to help clear as soon as Mr. Manners had walked in, so I bobbed in and out of the conversation as I carried dishes and condiments upstairs. I knew what he was saying anyway, and not just from the initial explosion. Mr. Manners had dropped some of his papers as he walked in, his hands shaking as if he had palsy. Picking them up, I'd found myself holding several pages of notes in handwriting I couldn't read. But there was also the newspaper clipping that showed Mrs. Horton at a protest against the Bomb, and that was explanation enough.

"I've been looking into it," Mr. Manners said, sitting down. I heard him say that several times, like an incantation. I've looked into it. I've been looking into it. He might have been reading a psalm like Mr. Culver in church. Yea though I walk through the valley of the shadow of death, I shall fear no evil, for I have looked into it.

So much was going on that I didn't understand, and as I ferried the dishes up to the kitchen, any feeling of control I'd held over my life slipped out of my hands. Instead, I got an empty sense of how much happens over everybody's heads. How the most important things in life descend without giving people any say or warning. Suddenly they're here, the way Mr. Manners was here, and afterward, it seemed as if they always had been and always would be, at least inside you.

War, accidents, love, revenge. Parents.

My father and Mr. Manners talked for a long time, only coming upstairs after Bunny had sent me to bed. As I lay there quietly, pretending to be asleep, I heard Mr. Manners speaking in a rumble as the men walked toward the front door.

"If you insist on taking that position, Captain, I'd advise you to think long and hard about the consequences."

"Good night to you, Jim."

The front door closed, and I faced a difficult decision. I could stop pretending to be asleep and ask my parents what Mr. Manners had wanted, knowing that I could always get something out of my father. On the other hand, I tended to learn the more secret parts if I eavesdropped.

"What position?" Bunny asked, as soon as Mr. Manners was down the front steps.

"I need a drink," my father said.

He never said that, and it threw me. A rattle of cupboard doors, the freezer door, ice cubes tumbling into a glass. I hunkered down behind my cracked-open door.

"He wants to take it to the principals," my father said as they settled into the living room. "Insisting that Mike Duprée fire Jack Horton and Hank Eisenstadt get rid of Marian. He wants to get the pair of them driven out of town, and he wanted me to go with him."

"He knows you and Mike are friends."

My father must have shaken his head, since he went on to say that Manners had no proof they were communists, either. "He thinks he's got a case but he's only picked up rumours. Gaps when he can't figure out what the Hortons were up to.

"I think everyone has figured out they're on the left of the political spectrum," he told Bunny. "Marian going to Ban the Bomb protests and so forth."

"Her hair," she replied. "Bohemian . . . knapsacks."

I hadn't known knapsacks could be Bohemian.

"They're different," my father agreed. "But it's not illegal to be different. It's not illegal to belong to the Communist Party, for that matter. Or to have belonged to it, if they left the Party after the Soviets invaded Hungary."

"I wouldn't be so sure of that, myself."

"Manners is right in saying they haven't mixed, but we don't really know why. Maybe they don't want to parade any problems in their marriage."

"They're snobs," Bunny said, and I could almost hear my father dislike that. My parents seemed to be balanced on the verge of arguing, which was upsetting, especially when the subject was the Hortons. It made me remember that my mother didn't like them very much.

"My point is no one really knows them," my father said, "and that includes Jim Manners. Communists or fellow travellers, we have no idea.

In any case, I think we know that's not the real reason Manners wants to get rid of them."

Bunny made a noise I recognized as reluctant agreement, familiar from the times she let me stay up later than she thought was wise.

"Everybody knows," she said. "At least around here. Why on earth does he want to draw attention to it?"

"Deflect attention," my father said.

"Why not just get a bloody divorce?"

"Maybe he doesn't want one."

Bunny thought about that for a while. "So he's going to make a fuss. Nobody can say they support communists, not these days. Get rid of them that way."

"The worst part is, he seems to have convinced himself," my father told her. "I'm afraid he's going to hold pretty tightly to his public case for getting rid of Horton. That makes this harder to handle than if it were really about ideology. Which," he said, almost to himself, "it never entirely is."

Bunny was silent for a moment and then seemed startled. "What do you mean, handle?" she asked. "I thought you told him you weren't going to take any part in this. Don't tell me you're going to help Jack Horton?"

A pause. "Not what I want."

They went silent for such a long time afterward that I grew sleepy, so I only half heard my father get up and walk over to the phone.

"Mike. A word," he said.

I wondered what the word was. Then I was gone.

The next morning, before my father left for work, I came out of the bathroom with a neutral question prepared that would raise no queries about either provenance or eavesdropping.

"What did Mr. Manners want last night, anyhow?"

"Adult business," Bunny replied, before my father could answer. She was making lunches, working at her new speed, and didn't pause while folding our sandwiches swiftly into waxed paper. "You're not going to say a word. Not to Norman. Not to anyone."

But it was *about* Norman.

"Mr. Manners dropped by for a talk, Mary Alice," my father said. "It's not something you need to worry about, or to speak about at school. Your mother's right."

"Loose lips sink ships," Bunny said.

I was overtaken by a sudden mental picture of a boat carrying me and Norman down the creek, a crazy springtime ride over the rocks. Water foamed. We shrieked the way we liked to shriek on rides at the PNE. The picture was so arresting that my father managed to snag his lunch and get out the door before I could recover.

Yet as I picked up my lunchbox, I remained worried about Norman, despite what my father had said. If Mr. Manners went to the principal, it would set off a chain reaction that would involve Norman. I had no idea of the step-by-step, but I knew something would happen, and I walked down the street accompanied by a strong feeling of dread. I'd wanted to make Norman fit in, and over the past year, slowly, invisibly, that hadn't happened. But at least he'd become an acknowledged outsider, the teacher's son, my friend, accepted and ignored.

It was a slippery position to be in. As I walked up Norman's front walk, I felt weighed down by responsibility, knowing I would have to be perfect on the playground as well as in the classroom. I needed to protect Norman by becoming so popular that no one would be able to hurt him, even more popular than Debbie's skipping rope had made me. I didn't like being popular. It was far too much work. But I'd do it for Norman, even if I couldn't tell him what I was doing or why. When he came to the door wearing his knapsack, or his mother's knapsack, their bohemian knapsack, I felt tied up in so many knots that we walked to school without saying a word.

Nothing looked different as we turned into the playground. People played tag, climbed the jungle gym, stood in groups. And as I remember, things were the same for a couple of days after that. I tried to be perfect, complimenting girls on their hopscotch skills and Lucy Oliver on her new shoes. Nothing besides the shoes seemed different, although someone must have nudged a friend as Norman and I walked past. I wouldn't have noticed the first time. The first couple of times.

Then, a week after Mr. Manners came over, Norman and I walked into the schoolyard to find people turning to look at us. They craned their necks as if Mr. Eisenstadt had just given us the strap, first the closer kids and then the farther ones, attention gusting across the schoolyard like the wind. Little kids were no different than usual, running around disconnectedly. But people our age and older turned around and stared.

Then they turned away. Groups of people turned their backs on us as we got close, even if we had no plans to stop and talk. People standing on their own walked somewhere else. I wasn't sure what to do, and in my confusion, I couldn't even remember what we usually did when we arrived at school. I had to work out the trivial fact that we usually just rambled around the schoolyard. As nine o'clock neared, and people started to line up at the Boys and Girls entrances, we would join our lines and wait for the bell.

This time, after our ramble, the girls in my lineup not only turned their backs on me, they leaned together and whispered, glancing over at me and sucking their lips. Boys in Norman's lineup kicked the pavement in a superior fashion. We were being scorned out. I'd seen it many times, although I'd never gone through it myself. It felt strange being watched by dozens of eyes, as if tiny bugs were biting me all over, or flying around eating the air until there wasn't enough oxygen to breathe properly.

The strangest part was, Norman didn't seem to notice. Either that, or he was very good at pretending he didn't, standing absentmindedly in line before the bell rang. He behaved no differently in class, putting up his hand to answer the hardest questions as I fretted through the morning. Recess worried me. When the bell rang, I could barely tear myself away from my desk, which had never happened before.

September being marble-playing season, you compared your marbles with other people's at recess before competing for them at lunch. At our school, we created obstacle courses at the edge of the yard down by the ditch that marked the edge of the school property. You made a course by putting a prized marble at one end of a run of packed earth. Three or four feet back from it, you scored a line in the dirt. People wanting to play flicked their marble at yours from the marked line. If they hit your marble, they got it. If they didn't hit it after three tries, you got theirs.

Yet this recess, no one wanted to compare marbles with Norman and me, even though we'd laid out our allowances for a couple of superior cat's eye shooters the previous Saturday. When we started walking toward them, people turned and walked away, as if they'd just remembered something important. If I'd stopped to think, I could have predicted that. I knew what being scorned out involved.

Not quite taking a decision, I peeled away from Norman, telling him I was going to play hopscotch, hoping the girls would be more welcoming. But only little kids were jumping the hopscotch squares. Bigger girls had formed circles to whisper, huddling closer as I walked past. The only other girl wandering the playground alone was Judy Shribman, who wasn't shunned but friendless. I'd been right: Jeannie Stevens and Cathy Cole had dropped her after school started, preferring to talk to other girls in Mrs. Horton's class.

I smiled experimentally at Judy, but her entire body winced away. It hurt to see her brave up her shoulders and head over to Jeannie and Cathy, saying something the moment she arrived, a joke or piece of meanness. The other girls tittered, then craned their necks to look me up and down as if they'd never seen me before. Afterward, Jeannie and Cathy stepped apart to welcome Judy back into their friendship.

I needed Norman after that, and found him leaning against the chain-link fence, his legs crossed as he read a library book. Earlier that recess, Norman had said, "I forgot to tell you that my swordtail female had more babies," and I'd answered irritably, "If it was the male, you could sell them for fifteen million dollars," before heading off to look for girls. Now I leaned against the fence beside him, thinking this was all a mistake and someone would fix it quickly.

Yet it continued at lunch: the turned shoulders, the whispers, pavement kicking, smirks. I felt so lost that Norman was left in charge. At least, he did what he always did, motoring over to the marble courses while I followed, thinking this wasn't smart but not knowing how to stop it.

Fortunately, Norman headed straight for the course built by Darryl Wall, the policeman's son. Darryl was a crewcutted boy who liked marbles as much as I liked kittens, and kept his collection in an old purple Crown Royal bag. He was so intent on accumulation that he'd let anyone play his course, even sharpies. Today, he'd put up a steelie, and Norman knelt to play.

Darryl picked up his steelie and walked away. All the air fled the path and humiliation streamed in. Everyone smirked as Norman's slow blush rose up his neck. He stumbled a little as he levered himself to his feet, then looked back at the fence, ready to go back and read his book.

I refused, my stubbornness coming on strong. Hurrying a couple of courses along, I knelt down to play for one of Gord Brewster's cloudy blind-eyes: white marbles swirled on the outside with colour. Gord was a reliable boy, the one the teachers sent to get the janitor whenever spillage occurred. I didn't think Gord was capable of being mean.

Yet when I pulled out my shooter, Gord picked up his blind-eye and walked over to Darryl, even though they weren't friends. When I continued along, Kenny Potts picked up his cat's eye, and the next boy along proudly copied him. This was enough even for me. When Norman walked over to the ditch, I followed. We stood there for a very long time.

"See," I finally told him, conscious of disobeying my father. "Mr. Manners . . ."

"I know," Norman said.

I failed to grasp this.

"How he's going around trying to get people to sign his petition to get my parents fired," Norman said. "My mum told me."

"Who told her?"

"Your dad."

I couldn't believe my father hadn't said anything, or that I hadn't overheard.

Norman didn't meet my eyes. "You don't have to play with me anymore if you don't want to."

I didn't like the cravenness in his voice, the dash of self-pity, like the bitters my mother dashed into her old-fashioned. She'd let me taste the bitters one time on her little finger and I'd hated them. I didn't want to hate Norman, so I decided to ignore what he'd said.

"What are your parents going to do?"

"Fight it. My dad says things could get, like"—singing the *Twilight Zone* song. "But your father said your brother's a lawyer. So anyway."

"I guess they're communists," I said, before deciding to add, "which isn't illegal."

"They don't like the Soviet Union. My dad told me."

I heard Norman say, They don't like the Soviet Union so they're not communists. I didn't hear, My dad told me to say they don't like the Soviet Union. Yet it made me feel a little better, at least until Norman and I went back inside after lunch, and we found the contagion had spread to the classroom.

Maybe the kids had been buoyed by getting away with it on the playground, which was only lightly patrolled by teachers. I don't think I'd missed anything earlier. Our class had been normal in the morning. Now, when Norman put up his hand to answer, a number of the boys smirked, and a few of the girls. Fiona Krawchuk had a fine line in pre-teenage disdain that she was always happy to exercise, putting it on like eyeliner as she sighed loudly.

Some people looked embarrassed, including Lucy Oliver, Lucy being the one who had given me Barbie for my birthday. It might be better to say that Lucy looked as if she'd decided this was beneath her. A few of the girls looked more openly upset, including a nice girl named Laura

Stanton from choir. Being a pet meant that I was allowed to sniff around the edges of things, and most girls knew I was only curious and meant no harm. Seeing Laura's distress, I got my first vague sense of the way societies relied on different people to play different roles, at least within set boundaries. The girls knew they needed me, salt for the soup, and they didn't want to see me excluded.

Norman was a different matter. He was an outsider, and one who'd had polio, which made him both mythic and frightening.

"Spazz," Darryl Wall muttered, when Norman raised his hand.

Miss Oliphant must have heard him. Darryl intended to be heard. I will never forgive that teacher for the way she didn't reprimand Darryl and call the class to order. Instead, the rolled eyes and giggles and whispers made her look smug, so they grew amplified in the absence of adult disapproval, whispers bouncing around the morally vacant classroom like echoes. At the same time, Miss Oliphant seemed to notice Norman's raised hand less often as the afternoon went on, as if she felt buoyed, too. Toward the end of the day, she only gave him a nod when no one else was able to move her lesson along with the correct answer.

"Norman, again. A very well-informed child. What's our total, Norman?"

All this happened so suddenly, the day felt like a tidal wave crashing ashore. And it didn't ebb. The next morning, we faced more turned shoulders, more cries of "Spazz" and "Brain." The following day, more whispers. "His father." "*Her* father." The days became a week and the week, ten days. At times, people were content to offhandedly ignore us, although our exclusion from marbles and other games remained constant and enforced. Even the girls who felt uneasy fell into line, none of them brave enough to do anything other than smile at me covertly. It felt as if we were trapped inside the same movie playing over and over, nothing changing, the same weary story unspooling day after day after day.

If I'd abandoned Norman, they would have eased up on me, but I wasn't going to do that. If I'd told my parents what was going on, my father would have tried to stop it. But I didn't tell my parents about the Raincoat Man and didn't tell them what was happening at school. I thought I could handle it, although mainly I hoped it would go away, and it didn't.

By the end of September, Norman and I were in danger of being permanently scorned. Not for ourselves, but because of our parents, our families, and especially because of Mr. Manners's timing. He had started taking his petition just after the Soviet foreign minister had warned that if the U.S. invaded Cuba, it would mean all-out war. By that point, many of us were eating dinner in front of the television news. No one's parents had any idea what was going to happen, and everyone was anxious and upset. Then came a knock on the door, and there was Mr. Manners with his folder. The Hortons were communists? Hiding among us? A scandal, they agreed, their children acting as loudspeakers shouting their distress. And of course I had no idea how to stop it.

It was on the first of October that Norman finally decided to act. Or maybe it's better to say he decided not to act, and stopped putting up his hand in class.

I didn't know what Norman was planning. We never talked about what was going on. Maybe we exchanged a glance after one of the boys took an absentminded swat at Norman's rear end. But usually we just sat in a corner of the schoolyard talking about comic books, the latest *Superman* or *Batman*. When things got bad, we might argue about *Classic Comics*, whether they were boring or educational, and whether there was any difference.

From what I could pick up, Norman hadn't told his parents what was happening, either. I hadn't understood at first why his mother didn't stop it, but then I watched her walk through the schoolyard one day with her head down and her arms clasped like Mrs. Manners. Something was bothering her too, and I could see how that might have kept her from noticing us. In any case, the decision to stop putting up his hand was

Norman's alone, and he took it late. By then, Miss Oliphant was only calling on him when no one else could come up with an answer.

"I'm surprised at you, class," she said that morning. "Norman?"

It was the first time she'd said his name in a couple of days, and Norman shook his head. I could tell from the balled-up fists in his lap that he knew the answer but had decided not to tell her. I was surprised and looked from his fists to his closed face. A few nearby children knew something was going on and went uneasy, but Miss Oliphant didn't catch it and only gave a small smug smile before emitting the answer herself.

Not that I heard either the answer or the question. By that time, I was paying almost no attention in class, although I was learning a great deal about the many ways people could be nasty. Yet as I took in Norman's rebellion that morning, I understood that if he was going to assume my role as the silent one, I could start making noise. No more need to be perfect. I'd done that to try to protect him, and look how that had turned out. I knew far more of her subject matter than Miss Oliphant gave me credit for, and a mixture of knowledge, hurt, and fury began to churn in my stomach. Without precisely taking a decision, I knew I could no longer allow them to silence me.

Miss Oliphant was writing on the board about the Elizabethan age in England during social studies period. Her back was to us as she wondered aloud which monarch had reigned. From the look of polite ignorance going around the classroom, I realized that I was one of the few who knew the answer. *Classic Comics* had their uses.

"Queen Elizabeth the First," I called.

Miss Oliphant turned, her harlequin glasses glinting. "We raise our hand, Mary Alice."

I shrugged, which she noted. During arithmetic period, I worked furiously at an equation she'd written on the board, calling out the answer before she'd even asked for it.

"The result is one thousand, one hundred"—picking up Norman's whisper—"two hundred eleven."

"Raising our hand, Mary Alice!"

But now that I'd got started, I couldn't stop, and answers flew out of me like paper airplanes. The rest of the class stared as if I'd dropped from the sky myself, torn between admiration and disbelief. A small uneasy voice inside me started saying enough was enough. But in geography period, when she brought up the capital of Nigeria, I took it as a sign of approval from on high, especially when she called on Judy Shribman before she'd even asked the question. "Judy, can you tell us . . ." and Judy got it wrong.

"Lagos," I said. "I read it in the *World Book* encyclopedia, which makes it correct."

"That's sufficient, Mary," Miss Oliphant replied. "You *will* behave."

"Mary Alice," I replied, feeling my spine holding me straight. "Mary Anderson is Mary. I'm Mary Alice. But you can call me Tink if you want to, Miss Oliphant. Like my friends."

"Oh, I see. You have friends."

"All sorts of them."

The class held its breath.

"What you have is called an attitudinal problem," Miss Oliphant replied. "Sulky for a month, then cheeky. I observed the same thing in grade three, and I'm disappointed, *Mary*, to find you haven't improved."

She looked down at her lesson plan as if she'd defeated me, but I felt triumphant. I hadn't known that I'd needed vocabulary, but now that I had some, I could prove I was telling the truth. Until now, Norman and I had suffered a cascade of deniable smirks and half-audible whispers. "Attitudinal problems" was undeniable, since I couldn't have made it up. When the bell rang at three o'clock, I ran home fast to make it stop.

Mrs. Oliver was in the kitchen when I barged in. Bunny usually took guests into the living room, but Mrs. Oliver was standing up from the kitchen table, picking up her purse, ready to leave.

"Well, here's Tinker," she said.

"Hello, Mrs. Oliver," I replied, noticing that while Bunny had served coffee, there was no sign of squares.

"How was school today?" Mrs. Oliver asked.

I tried to think how to put it.

"People were mean?" she persisted, astonishing me, although of course her daughter Lucy was in my class.

Mrs. Oliver looked at me as if I was a specimen, I wasn't sure of what. This made me reluctant to speak of attitudinal problems in case she took it the wrong way.

"Look at her face, Buns," Mrs. Oliver said. "The child's being victimized. I'd ask Hall to reconsider his position, I really would. What are the Hortons to any of us, really?"

Mrs. Oliver said her goodbyes and left. Afterward, my mother slumped back down in her chair.

"So you're being teased," she finally said.

It wasn't teasing. But I poured myself some milk while deciding how to phrase it.

"You weren't going to tattletale."

That struck me as obvious.

Bunny launched herself up as if she'd been catapulted, grabbing her dishcloth and scrubbing the table down meanly.

"You're going to stop seeing Norman Horton," she said. "This isn't our problem."

Yes, it was.

"The radio saying there's going to be more turmoil in Cuba than Castro ever imagined."

I had no idea what Cuba had to do with anything, and felt thrown off-topic.

"Norman's my friend," I said, trying to recover.

"Not anymore. That nice Judy Shribman . . ."

"Who gives me the stink eye," I said. "Who sucks up to Jeannie and Cathy when they didn't even invite her to the Columbia River dam. Who says the Howards' poor little baby should go into a home . . ."

"We're talking about Norman Horton . . ."

"Who's my *friend*."

"What did I tell you?" Bunny asked, raising her hand.

She was clutching a dishcloth, and I stared at it. My parents never struck me and I didn't fully register what was happening. Bunny looked up at the dishcloth, too. Colour bloomed and faded in her face, although her expression remained angry as she lowered her hand.

"He's not welcome in this house. And you're not to go to his."

I didn't fight her, but Bunny knew I'd go. I also knew that my father wouldn't make me stop going, especially after I told him about my so-called attitudinal problems. Yet Irene Oliver was my mother's friend, and at the centre of their social circle. The idea of falling out with her made Bunny slump as if she was a plant that needed watering.

"All the decent teachers getting married," she muttered.

I didn't understand the connection, but I agreed with her.

"Oh, get yourself a damn cookie and go outside."

After changing out of my school uniform, I unscrewed the lid of the cookie jar. Oatmeal raisin. My least favourite, so I took three.

Andy Manners was sitting at the edge of the creek when I got down there, looking as upset as I felt. Having such a warm day so late in the year was eerie and untoward. The trees might really open their eyes, and ancient hunters stalk deer at the edges of sight. It was a magical place, humid and dense, and we were lost there.

Andy turned when she heard my footsteps, but then only shrugged and looked back at the creek. I took this as an invitation to sit down on a rock close to hers, working it out that Andy had been told not to be friends with Rosa. Either that or Rosa had been told not to be friends with Andy. I picked up a stone to throw in the creek, but kept it in my hand instead, smooth and pleasantly cool.

"What's an affair?" I asked.

"None of your business."

"Me and Norman are being scorned out," I said.

Andy winced and thought for a while, then told me what it was. In her description, an affair favoured the man, who was only looking for sex, not affection, and took off the moment things got complicated.

"Okay," I answered, seeing that Mr. Horton had taken off, at least from her mother. "But what's sex?"

Smiling this time, Andy explained it matter-of-factly and without using slang. She might have been saying, This is how a tree grows.

I had never been so shocked in my life.

"Glad you asked?"

I had no answer and tried to put things together. It took me quite a while to try to fit all this new information into my head, which complained of the burden. I didn't want to know these things and certainly wouldn't be able to discuss them with anyone. Yet I could see that you had to know them to understand the way the world worked, which was not the way I'd imagined.

I remembered again the verse that had come to me at Halloween, how all things should be done decently and in order. I'd got such an uncanny sense of the clockwork order of the world, even while feeling trapped inside it. But from what Andy said, the world wasn't the least bit decent and not all that orderly. The clock we lived inside could fly apart at any moment, destroyed by the pressure of human weakness and desire, its crystal shattering, its hands shooting out like arrows, the metal gears grinding a path through the air until their edges struck you down.

"Don't worry about it."

Looking over, I realized Andy had been watching me.

"It hasn't got anything to do with you. Not for a while, anyhow."

I didn't know what to say. Then I remembered: "Who said you and Rosa can't be friends?"

Andy kept looking at me without answering, a funny smile on her face.

"My mother says I can't be friends with Norman anymore," I said, and took heart. "But when my father gets home, he's going to say it's all right."

Andy nodded, half to herself.

"It was her mother. And my father, telling me not to see her. Except that I'm not going to listen to *him*."

As she brushed back her hair, I noticed that Andy's wrist was badly bruised. When she saw me looking, she pulled down the arm of her sweater to cover it.

"I fell," she said. "He's not *that* bad."

I thought Andy meant her father hadn't thrown her to the floor again. She must have taken a tumble, either playing tennis or going sailing, although I had an idea that it was late in the season for both.

"But her mother," Andy said, picking up the thought. "Maid Marian. She's the innocent party. So there's nothing Rosa can say to contradict her. Me neither, ya know?"

I thought about what my father had said. "Mr. Horton is disappointed in Maid Marian."

Andy smiled again, but bitterly. "He just has lousy taste in women."

She stood up and turned to look farther down the creek, where the forest was soft with beams of late sunlight, tiny insects dancing through. I got up beside her and marvelled.

"That's not even true," Andy said, as if the light had softened her, too. "My mother is infuriating, but she's all right. She's okay. She's beautiful."

"Like Katharine Hepburn."

Andy smiled more happily. "We never heard the end of that. I mean, I get it now. She figured out that Norman had picked it up from his father."

I shook my head. "That was Norman. We were trying to sell cookies. He told Mrs. O'Neill she looked like Ingrid Bergman, when Ingrid Bergman isn't hefty."

Something happened to Andy's face, hilarity or tears. But I'd remembered the oatmeal cookies in my jacket pocket and grew preoccupied with fishing them out. I handed Andy the least damaged one, which she took before wiping her eyes with the back of her bruised right wrist. I kept the other for myself, planning to dig out the broken crumbs of the third cookie once she'd left and there was no more need to be polite.

"Homemade," Andy said. "Your parents are the definition of normal. How come you're not?"

"I am."

"No, you aren't," she said. "Welcome to the club."

Neither Andy nor I felt like going home. After we ate our cookies, I poked around in my pocket and we shared the bigger crumbs, then walked down to the little bridge and spit over the edge on leaves carried along by the water.

The leaves were turning. The forest was chiefly evergreens but there were alders and maples burning red and golden like cold fires. I considered asking Andy if she wanted to collect some leaves to iron between sheets of waxed paper, then realized she probably wouldn't. It was hard to figure out what Andy liked. She disliked sailing and tennis, and school, and most of the people in it. She liked her big tan work boots, which were the same ones she'd worn last year, additionally scuffed. She liked Rosa. Aside from that, I couldn't name anything Andy had ever spoken of favourably.

We were still standing on the bridge when we heard footsteps, male footsteps blundering toward us over the uneven ground. Andy went alert, and I was worried it might be the Raincoat Man, who probably wouldn't like to find us on his bridge. When a branch cracked underfoot, fear steamed off Andy. I caught it, feeling twitchy and trapped and ready to run, although I also enjoyed the feeling because I was almost certain it was my father. It sounded like his walk, and both Andy and I relaxed when we saw his navy blue cardigan through the trees. I don't suppose Mr. Manners wore cardigans. When he reached the creek, my father hesitated, surprised to find Andy with me on the bridge. Then he nodded and walked up the steps to join us.

"Hello, Mr. Parker," Andy said, pushing back her hair to be presentable. When she realized this uncovered her wrist, she pulled the sleeve down quickly.

"Hello, Andrea," my father said. "Mary Alice. You don't seem to have heard your mother calling you to dinner."

I shook my head rapidly, ready to explain.

"We didn't, Mr. Parker," Andy said. "The creek's pretty high. We've been standing here for a while."

My father nodded. I was hungry and ready to go back, but he seemed inclined to linger, putting his forearms on the railing and leaning there comfortably, his hands clasped in front of him. Andy leaned on the railing the same way, although she didn't seem to be trying to copy him. I was too short to do it myself, but I stepped up on the bottom rung of the railing and held onto a couple of spindles, which put me high enough to rest my chin on top.

We maintained a companionable silence until my father said, by-the-way, "You might both be interested in knowing that Mr. Eisenstadt isn't going to let Marian Horton go. He feels very strongly that people's private lives are their own business. She's a good teacher, and that's enough for him."

"What about their dad?" Andy asked.

It choked her to mention Mr. Horton, and my father looked uncomfortable, leaving a long pause as he worked out what to say.

"But Mr. Duprée is your friend," I said, and realized from Andy's surprised expression that this counted as blurting.

"Mr. Duprée is the principal of a large high school," my father said, showing me only a slightly raised eyebrow. "He needs to consider all his options."

Feeling younger than I had just a few minutes before, I told Andy, "I'm not supposed to say they're friends. Not to people in high school."

Andy shrugged in a way that meant she wouldn't say anything. I wondered if my father understood that but decided not to ask. None of us said anything for a while, although I realized dinner must have been waiting at Andy's house, too.

Finally, my father levered himself upright.

"If you need help, Andrea," he said, in the same companionable voice, "you can come to our door any hour of the day or night. I want you to know that."

Andy didn't answer for a moment, then made a noise halfway like a laugh.

"It was kind of funny, actually," she said, and looked down at her wrist. "So he was beating up on my mom, and I kind of . . . inserted myself. That's not so funny, I guess. But he got hold of my arm. It's like a bracelet, when you look."

Andy held up her wrist so the sweater fell away, turning it as if she was really showing off a new bracelet, amethysts catching in the sun.

"Anyway, he kind of, yeah, he threw me. Onto the floor? Then he broke her arm over the back of the chair. And took off. And she couldn't drive, not with the stick shift. And Cal has his licence but he wasn't at home. Cal's never at home anymore. So anyway, yeah, I had to drive her to the hospital. Which was pretty cool, actually."

Andy wasn't quite crying, but she pulled up her sleeve to wipe her eyes.

"So she's sitting there in the passenger seat kind of teaching me to drive. You know? And I'm stalling it every six blocks. We're looking for the cops the whole way. Except that I got her to Emergency, un, un, unmolested."

Barking out a laugh. "And they X-ray her arm and put on the cast. And I get her home okay, even though she's like woozed out on pills and can't, what do you call it? Navigate. Or driving instruct. So I'm probably ten steps ahead on getting my licence."

"Andrea," my father began, but Andy hugged herself and pirouetted away. My father started putting out his hand to stop her, but snatched it back as if she were on fire. Andy talked over her shoulder as she walked off, drowning out anything he might say.

"I need to go cook dinner for my little brothers. And her, you know? She's a crap cook, anyhow. I'm going to take care of them, all right?"

Andy swivelled again as she reached the top of the steps, her expression growing haughty.

"And if you believe all that, you can ask your friend Mr. Duprée who I am. Go to the cops, and I'll tell them I made it all up. To *gain attention*. And she'll tell them I'm the bane of her existence. Katharine Hepburn. No one's going to seize my little brothers and put them in some Dickensian orphanage. And I do know what Dickensian means, thank you Mrs. So-Called English Teacher Who Reads Less Than I Do."

"Andrea, there's no question of seizing your brothers," my father began.

But Andy ran down the stairs and strode off into the forest, arms hugging her chest the way her mother hugged hers, appearing and disappearing between the trees as she took big strides in those tan leather work boots. I slipped my hand into my father's and looked up at him, watching the way he watched Andy until she disappeared.

Afterward, he looked down at me.

"Oh, that little face."

The words seemed torn out of him, and my father held my hand all the way uphill, blundering on the uneven ground as I kicked a worried path through the leaves.

PART THREE

PART
THREE

14

As if things weren't bad enough already, Typhoon Freda hit Vancouver two weeks later. There was little warning. The day before, high winds had knocked a tree on top of a car in Stanley Park, but the weather forecasters thought that would be the end of it. The tree didn't hurt anyone, although the accident caused traffic to back up over town, and my father was late for dinner. Being late usually meant he was working overtime, paid or not, and he would call from the office to warn Bunny. This time, she only knew what was happening because of CKNW.

"Sorry about that," my father said, kissing her cheek as he came in. "Things keep going wrong, don't they?"

"They're calling for more rain tomorrow," Bunny said. "Wind, but not nearly as bad."

"And how was school today?" my father asked.

By this time, my parents were keeping as sharp an eye on school as they did on the weather. After we'd come back from seeing Andy down the creek, my father had got everything out of me at dinner. Not that it was difficult. Dams burst less noisily.

They won't talk to Norman and me. Won't let us play. Calling Norman Brain and Moron and Spazz, and teacher called me Mary again and said I have an attitudinal problem, and I can't make that up. And I was right that the Elizabethan age was named after Queen Elizabeth the First, and what does Virgin Queen mean anyhow?

My father knew that Mr. Eisenstadt went to work early, and he phoned him first thing the next morning. Mr. Eisenstadt must have spoken to Angela Oliphant at lunch. Not long after class got back that afternoon, one of the boys made a rude noise after a boneheaded answer from Gord Brewster, and Miss Oliphant went off like a rocket. Behaviour like that wasn't tolerated in her classroom. She insisted on civility, and asked Lucy Oliver what that meant.

"Being nice to each other," Lucy replied, looking straight ahead.

"Precisely." Miss Oliphant gave a generalized glare at the classroom while taking no particular notice of Norman and me. Most people got the point, of course, and it was reinforced when she called on Norman not long afterward for a difficult answer, even though he still wasn't putting up his hand. When Darryl Wall tried an experimental snort, Miss Oliphant strode over to his side and rapped her knuckles on his desk as she said each syllable.

"What did I say, Dar-ryl?"

It was a relief to find respite in the classroom, even though Miss Oliphant was still our teacher. Of course, nothing changed on the playground. Norman and I remained excluded, and while the teasing grew more sporadic, it was nastier when it occurred. Norman's knapsack was thrown into the ditch. A boy tried to trip me as I skipped rope.

Mrs. Horton patrolled the schoolyard more alertly in those tense days, and that might have been part of the problem. The meanness built up and erupted more violently when her back was turned. Norman's knapsack wasn't just thrown in the ditch. It disappeared from his hanger in the cloakroom and was only found after school floating in the rank water. The boy who tried to trip me ran up from behind, and he might never have been found out, either. But I caught a glimpse of something coming and managed to take the boy down, kneeling on his back so I could pick up his head by a handful of curls, revealing Kenny Potts.

My father had started to question me minutely at dinner, not just about what did you learn today, Mary Alice, but is there anything you're not telling me.

No, I'd say repeatedly. It went fine. Kenny Potts and I were sent to the office, but everything was fine.

"You were sent to the office," my father said.

"I told him Kenny tried to trip me, and Mr. Eisenstadt didn't give me the strap. He just said, 'Call a teacher next time.'"

"So you'll do that."

"Of course she won't," Bunny answered. "Did you?"

By then, we were back to eating dinner in the kitchen instead of in front of the TV. I knew that my parents were trying to protect me from further upset, but that was impossible. Everyone else was watching the news. Bunny had been one of the first mothers to stockpile food, but from what I heard, everyone else was following. Darryl Wall's father had taken night shift so he could spend the day digging his bomb shelter, even threatening to bring in a backhoe. And Darryl's younger brother, Scott, had started rocking back and forth in his desk in grade three, humming quietly to himself.

All this, and Mr. Manners refused to stand down. From what I overheard, Mr. Duprée formally warned Jack Horton to teach the curriculum and suspended him for two weeks without pay. Yet my father said that Mr. Manners still wanted the Hortons fired, and that he was taking the matter to the school board. After my father had a couple of drinks with Mr. Horton one evening, I heard him tell Bunny that the board was going to schedule a special session.

"Having been presented with a petition as long as your arm."

I understood by then what a petition entailed, and knew that Jim Manners had been collecting signatures not just in our subdivision but throughout Grouse Valley. I watched him set out every evening after work, sometimes on foot but mainly in his car, ready to go door-to-door like an encyclopedia salesman. From what I picked up at school, he'd been telling people who didn't know him that he was their neighbour, a fellow ratepayer, a householder, even though he'd become more like a tenant living in the Manners basement.

That part wasn't public, but observation showed.

"What are you doing out on the sundeck in this weather?" Bunny asked one day, not long before the typhoon.

"Mr. Manners came out from his basement again. He didn't close the door properly, and you could see inside, how there's a bed made up on the rec room sofa."

A brief pause. "That's other people's business, Mary Alice. Come inside and help me peel some apples." When I balked: "You can throw the peel and see who you'll marry."

"I'm never getting married."

"Fair enough," Bunny said, surprising me with her tone, the one she used to speak about the cost of living. It was surfacing more often these days, especially when my father got home from work.

"Another call," she'd say, although she refused to go into details in front of me.

I knew anyhow. Bunny's friends spoke to her in person, too. Mrs. Armstrong told her in the bank lineup one afternoon that she and Mr. Armstrong didn't like what Jim Manners was doing, but they didn't like communists either. Cathy Cole's mother told her in the drugstore, "I don't agree with him, but everybody's signing, and we're backed into a corner." Then there was the day the egg man had a flat tire and only showed up after school. Mrs. Wall turned away when she saw us waiting for our eggs as if she'd remembered something important, her retreating back looking awfully familiar.

"Herd mentality," my father said that night. "It's not something I have any use for."

By then I was spending a good deal of time eavesdropping just inside my bedroom door.

"So when you were overseas," Bunny said, "you let your men do whatever they damn well pleased."

My father's exasperated silence.

"The communists want to take away all the freedoms you fought for," Bunny said.

My father was about to answer when I called through my cracked-open door, "Norman's father told him he doesn't even like Russians."

In the silence that followed, I got up and went into the kitchen, the feet of my flannelette pyjamas making a swishing sound on the linoleum, which I normally enjoyed. I was breaking the rules of eavesdropping, but everything else was breaking. Glass, friendships, my heart.

"His mum and dad aren't your friends," I said. "But Norman's mine."

"Sweetheart . . ." my father began.

"I want it to stop. Why aren't you making it stop?"

Even I could hear the waver at the end of my question. My father held out one arm so I would come over and sit on his lap. When I ignored him—and this was the first time—he took his hand back and rubbed his eyes behind his glasses.

"Your brother has been coming over," he said, lowering his hand.

I had to concede that much.

"There are laws and procedures in a case like this that need to be followed. Your brother is finding out what they are."

"As if the law's going to decide this," Bunny said.

Seeing the conflict between them, I began to shake. It started in my knees and spread to my stomach, which began to churn. My heart thumped hard and my shoulders quivered and my teeth began chattering so uncontrollably that I became like our house the next evening, juddering through a typhoon.

"Come to bed, now. Come to bed."

My father carrying me to comfort, a warm parent on either side as I failed to fall asleep.

The meteorologists hadn't predicted Freda because it was a once-in-a-century event. My father told me afterward that the storm had formed west of Hawaii, as typhoons usually did. But the winds had weakened as they approached North America, which was also usual, and Freda was downgraded to a tropical storm. On the radio beforehand, the forecaster had said we would suffer nothing worse than wind gusts and rain.

Yet this time, the system had hit a powerful jet stream, picking up fury until it made landfall in California, roaring north through Oregon and Washington State at a peak velocity approaching three hundred kilometres an hour. The West Coast hadn't seen stronger winds in all the twentieth century, winds like a cavalcade of warplanes, one after another and another knocking down power poles and billboards and trees as Freda roared toward Vancouver.

It was already raining solidly as Norman and I walked home from school. Steady downpours weren't unusual in Vancouver, and especially on the North Shore, where clouds could get trapped against the mountains and drop their rain. It had rained far harder the previous week, making the creek run so high we could hear it thundering from inside the house.

My parents had forbidden me to go down the creek, but I didn't want to go anyway. When Norman and I reached his house, we made plans to meet in the morning and spend our allowance in the village. With no use for marbles, we'd got in the habit of buying the drugstore out of comic books. Plus, Norman had started wanting to go to the fruit and vegetable store every week for penny candy. He was eating so much candy he might have been working through a hoard, even though Halloween was still three weeks away.

Mr. Horton's suspension had started the previous day, so he must have been inside the house as we stood in the driveway, although I saw no sign of him. Maybe this was the reason Norman didn't invite me in, or ask to come to my place. In my heart, I was glad. I was growing tired, not of Norman but the Hortons, or at least what was attached to them. Norman might have been tired of me too, the witness of what was going on. In any case, I slogged home alone through the rain, saddened and wet right through, before walking through the front door to a surprise.

Bunny was waiting in the hall with a big fluffy towel still warm from the dryer. Without a word, she wrapped it around me from my wet hair to my water-logged shoes, enfolding me gently. I disappeared inside the warmth of that towel and the strength of her arms, her reliability and tenderness, and never wanted to emerge.

"It's really starting to blow out there, isn't it?" Bunny said, and slowly began to swab me down. "Your father's getting off early after a meeting. How was school?" Without requiring an answer, she took away the damp towel and said, "Now go get out of those wet clothes. There's clean ones on the bed."

Afterward, we sat in the living room with coffee, Bunny having made mine according to Debbie's recipe, mainly hot milk and sugar. The wind was gusting rain against the windows now but we weren't concerned. We didn't have the radio on, not bothering with the news.

"I guess Mr. Manners isn't going to go out today," I said.

"Coward," Bunny said. I was surprised, although she sounded more reflective than accusing. "That seems to be what he goes around thinking about himself. That's the real problem."

She seemed to be talking to Debbie, or maybe to her reflection in the darkening window. She glanced at me briefly. "That doesn't mean I think very highly of Norman's father."

"He dumped Mrs. Manners," I said. "Andy Manners told me. She told me what affairs are, since I'm old enough to know."

Bunny digested this.

"*Men*," she said finally. "It's always about them. Now here's all my friends phoning me, or more to the point *not* phoning me, all because some man couldn't keep it in his . . ."

A hard gust of wind, a snap, a flash up the road and our lights suddenly went out.

"Away from the window," Bunny ordered, jumping up to draw the curtains. When I sat paralyzed, my mother herded me into the kitchen, still holding my coffee in both hands. Grabbing a flashlight from the string drawer, she guided me from behind by the shoulders, steering me downstairs to the rec room. Leaving me there, she continued without speaking into my father's workshop, where she seldom went, coming back with candles and matches. I watched her light one, dripping wax into an old chipped saucer and securing the candle in place, where it glowed feebly in the twilight.

"That looks lonely," she said, and lit another.

"I guess there isn't any TV," I said, and Bunny held up a finger. Going back into my father's workshop, she returned with his battery-powered radio and tuned it to CKNW.

"Typhoon," a newscaster said, and Bunny snapped it off.

We looked at the radio for a long blank moment as wind rattled the house.

"Well," Bunny said finally, "tell me what comics you got last weekend."

"You don't care about my comics, Buns."

If she wanted to be adults, I would try to be adult.

My mother looked at me for longer than we'd looked at the radio.

"Drink your milk before it gets cold," she told me.

"Coffee," I said.

My father found us in the dark rec room with three lit candles and two cans of pork and beans bubbling on the camp stove. On the coffee table was a plate with thick slices of bakery bread, the butter dish with the square of ice-cold butter I'd begged, a plate of sliced tomatoes and another of sliced dill pickles for colour. The pork chops we were supposed to have for dinner had gone back in the fridge.

By this time, the wind and rain were loud. People use words like roar and howl, and the wind did that, making animal sounds. But as the night

grew darker, it started sounding like giants punching the house and rattling the windows to get inside. The wind whistled through any cracks it
could find, making the candle flames flicker. After our excellent dinner,
I felt gusts of it on my cheeks and hands, puffs of humidity that were
surprisingly uncold. Meanwhile, I kept telling myself that none of this
frightened me. It was just the wind, which was air, and there was that
expression my Uncle Punk used: safe as houses.

"What I heard on the way home," my father said after dinner, having
to talk more loudly than usual. "What we should be prepared to see
tomorrow. The wind is knocking down trees on the boulevards over town.
It's uprooting trees in Stanley Park. But the trees behind us—I've shown
you this—they're fir and cedar, some of them old growth. Grouse Valley
wasn't logged out to the same extent the forest was elsewhere. Smaller
operators worked the land and they didn't clear-cut. That's part of what
makes this a special place. Are you listening, Mary Alice? The trees are
going to keep us safe."

Safe as houses. Safe as trees.

Some of which became houses, when you thought about it.

"You can listen to CKNW if you want," I said, being polite, and
hoping he wouldn't take me up on it.

"If the transmission tower hasn't blown down," Bunny said.

"They called it a typhoon," I found myself saying. "Is that like a
tornado?"

"No, it's not a tornado," my father said, although the wind outside
had grown as loud as the wind in *The Wizard of Oz*. "A tornado is a big
whirlwind. This system is blowing in on us straight. Almost horizon-
tally." And because he was congenitally honest, "Like a hurricane in
the Atlantic."

"Or the Bomb?" I asked.

A crash, and glass splintered upstairs, a branch, a projectile shattering
a window. Then I was screaming and screaming, panting in my father's
arms as he carried me and a flashlight into his workshop, where I was

astonished into silence by the sight of our patio chairs set up, complete with green-and-white cushions, and the plastic tables beside them.

"Okay, we're going to be safe in here. We're going to be safe, Mary Alice," my father said. "You know there aren't any windows. Look and see. There aren't any windows in here."

And the astonishing thing was, resting in my father's arms in a patio chair in his underground workshop, I soon fell fast asleep.

The next morning, Vancouver woke up to find that seven people had been killed and there were many millions of dollars in damage. Four thousand trees were down and some people would be without power for a week. But Grouse Valley hadn't been badly hit. All we saw out our windows were fallen branches strewn over lawns under a light sporadic rain.

We were still without power, although the breaking glass that had frightened me so badly was only the bathroom window being shattered by a runaway street sign. The bathroom was almost completely tiled, so Bunny mopped up the rain easily, and the window was small and quickly repaired.

Since we'd made plans, Norman soon came over, maybe a little obliviously. My mother had to tell him that without electricity, the stores wouldn't be open in the village. Nor could we go down to the creek in high flow.

"Maybe you've got enough comic books already," Bunny said.

"How did your house come through?" my father asked. "Keeping your father busy?"

"My mum," Norman answered warily.

It remained very damp. My father soon took us outside in our rain gear to help clear the yard and then the street of branches. Further up Far Creek Road, a neighbour revved up his gas-powered chainsaw to cut up one of the few fallen trees.

I liked being of use, but Norman was less interested and soon went home, then came back out of boredom, then left again when I wanted to watch my father saw the bigger branches for our woodpile, handing him the ones I could manage. When the power came back on early that evening, Bunny cooked up the pork chops, saying they wouldn't be good tomorrow, even though we'd only opened the fridge for milk, keeping in the cold.

None of us anticipated what would happen the following week, when the missile crisis would begin, so it felt as if the bad times had ended and we'd made it through. Or mysteriously, the reverse: we'd made it through, so the bad times had ended. I told myself that when I went back to school the next week, people would treat me normally. Our street was back to normal, my father as greeted as he'd always been, even though many of our neighbours had signed the Manners petition. Maybe it would have been different if Mr. Manners had been there, but he'd been caught over town by the storm and hadn't come home. This was according to Andy, who helped us clear branches from the street while Cal and the younger boys raked up their yard.

"Hall Parker," Mr. Wall said, dropping by. "Harvesting yourself some firewood."

"Need any of it, Mac?" my father asked.

"My cherry went over in the backyard," Mr. Wall said. "I do like the smell of a cherry wood fire."

"How's the excavation?"

Mr. Wall looked less cheerful. "Swimming pool," he said.

Behind him, Darryl Wall nodded at me. But boys only ever nodded at girls in the presence of their fathers, so that was all right, and I figured everything else soon would be.

Maybe you can remain pessimistic and frightened for only so long. Or I could. Norman's father was still suspended from work and the school board hearing loomed. But both these things felt small in the face of the typhoon and easily blown away. When Uncle Punk and Auntie Nita brought my brother over the next afternoon, I wasn't surprised to find that for once, Bob and my father greeted each other easily.

Football wasn't on the menu, post-typhoon. But my father had fired up the barbecue on the patio outside and my mother had made potato salad and one of the jellied salads that Uncle Punk liked, even though jellied salads were becoming unfashionable and she wouldn't have served it to one of her friends.

I was a little worried, having heard my mother mention how thoroughly Uncle Punk disliked my father's support for the Hortons. She and Auntie Nita had talked on the phone, and serving my uncle's favourite food seemed meant to indicate her agreement with his position. I'd noticed that Bunny often did this with food, signalling approval or maybe her wish for approval. Mrs. Oliver loved date squares, so Bunny always baked them when her friends came over, even though no one else liked them. Mrs. Oliver had to take most of the leftover squares home wrapped in tinfoil, to which I didn't object, especially if there were Nanaimo bars left over.

"So how's it going, Don Quixote?" Uncle Punk asked, lumbering through the rec room toward my father, who stood just inside the patio.

"And here we are, having a nice family barbecue," Auntie Nita said.

It was a warning and Uncle Punk took it, stopping in place, then retreating to an armchair.

The air remained heavy outside and our woodpile had got wet, but my father and I had scavenged enough dry logs to light a fire. It crackled and burned as I sat by the fireplace, toasting my back while Auntie Nita asked after my sister Debbie. As Bunny answered, my brother sat upright and impatient on the arm of his chair. Bob never had any use for small talk, and today he'd barely managed to survive saying hello. He looked at our father, who stood by the window frowning out at the barbecue, having had to light the coals twice already.

"I managed to get hold of Jack Horton's union rep," Bob told him, the moment Bunny finished speaking. "It's about what I suspected.

They're not prepared to go to the wall, not on this one. The rep will be at the school board meeting, but it doesn't sound as if he plans to say more than 'Hi, how are ya.' They're worried about being tainted by communism, especially when it's a lost cause. Rep told me there's a morality clause in the collective agreement, how teachers are bound to uphold decency. The wording is vague enough that the board can define decency any way it wants. So they can use it not just for moral failings, but for political ones."

My father was going ramrod by the window as my brother spoke.

"I looked at the wording," Bob went on. "The rep's right. It's ambiguous. Which is smart. You don't want a list of reasons for dismissal that ends up being exclusionary, leaving out someone with an unprintable predilection for . . ."

My brother stopped when he realized I was listening and shook his head.

"I'm afraid it's a lost cause," he repeated. "The trustees can do anything they want."

"So there you go, Don Quixote," Uncle Punk said. "Even his union won't back him."

My father remained silent.

"He doesn't have a comeback," Uncle Punk needled.

"Actually, I have a problem when politics are confounded with morality," my father said.

"I agree there's usually no connection," Uncle Punk replied.

"And if you were dismissed for your political views," my father asked, "using the excuse of a morality clause in your collective agreement? I'm not sure I like the precedent."

Uncle Punk was left without a comeback, while my brother thought it through, then smiled.

"Here's the irony," he said. "Strictly speaking, Jack Horton *is* in breach of the morality clause. Having an affair with a pupil's mother is exactly what it's designed to address. Moral turpitude. One gathers that

Jim Manners won't be pressing that particular issue. But under his contract, Horton is absolutely liable to be fired. Just for reasons other than Manners is arguing."

"You said yourself he was implicated," Bunny told my father, speaking in her wavery voice.

"Horton taught an ill-advised class, or part of a class, outside the curriculum," my father said, "and received a two-week suspension without pay. That was harsh, and a warning, and no one wishes more than me that it had stayed there. As for the rest . . ."

He stopped, glancing at me.

"Oh, the Manners girl told her what's going on," Bunny said.

"Mr. Horton dumped Andy's mother," I said, wanting to be helpful. "And he told Norman he doesn't like the Soviet Union."

My brother smiled again.

"Here's something to chew on, Tinker," he said. "You can be a communist without liking the Soviet Union. People can hold to the ideal without liking the reality."

He turned to the others. "I put the question to Horton point blank. He says he's not a commie."

"Does he?" Uncle Punk asked.

"Says, 'I'm not,'" Bob continued. "Present tense. Ask him about the past, and here comes temper. Scorn might be a better word."

I shifted on the hearth, stung by the word.

"Which brings me back to my question," my father said. "Whether someone should be fired for his private political views. Especially if he no longer holds them."

Uncle Punk paused.

"I'll give you this much," he said. "We ought to get rid of morality clauses. Leftover from days of the Women's Christian Temperance Union. Apply them by the letter and you'd lose half your membership. We ought to consider it for the next round of bargaining."

"And meanwhile, you have no qualms about the man being fired."

"Much less his wife," Auntie Nita said unexpectedly.

Uncle Punk sounded exasperated. "The man had an affair. Yes, the poor wife. Who probably ought to spread her . . ."

"Donald!" my aunt said, and everyone went quiet for a surprisingly long time.

"Actually, Dad's right," Bob said.

His words struck like a whipcrack, making my father look surprisingly hopeful. An outsider might have thought he hoped Bob would help the Hortons. But everyone in our family understood that what really moved him was that my brother had said he was right, taking a step back from their long disagreement.

"It's a hard one," my brother said. "But there might be a way to handle it."

In the discussion that followed, the only thing I understood was that my father and brother were speaking over Uncle Punk's head. My father stayed by the window, keeping an eye on the barbecue, and it didn't occur to my brother to join him. They spoke companionably, the way fathers and sons were supposed to speak when discussing joint projects. Moving the woodpile. Cleaning out the gutters. Not that my brother did any physical labour, but that was the feeling between them.

Meanwhile, I could see that Uncle Punk was getting restless. He chafed at Bob's long talk with our father, disliking not only what they agreed about, but the fact they agreed. I knew how proud he was of my brother, and understood how much credit he liked to take for Bob's achievements. Whether his attitude implicated Uncle Punk in the long discord between my father and brother is something I couldn't see the bottom of. I knew that Uncle Punk would have been shocked and wounded if I'd said that it did. But my mother's word *implicated* hung in the air, and I knew it meant something like tangled-up wool. I also knew families were like that, implicated in each other.

"I'd just be sure," my uncle put in finally, when there was a break in the conversation. "You better be sure that Horton isn't lying about being a member of the Party. My understanding being," he told Bob, "lawyers like to be sure of the answer to a question before they raise it."

My brother got up and pressed an affectionate hand on Uncle Punk's shoulder, which had the effect of settling him further into his chair. Afterward, he and my father went outside to continue their discussion by the barbecue. Through the window, I saw them both looking genial, and marvelled at the healing of the breach between them. The typhoon had carried us to Oz, where magical things happened. Uncles became just uncles, if disgruntled ones, while fathers turned back into fathers. When I returned to school, I was certain that people would welcome me and Norman back, too.

The next morning, Norman and I walked into the schoolyard to find the playground louder than usual. A chaos of running, skipping, hopscotch. Everywhere, rampant glee. Grouse Valley had survived the typhoon and everyone was proud of themselves. Younger kids ran around happily, and big girls played little girls' clapping games, giggling to find themselves doing a baby thing and enjoying it.

Nearby, the bigger boys kicked a ball around, with Jamie Manners providing the type of running commentary we heard on B.C. Lions games. Jamie was the grade six Manners, louder and rougher than his younger brother Harry. Yet even though Jamie was in charge, no one booted the ball at Norman or called him names. They didn't acknowledge him either, but a few of the girls who hadn't managed to see me for a month smiled in my direction. Laura Stanton from choir even came up and asked if our house been damaged. Theirs had lost shingles, she said.

In the classroom, even Miss Oliphant was buoyant. She started the day by singing along to "God Save the Queen," which she'd never done before. I was surprised to hear a pretty voice, sweet and melodic. She would surprise me again that afternoon by saying that her mother had slept through the typhoon, but their budgies had been a bother.

Miss Oliphant had never mentioned her home life, even when she was Mrs. Persson. I realized she must have gone back to live with her mother after her divorce the way Mr. Duffy had. That teacher possessed a hard shell, which was part of what made her so dislikeable, a beetle in glasses. But as I glimpsed a few personal details, I wondered for the first time if Miss Oliphant might be human.

It was dry that afternoon, neither warm nor cold, nothing special. Yet I went home feeling blithe, certain that the scorning would soon be over. And it's true people were friendly enough for the rest of the week, certainly in comparison to the past year, or what felt like a year. They continued to ignore Norman, but he wasn't taunted, and more girls risked sidling up to me and speaking.

The buoyancy of that first Monday dissipated from day to day in a slow leak. But the level of what we thought of ourselves, or expected of ourselves, seemed to have risen a little, like a lake after a storm. We had lived through something big and we'd become bigger, and it's possible that Norman and I would have been accepted back if the universe had given things a little longer to settle, and the petition Jim Manners was circulating had grown less urgent.

But Cuba came back in the news as the typhoon receded, turning everybody harsh. More talk of the Bomb, of the Soviet Union. Adults became punitive and superstitious, children panicky. Then the Cuban Missile Crisis arrived, and we all grew terrified that the world was going to end, as it very well might have.

Or maybe I should say, as it did, since some worlds can come to an end even as our poor old Earth keeps spinning.

15

onday, October 22, 1962. It was the start of a very long week,
which quickly came to seem like the longest of my life. When
I got home from school, Bunny was on the phone to my father. From
what I could pick up, President Kennedy was going to make a speech that
evening. Since the White House had scheduled a live television broadcast,
everyone knew it would be important. CKNW Radio, on low in the background, spoke of the mood in Washington as grave, which I knew meant
something beyond serious, with a shivery intimation of burial.

"I know," Bunny was telling my father. "I know that. But we can't
protect . . . Not from everything, Hall." A long silence on her end as
my father spoke quietly, which allowed Bunny to nerve herself up to be
brassy, "Well, I want to hear it," she said. "I know it's too much. Believe
me, I've had just about enough of everything myself. But I can't send her
down the creek, and she picks it all up anyway." A shorter reply involving
the overhead words, stop you. "No, you can't," Bunny said. "Ribs for
dinner."

After she hung up, Bunny looked over at me as I innocently poured a
glass of milk.

"When me and Punk were kids, we didn't *want* to hear what our parents
were saying. I'll leave you to think about that one." A brief pause. "Punk
and I."

The president was due to speak soon, at four o'clock our time. With the days shortening, we'd already entered the long northern gloaming that made the outdoors too meaningful for the mood I was in, even if I could have gone down the creek. An elfin light, mysterious, when I still felt unsettled from living through a typhoon, more so than other children seemed to feel anymore, certainly than Norman, although it's true he didn't demonstrate moods.

It was darker in the basement when we went downstairs, and Bunny turned on a floor lamp that was circled by its own metal tray. I claimed it for my milk and cookies, and Bunny put down a paper serviette beside them, a little damp and curled from her palm. With no other ceremony, she turned on the television, at first finding a commercial.

Then it began, tinny horns announcing the president of the United States. Without much preamble, President Kennedy launched the missile crisis, revealing that the Soviet Union had put nuclear missiles in Cuba, and saying they were aimed at us. I felt my stomach knot, a queasiness made worse by the fact I had trouble understanding what he was saying. I wasn't used to accents, and Kennedy's strong Boston accent confounded me. I only managed to understand that my father's guess wasn't far off. The Soviet Union was building nuclear bases in Cuba.

"The purpose of these bases can be none other than to provide a nuclear strike capability against the Western Hemisphere," the president said, telling us that the Soviet missiles could strike as far north as Hudson Bay. I assumed he was referring to the Hudson's Bay store over town, which meant we would be blinded in a Russian attack. I was also frightened by the way he kept calling the Soviet leader a liar, saying that Mr. Khrushchev had denied both publicly and privately that his country had put nuclear weapons in Cuba, while Mr. Kennedy now had photographic evidence that it had.

Any child could tell you that calling someone a liar was a good way to start a fight. Someone would take a sock at you, or call you a name, and that meant you had to push them away hard. I missed most of the rest of the speech as I pictured this fight, which would involve communist missiles. That was the other thing I retained, that the president said Soviets had put "communist missiles" in Cuba. The mushroom clouds I pictured took on a pinkish hue. Sunset. The end of the world.

As the president signed off, the network promised commentary, but after Bunny sat very still for a minute, she got up and turned off the TV.

"Come set the table," she said. "We might as well go out in style."

It started that suddenly. The shunning and the typhoon had both been sudden and the missile crisis was the same, even as the Hortons' troubles simmered in the background. I didn't understand what was going on, and the effort of trying to figure it out left me unfocused, my head hurting and my feet uncoordinated. I dropped cutlery getting it out of the drawer, making a clatter that left my stomach heaving.

"The forks go on the left," Bunny said. "You know that. And steak knives for the ribs."

My father got in while I was putting down the salt and pepper, maybe setting them up a little too straight. I could feel him watching me, even as he took off his hat and overcoat and put them in the hall closet. My mother appeared out of nowhere and gave him a drink on the rocks.

"Just like on the TV shows," she said, clinking her glass against his.

As my father examined his glass, she added, "Not the kind of TV we watched this afternoon."

"We heard it on the radio," he said. When Bunny gave him a questioning look, my father added, "I gave Dan Lake a ride."

"And what did two old army men conclude? That war plans are an oxymoron?" she asked. "I looked that up in the dictionary, by the way. A contradiction in terms."

"Can I sit down?" my father asked, taking his seat at the top of the kitchen table and looking around hopefully. "Something smells good."

"The last meal before execution."

"Muriel . . ."

"I don't like that word," I said. "They called Norman a moron and he's really smart. You can't call someone a Moron and Brains all at once."

"Haven't they stopped?" my father asked.

When I shook my head, he started to put out his arm, then hesitated, probably remembering the way I'd rejected it last time.

I went over and leaned against him.

"Dan pointed something out," my father said, putting his arm around me but speaking to my mother. "Kennedy wasn't announcing an invasion of Cuba. None of this, 'At 8 a.m., our troops landed, or will land.' He's just putting a naval quarantine around the island. Dan pointed out that he used the word 'quarantine' when the military term is 'blockade.' The fact he avoided saying blockade means he's trying to avoid military action."

"Words," Bunny said.

"Well, they're important. And as Dan says, everyone on the reserve has a Ph.D. in interpreting white men's double-talk."

"He's speaking about the president of the United States!"

"With respect for his intelligence. Which we're going to have to rely on."

The next morning, I stumbled around the kitchen, having spent a restless night. Hudson's Bay. The mushroom cloud. When I pushed aside my bowl of cereal, my father insisted on walking me over to the Hortons' place to pick up Norman for school. I dragged along wishing that he wouldn't, having had enough of adults to last me a lifetime.

Mrs. Horton met us at the door in her dressing gown, saying that both Norman and Rosa had stomach aches.

"I'm keeping them at home," she said. "And called in sick myself, in case we've picked up a bug. We wouldn't want to spread anything."

She and my father looked at each other unblinkingly, then he looked down at me.

"How's your stomach, Mary Alice?" he asked. "You think you'd better stay home, too?"

I shrugged.

"It might be a good idea," Mrs. Horton said. "These things can be catching."

I thought of the girls who'd begun to talk to me, and how that might be catching, too. I didn't quite admit to myself that they might be even friendlier if Norman wasn't there.

"My stomach doesn't hurt," I said. "My head hurts from all the nuclear missiles. But my stomach's okay."

"If you've got a headache . . ." my father began.

"Let's go," I told him. This caused Mrs. Horton some degree of amusement. She seemed ready to close the door, but my father lingered for a moment.

"Then I'll see you at the school board on Thursday."

"Presuming we're all still here," she said. "And they don't postpone."

"I imagine that's a possibility," my father replied, adding, "Postponement."

For some reason, this made them both smile, although crookedly.

I found the whole incident unclear and annoying, and at the end of the Hortons' driveway, I told my father I could go to school myself. I knew the way. What was the problem?

"Well, without Norman," he said, thinking it through, "you're probably right."

Even so, I could feel him watching me all the way along Connington Crescent until I turned downhill.

This was Tuesday. Walking into the schoolyard, I had to try to remember again what to do when I got there.

"Where's the commie?" Jamie Manners called, swaggering toward me. Jamie was the grade six Manners. No one claimed he'd inherited anyone's brains. "Where's your commie friend?" he repeated, stooping down to stare in my face.

Everyone was watching. I stepped back, balling my hands into fists in case I had to fight.

"I'm your sister's friend," I said.

This confused Jamie. "You're not her friend," he tried saying, but sounded unconvinced. He tried again: "You're not her friend. You're her pet."

I was ready to fight him on that one. But Harry Manners arrived and lifted his chin subtly, signalling his brother to look to one side. Looking over myself, I saw Mr. Eisenstadt watching from under the awning. He seemed to be watching me, not Jamie, and I met his eye. Not that it told me anything, not from so far away.

When I turned back, I found Harry leading his brother off, even though Harry was the younger one. Everyone else looked away from me, so we were back to that. Lining up, going to class, sitting down next to a vacant desk—there were quite a few—I was generally ignored.

Or inattentive, as I half heard Miss Oliphant say.

"Are you listening, Mary Alice?" she asked loudly, not long after lunch.

"No, ma'am."

I looked at the map of South America that she'd unrolled over the chalkboard, wondering what question I was supposed to answer.

"Russian missiles can reach most of Latin America from Cuba," I said.

A hysterical cry from Fiona Krawchuk. She was a dramatic girl, but she meant it.

"Well done, Mary," Miss Oliphant said.

"Alice," I replied.

Miss Atkinson would have hugged Fiona, who had broken out sobbing, but Miss Oliphant just hovered at the front of the room like a balloon on a string.

"She can go to the nurse's office, Miss Oliphant," I said. "She knows the way."

"I'll take her," Lucy Oliver said. She did a quick sliding double step as she stood up, and I looked over to find that someone had wet themselves near Lucy's desk. I would have said to send Gord Brewster for the janitor, but Gord was so red he must have been responsible.

"I'll get the janitor," I said.

"You'll do nothing of the sort," Miss Oliphant said.

But I opened the door so Lucy could lead Fiona out of the room, and once they were on their way to the nurse's office, I got the janitor, Mr. Mountcastle, and his bucket of sawdust. He was a spry old man who smelled of cigarettes and a particularly strong aftershave. After he'd cleaned up the puddle, Mr. Mountcastle told Gord Brewster, "Gordon, why don't you come help me with this," and Gord sidled out of the room close to his side.

After it was all over, Lucy and I exchanged a nod, proving that I was growing more visible again, a wavering presence. Afterward, I settled back and waited for the three o'clock bell.

The air raid siren revved up half an hour before dismissal. That rising, throat-clearing *er-er-er* followed by a long metallic shriek holding endlessly without human intake of breath. It hurt my chest, but I didn't panic. None of us panicked. It was more a case of being paralyzed, including Miss Oliphant.

The P.A. crackled with Mr. Eisenstadt's voice. "Teachers, this may not be a drill. Your classes to the auditorium in orderly fashion. I repeat, this may not be a drill."

We got out of the classroom to find ourselves in the hall in rows behind other classes in rows, including Mrs. Horton's class with a substitute teacher. I knew who she was but couldn't remember her name, although coming up with it struck me as important.

We were on the upper floor so we had to go down the stairs, accompanied by teachers' cries. "Orderly fashion! Orderly fashion!" Downstairs, turn right, go down another hallway and we reached the gym, which was also the auditorium. It was a huge empty square with small windows along the top of the side looking outdoors. Banners hung on the walls, and there were basketball hoops, and the big caramel-coloured wood floor wasn't scuffed up too badly, since it was a fairly new school. At the front was a stage with a red curtain and chairs stacked across it. The wail of the air raid siren bounced around inside those walls like a banshee.

When I got into the gym, I saw people being told to crawl under the stage through the open storage doors. Usually, the chairs were stored under there. That must have been why they were stacked on the stage. Mr. Mountcastle had been busy.

My heart clenched. I didn't want to go under there. I wasn't afraid of spiders, not more than usual, or of the dark, not that much, or of suffocating when the roof caved in like the famous Springhill Mine Disaster. But all these things combined to make me pull back from the stage even as I was carried toward it by the shuffle of people around me. My back wanted to retreat as my front moved ahead, and something inside me felt stretched between them.

I wasn't the only one. A boy balked when his turn came to go under the stage, holding up the line. His teacher barked at him and he whimpered but did it.

"Quickly now!" the teacher said, then followed her class underneath.

It was a small school but we had a big gym. The standard auditorium had been built to allow for the school's expansion as the suburb grew. Yet I knew we'd only get a tiny space to ourselves and be closely packed in, and didn't like the way I'd have to rub elbows with people who were scorning me out, especially Miss Oliphant.

At least there weren't any windows, I told myself, and ducked underneath.

The smell of dust tickled my nose and there was a strong whiff of Mr. Mountcastle's aftershave. Little children were sneezing like kittens, and there was a fugitive sound of glass rolling on the concrete floor. I heard a teacher say, "Bay rum," which left me frightened about the Hudson's Bay. There were a few cries when the doors were closed and the light went dim, but at least the siren was muffled.

"Well, isn't this cozy," my old grade one teacher, Miss Barnes, called loudly. "Why don't we sing a song?"

I suppose she was the senior teacher, or at least the oldest, and that made her the one to take charge. Yet having said that, she didn't seem to know what to sing, and another teacher started "God Save the Queen," which we all knew from the P.A. announcement every morning.

It was eerie, singing "God Save the Queen" under a stage as an air raid siren wailed, threatening us with the end of the world. A number of the littler ones sobbed, while a few of the bigger ones whimpered quietly. We were cramped together amid dust and cobwebs and spiders with heavy doors holding us in as if we'd been locked inside a mausoleum. Grave. The word beat in my head even as the anthem beat out. Long to grave over us. God grave our grave.

"Again!" Miss Barnes cried.

When I went to sing the second time, my throat choked up. In this moment I knew I would die. Not that I would die soon in the missile crisis, although that could happen. It was the solid certainty that I would die one day like everybody else. I'd always been afraid that my parents would die and leave me alone. But now I knew for a fact that I would go too, and I felt riven. Our minister, Mr. Culver, and the hope of heaven turned as insubstantial as echoes. I was unsubstantial, here on Earth so fleetingly, and I vibrated with horror.

The siren ended, an abrupt absence that made people raggedly trail off singing.

"Now we wait for the all-clear," Miss Barnes called, and everyone held their breath.

In the silence, I heard Miss Oliphant muttering to herself, and realized from the rhythm of her words that she was praying. She wasn't far behind me in the darkness, which was growing increasingly odorous and stuffy. I didn't know you could feel sorry for teachers, but my sore heart cracked open and I felt sorry for her.

"You should sing, Miss Oliphant," I told her. "You've got a pretty voice."

"Who said that?" she asked sharply.

"God," Nancy Workman replied sonorously. She'd deepened her tone like a comedian, but I knew it was her. Mrs. Horton's class was next to ours under the stage, although of course with the substitute teacher instead of Mrs. Horton.

"All right, Nancy, that's enough," the substitute said.

Mrs. Walton. Remembering her name felt like a victory. She was a nice substitute, sparky, although she was like all of them in having several pairs of eyes in the back of her head. She also sounded as if she was having trouble not laughing, and it's just as well she didn't, or the entire school would have crashed into hysteria.

The drill ended soon after that. A drill, teachers reassured us. Of course it was a drill, and people emerged in just as orderly a fashion as they'd gone in, except looking dazed.

Miss Oliphant looked more dazed than most, and in the few minutes before class was dismissed, she gaped awkwardly at our faces, trying to figure out who had praised her singing. I suppose that being under the stage had distorted my voice because she should have recognized it. Maybe she had a block: I couldn't have possibly said anything nice to her. I loathed that teacher, but understood as she gaped that there was something off about her. Standing at the front of the class, she couldn't identify a telltale smirk, since I was innocent and looked innocent, and she finished the day in a defeated droop while I walked home traumatized, but at least unscolded.

Wednesday. The Hortons still had stomach aches. The nice substitute Mrs. Walton patrolled the schoolyard with her several pairs of eyes so I was roughly all right. After school, Bunny and I learned from the radio that there was no response from Chairman Khrushchev to the American insistence he get his missiles out of Cuba. I wondered what my father would have to say, and went to the picture window in the living room to look for the car.

A long sleek silver airplane flew in low over the city, just above the rooftops of the highest buildings. It was coming in from the east but headed for the west of the city, which was a relief. Then it banked around and circled back. I was paralyzed, and my father came in to find me clinging to the back of his lounge chair, panting like a frightened cat. He picked me up and sat me on his lap and waited.

"We're all going to die from cancer like the people in Hiroshima," I said. "After the radiation gets here."

"That's not going to happen, Mary Alice."

"But we're going to die."

"Not for a very long time, I hope."

"But we're going to die."

"It's an airliner coming in to the airport. See how he's circling, waiting for permission to land. The pilot's giving his passengers a good look at the city."

He sounded like Bunny, and I felt forlorn.

Thursday, the day of the special evening session of the school board. It hadn't been postponed, and my mother didn't know why not. I heard her say so when I was standing outside my parents' bedroom door. I needed to ask whether I should change back into my school uniform or if ordinary clothes were all right.

"Why are you insisting on doing this? Sacrificing your family for the sake of what? Sacrificing your daughter. Just like the Hortons, running roughshod over their children."

I hadn't intended to eavesdrop. I'd more or less stopped eavesdropping because Bunny was right, I no longer wanted to hear what people said. I no longer wanted to hear anything. I just wanted it to all go away. Or at least, go back to the way it was before, when we were safe.

I went and changed into my Sunday clothes, which I had decided would be best, then headed for the living room to wait. Hearing a rattle in the kitchen, I looked in and found Debbie putting away the dinner dishes, which had been draining. When she turned and smiled, I saw that her mid-section was bursting out round and shiny under her navy blue maternity dress, which had a white collar and cuffs. Debbie refused to wear maternity clothes with flounces. She hadn't lost her sense of style, she said. She was just pregnant.

I realized Debbie was looking at my clothes as seriously as I was looking at hers.

"Oh, little Tinker, there you are," she said. "And they haven't told you you're not going."

A truck hit me.

"It's all right. I'm here to babysit."

"But Norman's my friend."

"Well that's true," she said. "But I'm afraid you're not going."

My father and mother came in, both of them in Sunday clothes as well, my mother even carrying a pair of gloves. Neither looked happy. I was going to speak when Debbie cut in.

"Tink didn't realize she's not going with you. But we'll be all right."

Debbie put a hand on my shoulder the way Bob had put his on Uncle Punk's. I hadn't realized before then how heavy a hand could be. It kept me rooted in place as my parents left.

But it wasn't all right. After they'd gone, I felt like howling. When Debbie let me free, I raged around the living room, feeling as trapped as if they'd put me under a stage. Barred the doors, forgotten me. I threw myself into my father's lounge chair and leapt out. Threw myself on the chesterfield and jumped up. Threw myself against the wall, which hurt my shoulder.

"Hey, hey, hey, Tinker," Debbie said. "I'm going to have to ask you to calm down."

She came over and tried to hold me against her belly. I knew to be gentle, but spun away and stood there furiously.

"Norman is *my* friend. Daddy doesn't even like Mr. Horton, and Bunny hates him. She *hates* him."

Debbie looked down at me; at my hands balled into fists. My cat was looking at me, too. Wilma sat in the doorway, ballooning out behind her front legs. She was expecting as well. The only thing that would have distracted me was if she'd started having kittens right there.

"All right," Debbie said. "Go get your coat."

I wasn't sure I'd heard that.

"Go get your coat." Smiling. "I want to go, too."

16

W hen we got to the civic centre, we followed signs to the special session of the school board. It was being held in the Grouse Valley council chamber at the centre of the complex, a hexagonal room under a small glass dome. Bunny had hoped that the missile crisis meant few people would come. But when we walked into the chamber, the room was as full as a carnival tent, people laughing and chatting, the walls vibrating with outlandish joy.

The council table was at the front of the room, which had been designed like a church or a courthouse with wooden benches fanning back from it like pews. There were two banks of benches, and an aisle ran down the middle. I didn't see my parents or the Hortons, but Mr. Manners already sat on a bench at the front with his son, Cal, and an old man I thought must be his father, Calvin Senior. Andy and the younger boys weren't with them, but as I sat down, I glimpsed Mrs. Manners hovering at the back of the room wearing a scarf over her red hair.

"So you brought Tinker," my Aunt Magda said.

Startled, I turned to find that Debbie had led me to a bench toward the rear of the room where my aunt was already sitting.

"Magda," Debbie said, leaning over her stomach to give our aunt a kiss. "She was like a little bird flying into the window."

"I have no use for the overprotection of children. Better to see what crowds are like. Nasty things. It's good to toughen them up."

"Norman got toughened up by polio," I said.

"Just as well," my aunt replied.

It came to me that when Norman lay in the iron lung, young as he was, he must have understood that he would die. Maybe that day, maybe tomorrow, but certainly one day. Looking around, I realized that everybody there knew they were going to die. Grown-ups all knew that. Maybe they changed a little after they knew it. I wondered if I had.

A bustle at a side door, and my father and brother came in with the Hortons and another man. They sat at the front on the opposite side of the room from the Manners family. When my mother slipped in afterward, she took a seat behind my father. Many of her friends were in the room, sitting behind the Manners to show their support and fanning out from there. I could pick out Dentist Winters, and Mr. and Mrs. Wall, Mrs. O'Neill, Dr. and Mrs. Longford, nice Mrs. Armstrong and her husband, who was a pharmacist, along with many others I recognized, although I didn't know their names. The ice cream truck man was there, and a teller from the bank, shopkeepers from the village. I'd never thought about it, but of course they had children, too.

Principal Eisenstadt and Mr. Duprée sat neutrally on the aisle in the middle of the room. Neither of their wives was with them. Mr. Duprée didn't look at my father after he came in, nor did my father look at him. I'd heard my father tell Bunny that Mike Duprée was sick of Jack Horton and didn't appreciate any effort to keep him employed. Both principals were silent, but people around them continued to chat in loud whispers, looking pointedly at the Hortons. There was no protest out front, no signs, no slogans. This was an orderly community. But the feeling against the Hortons was so strong, people might have been gathering to stone them.

When the door opened again, the five trustees came in to take seats behind the large oak table at the front of the room. I recognized Mr.

O'Neill, who came in first and took his seat at the head of the table, where there was a chair with a high back and wooden arms. Mr. O'Neill was married to the neighbour who made candy apples, and I knew he was chairman of the board. A tall man, and thin.

I didn't know the three other men coming in behind him but was surprised to see Mrs. Oliver follow them to the table. I knew she was in politics, but I would have said she was head of the local PTA. Now she sat down importantly with a thick file in front of her. The four trustees sat two-by-two on each side of the table, taking up very little room.

"A gathering of intellectual giants and wits," Aunt Magda said.

"You're going to get us in trouble," Debbie whispered.

"And that's him," my aunt said, nodding at Mr. Horton, whom she'd been watching.

"Jack Horton," Debbie agreed.

"Horowitz, more likely," my aunt said.

"Call this meeting to order," Mr. O'Neill said, not particularly loudly. He waited a moment, and since this was Canada, the meeting came to order.

Mr. O'Neill looked around the crowd, scanning it as if he was looking for someone, maybe a Lone Ranger ready to rescue him from peril. Something around his mouth told me that Mr. O'Neill didn't want to be there. After his fruitless scan, he turned his attention back to the near seats and set his shoulders, as if knowing he would have to bear the burden.

"We're fortunate to have the Reverend Culver in attendance," he said, although I had an idea that the O'Neills were Catholic. "The Reverend has kindly offered to start us off with a blessing before we get to the business at hand."

With a slight bow of his head, Mr. Culver stood up from the row behind Mr. Manners, revealing Mrs. Culver beside him. He made his way to the front of the table, raising his hands as if he were in the pulpit. Mr. Culver was wearing his black suit and white collar. I'm not sure I ever saw him dressed in anything less formal.

"Oh Lord," he began. "We live in perilous times. Grant your wisdom to *all* our leaders, that they may protect us from threat. For we face Godlessness and evil"—looking pointedly at the Hortons—"and it can be called nothing lighter nor less. Your children seek refuge in your sanctity, dear Lord, innocent lambs *not* for the slaughter. Spread your protection over them, that those who love your name may rejoice in you. Amen."

"Amen," the room agreed enthusiastically.

"Thank you, Reverend," Mr. O'Neill said. "And thanks to principals Duprée and Eisenstadt for joining us, and to so many of our ratepayers for taking the time to be here."

Both Jim Manners and Jack Horton sat up alertly, as if expecting to be acknowledged as well.

Instead, Mr. O'Neill went on, "I'll take a moment to set out the issue we're facing here, which revolves around the sanctity of the schools. Teachers are bound, legally and morally, to conduct themselves as examples to our students."

"No bad apples," someone called.

"We can't tolerate breaches in behaviour," Mr. O'Neill agreed, "and we're here to consider an alleged breach of great significance."

The word *alleged* made Mr. Manners impatient. His father, Old Calvin Manners, turned even more bullish, looking like the bust of Beethoven that frowned over our school music room.

"As all of you know, two teachers in our district have been accused of being adherents of communism, a political movement that Ambassador Adlai Stevenson characterized at the United Nations earlier this week as seeking world domination. In fact, it's an evangelizing force of near-religious zealotry . . ."

"Anti-religious," the Reverend Culver corrected loudly. "Atheistic."

"The point is, Reverend, they look for converts," Mr. O'Neill replied in a reasonable voice. "Wherever they can find them, I would guess. But what concerns us here is whether they're seeking them among our children."

There were murmurs of agreement, and Mr. Culver acknowledged the point graciously. Across the room, I saw my father keep his eyes on our minister, even as Mr. O'Neill continued to speak, naming Mr. and Mrs. Horton, which made Mr. Culver shake his head sadly. From the expression on my father's face, I could see that we weren't going to go to Mr. Culver's church anymore, and wondered what that meant about choir.

Mr. O'Neill went on to make specific reference to the collective agreement, along with the morality clause and other terms I'd picked up at our family barbecue, even though I still wasn't sure what they meant. But my mind must have wandered, because suddenly there was silence in the room and I realized that Mr. O'Neill was looking expectantly at Mr. Manners. A buzz from the crowd, a throat-clearing bustle, and he stood up and walked to the wooden table.

Mr. Manners took a position at one corner of the table and put down a file. A tall broad-shouldered man in a business suit. A square-faced, black-haired lawyer considered handsome by my mother and her friends. A former prisoner-of-war with a bad shoulder and a tremor in his hands that was visible even from where I sat. A husband and father who hit his family.

"I've looked into this," Mr. Manners began, "at some length, after my eldest son heard communistic language used in the classroom. Many here know my concern, and how I started . . . looking into this. In fact, since I first talked to many of you, I've continued to find other evidence," he said, and people leaned forward. "Particularly about the history of the Hortons' employment."

Mr. Horton shifted angrily on the bench as Mr. Manners opened a file. I knew most of what he mentioned: that Jack Horton had gone to McGill University—"on the public dollar"—and that a cousin of Mr. Manners, who had been there at the time, said he was known for his incendiary views. Also his membership in campus "clubs," which was said disdainfully. The police kept an eye on him. Mr. Manners's cousin knew this for a fact. After he graduated, the Hortons moved from Montreal to Sudbury, although not immediately, leaving what Mr. Manners called a puzzling year-long gap.

"To all intents and purposes," he said, "the Hortons disappeared from the face of the Earth. Or, arguably, from this country, perhaps to another with ironclad borders."

"Oh, come on," Jack Horton called.

Mr. Manners looked rattled but ignored him.

"After living in Sudbury for four years, they took themselves off to Prince George, and from there to Vancouver. And the question is," he asked, scanning the crowd, "what were they up to?"

"Looking for work," Mr. Horton called, and Mr. O'Neill gavelled him quiet.

"Only yesterday," Mr. Manners said, "I spoke to the principal of the high school where Jack Horton taught in Sudbury. An industrial town, I would point out, rife with communist activity, where agitators are frequently uncovered."

More angry shifting from Mr. Horton. Beside him, Mrs. Horton looked down quietly, so I could only see the crown of braids around her head.

"In all fairness," Mr. Manners went on, "I can tell you that the principal, Mr. George Hausmann, had no complaints about Mr. Horton's teaching. This despite what he called 'Jack's prickliness, his arrogance, and his red-tinged views.'" Murmurs of agreement from the crowd. "He also told me that the principal of the elementary school was very high on Mrs. Horton, even though she was closely involved with that well-known communist union, the Mine, Mill and Smelter Workers, cooking meals during a notorious labour dispute."

"She took dinner to our neighbours," Jack Horton called. "When the parents were on strike and the children were hungry."

"But," Jim Manners went on, "despite the principals' forbearance, the Hortons left them in the lurch. With minimal notice, Mr. Horton packed up his family and left town. As if, as Mr. Hausmann put it, they had no real concern for the schools but were working for a different employer. Which, he told me, he'd seen before. So had the local police force, which Mr. Hausmann knew for a fact had kept a file on the Horton family."

"Insinuation," Jack Horton called. "All of it."

"All right, Horton," Mr. O'Neill said. "You're in danger of losing your turn to respond."

"My right to respond," Horton said, and my father put his hand on Mr. Horton's arm.

"Members of the board have a right to speak at our meetings," Mr. O'Neill told him. "Being unelected, Mr. Horton, you speak at my forbearance. Which I warn you is beginning to fray."

As Mr. Horton settled unhappily back into his seat, I was left with a memory of Norman saying something about his parents leaving Sudbury that I couldn't quite call to mind. Nor did I find it very interesting to hear from Mr. Manners about Prince George being another industrial centre, also rife, or to see the newspaper photograph he held up of Mrs. Horton protesting the Bomb. More interesting was a police photograph showing her at a bigger protest. When Mr. Manners said that a civic-minded member of the force had passed it on, everybody in the council chamber turned to look at Mr. Wall, who remained as stony-faced as if he was giving out another ticket to Mr. O'Neill.

"Many people here have heard me say this," Mr. Manners said, "or heard most of it, and they've signed their name to a petition. From which, Mr. Chairman, I would like to read the names of the signatories, to indicate the range of support I've received for the removal of the Hortons, like an infestation, from our schools."

"Infestation," Aunt Magda murmured, and leaned over to me. "If you are called an infestation, you must run."

I remembered the numbers tattooed on her arm and nodded, although I was soon caught up in the roll call of names. I heard Potts and Shribman and Brewster and Workman and Cole, surprised to recognize many as parents from my school and the high school. It hadn't occurred to me before that people who'd signed the petition would have children in Mr. and Mrs. Horton's classes. Nancy Workman and Cathy Cole were both in Mrs. Horton's class, and if Cathy Cole's parents had signed, Jeannie Stevens's would have, too. Mr. Horton had been suspended, but I hadn't realized Mrs. Horton had been looking every day at the faces of people whose parents wanted her fired. Hearing Mr. Manners read out their names so sonorously—and here was "Stevens"—I didn't know how either of the Hortons would be able to go back to their schools. I craned toward Mrs. Horton. It didn't look as if she expected to.

Mr. Manners took a long time to read the names, and the list created ripples of pride in the audience as people heard themselves mentioned. Old Calvin Manners looked proud as well, and nodded in satisfaction when the list was finished. A thought came to me. He looked proud as a mountain when his son sat back down beside him, and cleared a good space for him on the bench. When I turned to my father and brother, I saw the same tie between them, and got a sense of the rugged bond between parents and children. Rugged, robust, jagged as rocks, and entirely inescapable.

"Jack Horton," Mr. O'Neill said, calling me back to order.

"Sir," Mr. Horton replied, not without irony.

"I'm going to give you a chance to respond, Jack. Which is more, I would note, than I would expect to happen in the Soviet Union, where dissent is crushed. I think that's a fair word."

"You're assuming I have any use for the Soviet Union," Mr. Horton said, speaking even as he walked toward the table. "Which I don't."

There was a wary rustling in the crowd as Mr. Horton reached the table, carrying none of the notes Mr. Manners had relied on. I remembered my brother saying that you could be a communist without supporting the

Soviet Union, and looked over at Bob, whose long grave face gave away nothing more than our father's.

"But this isn't about the Soviet Union, is it?" Mr. Horton asked, and electricity ran through the crowd. Judging from their raised eyebrows, a good number of people seemed fully aware of his affair with Mrs. Manners, and that included the trustees.

"I have to say, it's been very odd to hear my decisions cast in such a melodramatic light," Mr. Horton said. "But here's the mundane story. I don't know Jim Manners's cousin and have no idea how he purports to know about my career at McGill. Where, as a matter of fact, I was an eager member of the outdoors club."

Mr. Manners shuffled through his papers, but couldn't seem to find what he wanted.

"After leaving university, I was unable to secure work teaching high school in Montreal, my French being inadequate. My wife and I took the decision to cross the so-called *ironclad* Ontario border to try our luck in Toronto, thinking we'd both be able to find jobs in the big city. When we couldn't, I ended up working in a meatpacking plant."

"No doubt trying to organize the workers," Mr. Manners called.

"Earning a paycheque, sir. Which is something that concerns most of us deeply."

Mr. Manners looked ready to respond when Mr. O'Neill cut in.

"Jim," he said, "I asked him not to interrupt. I'll ask the same of you."

Jim Manners sat back in his seat.

"Fortunately, we were finally able to get jobs in Sudbury," Jack Horton went on. "It suited us. My wife likes the outdoors as much as I do. We got a canoe. Went hiking. And yes, my wife took food to several of our neighbours when they went on strike. We had paycheques when they only had strike pay. And children."

He looked around the council chamber, speaking to the people there as if they were friends, although he hadn't tried to make any.

"My wife and I had a daughter ourselves," he told them, "and our son was born in Sudbury. Unfortunately, he wasn't a well baby. And why I'm forced to bring up these personal details in a public meeting when this could have been settled in a strictly private conversation . . ."

Jack Horton and Jim Manners glared at one another. The room was titillated now, and Mr. O'Neill looked uneasy.

"He's very clever," my aunt murmured to my sister. "I don't quite trust him, of course. Nor do I particularly like this Manners. Certainly, his wife has exhausting taste in men."

I turned to look at Mrs. Manners, who was staring at Jack Horton with a look of abject devotion on her face.

"My son was subject to repeated colds and lung infections," he said. "To the point where the doctors advised us to get him out of Sudbury. The Big Smoke, they call it. Once again, we started looking for jobs. Not that we advertised this to our principals, having no guarantee we'd be able to find anything. It's not easy, getting two teaching jobs in the same city. But we finally found work in Prince George and gave our notice in Sudbury. Not negligible notice, as has been claimed, but as much as we could, and certainly as much as was legally required."

I remembered it now. Norman had said that his parents were sent to Prince George. It seemed as if they were sent by the doctors, and I wondered why Norman hadn't just said so.

"We liked Prince George. We like outdoor pursuits, as I've mentioned. But as some of you know, our boy contracted polio, and we had to come down to Vancouver for his treatment. And here we are, maligned for decisions of the type anybody in this room might have made for the sake of their work and their families."

Uneasy shifting in seats. No one had expected this.

Mr. Manners stood up, not quite steadily, and grasped for the back of a seat ahead of him that wasn't there. After he found his footing, he faced Jack Horton belligerently.

"But are you a communist, Horton? You seem to have left out that part."

Mr. Horton looked at him steadily. "For the record," he said, "I'm not a member of the Communist Party, no. I'm not a communist. Thank you for finally asking."

Mr. Manners refused to stand down. "From this, perhaps we can take it that you're not a member today," he said. "Yesterday is a different question."

Mr. Horton gave him a smile that was equal parts forbearing and furious.

"I'm on the liberal side of the equation, no doubt. And to dispel any doubts, I will tell you carefully, sir, that when I was in the army, in a role I'm unable to talk about, use was made of my languages. I grew up in Winnipeg, which you may know as a city of immigrants. Our northern Chicago, we liked to say. As a boy, I learned to speak Polish, Hungarian . . ."

"Czech," Aunt Magda murmured.

". . . and a decent amount of Russian. You'll remember that the Soviet Union was our ally in the war against Hitler. You'll remember the Battle of Stalingrad, when the Soviets beat back the Nazis. They crippled Hitler, and at terrible cost to themselves. I admired that. They're tough, those Russians."

Looking around the room, I could see people growing even more intent, with some of the men nodding reluctant agreement.

"And it's true, I looked into it. Communism. And in fact," he said, speaking each word clearly, "I didn't like it, nor did I like the Soviet Union. I've mentioned that. I've never been a member of the Communist Party. Does that answer your question, sir?"

Jim Manners looked at him for a long time, thinking it through before shaking his head. "You're so slippery you could grease a wheel," he finally said. "O'Neill . . . Mr. Chairman. I don't trust him. How many years did you look into communism, Horton? And how closely? Maybe you didn't join the party, but you travelled alongside it pretty closely, and I would suspect for a good long time. My boy was in your class. He heard what you said."

"He heard an analogy, Manners," Mr. Horton said, growing testy. "We spoke of the Greek empire, the Roman empire, the British empire in the last century, and the growing American empire in this one. I don't think anyone in Washington would dispute the analogy. Half the buildings in Washington have Roman facades." He controlled his anger, but still sounded irritated. "It's true I took a ten-minute deviation from the curriculum, as teachers often do, and landed a two-week suspension because of it. Without pay, Manners, which I repeat, means something to me. When I'm still paying off medical bills for my son's polio."

Reluctant sympathy rippled through the room. A sense of uneasiness. Jack Horton wasn't the bear they thought they'd be baiting.

He turned to Mr. O'Neill.

"I need my job, sir. My wife needs hers. My parents are dead and hers were farmers with a big family. Jobs are what we've got." He rubbed his jaw. "And a mortgage."

After thinking for a minute, he added, "That's all I've got to say."

Nobody knew what to do, including the trustees, who leaned across the table to confer. I looked over at my father and brother, who talked quietly. Jim Manners and his father were doing the same. Members of the audience were more noisy, and it looked as if some people were disagreeing with their neighbours. The only one in the room who remained still and silent was my Aunt Magda, who came out of a reverie when she realized I was looking at her.

"So, what do you make of your friend's father?" she asked.

"Norman said his family was sent to Prince George," I replied, unsure whether they could have been sent by doctors.

"Yes, I would imagine so," Aunt Magda said.

By this time, the board had finished conferring, and Mr. O'Neill called the meeting back to order, inviting any members of the audience to speak, who wanted to say their piece.

My father stood up. "If I could add a word."

"You don't have a child in the high school," Mr. Manners called, and turned to Mr. O'Neill. "He doesn't have a child in high school. And we're talking about Jack Horton."

Mr. O'Neill thought about this, and the trustees leaned together again to consult.

"Afraid that's a good point, Hall. Is there anyone with a son or daughter in the high school who has some light to shed on the situation?"

My father sat down reluctantly. People looked at each other, or looked away from each other. I turned to see Mrs. Manners still standing at the back of the room, not as still as before, but vibrating in place, a ballerina dancing on pointe on a darkened stage.

"There's something I could say," came a voice from the rear.

Everyone rippled with surprise as my father's friend Mr. Lake walked down the aisle. I don't think I'd noticed before how gracefully he walked. He stopped facing the board members, not standing behind either Mr. Horton nor Mr. Manners, but in the centre aisle.

"Well, here we go then, Chief," Mr. O'Neill said. "Give you the floor."

Mr. Lake paused. "I'm not a chief," he said. "I'm Dan Lake, and I've got a boy in grade eleven."

He paused again, not proceeding quickly. This sounded companionable when working under a car hood, but didn't entirely fit in the council chamber. I could see that Mr. Lake knew this and disliked it. He disliked being here.

"I want to talk about what started last year, when Jack Horton came to the reserve, offering to tutor some of our boys. The idea was to see if they could get into university. We didn't ask him to come. It was his idea, to tutor them on Saturday. He knew the boys from school and thought he could help."

"Thought he might get some recruits," Mr. Manners said loudly.

Mr. Lake looked at him equably. "When this came up, I spoke to our boys," he said. "I was interested to see if there was any of that going on. By that time, he'd been working with them for more than a year. All of the boys said there'd been none of that. He just helped them with their schoolwork, and got them ready for exams."

"Well, good for them," Mrs. Oliver said, breaking in suddenly. "We all know what it's like to get teenagers to study on the weekend. How did they do? On their exams?"

These struck me as trick questions, although I couldn't see the trick.

Mr. Lake seemed to, and smiled.

"He did a good job, Mrs. Trustee. The boys all pulled up their marks. The oldest one got a scholarship, and he started university this fall."

"Well, *good for him*," Mrs. Oliver said. "Scholarship from where?"

"The Kiwanis."

"Good work. Studying what?"

Mr. Lake paused, as if waiting to be handed a tool.

"Science," he said. "The young man intends to go into medicine. Be a doctor."

They hadn't expected this, and it set the trustees back. I didn't know why they would be surprised at a young man's plans to be a doctor. I remembered things I didn't quite understand about prejudice. But Mr. Lake understood it very well, and smiled slightly, not in amusement.

"We owe Jack Horton a debt for his help with our boys," he said. "I came here to pay it. He didn't charge a nickel, and he very seldom missed a session, even when the boys might have welcomed a break."

Mr. O'Neill thought about this.

"Thanks, Chief," he said. "That's actually quite useful."

"Appreciate the promotion, sir," Mr. Lake replied, making Mr. O'Neill glance at him sharply. "If I can add?"

Mr. O'Neill nodded.

"Actions are what speak to me. Questioning a man's motives, that's up to himself."

Without saying anything else, Mr. Lake turned and walked back up the aisle, leaving one of his silences behind him. It took Mr. O'Neill a moment to get past it, but when he did, he turned to Jack Horton.

"However," he said, and paused to think it through. "However, I'm curious, Horton. What took you down to the reserve?"

Mr. Horton stood up again, looking uncomfortable. "Well, I thought I could help." Looking around the room, he said, "Many people here—if their children are falling behind, they can get extra help from the teachers. I saw some bright boys who weren't getting any help, and I thought I could provide it."

Mr. Duprée shot Jack Horton a look that would freeze an erupting volcano. Nor did Mr. O'Neill appear pleased.

"But why these boys?" he asked. "Some sort of missionary zeal, Horton? I mentioned that earlier, and I find the phrase coming to mind again. Missionary zeal. And from what perspective?"

"From the perspective of a boy who grew up poor in Winnipeg, O'Neill, in a family that had trouble getting its children the type of help I'm now able to provide."

"The North End, was it?" Old Calvin Manners asked in a carrying voice, speaking for the first time. "Rife with Jews and communists."

Most people in the room murmured in a way that meant they agreed, including Mrs. Oliver. I looked at my Aunt Magda and was surprised to find her perspiring, and rubbing the tattoo on her arm. Then her shoulders girded themselves. I remembered a quote she repeated from a man named Beckett. You must go on. I can't go on. I'll go on.

Jack Horton looked just as girded.

"Rife," he said, "with a great bulk of people damned sick of politics, which has too often caused them grief. People who just want to get on with their lives. Among them myself."

An uproar caused Mr. O'Neill to bang his gavel several times.

"All right. All right. We'll come to order," he called over the hubbub. "We'll come to order, and I'll ask you to watch your language, Horton."

As the room calmed down, the trustees put their heads together, conferring and nodding again, although this time it wasn't long before Mr. O'Neill sat back up in his chair.

"I don't think there's anyone else," he said. "Mike, you don't want to say anything?"

Mr. Duprée couldn't have shaken his head more vigorously.

"All right," Mr. O'Neill said, looking over the confused room. "I'm not sure any of us really want to be here, and not for much longer. I'll thank the public for coming. The board will meet to discuss what we've heard. Mr. Manners, I'd also like to thank you very much for your show of civic responsibility."

Mr. O'Neill didn't sound very thankful or very fond of civic responsibility. I tried to understand what was going to happen and couldn't.

"Jack Horton," he went on, after a pause. "I think you're very likely your own worst enemy. That in itself isn't enough to bar you from teaching. But what might do the trick is the truth. I have to say, I'm not sure, personally, that you've told the whole story. As Manners says, there are gaps, which you talk over with notable fluency. You got a meatpacking job in Toronto, but for how long? What was your wife doing? This means the board has a good deal to weigh, and a few phone calls to make. We'll let you know our decision . . ."

"But the wife," Mr. Manners called.

He scrabbled through the file on his lap, looking like an old man trying to find a slip of paper in his wallet. Finally, he held up the photographs of Mrs. Horton protesting the Bomb. People who had been gathering themselves to leave were forced to stop, looking annoyed. They had enough to talk about. They wanted to go home.

"Yes, the wife," Mrs. Oliver said, taking over. Eyes shifted from Mr. O'Neill, who couldn't have looked more relieved. Mrs. Oliver stood up, tall and formidable.

"Marian," she said. "Ban the bomb."

Mrs. Horton stood up calmly and turned so she could face her.

270

"I hope they do," she said. "I don't want anyone dropping it on my children."

"The Russians?"

"The Russians, the Americans, anyone else who might build it. Look what we're going through right now."

Mention of the crisis made people uneasy. We'd forgotten it for a while.

"If you want to know," Mrs. Horton went on, "I dislike the way we've got ourselves into this position. Daring to build such powerful weapons. I'd like to see them banned worldwide. If you want to know, I was under no illusion that going to a pair of small protests would do any good. But I have children, and I teach children. I love teaching. It's my vocation. So when a friend asked me to go to a couple of protests, I thought it was something I could do. I could stand up and try to be a decent person. I think that's what we're asked for in life. To be decent people."

Marian Horton looked up at the back of the chamber, where Mrs. Manners stood. Nobody missed this, although she seemed to do it without intending to make a point. She fixed Mrs. Manners with a long unwavering stare that looked very hard to take. Mrs. Manners stared back, and the lights caught the tears on her cheeks.

Marian Horton was the one to end it, shaking her head and sitting down. Jack Horton had been looking down at his clasped hands the entire time.

"Well," Mr. O'Neill began.

"But," Jim Manners called, and couldn't seem to think what else to say.

"If I can," my father said, and stood. "Having a child in the school."

"And in the council chamber," Mrs. Oliver interrupted. "Isn't it past her bedtime?"

Looking puzzled, my father turned and saw me on Debbie's lap. Not knowing what else to do, I waved at him brightly, and there was a ripple of relieved laughter in the auditorium.

My father smiled at Mrs. Oliver.

"The Horton boy is her friend," he said. "And she's worried about her friend. This sort of thing takes a toll on children. The Horton children, too."

"Who's look-to is that?" Jim Manners called.

My father looked at him for long enough for everyone to think, What about your children? But my father only said, "It's all our look-to, Jim, trying to protect our children. My wife said to me earlier tonight, 'Why do you have to get involved in this? It's hard on your family.' I'm proud to say my elder daughter and my son are both fine and responsible adults." He nodded at Debbie, then at Bob, who seemed to look inward. "But my wife is right, as she always is. Standing up here is hard on my family, and I couldn't be more sorry."

He looked at Bunny, who seemed both embarrassed and helplessly moved.

"But what's harder on them," my father said, turning back to the trustees, "is to let things slide. To keep from saying, No, this is wrong. As Jack Horton has said, much of what's going on here is personal, and it should have been handled privately."

I couldn't see Jim Manners, his bullish father was leaning so far forward, looking as if he could spit nails.

"But from your closing remarks," my father continued, "I can see that it's trapped the board in a corner. You're being forced to make a political decision.

"And I think it's wrong, Mr. Chairman, to discipline teachers for their private political beliefs, whatever they may be. The morality clause in the collective agreement wasn't written for that purpose. Wisely, I would say. If you feel a teacher oversteps politically in the classroom, to whatever side of the equation, deal with their actions as Principal Duprée did. A two-week suspension without pay. I wouldn't want to be out two weeks' pay myself, and I'd think long and hard about doing anything else that would put me in breach of contract again. If I did, if it kept happening, that would have to be dealt with.

"But we're speaking of Marian Horton, and I can't see firing a teacher for going to a couple of small protests outside school hours. Or one of the larger Ban the Bomb marches, if it came to that. I don't want my children to live in a world where they can't join a legal protest—or for that matter, a legal political party—without jeopardizing their livelihoods. I don't think that's right. I may disagree with some people's choices, and I often do. But one of the freedoms we enjoy in our society is the right to make unpopular choices. No violence. Nothing illegal. But attend your rally or join your small political party. That's your right, and I hope it remains our children's right.

"I would ask the trustees to consider that in making your decision. Thank you."

When my father sat down, there was a long silence. I would have expected clapping, but there was none. Uneasiness. Reluctant admiration. Pockets of bullish disagreement.

Finally, Irene Oliver asked, "But you're not a communist, Marian? Just to clarify."

Mrs. Horton stood up again calmly.

"Yes, I am," she said.

In the immediate hubbub, Marian Horton smiled at her husband, a wash of victory, bitterness, and amusement fleeting over her face. Raising her voice over the clamour, she said, "I joined the Communist Party of Canada when I was young, and after it was outlawed, I joined the Labour-Progressive Party . . ."

"A communist front!" Jim Manners called.

"Yes, it was," Marian Horton called back amiably. "And while I left the party over the Soviet invasion of Hungary, and Premier Khrushchev's revelation of Stalin's crimes . . ."

Old Cal Manners was beside himself, clapping his knee, then slapping Jim Manners's head with a flat palm and the greatest bonhomie.

"I continue to feel that communism, as a philosophy of economic justice and social equality . . ."

I turned to look for Mrs. Manners, but she had disappeared.

"Well," Marian Horton said, "I just agree with it, that's all."

Turning back, I was just in time to see Jack Horton give his wife a look of profound admiration. She didn't meet his eye, but smiled abstractly and made the oddest gesture, stroking her chest as if it were a cat.

"And your husband, Marian?" Mrs. Oliver asked, calling Mrs. Horton back into the room.

After thinking for a moment, Mrs. Horton gave a funny little smile.

"My job, my vocation is to teach children to put two and two together," she said. "Not just in arithmetic, but in terms of learning how to reach informed conclusions. I consider it my job to help them develop a critical frame of mind."

"There you go," Old Cal Manners called. "Undermining society."

Mrs. Horton paused politely while he spoke, but otherwise disregarded him.

"That also makes it part of my job, my vocation, to pose difficult questions. The sort of questions that cause children, and cause us, to put two and two together outside arithmetic, adding together disparate facts that we know—we *do* know—in order to reach a reasonable conclusion."

"We understand that, Marian," Mrs. Oliver said patiently.

"Does my husband honestly strike you as a person who could endure the discipline of belonging to a political party?" Mrs. Horton asked. "Any more than he enjoys the discipline of marriage."

Mrs. Oliver didn't know what to make of that.

"Good luck in deciding what to do with him," Mrs. Horton said, getting her coat, ready to leave, but pausing to look down at her husband. "I've never found it easy, myself."

17

" They're going to fire the Hortons," Bunny said, as we drove home from the council chambers. "Drive them out of town."

I thought she was probably right and pictured the moving van appearing again outside their rockery, which people still called the Milewski's rockery before correcting themselves. The corrections would stop now, the Hortons forgotten by everyone but me.

"Cam O'Neill might surprise us," my father said, keeping his eyes on the road. "Nothing ever happens the way you expect."

I didn't find this reassuring, given the situation in Cuba. When we got home, I went to bed without being asked and didn't even try to eavesdrop. Yet everything felt so uncertain that I couldn't sleep for a very long time, and woke up the next morning wanting this to end. I also knew that it wasn't ending, not unless everything was ending, which it might. As I tried to eat my breakfast, the radio said that Russian ships were steaming toward the quarantine line that President Kennedy had set up around Cuba. The Q line, the announcer called it. If the Russians tried to break through the line, there could be a nuclear war.

My stomach started churning, life already more than I could encompass, when the telephone rang. Bunny answered, then held out the receiver to my father, saying it was Mrs. Peabody.

This was the secretary of the regional manager of the railroad, who was far above Mr. German in terms of being my father's boss. Mrs. Peabody had such a penetrating voice that when my father took the receiver, I could hear her say that Mr. Calvin Manners had called the manager directly after the school board meeting. My father said he was sorry that Mr. Manners had bothered the manager at home, but the secretary corrected him. Called him at home, she repeated. Now she told my father that he didn't need to come in to the office until Monday, when the manager would have time to speak with him.

When he hung up, my father looked pale.

"I'm sure we can clear it up next week," he said, but my stomach churned harder. You got frightened when you saw your father looking so pale.

"Why did they ever have to move here?" my mother wailed. Her cry was so loud and torn, it sounded as if a crow had flown into the kitchen, cawing and flapping. I knew what that meant. A bird in the house meant a death in the house. My stomach cramped harder, even though Bunny went to lean against my father in a way that said she wasn't mad at him anymore, and my father put his arm around her.

That seemed to be as far as he could go. My father stood in the middle of the kitchen looking pale and paralyzed, one arm around Bunny's shoulder. I watched as my mother's jaw clenched, and she broke free to hurry over to the picture window.

"Manners always leaves for work around nine," she said, scanning the street. "*Not* on the dot. I'm going to beard him right there in the driveway."

My father spoke very quietly. "There's no point in that."

"And if I say there is?"

My father turned abruptly and went downstairs to his workshop.

Bunny looked after him, then saw me hunched very small against the kitchen doorframe. She stared at the doorframe absently for a surprisingly long time before coming to herself.

"Come on," she said, turning bright. "Let's build a tent."

I hated it when Bunny talked like that. Without expecting me to help, she pushed two armchairs parallel to each other in the living room. Afterward, she got my father's old army blanket and draped it between them. One open side was up against the picture window, which struck me as dangerous, given the Bomb, although I didn't seem to have any say in the matter.

"Keep a watch out while I do the dishes," she said, and I must have looked stupid. "Manners going to work?"

Bunny brought me some comic books, but I had to look out the window, not just because I'd been ordered to, but because that was what I did. Fortunately, I hadn't been there long when Jamie and Harry crashed out the garage door on their way to school. Behind them, I could see that the chesterfield in the rec room was back to being a chesterfield and not an unmade bed. I didn't understand adults, but I doubted that Mr. Manners had slept upstairs, judging from Mrs. Manners's face last night, which meant he hadn't gone home after the board meeting. I wondered if he was staying with his parents like Miss Oliphant and Mr. Duffy.

Crawling back under that old brown blanket, moth-eaten and frayed at the edges, I caught a glimpse of how crushing it must have been for Mr. Manners to see how many of the people at the school board meeting knew his wife was having an affair. I remembered my father saying he might not have filed for divorce because he didn't want to. He'd probably have to get one now. It struck me as interesting that the petition hadn't saved his marriage but had got him back in his father's good books instead. Mr. Manners seemed to have won a very peculiar eleven o'clock special, a set of matched luggage that was taking him out the door.

The thought of the luggage halfway cheered me up. Mrs. Horton had packed her clothes in Norman's nesting set when she drove him and Rosa back east for summer camp. In retrospect, this struck me as a fair trade for the bohemian rucksack. It was made of sturdy canvas while the suitcases were cardboard under vinyl.

"Well?" Bunny asked, putting her head in the tent.

"He's not there," I said, and crawled out to explain.

We were standing at the window when Mrs. Manners opened her front door and walked outside. She looked well put together in a tweed skirt, silk blouse, and pumps. After walking quickly down the front steps, she continued to the end of the driveway, where she stopped and looked down Connington Crescent toward the Hortons' house. Mrs. Manners wore another scarf over her red hair, and I wondered whether her roots were showing. She'd walked this far easily, but now she didn't seem able to leave the driveway, even though it was spitting rain. Instead, she stood staring at the Hortons' house, crossing her arms in a way that made her cast stand out.

I wondered if my mother could beard Mrs. Manners instead. As if I'd said it aloud, Bunny told me, "I don't drown kittens."

I already knew that, although I didn't see how it was relevant and Bunny didn't explain. Instead, we watched Mrs. Manners staring down Connington for a very long time. Then she turned and walked back into her house.

That afternoon, CKNW told us that a flotilla of Russian ships had stopped just short of the Q line. I liked that word, flotilla. I particularly liked the fact that there wasn't any fighting. The Americans permitted some of the ships to continue on to Cuba, the ones that carried food and medicine. Others turned back voluntarily. Bunny was relieved enough to tell me that we might just get through this, at least if the generals didn't overrule the captains and bunk things up the way Old Cal Manners had.

There had never been any chance of going to school that day. I spent the morning watching TV and drinking ginger ale to calm my stomach. After the news that afternoon, I took a sandwich down to my father in his workshop and ate one myself, then helped Bunny bake hermit cookies, eating three as a test.

As I contemplated a fourth, Bunny said narrowly, "Go outside and run that off."

Taking a cookie, she added, "Do as I say, not as I do."

The rain had stopped, and I took my soccer ball into the backyard, where I kicked it around the wet grass. It wasn't a particularly interesting thing to do, and I was about to go back inside when Norman appeared. Usually Bunny would have let Norman in upstairs, and he would have come out the rec room door to join me, preceded by my mother's voice. This time, he must have heard me kicking the ball and come straight through the garage. That meant Norman arrived so suddenly I was startled into missing a kick, which made him giggle.

"How was school?" he asked shyly. So much had changed overnight that we weren't on easy terms with each other.

"Didn't go," I replied, and went back to dribbling the ball. "Stomach ache." He stayed silent until I asked grudgingly, "How's yours?"

"Non-existent," Norman replied. His adult jokes always made me feel better.

"We had an air raid siren the other day," I told him, picking up the ball. "They made us go under the stage in the auditorium. It was full of bottles from Mr. Mountcastle's bay rum."

Norman nodded as if this didn't surprise him. "We heard the siren," he said. "My mum said there wasn't any point going down to the basement. If it was a bomb, we'd probably want to die, anyhow."

I considered this. "Not if the windows broke and they blinded your eyes."

"If you got radiation and your hair fell out."

"If you got cancer."

"If your eyeballs melted into puddles."

"If your eyeballs melted into glass, and they turned into marbles."

"Gross," Norman said happily. "You want to go down the creek?"

This shut me down again. "I'm not allowed. The water's running too high."

"It doesn't matter if we don't get close."

"But it's cold," I said, far more worried than usual.

"It's not as cold down there under the trees."

Safe as trees, I thought, and decided Norman was right.

"I'll just go tell her."

"Then we won't be allowed," he said.

Right again. Although it's true that I hesitated before leaving my ball by the barbecue, and took a glance upstairs.

As we headed through the back gate, I thought Norman looked a little heftier from eating all that candy. He was also eager to get down the creek, and his good cheer was notable. Norman was almost like the people in the council chamber, at least the way they'd been at first, looking as if they were attending a carnival. He couldn't wait to run down the slope, even though it was slippery from the rain.

It was also as warm in the forest as Norman had said, especially once we started running around. He wanted to play sword fighting, which we hadn't done for a while, and we found good sticks. Norman was Zorro and I was Zorro, since there was no reason not to be. We didn't say, Remember when we did this and Mrs. Manners appeared? We just clashed sticks with one hand on our hips, at least until Norman hid behind a tree, going "Pschew, pschew." Our sticks turned into guns, and we ran around the cactus mountains shooting bad guys, which wasn't just each other, but also ferns.

Yet there were questions I wanted to ask, or at least a question. Finally, when I was hiding behind a tree, I called out loudly, "So who sent you to Prince George, anyhow?"

"I don't know," he called back. "I was just a baby."

Norman kept shooting, more like a machine gun now. *Ack-ack-ack-ack.* But I refused to be distracted and let my stick drop, feeling bored with lies. Stepping out from behind my tree, I asked, "But who did?"

I didn't say, You owe me, because no one said that. But Norman owed me and he knew it. He came out from behind his tree and lowered his stick.

"Rosa said the Party sent our mum. She was packing up, ready to take us, when our dad said he'd go, too. So he got a job and we all went."

"I guess he was having an affair."

"It's not always like that," Norman said. "Sometimes they just fight about my mum going to stupid protests. A lot of the time, they don't fight at all. We go camping, and they teach." He thought about that. "Vice versa."

We were no longer interested in our sticks and walked down toward the creek. After the typhoon, it was running so high it looked like a river. Andy Manners and I would have gone on the bridge and spit down at it, but Norman had never been interested in the bridge. He just stood a little back from the creek and started heaving stones at it, which I followed. If you got small flat ones and threw them right, the current carried them downstream as if they weighed nothing.

It was getting toward gloaming, that mysterious light, particularly between the old-growth trees. Without speaking, Norman and I started to head back uphill, not talking about anything but not meaningfully silent either. Maybe a little hungry, thinking about Bunny's hermit cookies.

We were partway up the slope when we heard a big rustling above us, a group sliding and stuttering downhill, sounding like teenage boys ready to take packages of cigarettes out of their back pockets. I stopped warily.

"I knew I saw them," a male voice said.

Cal Manners—young Cal, not the grandfather—arrived downhill with four boys from his football team. I didn't know them. Then I recognized Michael Shribman, who wasn't on the football team but ran track. They started to circle us, playing bad but grinning.

"Look at the little retards," Cal said.

"Hi, Cal," I said uneasily.

He picked up a stick and prodded it toward Norman, although without touching him.

"What's that?"

"You know it's Norman. It's Norman and Tink," I said. "We play down here."

"He can't speak for himself?"

"He prefers not to," I said with dignity.

The boys found this tremendously funny.

"'He prefers not to,'" one of them called, mimicking me.

"Chinless little bastard," Cal said.

I didn't understand how things could go bad so quickly. Getting scorned out. Typhoons, Cuba, and now it was happening again. Cal had his father's expression on his face even though he looked like his mother. I wondered if we could escape over the bridge, but when I glanced downhill, I saw that the Raincoat Man was standing in the middle. There was no way to escape uphill past the boys, and now we couldn't run downhill, either.

Cal prodded Norman in the stomach.

"Say something."

"I don't have anything to say."

"Well, your father has plenty to say, doesn't he? Can't shut the fuck up."

"It's not his fault," I said.

"Well who's fault is it, then?" Cal asked.

"I mean it's not Norman's fault." I was inclined to agree it was all Jack Horton's fault, but I wasn't going to say so.

"It's not my dad's fault, either," Norman said, and Cal poked him hard in the chest.

"Isn't it?" he asked. "Isn't it? The fucker."

Norman backed away and Cal followed, poking at him.

"You're a little fucker and he's a big one. Aren't you? Isn't he? Tell me the truth."

"Yeah, that's what he is," Norman said, finally stopping and standing his ground. "And it's your mother he's . . ."

Cal brought the stick down sharply, but Norman leapt under it and started running uphill. We knew the forest better than the big kids, but Norman had miscalculated. These were members of the football team, and Cal had Norman on the ground almost before he'd taken off. I caught a glimpse of Norman going down, and the bad way his head hit a tree trunk on the way.

"Leave him alone!" I yelled, and launched myself at Cal.

He grabbed me and threw me aside so I went tumbling, hurting my right leg. I couldn't help crying out, and when I tried to get up and get back to Norman, I was so dizzy I fell back on my hands and knees. As I knelt there, I caught a glimpse of an awkward male figure running toward us from the bridge. When I tried to get up again, one of the other boys grabbed my arm and held me away from Norman.

Up the hill, I glimpsed something brighter: Andy Manners and Rosa racing toward us.

"Leave them alone!" Andy called. "For God's sake, Cal! What do you think you're doing? They're babies!"

Cal stood up stupidly. Norman was still on the ground and Rosa ran over.

"His head's bleeding."

Andy gave Cal a mighty push and ran over to me, making the boy drop my arm.

"We've got to get him out of here. He needs a doctor," Rosa called.

She picked Norman up and held him awkwardly over her shoulder. I didn't see how she could get him out of there even before Cal dropped his stick and grabbed her arm.

"Not until we get our stories straight," he said.

"What story?" Rosa asked. "You're just like your father, breaking your mother's arm."

Cal jerked Rosa's arm so hard she nearly lost her balance, burdened as she was with Norman. I could see more now that Andy was picking me up too, holding me on her hip far more easily than Rosa could carry Norman.

I was afraid the two girls weren't strong enough to get us out. They were also being too mouthy, and I didn't know what to do about it.

Then I saw the Raincoat Man watching us from behind a tree, as if he wanted to step in but was afraid to.

"Please help us!" I yelled.

He looked directly at me, and that's when I saw who it was. The Raincoat Man was Mr. Duffy from the pet store. When he saw that I'd recognized him, Mr. Duffy shrank behind the tree, then started to back his way downhill. He was crouching, one hand on the ground for balance, still watching us but retreating.

"Leave him alone!" Rosa cried.

I was confused, then saw that Cal Manners was back to tormenting Norman, who was sobbing quietly. Holding Rosa's arm with one hand, Cal swatted Norman with the other, telling him to stop being a baby, stop being a baby, he was going to shut up.

"It's the pervert!" I yelled. "The pervert from the bridge. Over there! He's getting away!"

Mr. Duffy broke into a run, crashing downhill.

The boys turned to look, trying to figure out what was going on. Even Cal was distracted. When Rosa tried to jerk free, he grabbed her again roughly, making Norman whimper.

"The pervert," I yelled. "The Raincoat Man. You have to go get him. He can't do that!"

The boys knew exactly who I meant. They'd all played down here, and not that long ago.

"Jesus," one boy said. "It's Duffy from the pet store."

Mr. Duffy tripped, landing on all fours.

"Come on!" Michael Shribman yelled. "We can get him! Manners!"

The boys took off, going after Mr. Duffy as he scrambled to his feet. A moment's hesitation, then Cal dropped Rosa's arm and ran after him, too.

"Get the story straight," he told Andy over his shoulder, before picking up speed.

Rosa was already on her way uphill, holding Norman as best she could. "Andy! Let's get out of here!"

When Andy didn't follow, Rosa stopped. "Andy! Her leg's bleeding all over the place."

"Maybe we should go?" I whispered, trying not to shake. Yet Andy was transfixed, watching the boys run after Mr. Duffy.

With an exasperated hiss, Rosa left, struggling as she carried Norman uphill.

Mr. Duffy was fit from riding his bicycle, but the boys were younger and faster, and Cal was smart. He ran directly to the bridge, blocking Mr. Duffy from using it to get away. Bereft of his bridge, all Mr. Duffy could do was run to the edge of the creek, where the boys formed a semicircle around him. The creek was too loud for us to hear what they were saying, but we could see they were sneering, and everything about their postures said scorn, scorn, scorn.

Cal picked up another stick and brandished it.

"What are they doing?" I asked Andy, having failed to imagine anything like this.

"I don't know how to stop them," she replied.

With the sound drowned out, it was a pantomime, the boys circling Mr. Duffy restlessly. I couldn't see anyone's face. Mr. Duffy was wearing his fedora and keeping his head down as if he could hide himself that way. He didn't move, hunched in on himself. Then one of the boys darted up and snatched his fedora, throwing it into the creek. Mr. Duffy fought for it too late, awkwardly, reaching for something that wasn't there.

"Pervert!" I heard one of them call.

Without his fedora, Mr. Duffy had to face the boys bareheaded. This excited them even more. Cal danced in, prodding Mr. Duffy with his stick. Another boy flicked his wrist, and I saw he was flicking a stone. Flicking a second stone at the raincoat.

"Stop it!" Andy yelled, taking a step forward. "It's not your job . . ."

She had to fumble to hold me on her hip and couldn't go on. Nor did the boys stop tormenting Mr. Duffy, moving in on him slowly, forcing him back toward the creek. Soon he stood right at the edge, water splashing on his black brogues. Being the Raincoat Man was bad, but I knew this shouldn't happen. Andy was right. It was adult business. The boys should let our parents handle this.

Instead, they kept baiting him. Rocks. Branches. Finally, Mr. Duffy swore so loudly even we could hear and made a sudden break for it. Yet as he lunged, he lost his balance on the slick round rocks. His feet shot out from under him and he fell backwards into the creek. I saw the snap of his head as it hit a rock. Then he went limp and the water carried him away.

Dr. Longford stitched up my leg in his office afterward.

"I'm going to leave you a scar," he said. "That way you'll remember to behave yourself. Don't go where you've been told not to go, or play with people you shouldn't play with."

I didn't want to hear about playing with people. I wanted the sewing to hurt. But Dr. Longford gave me an injection and I didn't feel a thing. Afterward, he bandaged my leg, and Bunny took me home.

"She's nine years old," I heard my father tell a policeman. "She's had a nasty experience and got a nasty cut. Eleven stitches. The doctor gave her painkillers that make her woozy. Can't this wait until the morning?"

"What we'd like to know," the policeman said, "is whether your daughter has any idea where they've taken the Horton boy. They're not at Grouse Valley Hospital. The Shribman kid feels plenty bad and gave us a clear picture of what happened. The girl next door confirms it. There's no urgency to talk to your daughter. But we'd like to find the Hortons, and the Manners girl doesn't know where they are."

I thought she probably did, which meant we weren't supposed to say. Not that I knew anyway. But if the Hortons wanted to keep away from the police, the least I could do was try to help. Propping myself up in bed, I called, "It's my fault. The Raincoat Man."

After a brief silence, my father came in my bedroom and sat on the side of the bed. The light was on, since I wanted to keep it on. Bunny sat in a chair on the other side of the bed. I could see that my father was back to being himself, another battle fought and won.

"Is that what you called him?" he asked. "The Raincoat Man?"

I knew that the policeman was listening outside. My father hadn't closed the door.

"The Raincoat Man," I agreed. "He stood on the bridge and opened his raincoat."

"Has he done this for long?" my father asked.

"Forever."

Earlier, I'd heard the policeman saying that they were dragging the creek, which wouldn't take long. There were only so many places it could go. It, he'd said. Not him.

"We didn't know it was Mr. Duffy," I said. "We always ran away, and he never hurt us." I tried not to shiver, and wanted my teeth to stop chattering. "I didn't mean to hurt him."

"It was an accident, Mary Alice," my father said. "The boys shouldn't have teased him. But in the end, Mr. Duffy slipped and fell. You were only trying to keep Norman safe."

I remembered how my father had told me in September that I had a choice of teachers. I could stay with Norman in Miss Oliphant's class or I could go into Mrs. Horton's. It was my decision, he'd said, and it came with consequences either way.

This time, Norman had needed to get to a doctor. If I hadn't distracted Cal, there would have been consequences for Norman. But there were consequences for Mr. Duffy when I did.

"It's not fair," I wailed. "Why isn't anything ever easy?"

"Because it's not," Bunny said. "And you're going to have to get used to it."

"Muriel . . ."

"Where's Norman?" my mother asked. "Did Rosa say where they were going to take him?"

That's when it struck me.

"He came over to say goodbye," I said. "And now he's gone."

The Hortons' next-door neighbour would tell police later that they'd got home at about two o'clock in the morning driving into the garage. She was a light sleeper, she would say. And in fact, when I insisted on going over there first thing in the morning, the garage door was closed. The car could have been in there. But as I walked up the driveway with my father, I knew the garage was empty. I let him knock on the door, but I knew that nobody would answer, and nobody did.

Yet the silence hurt me, and I insisted on walking around the house, looking in the windows. There was no one in the dining room, which was at the front of the house on the east side of the door, and which was empty. You could look through it into the living room, and no one was in the living room either, although the furniture was in place. I walked down the stairs at the side of the house to the lower level, which hurt my leg, and looked in the rec room window. The furniture was there too, and the TV. I looked hard but couldn't see any sign of people, nor hear them. After going back up the stairs, I found Rosa's tuxedo cat sitting on the front steps.

"You see," my father said. "They're not far away."

Walking around the other side, I got my father to boost me up to look into Norman's bedroom window. He had the bedroom at the front. Looking through the window, I saw that the aquarium was gone. In its place was one of Norman's cleaning buckets with a note scotch-taped onto it. I struggled out of my father's arms and ran back to the front door, making the bandage on my leg turn wet from blood. The door was unlocked and I ran inside.

"Mary Alice!" my father called behind me.

In Norman's bedroom, I found that the bucket contained his fish and plants, not all of them in very good shape. Norman had packed up his tank and all his equipment, including the oxygen pump, but he'd left the fish for me. The note said, "These are yours, anyway. Please take care of them, especially my catfish. Your friend, Norman."

I'd already known that Norman was gone. Now I knew that he was all right. Maybe he'd had to get stitches, but he had survived, and I'd helped him survive, the way Mr. Duffy hadn't. At least I'd done that.

Leaving Norman's room, we paused in the front hallway. On a table below the hook where Mrs. Horton had hung her knapsack, or Norman's knapsack, my father found three other letters. One was addressed to Mr. Eisenstadt and one to Mr. Duprée, who was never quite my father's friend again. These proved to be letters of resignation.

There was also a letter to the local bank manager. We would later learn it said that a friend of Mrs. Horton's would sell the house and furniture to pay off the mortgage. This turned out to be the lady in sandals who had taken care of the garden the previous summer. Her husband was a lawyer, and on their way out of town, the Hortons had got her husband to draw up a power of attorney in her name. As well as paying off the mortgage, the letter said, the lady would settle the medical debts for Norman's polio, this being before Medicare. It was a big mortgage and the debts were large, so it turned out there was very little left after the house was sold. The extra she'd been instructed to give to the Campaign for Nuclear Disarmament. The woman later said she had no idea where the Hortons had gone and didn't expect to hear from them. Maybe that's why she and her husband took Rosa's cat, as a memento.

I had a memento, too. Not the fish. I lost interest in keeping an aquarium, and Debbie's husband Ed got rid of it. Instead, I was left with a feeling of guilt, which walked beside me like a shadow, as it does to this day.

This all ended on Saturday, which proved to be when the Cuban Missile Crisis ended as well. The announcement came over the radio: Chairman Khrushchev had agreed to remove the Soviet nuclear missiles from Cuba. Years later, we would learn that a top-secret deal meant the Americans removed their missiles from Turkey in return, and promised not to invade Castro's Cuba. The mood in the world at large was mainly relief. There was no celebration. Gratitude, maybe, although not exactly to the world leaders who'd got us into the mess in the first place.

The mood in our subdivision was even more subdued. Mr. Duffy's mother would be all right, since there was a daughter. But the disappearance of the Hortons was understood to be an accusation against the neighbourhood. On reflection, people didn't like what had happened to the Hortons, or at least to the children. If Mr. Manners had stayed around, I think he would have been avoided out of resentment and embarrassment for the way he'd got people to overreact.

But Jim Manners had moved over town to Shaughnessy, going to work for his father and buying a house nearby. Cal Junior moved with him. My father wasn't inclined to press assault charges for my leg, not without the Hortons pressing similar charges over Norman. As a result, Cal faced no penalty, and went to a private school for the rest of the year. Andy refused to go with him, insisting on staying in Grouse Valley. Jamie wanted to live with his father; Harry stayed. Mrs. Manners got the house in the divorce and continued to bring up Andy and Harry. Or at least, they all lived together until Andy left for university a couple of years later.

People's strained feelings had this effect: when my father was let go from his job, given the continued pressure from Old Cal Manners, Mr. O'Neill got him taken on as an accountant with the school district, where he proved to be much happier. Bunny's friends invited her for coffee again. The following summer, we were even asked to swim at the Walls' new pool, which had started out as their bomb shelter. Not that we liked the Walls or they liked us. But as Bunny said, they couldn't *not* invite us, and she liked swimming.

Aunt Magda and Uncle Ray offered to send me to private school as well. However, when Mr. Eisenstadt hired the nice substitute Mrs. Walton to replace Mrs. Horton, I decided to transfer into her class, and after a while, I became friends with Lucy Oliver. The Olivers went to the United Church, and once we started going there, Lucy and I sang together in the choir. Not that I cared much for church anymore, and stopped going as soon as my parents let me. In the meantime, Lucy and I took piano lessons from the same teacher, and later we took guitar lessons, so that was all right.

I continued to float out of my body, at least until adolescence left me permanently unmoored. Twice more that I remember, I went very far into the sky. The suburb was laid out below me as it had been the first time, with peaked roofs spaced widely along the curving streets. Smoke came out of the occasional chimney, although I was never conscious of cold. Despite everything that had happened, I continued to feel surprisingly unafraid. Yet I had a sense of the strangeness of the world as I gazed down at those suburban streets, seeing the way they curved up the mountain like animal trails.

I knew by then that the forms I saw rustling along them at night didn't belong to deer and bears. Instead, they were red-haired ballerinas dancing on pointe and sappers going behind enemy lines; politicians sailing on heavy seas and principals watching planes take off. There was also a sister who would bring her son over for visits, and a brother who would move back to Grouse Valley with his wife and three clever daughters. And then there were our parents, older than most of their neighbours, who loved each other all their lives, just as I knew they loved me.

EPILOGUE

I have no idea what happened to Norman. A dozen years later, when I went out on the road with my band, I started looking through the phone books that would be hanging by chains from the pay phones in the lobbies of the cheap motels where we stayed. At first, I worked the white pages, but after a few years, I started looking in the yellow pages under physicians. I didn't expect to find Dr. Norman Horton, but looked for Dr. Norman Horowitz and then for other Dr. Normans, of whom there were seldom any. I made a few random phone calls, but nothing ever panned out. Nevertheless, I kept doing this until I finally realized I was well enough known that if Norman had wanted to find me, he could have got in touch. I heard from everyone else I'd ever met, at least when they wanted tickets to my shows.

Then one day I was in Toronto, walking north on Jarvis Street. This would have been around 1980. We were doing a show that night, but I had a little time to take a walk and clear my head. Something caught my eye and I looked up, seeing an older woman walking toward me. She had white hair coiled around her head in a surprisingly thick braid, and I said to myself, Just like Marian Horton. Then I looked closer and realized it was her. I thought it was her. As she got close, I took a step toward her and said, "Mrs. Horton?"

The woman was startled, and as she met my eyes, I knew it was her.

"Mrs. Horton, it's Tink Parker."

"I know who you are," she said. "I see your advertising. You don't know who I am, but I know who you are."

She was dressed very tidily in older clothes. It was cold enough that we both wore coats, but she didn't wear gloves. There was no wedding ring on her left hand.

"I've always wanted to see Norman again," I said. "How's Norman? I presume it was just a concussion."

"I don't know what you're talking about," she answered, and started walking away.

"Please," I said, and put a hand on her arm.

"No!" she cried, pulling away.

"I'm sorry," I said. "I didn't mean . . ."

She stroked her chest the same way she'd done at the special school board meeting. It looked as if it had become a habit, and it was slightly odd. Doing the arithmetic, I figured that she must have been around sixty, maybe a few years older.

"If you could give Norman a message for me," I said. "Tell him, please, that he can get in touch. We could catch up. Have a coffee. Norman's so smart, he could figure out how to get through to me. I'll make sure that people in management know his name."

Mrs. Horton paused to consider this, but shook her head, and started walking away. As I turned to look after her, she called over her shoulder, "Norman's fine."

Then she walked down Jarvis Street and disappeared.

ACKNOWLEDGEMENTS

This book is set on the North Shore of Vancouver, British Columbia. I grew up there, and I remember the landscape lovingly, but the story and characters are fictional, as is the municipality of Grouse Valley. However, I wanted to get the background information right. For help with the labour history of British Columbia, I would like to thank my good friend Jan O'Brien, who provided invaluable notes. I also owe a debt to another good friend, Rod Mickleburgh, a former labour reporter, along with his mother, the late Brita Mickleburgh, for our wide-ranging discussions of the time period.

The mountain and creek I describe are the traditional territory of the Squamish Nation, and I'm grateful to Squamish elder Sam George for reviewing the parts of the book involving the character Dan Lake, a fictional member of the nation. My thanks as well to the Squamish Nation's Language and Cultural Affairs staff who introduced me to Mr. George. Huy Chexw. Of course, their help doesn't represent any form of endorsement, and all mistakes remain mine.

Great thanks go to my editor Susan Renouf, whose incisive comments and impatience toward self-indulgence—that enemy of writers—have made this a better book. Susan has been my editor on four books and my friend for many years, and I wish her the most rewarding of retirements, when she can spend her time reading books she doesn't *have* to read, in shockingly beautiful places. The help of others at ECW Press has been invaluable: David Caron, Jessica Albert, Claire Pokorchak, Emily Varsava, Victoria Cozza, Jen Albert, and cover designer Natalie Olsen.

I am grateful to the Canada Council for the Arts for providing a grant that freed time to write this novel.

This book is also available as a Global Certified Accessible™ (GCA) ebook. ECW Press's ebooks are screen reader friendly and are built to meet the needs of those who are unable to read standard print due to blindness, low vision, dyslexia, or a physical disability.

At ECW Press, we want you to enjoy our books in whatever format you like. If you've bought a print copy just send an email to ebook@ecwpress.com and include:

- the book title
- the name of the store where you purchased it
- a screenshot or picture of your order/receipt number and your name
- your preference of file type: PDF (for desktop reading), ePub (for a phone/tablet, Kobo, or Nook), mobi (for Kindle)

A real person will respond to your email with your ebook attached. Please note this offer is only for copies bought for personal use and does not apply to school or library copies.

Thank you for supporting an independently owned Canadian publisher with your purchase!